STORIES

STORIES

CESARE PAVESE

translated by A. E. Murch

THE ECCO PRESS
NEW YORK

Copyright © 1946, 1953, 1960 by Giulio Einaudi Editore
All rights reserved
English translation copyright © 1946, 1966 by Alma Murch
First U.S. edition published by the Ecco Press in 1987
18 West 30th Street, New York, N.Y. 10001
Distributed in Canada by Penguin Books Canada Ltd.
2801 John Street, Markham, Ontario L3R 1B4
This edition published by arrangement with Peter Owen Ltd.
London, and Giulio Einaudi Editore

Printed in the United States of America

Library of Congress Cataloging in Publication Data
Pavese, Cesare
Stories.
Translation of: Notti di festa, Feria d' agosto, and
I racconti di Cesare Pavese.
I. Title
PQ4835.A846A25   1987   853'.912   86-11505
ISBN 0-88001-124-6

Publication of this book made possible in part by a
grant from the National Endowment for the Arts

CONTENTS

Festival Night

Introduction	7
Land of Exile	12
Wedding Trip	29
The Intruder	46
The Three Girls	58
Festival Night	74
Friends	107
Gaol Birds	123
Suicides	162
The Villa on the Hill	181
The Cornfield	195

Summer Storm

Introduction	215
The Evil Eye	219
Misogyny	227
Summer Storm	239
The Idol	259
First Love	290
Loyalty	314
The Beggars	330
Evocation	335
The Family	345
The Name	391
Freewill	395
The Leather Jacket	401

Festival Night

INTRODUCTION

After Cesare Pavese's tragically early death, (he was not quite 42 when he committed suicide in August 1950), the short stories in this volume were found in manuscript form among his papers. Each story bore the date when it was written and they were all produced between 5th July 1936 and 2nd August 1938. They are among his finest and most characteristic prose works, yet he never offered these particular stories to the world and they remained unknown until they were published posthumously in 1953 as *Notte di Festa*.

During his lifetime, Cesare Pavese, poet and novelist, was recognised as one of the great contemporary European writers; his novel *Tra Donne Sole* won for him Italy's foremost literary award, the Strega Prize; his public eagerly awaited everything he wrote; yet he kept this group of stories to himself until his life's end. His reason may well have been that they revealed too poignantly his own state of mind during those two bitterly unhappy years.

As a student at Turin University he devoted himself with intense concentration to the study of literature, in particular American literature because of its atmosphere of intellectual freedom, so different from the fascist-inspired, rigidly limited work of Italian writers from 1922 onwards. To make this spirit of artistic and social freedom known in Italy, he embarked upon a long series of translations from American and English writers. His translation of Sinclair Lewis's *Our Mr Wrenn* (1931) was followed by his superb version of Hermann Melville's *Moby Dick* (1932) and a long series of other translations that revealed new spheres of interest to the Italian reading public and had a profound effect upon Italian writers generally.

After obtaining his degree, (with a brilliant thesis on Walt Whitman), Pavese returned for a time to his old school to teach literature and languages, then joined the publishing firm just established by his close friend Giulio Einaudi, becoming editor of the review *La Cultura*. His series of well-argued, precise and factual criticisms of the Fascist régime, which appeared in that journal, attracted the unfavourable notice of the authorities and in May 1935, he was arrested with other members of the staff of *La Cultura*, charged with Anti-Fascist activities and summarily convicted. Pavese was sentenced to a year's preventive detention at Brancaleone (Calibri) and actually served ten months there, an experience that affected him deeply, spiritually and physically.

From boyhood, Pavese had suffered from chronic asthma; his weak eyesight compelled him to wear thick glasses; by nature he was extremely shy and sensitive, diffident, sometimes sullen, always keenly observant. His life as a political prisoner was purgatory to him, endurable only as a source of new material for his work. The bleak loneliness of this period, and his perception of a prisoner's state of mind, are reflected in the first tale in this series, 'Land of Exile,'[1] a theme Pavese used again in his novel *Il Carcere*,[2] written between November 1938 and April 1939,

[1] The title on the original rough draft was *Sterilità* (*Sterility*)

[2] Original title, *Memorie di Due Stagioni* (*Memories of Two Seasons*)

but not published until 1948, when it appeared with another short novel in the volume *Prima che il Gallo Canti*.

His personal experience of prison conditions forms the background of two other stories, 'The Intruder' and 'Gaolbirds.' The second of these, almost a short novel, gives a pungent commentary on the social and political atmosphere of the period.

Just after Pavese's release from prison he was dealt an even severer blow. During his final year at the University, he met the first woman he had ever truly loved. Her name is still a secret. She is known only by the phrase Pavese used to describe her in his poems, '*la donna dalla voce rauca*' –'the girl with the husky voice'. Until he met her, Pavese had been, as he himself said, a woman-hater[1]. 'With her,' wrote his friend and biographer, ' he became a new Pavese, human, happy, free of his inferiority complex and his introspective shyness for the first time in his life.'[2]

Their love affair lasted for five years, but soon after his return from Brancaleone she suddenly abandoned him, remarking casually to a mutual acquaintance that ' Pavese may write fine poetry, but he's no good with a woman.' Distress and disillusionment brought him almost to the verge of madness. All his hatred of women blazed up again more fiercely than ever; for him they were all deceitful, self-seeking, treacherous, yet he felt driven to seek their company to convince himself of his own virility. In all Pavese's later work there is not one happy, chaste woman. On 24th November 1949, he noted in his journal with some surprise: ' D. has remarked that the women in my books are all whores. She is amazed by it. My amazement is that it should be true. I have never thought of it.'

But never did he portray women more savagely or treat

---

[1] Cf. his journal *Il Mestiere di Vivere*, 10th April '36 (p. 28 in the English translation *This Business of Living*)

[2] Cf. Davide Lajolo, *Il vizio Assurdo* p. 105.

them more cruelly than in these short stories, notably 'Wedding Trip' and 'Suicides'. In 'Wedding Trip' his bitterness often yields to pity in spite of itself, but underlying the cold, objective language Pavese is revealing how he believes he would have treated a loving wife. In 'The Three Girls' he adds the idea that every woman is foredoomed to sorrow by her very nature. In 'Suicides', his brooding spirit of revenge against women reaches its extreme limit when the man not only makes Carlotta suffer but indirectly suggests to her the idea of suicide by telling her how a young friend of his had killed himself.

All his life, Pavese was obsessed with the idea of suicide. While he was still at school his only close friend, a boy named Baraldi, killed himself with a revolver as described in the tale told to Carlotta. At his funeral Pavese, wild with grief, was only at the last moment prevented from following his friend's example. Shortly afterwards another of his young contemporaries, the son of Professor Predella, killed himself. The subject was constantly in Pavese's thoughts, as the many entries in his journal clearly show, and he used it in some of his novels too, notably *Tra Donne Sole*.

Though all the tales in this volume were written rapidly and in mental anguish they were none the less constructed with extreme care, putting into practice the precepts he noted in his journal, during the period he was writing them. 'One must tell a story, knowing that the people in it have a given character and that things will happen in accordance with pre-determined laws, but the *point* of our story must lie neither in these characters nor in those laws.' 'The style of the twentieth century ... expresses but does not explain ... It is a never-ending revelation of inner life, manifesting it in moments when the subject of the story is the link between reality and imagination.' 'The art of the nineteenth century was centred on the development of situations; the art of the twentieth on static essentials. In the first, the hero was not the same at the beginning of the story as he was at the end; now he remains the same.'

These stories, then, reveal Pavese's transition from poet to novelist. Indeed, he used at least two of them as the underlying themes of later novels – ' Land of Exile ' was developed as *The Political Prisoner* and ' The Villa on the Hill ' as *The Beach* (*La Spiaggia* 1941). They are therefore of considerable importance in any assessment of Pavese, the writer, and Pavese, the man.

A. E. MURCH

Land of Exile

1

When a sudden, unexpected turn of events in my job drove me down to the far south of Italy, I felt very much on my own. The squalid village seemed to me a kind of penance – such as we each have to suffer at least once in a lifetime – and also as a place where I could withdraw from the world to sort out my ideas and find fresh experiences. And a penance it certainly was, all the months I stayed there; as for my anticipation of novelty and excitement, that fancy had me properly fooled. Being a native of Piedmont, I took such a jaundiced view of things down there that their probable significance escaped me. Yet I still remember it all – the little donkeys, the pitchers on the window-sills, the many-coloured sauces, the shrieks of the ugly old hags and the beggars – so vividly, so strangely, that I am truly sorry I did not take a more sympathetic interest in them at the time. And when I reflect how intensely I longed for the skies and the streets of Piedmont – where I am living so restlessly now – I can only conclude we are made that way. Only when a thing has passed, or changed, or vanished, can we really see what it is like.

The sea was there – a remote, colourless sea. Even today, whenever I feel depressed, I hear the surge of it in the back of my mind. On its bare, low beaches, every trace of land

Land of Exile

ended in a vague immensity. There were days when I sat on the shingle and stared apprehensively out to sea at the heavy clouds piling up on the skyline. I could have wished the whole world was empty beyond that harsh, inhuman shore.

The beach was desolate but not unpleasant. I was glad enough – since the country around was so uninteresting – to walk along it in the morning, or towards evening, keeping to the pebble ridge so as not to tire myself in the sand. I forced myself to take an interest in the little clumps of flowering geranium and the strong, fleshy leaves of the aloes. It always distressed me to come across a sandy shoot uprooted or crushed, the green pulp of its leaves all shrivelled up, showing the network of veins.

I remember one July morning when the heat was so intense that I could not make out where the sea ended and the sky began. A few yards above the line of shingle lay a cluster of shabby, weather-beaten old boats, one of them turned on its side as if resting after the night's fishing. The waves at the water's edge showed scarcely a ripple, as though they were cowed by the vast expanse of ocean.

Sitting against a boat in the shade I saw the convict from the open prison, a working man. He was gazing at the hill on whose summit stood the rocky white walls of an old fortress – the ancient village. He seemed fascinated by the limpid light in the sky that threw a bright veil over everything. He did not turn as I went by. He was wearing a peaked cap pulled down over his eyes and a brown suit, threadbare at the elbows and baggy at the knees. After I had gone past I heard him call me. A Turin newspaper was sticking out of my pocket in plain view.

While the young fellow was reading it, I squatted down in the shade of the boat to get my breath back. There was a smell of wood baking in the sun and of burning sand.

Festival Night

After a while I asked him: 'Going bathing?'

'All the papers say the same things,' he replied, fumbling in his pocket. 'Got anything to smoke?'

I gave him a cigarette and began undressing in the sunshine.

'I'm no politician,' he went on. 'What I want from the papers isn't politics. I like to read about what's happening at home. Instead of that, all they can talk about is politics.'

'I thought you might be....'

'I'm a communist,' he interrupted me. 'I had a fight with a soldier, but that was a personal matter. I am a communist,' and he pulled his cap down over his eyes.

I slipped into my bathing trunks and sat down in the sun. I looked towards the calm, quivering sea, savouring in anticipation the foam on my face as I swam, the cool freshness of deep water, the marbled look of the sun below the surface. I felt very conscious of that heavily clad body still lying under the boat, almost out of sight. Long sleeves, thick trousers, rough cloth cap. The man must be suffocating!

'Coming for a swim?' I asked again.

'I'd rather have river water,' he replied, lost in thought.

'There's none of that here,' I told him.

I came up the shore, dripping wet, and threw myself down on the sand with my eyes shut. When I opened them again and sat up, I glanced casually at the hillside. The sun was still beating down, giving a red glow to the drab dejection of the thick plants and the nearby houses. My clothes made a dark patch beside the boat.

'And are you a prisoner, too?' the fellow called from where he lay.

'We all are, here, more or less,' I shouted. 'The only escape is to go in the water.'

'And what relief is that, in winter time?'

Land of Exile

' In winter we dream of the place we came from.'

' I dream of it even in summer.'

He came over and sat down beside me on the sand. He had taken off his jacket and was wearing a dark sleeveless shirt.

' And the people who live here,' he asked, ' what place do you think they dream about?'

' They think about Northern Italy even more than we do.'

' Yes, but this is their own land. They aren't missing anything.'

Across the railway, between the beach and the first outlying houses of the village, came a group of women going to their own bathing-place among the rocks further up the coast; old women, heavily built and dressed in brown, but with them was a girl in white.

For something to say, I remarked, ' Swimming in the Po is nicer, of course. There's not so much sun and it's more convenient.'

' Where did you live in Turin?'

I told him.

' What are you doing in this part of the country, then?'

' I'm working on the new road. I'm an engineer.'

The convict wiped his nose against the back of his hand. ' I was a mechanic,' he said giving me a look. ' D'you get any mail from Turin?'

' Now and then.'

' I had some the other day,' and he dug out of his pocket a postcard with a view of the station. ' D'you know where this is?'

I looked at the picture for a moment, smiling, then gave it back to him, feeling embarrassed as I caught sight of the message.

Festival Night

' My girl sent it to me. The only time she writes to me is when she's fooling around with some other man. I know her.'

I didn't like his tone – he sounded truculent – so I lit a cigarette without answering him. I waited for him to continue, but he said no more. After a minute or two he handed me back my paper with a brusque word of thanks and walked away, stumbling through the sand.

2

Some evenings, on my way home from work, I came through the countryside bordering the coast, and, every time I did so, one thing struck me as incomprehensible. When a native of these parts has gone out into the world, how can he possibly think of this region as the one place on earth that means home to him, how can he feel proud to identify himself with it, regard it as life's haven? I was not thinking so much of the shortage of good fields and fresh water. the deceptive whimsicality of the thick stunted bushes or the bleak coast. Those things are merely natural features, and I myself was helping to modernise the place by building a good tarred road.

The very life of the people was harsh and empty, their speech and customs boorish and uncouth, warped by race-memories from the far-distant past. At any time of day, the men emerge from their wretched hovels and casually saunter off to the barber's as if they had nothing else to do. They never seem to take the day's work seriously. They spend their time in the streets or sitting gossiping on their doorsteps in a dialect that, in the far-off mountains of the interior, is used only by farm-hands or colliers. Perhaps they work at night, or hidden away in their close-shut,

Land of Exile

stifling little houses, but out of doors, from dawn to dusk, they behave like idle tourists with nothing to do but enjoy their leisure. And not one of them will allow his wife to be seen in the streets. Old women can go out, so can the children, but wives, women in the flower of their beauty, must stay out of sight.

In this respect, certainly, it was an unfriendly place. Even the men seemed aloof, not identifying themselves with the village or their street, as if they did not belong there. They seemed to lack roots, and their persistent vivacity betrayed a physical uneasiness.

Still, as dusk fell, even the village grew sweeter under the sky. A breath of air blew in from the sea and the half-naked children played in the streets, while the old women chattered in their shrill voices. From the open doors came a stench of frying. I would sit outside a tavern facing the deserted station, watching the herd of goats that supplied the district with milk as they made their way to their stable, or just drowsing in the twilight, enjoying the solitude. Sometimes I thought uneasily that somewhere beyond the mountains behind me, life in the great world was going on as usual, and one day soon I should have to find my place in it again. Someone was waiting for me there, and this certainly gave me a tacit detachment from everything around me, so that my very boredom encouraged me to indulge in day-dreams. I lit a cigarette.

Suddenly Ciccio appeared from nowhere. ' Got anything to give me, sir?' Rubbing his hands together in anticipation, he added: ' I'm a smoker, too. Thanks. Your servant.'

Ciccio was a little man, burned brown by the sun, with crafty eyes and a thin, straggling, grey beard. He was swathed in a dingy cloak and his feet were wrapped in rags secured with strips of leather. Whatever alms he was given he spent on wine, and then kept out of sight so as not to

Festival Night

make a spectacle of himself. He came from somewhere inland and he had a prison record. The people here spoke of him with pride, as they did of everything else they felt belonged to them.

Ciccio was a half-wit, and every so often a fit would take him. Then he would rush wildly through the streets shouting abuse at various phantoms that haunted him personally. His wife had reduced him to this state by comparing him adversely with some other man. So Ciccio gave up everything – work, home, dignity – and roamed these coasts for a year, seeking he knew not what. Then he was put in a hospital, but he would have none of it and came back to the places he knew. So he became the Ciccio we know – the typical beggar who prefers a cigar stub or a good drink to a plate of thick soup.

Men playing cards in the tavern would drive him away, finding him a nuisance, but when they were idle and bored, or when there was a stranger about, Ciccio was worth his weight in gold – the perfect example of local eccentricity.

When he first started begging, he had been put in prison several times further up the coast, and this gave him such a horror of being shut up that even in winter he slept under bridges. 'Otherwise what should I have to put up with?' he once asked me all of a sudden, and I have often thought of his words. Perhaps he had been overcome by pangs of remorse that now gave a purpose to his life?

Though Ciccio was a half-wit, he was not stupid all the time. A breakdown such as his, suffering that turned his brain, could well have brought on his stroke, real or assumed, and robbed him of the right to complain. But in that case, deprived even of the comfort of railing against injustice, Ciccio would indeed have been wretched. At that time I preferred to believe he meant nothing by what he said – as begging too often makes a man do.

Land of Exile

If people made vulgar or impertinent references to his misfortunes, Ciccio would reply with a jumbled explanation that changed the subject. When the blonde came from town, brought down in secret and accommodated for a couple of days in the slaughterhouse, the butcher himself remarked to Ciccio:: ' Look, Ciccio, you ought to murder that wife of yours. She's a whore now, you know, like this one.' But Ciccio, with a crafty look, said: ' If a woman goes wrong, the pleasure is hers and the sin is the man's – as far as we still know how to amuse ourselves . . . .'

3

At night, I used to make myself sleepy by sitting on the shore, listening to the wash of the sea in the darkness. Sometimes I stayed in the tavern studying the plans of the workings or glancing through my newspapers again, smoking and dreaming idly of the transfer that would have to come soon.

One evening, feeling restless, I turned away from the beach and was walking towards the country when I heard a voice call me. I swung round and managed to make out the workman from Turin, sitting on a bit of old wall. I was astounded, for I knew his rules forbade him to be out of doors at that hour. ' How are you, Otino?' I said.

He gave me a cigarette and we started strolling along the road flanked by olive trees. In the air was the pungent smell of September fields under a cold sky. The convict did not speak. We walked about fifty yards and back again, passing and re-passing the huts where he lived.

' This is a good way of staying at home and enjoying the fresh air at the same time,' I remarked at last.

Festival Night

The other remained silent. As far as I could see, his lips were tightly pressed together. He stared at the ground he walked upon.

'Is there much of your sentence still to run?'

Even this question brought no reply, but with a kind of effort, as though his throat was cut, he said without looking at me: 'I'm at my wits end about someone.'

I halted, took him by the arm. 'What the devil's happening?'

He broke away from me and stood still. 'I'm not telling you,' he muttered irritably, then went on: 'Women are rotten. Here I stay, living like a monk, and she just knocks around.'

'The one who sent the postcard? If you write to her....'

The mechanic gave me a look of hatred. 'She was my wife.'

I stared back at him, aghast.

'When I was put inside she came to see me every day, crying and wanting to come with me. But how could she earn a living down here? There isn't a factory in the place. Then I understood and wrote telling her to come, but she didn't answer my letter. At this very minute she's in bed with some man or other.'

'But aren't you....'

'We were always together...' He cleared his throat and I stared at the ground. 'Yes, of course,' I murmured vaguely.

We leaned on the wall where the mechanic had been sitting when I saw him first. The black fretwork of the olive trees made another wall around us. The man beside me took a shuddering breath as if he had broken a rib. Then he suddenly straightened up and said: 'Let's go on walking.' We started off again with great strides.

Land of Exile

'But,' I began, after a while, 'the fact that she didn't write to you still doesn't mean that....'

'Rubbish!' he cut me short. 'Not her. She's a bad lot. Even when I was there I never knew how to take her from one day to the next. She never let me know what was in the back of her mind. Not that she bossed me about, but she kept on and on. The only time I had any peace was when I saw her crying. For two years I kept her, and then she...' His words seemed torn from him against his will, and his clenched jaws made his face look even more gaunt.

'Why don't you write to her, Otino? Turin girls are kind-hearted. She'll willingly write back.'

'Not her. Six months ago I wrote, telling her to come at once. I've sent her three letters. You saw her reply.'

In his little furnished cell he went on talking. He explained to me that he was sent to prison because he tried to punch some sense into the head of a soldier who was having an affair with that wife of his. They gave him five years and he hadn't yet finished the first. He felt like battering his head against the wall.

'Why don't you petition for a reprieve?' I asked cautiously.

'A petition? I'll do that,' he replied, staring like a madman at the candle. 'Yes, that's what I'll do. I must... At this rate I'll get twenty years,' he added drily. 'If I come back.'

I looked at him uneasily. There was a worm-eaten table piled with crumpled newspapers, a filthy plate, and the lighted candle stuck in a bottle. Its light was dimmed by the stench from the bed, mingled with sweat and smoke.

He paced up and down while I watched him, seated on a stool. I knew the sort of man he was, surly and taciturn, and I couldn't think of anything else to say to him. At last

Festival Night

I ventured to ask: ' And you can't do without that girl any longer?'

' I? Do without her?' he cried. ' I've done without her for a year.'

He leaned against the wall. ' I can still do without her. But for her to do without me ... I don't want that. Now you know ... I'm speaking to you as a friend, even if we aren't. If you've got a girl, get her in pod. It's the only way to keep her.

' Calm down!'

4

All through the dull day, in that dull countryside the thought of him remained with me – the obsession of that prisoner tramping up and down his room or the beach, seeking in vain for peace, always alone, staring in front of him. He seldom let himself be seen – I remembered his suffering – but to see him wave to me from a distance, or to hear his name mentioned, was enough to make me aware, with an unaccustomed sense of shock, that I was not alone in that desolate region, and that someone was suffering there as I could have suffered myself. That exile's fury of resentment wounded me, filled me with a sense of remorse, and robbed me of any further interest in the life I was leading. Henceforth I longed to get away from it as from a desert island. Yet, as the probable date of my transfer grew nearer, I resigned myself more and more, with a sour complacence, to the depressing atmosphere of the place.

Among the navvies working on my road were some who had travelled the world without making any money – they squandered it if they did. I used to find them at dawn, their pockets empty, waiting on the doorstep of the hut we had erected at the head of the bridge over the valley, already finished. I would smoke a cigarette with them in the chill air, as we stood drawing in damp mouthfuls with our backs to the low horizon of the sea. The navvies chattered away among themselves: ' At New Orleans I used to stay in bed in the mornings with a woman. There wasn't much work and life was easy. A curse on the season that drove me back to work like this.'

' Luck is luck. If you work you are swindled.'

' You ought to ask Vincenzo Catalano about that. He used to clean the keels of the steamers, and slept on the ground with the blacks.'

' No need to be such a fool as that. It's the country people that swindle you.'

' As long as you're with a crowd you're all right.'

' If you can get to Northern Italy, that's good enough.'

' As long as you're not a fool, anywhere's good enough.'

' There was an avenue of palm trees along the seashore, and once I walked along it from dawn to dusk without coming to the end of it. At night I was back in the city again, and it was behind that café that I met....'

Now that the bridge was finished it was my job to act as watchman. All I had to do was to keep an eye on the three or four men who fired the boiler and planted pickets. Near the boiler was a scorched agave bush. The vapour from the tar combined with the brackish mist from the beach to veil the pale sun and sting one's eyes as it rose.

At such times I wandered away from the sea and up through the deserted street, looking up at those unknown mountains with half-shut eyes. In the street I sometimes met a peasant on his donkey, smaller than its master. The animal trotted placidly past me without glancing in my direction, while the peasant doffed his cap. He came from below those heights, a silent man from some thatched hovel

Festival Night

or an ancient fortified hamlet, and scrutinised me for an instant with listless eyes. For such people the sea was a vague azure cloud. Sometimes a humble country-woman dressed in brown, sunburned and wrinkled, passed by barefoot, with a large basket on her head or a piglet tied by a rope, scrambling along on its three free legs. She never glanced in my direction, but always kept her eyes steadily fixed on the road ahead. I never had enough of these chance encounters. This was an unknown race, living its own life on its own land.

I returned to the hut and found the navvies sitting waiting for me, some difficulty having arisen that it was not their job to settle. So came mid-day, then the evening, then the morrow, and with October the heavy rains began.

It was impossible to lay asphalt any longer. The rain was like a waterfall. I wrote to the firm to pay me off and let me go; meanwhile I spent my days shut up indoors, in the tavern.

One day the butcher took me on one side. 'Engineer,' he said, ' put up ten *lire* and join a few of us. I'm writing on Sunday. The goods will arrive on Wednesday, and by Friday, any time you have a fancy for it you can knock three times on the door and find love waiting for you.'

The blonde slipped out of the train one wet and windy night, the butcher covered her with an umbrella, another man took her case, and they all disappeared in the dark alley behind the church.

The whole village knew about it, but at the tavern it was mentioned only between a few trusted friends. 'Keep it dark,' urged the butcher, 'and we might get hold of another client or two for Concetta.' They fed her on meat and olives, but they kept her shut up. As one man left her, the next went in. I was there the second evening. As I went through the dark shop I caught sight of two disembowelled kids hanging from hooks over a tub. Then the butcher came across to me, opened another worm-eaten door, took me by the hand and led me in.

5

I often heard them discussing Concetta in the tavern. One man called her stupid, another suggested sending her away at once. The fact is that in the city, these girls are overworked. 'Next time we must get someone less tired.' They were particularly struck by the contrast between her dark, greasy skin and the exotic fineness of her fair hair. 'That comes from mixed breeding,' the barber explained. 'She was brought up at the foundling hospital. They're the best sort. When I was in Algeria, I went with an Arab woman as white as milk, with red hair. She said she was a sailor's daughter.'

I swore to myself that I'd had all I could take. Those discussions after love-making didn't please me much, either. There's something degrading about listening to men from another part of the world talking about women. To change the subject, I enquired. 'Has anybody seen the convict lately?'

'Sh!' hissed a young fellow, lowering his face to ours. 'Quiet! Not a word! Yesterday, someone from police headquarters came to question him. It was something about a murder.'

'That gang of twisters!'

'Who was killed?'

'Nobody. They didn't take him away. They only wanted to question him. It was about a crime that happened in North Italy.'

'What do you know about it?'

Festival Night

'Nothing. I only know I saw him last night wandering on the beach like a man out of his mind. He had no cap and it was pouring with rain.'

I ran to look for him. He was not in his hut. I enquired of the neighbours. He had gone out at dawn, as usual. I went back along the beach and came across Ciccio under an upturned boat, binding up his feet. Ciccio had seen him. 'I'll show you where he is. Don't rush me.' We searched the whole village, No-one showed the slightest curiosity. Then we turned our backs on the sea and climbed the hillside. At midnight we came to a gateway in the fort, overlooking the roofs far below. At the foot of a column sat Otino, staring at the ground. He lifted a face ravaged by grief and pain and saluted me with a vague gesture.

'What's happened, Otino?'

'What was bound to happen.'

Ciccio, who had run to the other column and sat down, gestured to me that he wanted a smoke. I told him to go to hell.

'I know that someone from police headquarters...' I began.

'Everybody gets to know everything,' said Otino gloomily. Then he glanced round and noticed Ciccio.

'He's a fool. Anyway, he's not listening,' I said. 'If you want to tell me anything, go ahead.'

'Is he the one whose wife ran away? He must be a fool to let that bring him to such a state.'

'Otino, I've been looking for you for half an hour. They told me you were ill.'

'I?' He sprang to his feet. 'There's only one thing wrong with me, that sticks in my throat,' the words came slowly, one by one, from his pale lips. 'It's that now I can't do it myself.'

'Do what?' I murmured.

Land of Exile

' But you know that,' he shouted in my face. ' You know it all. Why pretend you don't?'

' Otino,' I said, ' when I tell you a thing, you can believe me. I know that someone from the police came to question you, but what he told you, or what information he wanted, I have no idea.'

' Give me a smoke,' he said abruptly. I passed him a cigarette, then glanced at Ciccio and threw him one, which he caught in mid-air.

' Listen, then. My wife,' – and he tried to smile – ' my wife's been murdered by one of her workmates. She's lived with him for the past six months, but they'd been lovers for two years. Yours truly was questioned because " he used to frequent the victim – frequent! – and might be able to throw some light on important precedents".' Then, clutching me by the arm, he exclaimed: ' D'you know the best bit? He bashed her seven times, all in the face.'

He was no longer trying to smile. He spoke with a brittle lightness as though every word was forced from him, without raising his voice. When he had finished he sat there swinging his cap and staring at the cigarette, still unlit between his fingers. Then he started to his feet, crushed the cigarette in his fist and hurled it from him with a roar as if he could have thrown his hand as well. I felt the shock of it in my own arm, which he still gripped. Freeing myself, I said gently: ' Excuse me, Otino.'

' What sticks in my throat is that now I can't do it myself.' He gave another groan. ' Two years!' He took his cap in both hands. ' Two years!'

I turned away from that portico overlooking the sea, feeling callous and degraded. The two men who stayed there were not the sort to be good company. Yet I saw them a few days later in the square, sitting on a log. They were not talking, but anyway they were together.

Festival Night

I spent my last days wandering about, even in the rain. I avoided looking at the sea; it was dirty, turbulent, fearful. The village and the fields seemed suddenly smaller. It took me only a few steps to reach any part of the region and I returned unsatisfied. I could not endure it any longer. There was no colour left in the place. When the weather was bad, even the mountains disappeared – the background and the horizon of my earlier walks. The only thing still visible through the rain from the tavern window was the bare hill with the dirty-white fortress on its summit – the ancient village. This was the view that stayed in my mind's eye when, in the dazzling light of early morning, I moved on to follow my own destiny.

5th–24th July, 1936

Wedding Trip

Now that I, shattered and full of remorse, have learned how foolish it is to reject reality for the sake of idle fancies, how presumptuous to receive when one has nothing to give in return, now – Cilia is dead. Though I am resigned to my present life of drudgery and ignominy, I sometimes think how gladly I would adapt myself to her ways, if only those days could return. But perhaps that is just another of my fancies. I treated Cilia badly when I was young, when nothing should have made me irritable; no doubt I should have gone on ill-treating her, out of bitterness and the disquiet of an unhappy conscience. For instance, I am still not sure after all these years, whether I really loved her. Certainly I mourn for her; I find her in the background of my inmost thoughts; never a day passes in which I do not shrink painfully away from my memories of those two years, and I despise myself because I let her die. I grieve for her youth, even more for my own loneliness, but – and this is what really counts – did I truly love her? Not, at any rate, with the sincere, steady love a man should have for his wife.

The fact is, I owed her too much, and all I gave her in return was a blind suspicion of her motives. As it happens, I am by nature superficial and did not probe more deeply

Festival Night

into such dark waters. At the time I was content to treat the matter with my instinctive diffidence and refused to give weight or substance to certain sordid thoughts that, had they taken root in my mind, would have sickened me of the whole affair. However, several times I did ask myself: ' And why did Cilia marry me?' I do not know whether it was due to a sense of my own importance, or to profound ineptitude, but the fact remains that it puzzled me.

There was no doubt that Cilia married me, not I her. Oh! Those depressing evenings I endured in her company – wandering restlessly through the streets, squeezing her arm, pretending to be free and easy, suggesting as a joke that we should jump in the river together. Such ideas didn't bother me – I was used to them – but they upset her, made her anxious to help me; so much so that she offered me, out of her wages as a shop-assistant, a little money to live on while I looked for a better job. I did not want money. I told her that to be with her in the evenings was enough for me, as long as she didn't go away and take a job somewhere else. So we drifted along. I began to tell myself, sentimentally, that what I needed was someone nice to live with; I spent too much time roaming the streets; a loving wife would know how to contrive a little home for me, and just by going into it I should be happy again, no matter how weary and miserable the day had made me.

I tried to tell myself that even alone I managed to muddle along quite well, but I knew this was no argument. ' Two people together can help each other,' said Cilia, ' and take care of one another. If they're a little in love, George, that's enough.' I was tired and disheartened, those evenings; Cilia was a dear and very much in earnest, with the fine coat she had made herself and her little broken handbag. Why not give her the joy she wanted? What other girl would suit me better? She knew what it was to work hard and be short of money; she was an orphan, of working-class parents; I was sure that she was more eager and sincere than I.

On impulse I told her that if she would accept me, uncouth and lazy as I was, I would marry her. I felt content, soothed by the warmth of my good deed and proud to discover I had that much courage. I said to Cilia: ' I'll teach you French!' She responded with a smile in her gentle eyes as she clung tightly to my arm.

2

In those days I thought I was sincere, and once again I explained to Cilia how poor I was. I warned her that I hardly ever had a full day's work and didn't know what it was to get a pay-packet. The college where I taught French paid me by the hour. One day I told her that if she wanted to get on in the world she ought to look for some other man. Cilia looked troubled and offered to keep on with her job. ' You know very well that isn't what I want,' I muttered. Having settled things thus, we married.

It made no particular difference to my life. Already, in the past, Cilia had sometimes spent evenings with me in my room. Lovemaking was no novelty. We took two furnished rooms; the bedroom had a wide, sunny window, and there we placed the little table with my books.

Cilia, though, became a different woman. I, for my part, had been afraid that, once married, she would grow vulgar and slovenly – as I imagined her mother had been – but instead I found her more particular, more considerate towards me. She was always clean and neat, and kept everything in perfect order. Even the simple meals she prepared for me in the kitchen had the cordiality and solace of those

Festival Night

hands and that smile. Her smile, especially, was transfigured. It was no longer the half-timid, half-teasing smile of a shop-girl on the spree, but the gentle flowering of an inner joy, utterly content and eager to please, a serene light on her thin young face. I felt a twinge of jealousy at this sign of a happiness I did not always share. ' She's married me and she's enjoying it,' I thought.

Only when I woke up in the morning was my heart at peace. I would turn my head against hers in our warm bed and lie close beside her as she slept (or was pretending to), my breath ruffling her hair. Then Cilia, with a drowsy smile, would put her arms around me. How different from the days when I woke alone, cold and disheartened, to stare at the first gleam of dawn!

Cilia loved me. Once she was out of bed, she found fresh joys in everything she did as she moved around our room, dressing herself, opening the windows, stealing a cautious glance at me. If I settled myself at the little table, she walked quietly so as not to disturb me; if I went out, her eyes followed me to the door; when I came home she sprang up quickly to greet me.

There were days when I did not want to go home at all. It irritated me to think I should inevitably find her there, waiting for me, even though she learned to pretend she took no special interest; I should sit beside her, tell her more or less the same things, or probably nothing at all. We should look at one another with distaste and a smile. It would be the same tomorrow and the next day, and always. Such thoughts entrapped me whenever the day was foggy and the sun looked grey. If, on the other hand, there was a lovely day when the air was clear and the sun blazed down on my head, or a perfume in the wind enfolded and enraptured me, I would linger in the streets, wishing that I still lived alone, free to stroll around till midnight and get a meal of some sort at the pub on the corner of the street. I had always been a lonely man, and it seemed to me to count for a great deal that I was not unfaithful to Cilia.

She, waiting for me at home, began to take in sewing, to earn a little. A neighbour gave her work, a certain Amalia, a woman of thirty or so, who once invited us to dinner. She lived alone in the room below ours, and gradually fell into the habit of bringing the work upstairs to Cilia so that they could pass the afternoon together. Her face was disfigured by a frightful scar – when she was a little girl she had pulled a boiling saucepan down on her head. Her two sorrowful, timid eyes, full of longing, flinched away when anyone looked at her, as if their humility could excuse the distortion of her features. She was a good girl. I remarked to Cilia that Amalia seemed to me like her elder sister. One day, for a joke, I said: ' If I should run away and leave you, one fine day, would you go and live with her?' ' She's had such bad luck all her life. I wouldn't mind if you wanted to make love to her!' Cilia teased me. Amalia called me 'Sir' and was shy in my presence. Cilia thought this was madly funny. I found it rather flattering.

3

It was a bad thing for me that I regarded my scanty intellectual attainments as a substitute for a regular trade. It lay at the root of so many of my wrong ideas and evil actions. But my education could have proved a good means of communion with Cilia, if only I had been more consistent. Cilia was very quick, anxious to learn everything I knew myself because, loving me so much, she could not bear to feel unworthy of me. She wanted to understand my every thought. And – who knows? – if I could have

Festival Night

given her this simple pleasure I might have learned, in the quiet intimacy of our joint occupation, what a fine person she really was, how real and beautiful our life together, and perhaps Cilia would still be alive at my side, with her lovely smile that in two years I froze from her lips.

I started off enthusiastically, as I always do. Cilia's education consisted of a few back numbers of serial novels, the news in the daily papers, and a hard, precocious experience of life itself. What was I to teach her? She very much wanted to learn French and indeed, Heaven knows how, she managed to piece together scraps of it by searching through my dictionaries when she was left alone at home. But I aspired to something better than that and wanted to teach her to read properly, to appreciate the finest books. I kept a few of them – my treasures – on the little table. I tried to explain to her the finer points of novels and poems, and Cilia did her best to follow me. No-one excels me in recognising the beauty, the 'rightness' of a thought or a story, and explaining it in glowing terms. I put a great deal of effort into making her feel the freshness of ancient pages, the truth of sentiments expressed long before she and I were born, how varied, how glorious, life had been for so many many men at so many different periods. Cilia would listen with close attention, asking questions that I often found embarrassing. Sometimes as we strolled in the streets or sat eating our supper in silence, she would tell me in her candid voice of certain doubts she had, and once when I replied without conviction or with impatience – I don't remember which – she burst out laughing.

I remember that my first present to her, as her husband, was a book, *The Daughter of the Sea*. I gave it to her a month after our wedding, when we started reading lessons. Until then I had not bought her anything – nothing for the house, no new clothes – because we were too poor. Cilia

Wedding Trip

was delighted and made a new cover for the book, but she never read it.

Now and then, when we had managed to save enough, we went to a cinema, and there Cilia really enjoyed herself. An additional attraction, for her, was that she could snuggle up close to me, and now and then ask me for explanations that she could understand. She never let Amalia come to the cinema with us, though one day the poor girl asked if she could. She explained to me that we got to know each other best of all in a cinema, and in that blessed darkness we had to be alone together.

Amalia came to our place more and more often. This, and my well-deserved disappointments, soon made me first neglect our reading lessons, and finally stop them altogether. Then, if I was in a good mood, I amused myself by joking with the two girls, and Amalia lost a little of her shyness. One evening, as I came home very late from the college with my nerves on edge, she came and stared me full in the face, with a gleam of reproof and suspicion in her timid glance. I felt more disgusted than ever by the frightful scar on her face, and spitefully I tried to make out what her features had been before they were destroyed. I remarked to Cilia, when we were alone, that Amalia, as a child must have been very like her.

'Poor thing,' said Cilia. 'She spends every penny she earns trying to get cured. She hopes that then she'll find a husband.'

'But don't all women know how to get a husband?'

'I've already found mine,' Cilia smiled.

'Suppose what happened to Amalia had happened to you?' I sneered.

Cilia came close to me. 'Wouldn't you want me any more?'

'No.'

Festival Night

'But what's upset you this evening? Don't you like Amalia to come up here? She gives me work and helps me....'

What had got into me – and I couldn't get rid of it – was the thought that Cilia was just another Amalia. I felt disgusted and furious with both of them. My eyes were hard as I stared at Cilia, and the tender look she gave me only made me pity her, irritating me still more. On my way home I had met a husband with two dirty brats clinging round his neck, and behind him a thin worn-out little woman, his wife. I imagined what Cilia would look like when she was old and ugly, and the thought clutched me by the throat.

Outside, the stars were shining. Cilia looked at me in silence. 'I'm going for a walk,' I told her with a bitter smile, and I went out.

4

I had no friends and I realised, now and then, that Cilia was my whole life. As I walked the streets I thought about us and felt troubled that I did not earn enough to repay her by keeping her in comfort, so that I needn't feel ashamed when I went home. I never wasted a penny – I did not even smoke – and, proud of that, I considered my thoughts were at least my own. But what could I make of those thoughts? On my way home I looked at people and wondered how so many of them had managed to succeed in life. Desperately I longed for changes, for something fresh and exciting.

I used to hang around the railway station, thrilled by the smoke and the bustle. For me, good fortune has always meant adventure in far-away places – a liner crossing the

Wedding Trip

ocean, arrival at some exotic port, the clang of metal, shrill, foreign voices – I dreamed of it all the time. One evening I stopped short, terrified by the sudden realisation that if I didn't hurry up and travel somewhere with Cilia while she was still young and in love with me, I should never go at all. A fading wife and a squalling child would, for ever, prevent me. ' If only we really had money,' I thought again. ' You can do anything with money.'

'Good fortune must be deserved,' I told myself. 'Shoulder every load that life may bring. I am married but I do not want a child. Is that why I'm so wretched? Should I be luckier if I had a son?'

To live always wrapped up in oneself is a depressing thing, because a brain that is habitually secretive does not hesitate to follow incredibly stupid trains of thought that mortify the man who thinks them. This was the only origin of the doubts that plagued me.

Sometimes my longing for far-away places filled my mind even in bed. If, on a still and windless night, I suddenly caught the wild sound of a train whistle in the distance, I would start up from Cilia's side with all my dreams re-awakened.

One afternoon, when I was passing the station without even stopping, a face I knew suddenly appeared in front of me and gave a cry of greeting. Malagigi: I hadn't seen him for ten years. We shook hands and stood there exchanging courtesies. He was no longer the ugly, spiteful ink-spotted little devil I knew at school, always playing jokes in the lavatory, but I recognised that grin of his at once. ' Malagigi! Still alive, then?'

'Alive, and a qualified accountant.' His voice had changed. It was a man speaking to me now.

' Are you off somewhere, too?' he asked. ' Guess where I'm going!' As he spoke he picked up a fine leather suit-

Festival Night

case that toned perfectly with his smart new raincoat and the elegance of his tie. Gripping my wrist he went on: 'Come to the train with me. I'm going to Genoa.'

'I'm in a hurry.'

'Then I leave for China!'

'No!'

'It's true. Can't a man go to China? What have you got against China? Instead of talking like that, wish me luck! Perhaps I may stay out there.'

'But what's your job?'

'I'm going to China. Come and see me off.'

'No, I really can't spare the time.'

'Then come and have coffee with me, to say goodbye. You're the last man I shall talk to, here.'

We had coffee there in the station, at the counter, while Malagigi, full of excitement, told me in fits and starts all about himself and his prospects. He was not married. He'd fathered a baby, but luckily it died. He had left school after I did, without finishing. He thought of me once, when he had to take an exam a second time. He'd gained his education in the battle of life. Now all the big firms had offered him a job. And he spoke four languages. And they were sending him to China.

I said again that I was in a hurry, (though it was not true), and managed to get away from him, feeling crushed and overwhelmed. I reached home still upset by the chance meeting, my thoughts in a turmoil. How could he rise from such a drab boyhood to the audacious height of a future like that? Not that I envied Malagigi, or even liked him; but to see, unexpectedly superimposed on his grey background, which had been mine, too, his present colourful and assured existence, such as I could glimpse only in dreams, was torment to me.

Wedding Trip

Our room was empty, because now Cilia often went downstairs to work in our neighbour's room. I stayed there a while, brooding in the soft darkness lit only by the little blue glow of the gas-jet under the saucepan bubbling gently on the stove.

5

I passed many evenings thus, alone in the room, waiting for Cilia, pacing up and down or lying on the bed, absorbed in that silent emptiness as the dusk slowly deepened into dark. Subdued or distant noises – the shouts of children, the bustle of the street, the cries of birds – reached me only faintly. Cilia soon realised that I didn't want to be bothered with her when I came home, and she would put her head out of Amalia's room, still sewing, to hear me pass and call to me. I didn't care whether she heard me or not, but if she did I would say something or other. Once I asked Amalia, quite seriously, why she didn't come up to our room any more, where there was plenty of light. Amalia said nothing; Cilia looked away and her face grew red.

One night, for something to say, I told her about Malagigi and made her laugh gaily at that funny little man. Then I added: 'Fancy him making a fortune and going to China! I wish it had been me!'

'I should like it, too,' Cilia sighed, 'if we went to China.'

I gave a wry grin. 'In a photograph, perhaps, if we sent one to Malagigi.'

'Why not one for ourselves?' she said. 'Oh, George, we haven't ever had a photograph of us together.'

'No money.'

'Do let's have a photograph.'

Festival Night

'But we oughtn't to afford it. We're together day and night, and anyway I don't like photographs.'

'We are married and we have no record of it. Let's have just one!'

I did not reply.

'It wouldn't cost much. I'll pay for it.'

'Get it done with Amalia.'

Next morning Cilia lay with her face to the wall, her hair over her eyes. She would not take any notice of me, or even look at me. I caressed her a little, then realised she was resisting me, so I jumped out of bed in a rage. Cilia got up, too, washed her face and gave me some coffee, her manner quiet and cautious, her eyes downcast. I went away without speaking to her.

An hour later I came back again. 'How much is there in the savings book?' I shouted. Cilia looked at me in surprise. She was sitting on the stool, unhappy and bewildered.

'I don't know. You've got it. About 300 *lire*, I think.'

Nearly three hundred and sixteen. Here it is,' I flung the roll of notes on the table. 'Spend it as you like. Let's have a high old time! It's all yours.'

Cilia stood up and came over to face me. 'Why have you done this, George?'

'Because I'm a fool. Listen! I'd rather not talk about it. When money is in your pocket it doesn't count any more. D'you still want that photograph?'

'But, George, I want you to be happy.'

'I am happy.'

'I do love you so much.'

'I love you, too.' I took her by the arm, sat down, and pulled her on my knee. 'Put your head here, on my shoulder.' My voice was indulgent and intimate. Cilia said nothing and leaned her cheek against mine. 'When shall we go?' I asked.

Wedding Trip

'It doesn't matter,' she whispered.

'Then listen!' I held the back of her neck and smiled at her. Cilia, still trembling, threw her arms around my shoulders and tried to kiss me.

'Darling!' I said. 'Let's make plans. We have three hundred *lire*. Let's drop everything and go on a little trip. Quickly! Now! If we think it over we'll change our minds. Don't tell anyone about it, not even Amalia. We'll only be away a day. It will be the honeymoon we didn't have.'

'George, why wouldn't you take me away then? You said it was a silly idea, then.'

'Yes, but this isn't a honeymoon. You see, now we know each other. We're good friends. Nobody knows we're going. And, besides, we need a holiday. Don't you?'

'Of course, George. I'm so happy. Where shall we go?'

'I don't know, but we'll go at once. Would you like us to go to the sea? To Genoa?'

6

Once we were on the train, I showed a certain preoccupation. As we started, Cilia was almost beside herself with delight, held my hand and tried to make me talk. Then, finding me moody and unresponsive, she quickly understood and settled down quietly, looking out of the window with a happy smile. I remained silent, staring into nothingness, listening to the rhythmic throb of the wheels on the rails as it vibrated through my whole body. There were other people in the carriage, but I scarcely noticed them. Fields and hills were flashing past. Cilia, sitting opposite and leaning on the window-pane, seemed to be listening to something, too, but now and then she glanced swiftly in

Festival Night

my direction and tried to smile. So she spied on me, at a distance.

When we arrived it was dark, and at last we found somewhere to stay, in a large, silent hotel, hidden among the trees of a deserted avenue, after going up and down an eternity of tortuous streets, making enquiries. It was a grey, cold night, that made me want to stride along with my nose in the air. Instead, Cilia, tired to death, was dragging on my arm and I was only too glad to find somewhere to sit down. We had wandered through so many brightly-lit streets, so many dark alleys that brought our hearts into our mouths, but we had never reached the sea. No-one took any notice of us. We looked like any couple out for a stroll, except for our tendency to step off the pavements, and Cilia's anxious glances at the houses and passers-by.

That hotel would do for us: nothing elegant about it. A bony young fellow with his sleeves rolled up was eating at a white table. We were received by a tall, fierce-looking woman wearing a coral necklace. I was glad to sit down. Walking with Cilia never left me free to absorb myself in what I saw, or in myself. Pre-occupied and ill-at-ease, I nevertheless had to keep her beside me and answer her, at least with gestures. Now, all I wanted – and how I wanted it – was to look around and get to know in my heart of hearts this unknown city. That was precisely why I had come.

We waited downstairs to order supper, without even going upstairs to see our room or discussing terms. I was attracted by that young fellow with his auburn whiskers and his vague, lonely manner. On his forearm was a faded tattoo mark, and as he went away he picked up a patched blue jacket.

It was midnight when we had our supper. At our little

Wedding Trip

table, Cilia laughed a great deal at the disdainful air of the landlady. ' She thinks we're only just married,' she faltered. Then, her weary eyes full of tenderness, she asked me: ' And are we really?' as she stroked my hand.

We enquired about places in the neighbourhood. The harbour was only a hundred yards away, at the end of the avenue. ' Let's go and see it for a minute,' said Cilia. She was fit to drop, but she wanted to take that little walk with me.

We came to the railings of a terrace and caught our breath. The night was calm but dark, and the street-lamps floundered in the cold black abyss that lay before us. I said nothing, and my heart leapt as I breathed the smell of it, wild and free. Cilia looked around her and pointed out to me a line of lights, their reflection quivering in the water. Was it a ship? A breakwater? We could hear waves splashing gently in the darkness. ' Tomorrow,' she breathed ecstatically, ' Tomorrow we'll see it all.'

As we made our way back to our hotel, Cilia clung tightly to my side. ' How tired I am! George, it's lovely! Tomorrow! I'm so happy! Are you happy, too?' and she rubbed her cheek against my shoulder.

I did not feel like that. I was walking with clenched jaws, taking deep breaths and letting the wind caress me. I felt restless, remote from Cilia, alone in the world. Halfway up the stairs I said to her: ' I don't want to go to bed yet. You go on up. I'll go for another little stroll and come back.'

7

That time, too, it was the same. How I hurt Cilia! Even now, when I think of her in bed as dawn is breaking, I am filled with a desolate remorse for the way I treated her.

Festival Night

Yet I couldn't help it! I alway did everything like a fool, a man in a dream, and I did not realise the sort of man I was until the end, when even remorse was useless. Now I can glimpse the truth. I become so engrossed in solitude that it deadens all my sense of human relationships and makes me incapable of tolerating or responding to any tenderness. Cilia, for me, was not an obstacle: she simply did not exist. If I had only understood this! If I had had any idea of how much harm I was doing to myself by cutting myself off from her in this way, I should have turned to her with intense gratitude and cherished her presence as my only salvation.

But is the sight of another's suffering ever enough to open a man's eyes? Instead, it takes the sweat of agony, the bitter pain that comes as we awake, lives with us as we walk the streets, lies beside us through sleepless nights, always raw and pitiless, covering us with shame.

Dawn broke wet and cloudy. The avenue was still deserted as I wandered back to the hotel. I saw Cilia and the landlady quarrelling on the stairs, both in their night clothes. Cilia was crying. The landlady, in a dressing-gown gave a shriek as I went in. Cilia stood motionless, leaning on the handrail. Her face was white with shock, her hair and her clothes in wild disorder.

' Here he is!'

' Whatever's going on here, at this time in the morning?' I asked harshly.

The landlady, clutching her bosom, started shouting that she had been disturbed in the middle of the night because of a missing husband; there had been tears, handkerchiefs ripped to shreds, telephone calls, police enquiries. Was that the way to behave? Where did I come from?

I was so weary I could hardly stand. I gave her a listless glance of disgust. Cilia had not moved. She stood there

Wedding Trip

breathing deeply through her open mouth, her face red and distorted. 'Cilia,' I cried, 'haven't you been to sleep?'

She still did not reply. She just stood there, motionless, making no attempt to wipe away the tears that streamed from her eyes. Her hands were clasped at her waist, tearing at her handkerchief.

'I went for a walk,' I said in a hollow voice. 'I stopped by the harbour.' The landlady seemed about to interrupt me, then shrugged her shoulders. 'Anyway, I'm alive, and dying for the want of sleep. Let me throw myself on the bed.'

I slept until two, heavily as a drunkard, then I awoke with a start. The light in the room was dim, but I could hear noises in the street. Instinctively I did not move. Cilia was there, sitting in a corner, looking at me, staring at the walls, examining her fingers, jumping up now and then. After a while I whispered cautiously: 'Cilia, are you watching me?' Swiftly she raised her eyes. The shattered look I had seen earlier now seemed engraved on her face. She moved her lips to speak, but no sound came.

'Cilia, a husband shouldn't be watched,' I said in a playful voice like a child's. 'Have you had anything to eat today?' The poor girl shook her head. I jumped out of bed and looked at the clock. 'The train goes at half past three,' I cried. 'Come on, Cilia, hurry! Let's try to look happy in front of the landlady.' She did not move, so I went over and pulled her up by her cheeks.

'Listen,' I went on. 'Is it because of last night?' Her eyes filled with tears. 'I could have lied, said I had got lost, smoothed things over. I didn't do that, because I hate lies. Cheer up! I have always liked to be alone. Still, even I,' and I felt her give a start, 'even I haven't enjoyed myself much at Genoa. Yet I'm not crying.'

24th November – 6th December, 1936

The Intruder

My cell-mate rambled on and on in a mumbling voice that did not carry beyond the four walls. There was nothing to stop us quarrelling if we felt inclined, or even singing, with a certain amount of discretion. I was a young man, and every now and again would heave a painful sigh that ended in a groan, but I never heard my companion do anything but mutter away to himself. He lay on his bunk and stared at the ceiling. Sentences oozed from his twisted mouth in a quiet, inexhaustible stream. Often I imagined I was alone, and would carry my stool over by the door so that I could lean back into the corner and gaze at my empty bunk, but I noticed that Lorenzo's muffled voice followed every movement I made and even seemed to suggest the very thoughts that came into my head.

Lorenzo was an old man, tall and fat; his voice seemed crushed by his great muscles. In spite of his way of arguing with the air around him he was a taciturn fellow. If I asked him something, he invariably remained still and silent for a while, as if hesitating to speak, before making any reply. When it came it was short and sharp, spoken in an undertone.

In the mornings, of course we were both wide awake and active. We washed ourselves, then quickly cleaned everything in the cell, while all around us we could hear the

The Intruder

noise of clattering tins, splashes, voices. Then we went out into the corridor where we ate and saw a bit of life. It was during the long afternoons and when dusk was falling that my sighs would begin, and Lorenzo started muttering. Yet if something out of the ordinary happened – heavy footsteps passing the door, or a guard looking at us through the peep-hole – Lorenzo never let it startle him, as it did me. He just stayed where he was, standing up or lying on his bunk, and took no notice.

If I happened to be reading some book or other from the prison library, Lorenzo, who couldn't read, would stamp to and fro with that heavy body of his until at last he slackened his belt and collapsed on his bed.

'No-one ever saw anything like it!' he started muttering. 'Reading a book as if it was a newspaper! A poor sort of company! Not so much as a walking stick! That's the governor's idea! They let you read books in prison just to suit their own purpose. A man who reads will stay quiet and treat his superiors with respect. They can do what they like with him. The written law is what makes prison strong. Disgusting to see a young fellow in here lapping up all that stuff as if he was paid for it! In prison, nobody should do anything. Just let the time go by. The right sort of man has as much as he can do to get through the day. If he has to read to keep himself company, he's like those women who want a man about the place all the time. If they haven't got one, they keep a cat.'

'If you're talking to me, Lorenzo,' I told him once, 'you ought to know there's nothing like a book to kill time. Better than playing cards.'

'That's a fine way to talk,' he went on, still not moving. 'When you play cards you always have company, and in the end somebody pays. You see who's in luck and who isn't. It's a battle of wits; there are the rules! Only

Festival Night

scroungers play for the sake of winning a few *lire*, but it gives a man some satisfaction to win a drink for himself by his own skill. Do they allow cards in prison, d'you think? Of course not! It's obvious! Cards are one thing, books another.'

He might have been about fifty, and his crown of grey hair was always well slicked down on his skull, unruffled by his headstrong thoughts. When he was not talking, he chewed a fag-end like an ox chewing the cud. He never seemed to be seized by the hungry longing for tomorrow that tormented me every day at dusk. My sigh of relief that night would end my boredom, was tempered by the hopeless certainty that the next day would bring the same boredom, the same hope, the self-same longing.

When they brought me into this little cell, on that first evening, Lorenzo was stretched out on his bunk. He threw me a listless glance as the guard in charge of me stood by the wide-open door while others brought in utensils and blankets from outside. As soon as we were left alone I started talking to him with all the brash over-confidence of inexperience, and boldly asked if he were awaiting trial, but my fat companion waved me away and muttered irritably that we were neither of us in any condition to concern ourselves with questions of that sort. We should get along all right together if each of us minded his own business; if we treated one another with reserve; if, in short, we behaved like two gentlemen who happened to shelter from the rain in the same shed. No need for more, except to excuse him if he ever snored in the night.

At the time we had days of persistent rain pouring down on the prison roof and in the courtyards, saturating everything. Even the light coming through our barred window was the colour of lead. Our rough blankets were unpleasant to touch with our numbed hands; in the morning, every

The Intruder

object in sight was humid and depressing; the only warmth we had was when the rations came round and we could enjoy the genial presence of a scalding mess-tin squeezed between the knees. Lorenzo, ignoring me completely, would babble away at great length to his tin, bending over it so that the steam wreathed itself round him and warming his hands on it as if it were his own fireside. The rest of the time he lay at full length on his bunk, talking to himself. In those early days, I thought his behaviour was due to the bad weather. Even I wanted nothing better than to sink into a drowsy inertia and forget the squalid walls around me.

At last the rain stopped and great gusts of wind dried everything up, bringing clear skies again. We could see a patch of sky through the squares of our barred window, and I watched the white clouds as they passed. But still Lorenzo spent most of the time staring at the ceiling, grumbling incessantly. I quickly got used to stretching my legs in the narrow space between the corridor and the cell; in the same way I finally managed to ignore that continual muttering, as long as Lorenzo talked to himself. But sometimes, as inconsistent as a drunkard, he would pick holes in whatever I was doing, or question me, or let his random thoughts come to the surface, all about prison, cunning, stupidity or the tavern. Then there was nothing I could do but say something aloud, as if talking to the walls, but I soon found it did no good. It gave me no relief; instead, it left me unsettled, straining my ears.

Towards evening I managed to forget that Lorenzo was there at all and I dropped off to sleep, distraught by my old longing for tomorrow, letting the twilight numb me like a frost. This was my only means of solitude. As for Lorenzo, it was plain from his gloomy muttering that he had no desire at all to get out. One morning as I stood by the window, clutching the bars and taking deep breaths of fresh air, in the chill silence I heard him cursing me.

2

'What's the matter, Lorenzo?' I asked him, turning round. Lorenzo, sitting on his bunk, raised his head from a pair of shoes that he was lacing, and stared at me.

'What's come over you, Lorenzo?'

He still made no reply, but bent his head over his work and started mumbling, the usual sign of a conversation going on in his own mind. I paced up and down the cell, my thoughts in a turmoil. Often, on such mornings, I realised in an instant of terrifying lucidity how irreparable was my own condition.

'If you don't know how to control yourself,' – the muttering grew suddenly clear – 'how will you get on in prison, or when they let you out? You're like a sick man studying his own fever. Much better read your book; but if it doesn't even teach you how to stay in prison, that means you're really crazy, and in that case the police records are all wrong. If I were you, I should put in an appeal, a fine appeal on those grounds.'

'It doesn't suit me,' I retorted. 'I shouldn't be any better off than I am here.' I paused a moment, then went on: 'Listen, Lorenzo, what made you start getting at me? I haven't done anything to you, and I wish all this silly nonsense would stop. Already we're in prison. If we keep quarrelling, it'll be purgatory.'

My huge companion rose to his feet, wiping his nose on one of his massive hands that could have hurled me to the ceiling. 'Have you been dreaming, too?' he asked doubtfully.

The Intruder

'What do you mean by dreaming?'

'That's all right. You weren't dreaming. Then why were you acting like a kid?'

'I wasn't.'

'You don't know you're born, yet. And here you are in prison. You start smoking as soon as they give you a cigarette, because you need something to calm you. You can't calm yourself. Who have you got outside? Some girl who doesn't come to see you here?'

'I'm married,' I stammered.

'Then your wife can set her mind at rest. You won't get run over by a lorry in here. What did you do? Play with matches and set fire to your bed?'

'Lorenzo, you're old enough to be my father, so I let you talk. It's true that I'm in your cell. You weren't put in mine. But that's not my fault. Nor have I asked you why you are here. We are here, that's all that matters.'

Again the old man looked at me dubiously. 'Then remember that we are here, and understand what that means. Don't bite your knuckles and don't sigh. Don't run to the door whenever anyone goes by. Stretch out on your bunk and learn to be alone. Any kid going to the dentist knows more about life than you do.'

So that morning passed, too. The patrol went round, bringing our food. Lorenzo went out into the open air. I stayed behind in the cell, looking into my own mind, while the silence throbbed around me. Now and then I refused to go out so as to make a change, to do something of my own choice. But I was not at ease that day. I paced wearily up and down, imagining myself really alone; and I realised that until now this idea had really terrified me.

My wife had written to me that if I was convicted of the disgraceful charge brought against me at my trial, she would, for very shame, apply for a separation, and she

Festival Night

thanked God we hadn't had any children in our three years together. This information had passed over my head like a wave over a drowning man. I turned it over in my mind, before and after, and I soon learned that any man who is sent to prison gets a letter like that: clear and ruthless, or watered down in a long, inky screed, one day it comes through that little peep-hole; you hold it in your fingers and know that they want to be rid of you. That morning I saw myself as if enclosed in glass; no longer imprisoned by walls and bars but isolated in a void, a chill void that the world knows nothing about. This was the real punishment: that the world rejects a convict. What I longed for was not so much to be free, but that the world should come into my empty void and bring it colour, give it warmth with words and gestures. Reading was not enough, my cell-mate was right; what I needed was that someone, at least, in the world should think of me, send me a message now and then; not that everything should vanish in that dreadful, unnatural nothingness.

When Lorenzo came back, he was still thinking over what I had said about his being old enough to be my father, laughing ironically and muttering to himself. I was sick of reading and settled down to listen to him.

'In prison,' he began, after a while, 'a man has no need of illusions. Only fools create illusions for themselves. The government puts us in here to punish us: it's up to us to fool the government, and go out worse than we came in. Here a man sees things as they are. If there's any bad blood in prison, who's responsible for it? The prisoners, perhaps? No, Sir. The warders, who run here and there, always busy, always carrying tales, like porters at a railway station. They never leave us alone. That's why, if I find a Christian eating his heart out in this place, I want to knock it out of him. Nobody dies in prison.'

The Intruder

'They don't say so, but men do die of it.'

'It's a grand thing to do without other people,' Lorenzo went on, now absorbed in his soliloquy. 'What is this world, anyway? People say so many useless words: they're more full of tricks than a monkey. A man who can wander about as he likes is never at peace. He sees a woman and wants her; he sees a piece of land and tries to get hold of it. Along comes a policeman and asks him: "Why did you touch that woman? Why did you steal that land?" "But I needed her; I had to have it," all the fools reply. "Then come along with me, and you won't need anything any more".'

The police are right. But some of us are more cunning than any of them. 'No need to raise your voice. We weren't brought up together.' Even if the prison is full, there's always another cell. 'You have to be alone.' A clever man bursts out laughing. He's never been alone. 'I'd like to try it.' And from then on, he knows. His cell no longer frightens him, and he lets the guards run where they like. All the world seems upside down. A dead man here, a drunkard there, or a woman killing a child. 'Arrest them! Put such people underground! Run!'

Instead, a clever man does not run. In prison there's room for everyone. So many cells, and each man has his own. He has the right to stay in it alone. In here, people show what they are made of. Some go mad if they are kept alone.

3

At night-time, in the ghostly light from the tiny bulb, I listened restlessly to the breathing from the neighbouring bed. My weariness was all in my head. I never felt sleepy. I wondered whether I made the same raucous sounds as

Festival Night

Lorenzo whenever I had a nap. I stayed quiet, trying to go to sleep, trying not to disturb the painful thoughts I could feel crouching in my mind, ready to leap out and destroy my rest. Cautiously, almost furtively, I tried to find oblivion. But Lorenzo's mountainous bulk turned over, his bunk creaked, he muttered something, and I opened my eyes again to stare at the dim light. The patrol came round with a rattle of padlocks. I turned over to try and shut out the sound.

In the dead of night I grew drowsy and had incoherent dreams in which everything happened a long time ago and my mind, conscious of its own disorder, found no peace in them. I saw myself as a boy again, running off into the fields; or I was talking with my wife, caressing her with silly little gestures of tenderness.

In the grey light that comes before dawn I was already wide awake and waiting for the sudden clang of the bell, anticipating its deafening vibrations when the hammer fell. Lorenzo never even sat up until we could hear the first erratic tinkling sounds made by the patrol coming round to check the bars, and he had finished dressing by the time that patrol, working from each cell to the next, had reached our own. Then the door was thrown open, the head warder came in, another guard ran to the window and lifted his hammer.

One morning I heard my cell-mate exclaim: ' I tell everybody . . . .'

' Get on with it, you,' said the chief to the guard. ' What d'you want?'

In the deafening clamour, Lorenzo came forward excitedly and mumbled something. ' What is it?' the chief shouted. The guard was already waiting for him by the door.

The Intruder

My huge companion lowered his head as the clanging echoes died away into silence. His lips protruded, his face was slack and wet with tears.

'What do you want?'

'Nothing,' said Lorenzo. The chief rubbed the back of his neck in uncertainty. 'Have you any complaint?' he asked, pausing by the door.

Lorenzo turned to me and repeated quickly: 'Have you got a complaint?' The chief went out and the door was locked.

Lorenzo attended apathetically to the usual things. They came round to collect the rubbish and it was his turn to sweep out the cell. Then he mended a sock and chewed his fag-end. Then we both went out into the corridor. Lorenzo sat down on one of my illustrated magazines and leaned on the courtyard wall, his head between his hands. He wouldn't say anything and twice, when I spoke to him, he growled like a dog, so I lay down and looked at the sky, watching the flight of the pigeons.

When we were back in our cell, he planted himself on the stool, his head bent, and muttered: 'Did you have any complaint?'

'Lorenzo, this is no way to act,' I told him nervously. 'Learn how to behave in prison.'

'If you have a complaint,' he persisted obstinately, 'I want to warn you. You don't know what a complaint is. You must make it by word of mouth. Don't write it on a form, because they keep all the papers and read them at the trial. You've got to keep your wits about you, in prison. They hold you here on purpose to find out all about you and drive you crazy. They make you read, they make you write, then they can take it easy and keep track of everything that happens. Haven't you realised yet why they come round and hammer at the bars? It's not just to inspect them.

Festival Night

No one has ever broken the bars. They come and make all that noise, night and morning, in the hope of driving a prisoner off his head, making him cry out, getting him to talk. Then they tell him: " We'll see about it, we'll see. But now write it down and sign it." Then they inform the magistrate.'

Not knowing what to reply, I pulled a mouthful of bread from the fresh loaf and sat chewing it while I thought over what I had heard. ' Lorenzo,' I said. ' Did they reduce you to this state?'

Lorenzo peered at me suspiciously. ' No,' he replied softly, ' but they try it on with everybody. You've got to be cunning.'

That evening, when in the distance the persistent hammering began again, the morning's scene came back to my mind and I went over to Lorenzo's bed where he lay outstretched staring with dull eyes at the ceiling. I saw him move. ' Listen, Lorenzo,' I said brusquely, ' what did you want from the chief, anyway?'

Lorenzo closed his eyes drowsily. ' Lorenzo,' I repeated, ' Stop playing the fool. What was it about, that lie you told this morning?'

Without opening his eyes he raised his great hand and waved me away. Meanwhile, with brief pauses, the rapid hammering grew nearer. Irritated and worked up by the noise, I repeated my question and seized his wrist. With a furious wrench the giant released his arm and brought it crashing down on my chest. He jumped up and knocked me sprawling to my knees, then gripped me by my shirt and the flesh of my breast so convulsively that I felt no pain at first, only the shock of the blow. Two wild eyes glared at me, mad with rage.

' Nothing to do with you,' he roared in a voice full of hate. ' I won't talk to you, nor to any of the others. I don't

The Intruder

want to set eyes on you, even at night. This bunk is mine; this cell is mine.'

As I panted and struggled, all I could think of was that we must stop fighting before the patrol came in. The hammering grew even louder and sharper till my head swam; there was a roaring in my ears; and still Lorenzo kept spitting at me from his twisted mouth, driving me before him with a rain of heavy blows from his huge fists.

Then I felt someone pull me away; I saw the guards and fell crashing to the floor. Three men sprang on Lorenzo, trying to trip him and make him fall. In the struggle, one of them trampled on my hand. In the end they all rolled on the bunk where they managed to hold him down, still spitting and roaring.

'Take him down below,' said the chief coming forward. The whole group began to move. 'You stay here,' he shouted to the man with the hammer, who raised it and gave his usual deafening blows on the bars. Then they all went away, locking the door.

A moment later, the peep-hole opened. 'Did that lunatic injure you? Hold yourself ready to make a statement.' Then it shut again.

(30th December 1936 – 14th January 1937)

The Three Girls

It amazes me that Clara, Lucetta and even Signora Ugolina (who isn't a girl any more) are always so ready to exclaim that all men are disgusting, that they despise them and never know what to do with them. It's all they talk about. I don't think I've ever slept in silk sheets, but I've never said things like that or even thought them, not even when I was young and silly. Perhaps it's not really surprising in Clara's case. It even shocks her that I go boating. Clara is made of crystal and might break. Judging by the way she talks, that crystal is filled with some precious liqueur that must not be spilled. I suppose they enjoy it together, she and that ugly cross-eyed girl she takes round with her everywhere, even to the Winter Palace when it's open.

Lucetta says, for something to say: 'Men! They're clumsy, crafty good-for-nothings. Even if they're not born that way, they get like it.' Take that cheeky airman of hers, for instance, always chewing his cigarette or cupping it in his hand. His mouth is twisted and he keeps winking. She's so crazy about him that she has to tell me all about it. He gives her a dreadful time, says awful things to her, borrows money from her, and after all that he only has to grin at her and she throws her arms round his neck! She's softhearted, is Lucetta. I think he's a bit of a devil and she'd

The Three Girls

do anything to please him. Pity she's so mad about him! Sometimes, though, I fancy she tries to lead us up the garden. It wouldn't surprise me if she thoroughly enjoys all the things she complains about, finds them an outlet for her own feelings.

I shan't forget the evening when that accountant friend of hers met us from work. (This was before any of us at the Nirvana knew she had fallen for a new boy-friend). When I set eyes on that poor chap and his spectacles I felt like bursting out laughing and going off by myself, but Lucetta made me stay. I knew by the look in her eyes she had some scheme in mind. She insisted that her serious-minded Gino should walk arm in arm with both of us, so that's how we started off. I was quiet and well-behaved, but Lucetta bounced along, digging him in the ribs with her elbow now and again, shrieking with laughter so that everybody stared at us.

'Quiet, Lucy! Keep quiet!' he urged her. With me, he pretended to be unperturbed. He was more polite than ever, to offset Lucetta's wild behaviour, and told me about his life, his likes and dislikes, his hobbies and recreations. He put me in mind of a bed-bug, trying to hide himself behind me as if I were a sheet. Lucetta pestered him unmercifully, made him raise his voice and shook him until even I could hardly keep a straight face. 'Old Bellyache!' she called him, and carried on as if she was crazy. Stammering and terrified, he cut short his flow of oratory and faltered: 'Shut up, Lucy! Be quiet!'

'So you're the sort of man who can't bear to be seen out with girls like us! We're not posh enough for you! Who d'you think you are, anyway? Go on! Run away and hide! Jump in a ditch! What d'you expect to get out of us? If you're ashamed of us, say so! We don't care!' All this in

Festival Night

front of the Central! I gave him a tolerant smile, like an indulgent mamma trying not to be upset by all the fuss.

That's the sort of thing Lucetta would do. And she had the cheek to call men spiteful! But she's thoughtless and lives for the moment now gay, now sad.

She gets depressed when that cynical lover of hers tells her straight out that he has no intention of marrying her. She's not stupid – just a bit crazy. She expects too much from life. Out in the street she's free and easy and she thinks men are a joke, but it's the easiest thing in the world to catch her unawares with her eyes wide with desire. Sometimes it seems to me that she's walking about naked and doesn't know it. One day as we were leaving work a stupid lout came up and tried to pal up with us. I pulled her away and would not answer him, but a few minutes later Lucetta remarked peevishly: ' Pity there weren't two of them.'

I don't envy these city girls. I grew up running barefoot among the vineyards, then I was kept at school. My father is a simple farmer who still spreads the manure himself, but it seems to me that I know a lot more about life than they do. I don't consider men are disgusting or harmful, but then I don't run round after them like a cat. I get lots of ideas as I walk through the streets. Boys look us up and down, seeing how we are dressed but knowing no more about us than that. It's easy to overlook the fact that we really know nothing about them, either. I think it's great fun to study fashions, choose colours, learn how to walk and use one's eyes, but the point is that I know it's a game. Lucetta takes it seriously.

The one who puzzled me most is Signora Ugolina. When my aunt first took me to call on her, she embraced my aunt, then me. So far, so good. But almost as soon as we sat down she began to colour up and devour me with those dull eyes of hers. As my aunt went on talking she turned and shook

The Three Girls

her head at me, which annoyed me so much that I laughed in her face.

After living in her house for a while I got to know her better. By now I can read the meaning of every tiny wrinkle on her face, and notice how her colour flares up when her passion rises. She is not an old woman, but she is thin and bony: yet, watching her, I feel sure she is better-looking now than she was as a girl. Clara, who sometimes comes to supper, once whispered to me with half-shut eyes that even now our hostess is an amorous woman.

In my early days there, she was very tactful with me, making casual comments that broke me of certain provincial ways; without seeming to do so, she would advise me how to dress to make the most of myself; sometimes she would stroll round the town with me; but mostly she let me do whatever I liked and find things out for myself.

'You girls!' she sighed one day. 'It upsets me that you go out to work. This bachelor-girl life you lead doesn't suit you at all, Lidia. The moment you wake in the mornings you throw on your clothes and dash out, while I stay here feeling I'm the only woman left in the world. What do your days mean to you? Just leaves on a calendar! Don't you ever think of doing better for yourself in the future, Lidia? Take care! Some day, other girls will come along even harder than you are, and brush you aside as you do us older women, leaving you shut up at home with your memories. If you want to stay young, you must enjoy being young.'

At other times she is relaxed and gay, and then her face glows. Once I was more in her confidence and she felt she could talk without reserve, we were soon on very good terms. Except in years, she is no older than I am; in everything else – thoughts, desires, fancies – we are much the same and can talk as friends. Now and then I catch

Festival Night

glimpses of a certain bitterness that surprises me, so well does she keep it hidden behind an amiable, conventional façade, and I try to find out more about it.

'Lidia,' she said to me once in an anguished voice, 'it's the most dreadful thing to reach my age and realise that everything is an illusion, a filthy horrible illusion. You can give them everything, give up everything for them, make the ultimate sacrifice, even go down on your knees. As long as we have a little grace left, a little warm blood, anything they can take from us, they put up with us; and then, when they no longer know what to do with a woman, they blame her for their humiliation, though she has suffered the same from them. If you're nice to them, if you have once given them pleasure, you ought to be able to do it all the time. Even this can happen. That's a terrible thing to have to tell you, Lidia, at my age.'

'Then leave me my illusions, Signora.'

'Ah, you're joking Lidia. You make my blood run cold at times. I know what you girls are like. You think it's enough to look men straight in the eyes like dogs, and dominate them. You don't know that the vilest, meanest, most stupid man can trap a woman, humiliate her, break her life in pieces. That's the way of Nature.'

She says things like that at table, fixing me with her eyes, changing colour, venting her spite on the food she has just put in her mouth. I feel trapped there and eat quickly, looking her up and down. That hard look in her eyes makes it difficult for me to understand her. She isn't the poor, downtrodden woman she tries so hard to appear; she rages too fiercely against what she calls her humiliations. If anything had humiliated me as much as that I could never bring myself to talk about it. Or perhaps she likes to exaggerate, so as to feel more feminine.

Still, it is true that in a city one cannot live without think-

The Three Girls

ing of it. I am conscious of it while I'm dressing, walking about, looking around. I can understand, now, why I felt so gay when I first came here, so eager to go out walking and look around me, happy to see the strip of sky above every street. In the country, such things don't mean anything. There's too much sky there, doing no good to anybody. But it isn't only the sky. Whether I'm up in my room or down in the street, I'm thrilled by the fresh, clear light, the sunshine and shadows, people walking up and down on the pavement. But even that isn't all. There's the surprise and delight of realising I'm a woman, independent, owing nothing to anyone, being able to look a passer-by in the eye and know I'm his equal. But more than anything else, it is a quiet tenseness, a desire ripe for harvest, a wild expectancy.

I can't help thinking of it. It's great fun and gives meaning to the bustle in the street, the colours, everything around me. In a way, I can understand Lucetta. I listen to her telling me the usual things – spiteful jokes, all about her silly fits of depression – but what I understand is something different, something given away by her eyes. In my early days a voice in the street, a smile or word of greeting from the first man I met, was enough to exalt me, fill me with a limpid, golden bliss that was all the keener for being secret. Automatically I amused myself by fancying the whole street shared my intoxication, while I eagerly absorbed a vague impression of the unknown. And then I would grow numb with astonishment, realising that the underlying cause of it all was a casual glance from a man who was probably married, anyway. So much for my flights of fancy, born of nothing more than a smile! Oh! How our blood surges through our veins!

But even in moments like this I am still myself, enjoying my own company on my walk. I can look at the stones in the walls or the cars flying past so as not to lose my grip on myself, because that's where the danger lies. Losing our self-control, giving ourselves away. Signora Ugolina and Lucetta are always giving themselves away, and that's the real reason for all their imaginary troubles. They reveal that they are taking something seriously when it's really only a game.

How self-assured the Signora was, the time when Nanni called for me at the house. Studying her thick knuckles as she talked, she asked him what he called me; whether he really liked boating or went just to please me; whether he always wore that white pullover; whether he lived with his parents or in lodgings; in short, she pumped him in her gushing, gracious way, quite convinced she was doing it for my sake. Nanni sat there listening to her with his usual calm, his jacket slung over his shoulders, just managing not to laugh at her. When we were outside he took my holdall and asked me bluntly: ' Does she always carry on like that, even with you?'

' We all do that sort of thing,' I explained to him. ' When I was a little girl I used to kiss the cat and talk to it just as the signora did to you. When we grow up...' (Nanni chuckled at that) ' and are old enough to fall in love, some of us understand that men want something different, and some of us don't. Still, it's a rare gift to remain childlike, as she has.'

' What a woman you are!' Nanni exclaimed.

During our last month together we saw each other every evening. He worked in the same street as I did and came to meet me after work, then we would go and have supper together. He always telephoned the signora first, to tell her I should be home late, but she always waited up for me looking anxious and worried, calling me an abandoned woman and warning me not to let him go too far. She was

The Three Girls

baffled by his casual manner, his steady eyes and his way of slinging his jacket over his shoulders. She imagined him capable of the most sinister designs and asked me how he looked in shorts.

But Nanni understood me, or perhaps he had always been like that. I still remember his silences, those evenings when I went up to his room, and the dim light streaked with spirals of smoke. He did everything so simply, the way I like it – as if he were a boy eating fruit – never asking if I belonged to him. Then I watched him grow restless and every time I was afraid he would say something stupid. Instead, he came out with a tentative suggestion that we should go down, move on, amuse ourselves somewhere else.

The moment we were outside he was gay again, as if he owned the street, and off we went on the best of terms. He never got tired, but I very soon did and would bend down with a smile to rub my ankle. Then Nanni would resign himself to a café.

We talked of trivial things: he told me of his craze for travelling and how he wished he had been a sailor; he asked me about my part of the country, and whether I wanted to go on working in an office. He did not like city-life and advised me to get away from the people here and go back to my own village. He couldn't understand why a woman should want a job. As I listened, it always surprised me that he expressed his thoughts so plainly and simply. With him, I seemed to see myself reflected in a mirror, hearing him calmly discussing things I would say only to myself.

When he went off to the mines (he was fed up with sitting at a desk), he was shame-faced as he told me about it, as though it were something wrong. ' But, Nanni, you're doing fine! You'll live as you like and not have to bother about keeping clean or wearing a jacket. Don't they wear high

Festival Night

boots in a mine? And there aren't any women down there. I wish I could come, too.'

Nanni moved his lips to speak, but then decided to say nothing and just smiled at me. If I remembered nothing else about him, the memory of that smile would always make me close my eyes in tenderness. I was so glad he asked nothing of me, for if he had spoken I'm still afraid I should have said yes.

Like a fool, I was terribly upset to see him go, and have to go back to the office. I went to the station with him, and the smell of the coal (it was a cold morning) made me want to jump in a train and get away somewhere. I thought of the barren smoke-filled places Nanni liked so much, those chill bottomless pits he would go down, and I lifted my eyes to the airy sky as Nanni would raise his when he came to the surface again.

I was so lonely that, for days, I talked about him to Clara. She gave me a wink and asked whether women were allowed to go boating by themselves. I advised her to wear her bathing costume under her dress, and one Sunday we found ourselves on the river. Clara brought along the cross-eyed girl – who seemed to have a chip on her shoulder – and they lay at full length in the bottom of the boat, stroking their legs and undressing bit by bit. We glided to a deserted spot where the bank was fringed with trees. Clara slim and blonde, was wearing a lovely little white costume. I was rowing and the other two were quarelling, glaring at one another, turning their backs, exchanging insults or sulking in silence. The sun was very hot and as I rowed I half-closed my eyes, thinking of the past, as if Nanni were still there, pulling at the oars, while I lay back and looked at the clouds.

Clara knows how to talk, and her own special friend was being cold to her, so she started teasing me because I was

The Three Girls

rowing slowly. The other girl gave a sneering laugh, so Clara stuffed a caramel in her mouth to make her shut up. There she sat, pale and bony in her bathing costume, scratching her hairy calves, sucking her caramels and grumbling all the time about the sun. It beats me how Clara, who fancies she's like fine crystal, can be on such intimate terms with so much ugliness and stupidity. If that's what they want, I suppose it's all right. It's up to them. But why show her off to me – in a bathing costume, too? And why grumble at me because she doesn't like sunshine?

I felt irritated and disheartened, and was no longer enjoying the excursion. They had destroyed my peace of mind and I felt like knocking their heads together with an oar. It depressed me to remember how often, between these same river banks, I had been so idiotically happy.

As it happened, it was the cross-eyed girl who took my mind off my troubles. A boat came along, full of happy-go-lucky fellows who yelled the usual things at us, so she slipped of her bath-robe and waved it wildly above her head. Naturally the boys decided to come closer and rowed across. One of them nearly jumped into our boat, but Clara gave her precious friend a sound box on the ears and I strained at the oars to get away from them, so the fellow fell in the water. There were shouts and laughter and in the end we got away, but only just.

Clara and her friend were no longer fit to be seen; one was furious, the other trembling, and both quarrelling as if they would never stop. At last I stopped rowing and hissed at Clara: ' If you want to make that sort of scene, do it at home. Out of doors you should behave discreetly when men are about.' And Clara just stared at me and couldn't say a word, so she gave that wretched creature a final scowl and snapped: ' We'd better go back.'

So now they're shocked at me for going boating. But I

Festival Night

don't regret that outing because, whenever I think of it, I regain that sense of independence I had almost forgotten. Clara doesn't matter to me, nor does Ernestina. I'm on my own again. They are just intruders. When I got out of the boat, all my sadness fell away from me as if I had shed a heavy load. No longer did I regret the fun I had had with Nanni, or find my memories painful. Nanni had been a dear friend to me, as I had been to him; we had satisfied one another, embraced each other and then had parted. That was enough. Without realising it, we fully understood each other. Now and then we had found complete serenity, and nothing should tarnish our memory of it. Those friends of mine, and the way the days dragged so heavily, didn't matter at all. The vital thing is to take what comes and be true to yourself. There's no reason why you shouldn't go on the river again and dream of what is past, but watch your step, don't give yourself away by a look. Much better to shut your eyes.

It made me so gay and light-hearted to regain my self assurance and feel mistress of myself again that for the next few days I could hardly contain myself. Lucetta, who can recognise happiness when she sees it, said to me: ' What's got into you, Lidia? Is that rowing friend of yours coming back?' I smiled. Then I asked if she would like to go to the dance with me, but that tormentor of hers had promised to take her, so we spent the afternoon laughing and joking round the little table until they went off together, arm in arm. I joined them again after supper, at the Nirvana.

By this time, even Signora Ugolina has noticed that Nanni isn't around any more. In the evenings she watches me anxiously, as if I were ill. She sighs, turns red and chatters even more wildly than usual, trying to probe my troubles. She cannot understand how I can bear to go boating again, all by myself.

The Three Girls

'Ah, Lidia, I knew it would end like this! I can put myself in your shoes, just as if it had happened to me. You were so keen on him, I could see. What are you going to do now? Forget him, Lidia! Do you write to him? Oh, I know how you're suffering, Lidia. Such pain takes your breath away. We should be ashamed to let them hurt us so! What did he tell you? Did he promise you anything? Don't believe such promises, don't believe anything! Poor child! Did he take you to his room?'

I let her talk, and answer her now and then, but I do not tell her what she wants to know, nor do I mention any indignities or humiliations. In the hope of leading me on, the signora probes into the cesspool of her own past and whispers her secrets to me. Amazing that she doesn't even blush! Instead she turns pale and perspires.

Yet I could have told her things that would have surprised her. I had hardly left school when the fever of love first seized me. I really was ill then, yes, indeed. But would she understand how such beginnings could end in such peace? Sometimes even now, if I wake in the night, clutching my pillow with burning hands and too terrified to move a finger, I remember what it was like then. Again I feel uprooted, lost in misery. I see myself skipping eagerly across the field, stopping every now and then with my heart in my mouth and my nostrils flaring, terrified by what I was doing, but even more terrified at the thought of not doing it. Giusto would stroll along, whistling, and smile at me, calling me: ' Poor little kid.' He would slip his arm around my waist, feeling the wild beating of my heart. How he flattered me! Then he wandered into the glen: I followed him.

There was a chestnut plantation on the bank, (long afterwards I found a chestnut leaf pressed in one of my books), and beds of fern, lumpy and rough, with patches of moss

Festival Night

here and there. Giusto would throw me down on the ground wherever he happened to be. The first few times he would laugh if I broke away because a stone was sticking in my back. One day he said he knew how fine and virile he was, and if I kept coming there it meant that I found him satisfying. Like a silly fool I hid my face against his chest and determined not to complain any more. I didn't even realise I was stronger than he was.

But though these meetings turned my life upside down, at least they cleared my mind, leaving me to go home alone and exhausted, yet sometimes even serene. I would sit by myself on the threshing floor and think over what had just happened, my cheeks aflame. I was like a bitch on heat: I tremble, now, to think of the risk I ran, but perhaps the very violence of my desire, my fears and everything, protected me. Giusto, fresh from his wife, never gave it a thought; I was sixteen.

I could tell all this, but how could I describe the state I was in at home with my family? The sleepless nights, my disgust with myself when I woke, my wild anguish when I thought of the future and dared not hope that this foolish attachment would ever come to an end? I could tell Lucetta, perhaps, if only she did not admire me quite so much.

Giusto had been married for a year to a pale, devoted little woman who, as I learned later, was already pregnant. She had enough to do in the house and the business – a drapery shop on the edge of the village. I was attracted to Giusto simply because of the thrill it gave me, that summer, to run from home to the new shop and choose a material for the first dress Mamma let me have after I left school. Under the very eyes of his wife, Giusto squeezed my hand inside the folds of a green silk muslin that made me tremble all over because it was so beautiful. And though I knew,

The Three Girls

even then, that he was a mere upstart from the gutter, it still disturbs me to remember how his bold eyes changed and flashed between the rolls of cloth.

His timid wife smiled at me every time I went by. She knew, I think, that her husband was already false to her, but not with whom. She would not ask him, but grieved about it alone. She often went to church. Now I know I wasn't even the first. I could understand that woman: I was not jealous of her, but in her degradation and mine I saw a kind of link between us, a joy and suffering we had in common. (She was not yet twenty.) One thing I remember well: I never envied her for being his wife, and that means that something inside me resisted what threatened to destroy me. Perhaps it was only an instinct, a faint yet steadfast voice from myself as a child, as I could be again. When I think of the danger that nearly engulfed me, and how I was saved by instinct, by some unconscious power, I really believe that everything happens to us as it will. We can do nothing about it; judgment and will-power are just words. No one can lose himself or save himself, but as we are born, so we shall always remain.

Giusto wanted to use me; instead, what happened is that in his hands I became a woman. What gave him power over me was my own desperate need to get away from the country and come to the city, to know myself better, as I had dreamed of doing at school. He found me timid and fearful; he only had to raise his hand to imagine he had seduced me. But the real truth is that any pleasure I felt from his crude intimacy and cold eyes was like looking at myself in a mirror. In fact, nobody has managed to seduce me since.

Meanwhile, drifting as I was, I put up with it. I was even rash enough to talk to him about my dreams for the future, and this made him often call me a typist. One day, feeling

Festival Night

reluctant, I said to him: 'You're mad! I shan't come tomorrow!' and he tried to frighten me with an icy glare. But that summer was very hot and I couldn't keep away. Still, I no longer felt any desire for him. My natural self-assurance must have been dormant then, though later it was strong enough for me to persuade my aunt to find me work here in the city, and get my family to agree. I just bent my head and kept my suffering to myself.

Then, suddenly, I was free, without wanting or even trying to be. No more putting up with it, no more inner conflict. At first I didn't even understand it. I felt on my own again, breathless and a little tired, but at peace, serene and clear as water – clearer than the sky had been all that summer. It happened one day as I was walking through our vineyard on my way to the path by the chestnut trees; it was already late in the afternoon and a big translucent moon was rising over the plantation. I had nothing special on my mind that evening, or any feeling against Giusto. On the contrary, I was convinced that he was serious about me and his roughness was due to his fear of losing me. I had left home in a hurry, thinking it was perhaps rather late. As I walked between the rows of vines I was thinking of our meeting and feeling surprised at myself. My steps faltered; I stumbled over the clods of earth, annoyed with myself for going; and all at once I knew I was free. I paused, held myself straighter, asking myself what Giusto meant to me. I smiled to myself, imagining him waiting there alone, looking so ill-tempered, crafty and uncouth, and I heard myself laugh out loud in the silence. Suddenly I felt an urge to test him, to wound him, and I took a step forward. Then I stopped and smiled once more, while the bats darted to and fro across the moon. I raised my arms as a baby does, then burst into shrieks of laughter like a silly girl and turned to go back. I was alone; that was enough for me.

The Three Girls

I even forgot my spiteful impulse to see how Giusto liked being jilted. I was free and on my own.

Neither that evening nor on any day that followed did I go with Giusto again. At first I stayed home, saying I was tired, and so Giusto heard that I was not well. The truth is that I was still rather afraid of him and hardly felt equal to meeting him. I could scarcely believe that the fever which had burned in my blood all that summer had really left me, but at last my tiredness went and I no longer felt reluctant to go out.

I saw him still hanging about the fields, looking for me, following me. Once he came face to face with me, scowling and humiliated, but his threats and pleading only made me lose patience. Soon his quarrels with his wife were the talk of the market-place and shocked everybody. He never had anything more from me. When his baby girl was born I decided to come to the city and I haven't heard of him since.

(23rd January – 12th February 1937)

Festival Night

1

Over the threshing floor, smooth and firm as a marble table, the evening air was rising, fresh and cool. When the setting sun has only just dropped behind the brow of a hill, the earth around the base of it seems to glow with a light of its own, a clear, serene radiance emanating from the stones and the bare soil. In the still air behind the cowshed, snatches of dance music could be heard, borne by the wind and broken by the distant hills, as if shrill voices were quarrelling far away.

Two boys with bundles of leafy branches were sweeping the threshing floor, their bare feet shuffling over its cold, hard surface. Darting sly, sidelong glances at the Padre, they seized their chance at a moment when he leaned inside a barrel and boxed each other's ears. A third boy, also barefoot, wearing long trousers, was sitting on a low wall, tying up his own bunch of leafy twigs with a strip of willow bark. Every now and then his hair fell over his face and he tossed his head to shake it out of his eyes. As the other two began squabbling he looked craftily at the Padre, who, with his cassock well tucked up, was still bending into the barrel trying to retrieve his stick, and hissed to the smaller boy: 'Soak him with that liquid manure.'

Festival Night

Another barrel stood open on the threshing floor and from that one, too, came a powerful stench, its pungency softened as it rose through the cool dusk. The boy lifted his bunch of twigs to dip it in this barrel, but let it fall from his hand as the Padre straightened up, red in the face, and began wiping his fingers on his sack apron. The boy ran away, crying: 'Padre! Rico's trying to mess me up, Padre.'

The Padre glared, then turned to the lad sitting on the wall. 'You're at the bottom of the trouble! You're the rock of offence!' he shouted at him, wiping the sweat from his forehead with the back of his hand and coming to a halt in the middle of the threshing floor. 'It's always you, Biscione. What are you doing, sitting there? You've already had your supper, I suppose? Your belly's swollen! We're all good at making manure, but mixing it means hard work. Get on with it! Clean this threshing floor! It will soon be dark.'

'The floor is ready,' said Biscione, without moving.

Along the path from the dung-heap came the schoolmaster with his coat over his shoulders, buckling the belt of his trousers. 'What nice fresh air there is here,' he murmured, walking close by the wall of the cowshed where the floor was not beaten so smoothly. He came and sat down on the little trough by the pump, a shallow basin filled with rubbish, and stretched out his legs, breathing through his nostrils, his eyes half shut.

'Look at all these ants! Just here!' cried the Padre, his face to the ground. 'Look out, Biscione! They're on their way to a festival, too! How they run! They seem to know the maize is coming. We shall spread it out for them.'

'Rest for a minute, Padre,' the schoolmaster broke in, filling his pipe, 'and listen to the music. It seems as if heaven itself is singing and the very wind making music tonight.'

Festival Night

Biscione was sparring with the other two by the pile of branches. The Padre turned and went over to the schoolmaster, between the barrels. 'It's a fine rough wind that has brought us this music,' he said, 'and you talk of heaven! Anyone who wants to find our boys should go there and look for them among the circus tents. Sideshows and animal cages, cages and sideshows! How many came to school today?'

'Two.'

'Fine! And the parents are even worse. They eat and drink, drink and dance. They might at least listen to the music. Yesterday I was passing through the square... it was six o'clock in the afternoon... and, would you believe it?... I saw that woman... that station-mistress... and she's old enough to know better... arm in arm with her father... her own father, I tell you. They got into one of those dodgem cars and started going backwards and forwards, shrieking, bumping into the other cars, crashing against one another like animals. Imagine what goes on in those cars at night-time. One man, they told me, had his hand crushed between two machines.'

The schoolmaster, with a wry smile, was watching the smoke of his pipe, and beyond it, as though through a cloudy mirror, the two boys who were tying up branches. Biscione had disappeared.

'We mustn't judge, Padre. Not all unmarried people are penitents like us.'

'But you know yourself,' grumbled the Padre, digging a bit of tobacco out of his cassock and chewing it briskly – 'you hear the young people coming home all night long on the main road, staggering from one ditch to the next, so drunk they can hardly stand, spewing out all the foulness they know or don't know, kicking at our door as if it were

Festival Night

a tavern. And there's no shortage of women among them, either.'

'All it means is that when the September Feast of the Madonna comes round a fine procession will sprinkle holy water on your door, too.'

'That's all very well!' snorted the Padre. 'Those circus gypsies know when they're on to a good thing and they won't leave the valley all that quickly. With all due respect, they're like this dung we're getting ready. Once you put your hands in it, you never get rid of the smell of it.' And the Padre again began rubbing his fists on the sack hanging from his neck. They were huge brown fists, streaked with black in every crease, under the nails and around the wrists. They looked like wood or shrivelled meat. Below the edge of the sack protruded his bare feet, and those, too, were knotted, covered with earth and twisted like roots.

'This smell isn't bad,' said the schoolmaster mildly. 'It shouldn't be unpleasant first thing in the morning, spread between the furrows.'

'As long as it's cow-dung, I agree,' said the Padre. 'But this lot, here, makes your eyes run. So scalding and acid it's no use even as manure.'

The schoolmaster puffed away at his pipe. 'For me, this is a sign of the good and bad aspects of our condition. In our body there is a devilish element – ill will – that poisons even what we expel. The acidity is of the spirit –' and he peered through the rank smoke at the Padre's fleshless face.

'Very likely!' the Padre answered. 'Nothing easier... Biscione! Are the brooms ready? Where has that rascal gone?'

As Rico and the other boy came forward, waving long bunches of alder, Biscione hastily reappeared, hitching up his trousers. The Padre went over to meet him, looked hard

Festival Night

at his face and seized him by the wrist. Biscione was almost as tall as he was, but slender and not so deeply tanned.

'You went off for a smoke, eh?' said the Padre, his face close to the boy's. 'Where did you get the money?' Without replying, Biscione tried to wrench his arm free, while with the other he pretended to be fastening his trousers. 'You've been smoking,' the Padre repeated, without letting go of him. 'No nonsense! I can smell your breath. Where did you get the money?' Biscione did not answer.

'He'll collect fag-ends,' said the schoolmaster, from the pump.

'Fag-ends, indeed! I've even found fag-ends he's dropped,' snarled the Padre. 'He goes round selling baskets of peaches for me; if he doesn't do worse. Do you know you're stealing what belongs to the Lord? D'you know that?' Panting, he ransacked the boy's pockets, twisting his arm. He found nothing. 'At sixteen! These are the poor little boys we take in for charity's sake. "Idiots," the Father Superior calls them. In the ordinary way they'd sleep in ditches and come to a bad end. You're a fool, you are! So am I, and the schoolmaster. You're sure to end in a ditch, if not worse. Vagabond!' and he punched him in the face. 'Just you try and give me the slip another night, to go to San Rocco!' He hit him again. 'You don't know what you're doing!' And with a kick from his bare foot he sent him staggering three yards away. 'Get a broom and work, Biscione. That name is just right for you.'

But Biscione, who had let himself fall to the ground, jumped up and was on the point of hurling himself at the Padre. He trembled visibly, raised his arm, gripped the skin of his flank through his clothes and leaned forward. The Padre, furious, stood ready and waiting; his cassock had dropped down to his heels again, at the back. Biscione spat at him, gave a roar, turned away his head, then the

Festival Night

rest of his body, started to run and disappeared behind the cowshed.

The schoolmaster had risen to his feet and was waving his pipe in one hand.

The Padre stayed a moment open-mouthed, as if on the point of crying out, then gave a shrug and turned to the others. ' Are the brooms ready? Now for the barrel! Remember, the hangman's bell-ringers don't stop working even for the Ave Maria. Come on, you others.'

The schoolmaster turned to sit down. The limpid air, clear as glass, was beginning to darken, softening and isolating the sounds that all seemed fresher, sweeter, under the bowl of the sky. Beyond the mulberry trees rustling on the nearby slope the hills stood black and distant. The bursts of music were more frequent now, more ethereal, throbbing in the tranquil air, freeing themselves in the sky from the tumult, the excitement and the wine that gave them birth – a sound as pure, as remote from humanity as the voice of the wind.

Bare feet were shuffling on the pale, hard threshing floor. The two boys were stooping in front of the barrel, ready with their alder brooms. They no longer looked at one another and seemed intent on some game. The Padre planted himself behind the barrel, his legs wide apart in their light-coloured underpants, his arms spread out to clasp the top of it. Like a wrestler he heaved at the huge cask, rocking it to start the contents moving. ' Ready!' he hissed. The two boys waited, tense and still. Then he gently tipped the cask forward, directing its mouth between them, towards the threshing floor. For a moment he balanced it there, at an angle, then slowly, cautiously, let it slant a little more, his body going with it. Panting and grunting, he braced the weight of it with his arms, his spine, the back of his legs and his heels. Away from him and between the

Festival Night

two boys the dark evil-smelling slime began flowing in a rush of foam, dropping and spreading like oil. The boys leapt back. 'Get at it, you two!' roared the Padre, straining every muscle. 'Get into it! Spread it!'

The two boys bent forward, busy with their brooms. Every time one of them fell, the frothy mass splashed in all directions. Their feet made splashes, too, as they struggled frantically at their task, raising their hissing brooms, then quickly lowering them again to avoid the drips, their eyes screwed up tightly, their noses turned aside, sometimes bumping into each other, deaf to all else and working as if possessed. 'Rogues!' yelled the Padre with all his strength. 'Good-for-nothings! That's enough! Let it flow. A bit more round the side. You should be able to use up the lot... Get some at the side... Gently, now... Go along with it... Ah!' He kept on spitting and clearing his throat, still bent over the cask, still gripping it tightly as, slowly, relentlessly, it poured out the mixture.

Some semi-solid, semi-liquid splashes from the stinking flood even reached as far as the schoolmaster. He felt his head swimming as the fumes stung his eyes and nostrils, the distant music rang in his ears, and a wild impulse seized him to shed his shoes and stockings, strip off his clothes and plunge into the heaving mass, leaping and shouting, his beard flying in the wind. But he didn't bat an eyelid, except for the tears that streamed from his enflamed eyes.

The two boys had already calmed down. In response to the Padre's voice they obediently took short, careful steps and with their long brooms, now unrecognisable, they bent over and slowly swept the bubbling mass to get rid of the froth, pushing it away from them as they moved forward, glancing at each other now and then. As the last dregs drained from the steaming cask the Padre let it fall

Festival Night

to the ground and collapsed on top of it in a single, shapeless heap.

'This smell, Padre, goes to a man's head like new wine,' the schoolmaster remarked from the shadows where he sat spitting.

'We're all a bit responsible for it.'

2

Rico set the big lantern down on the window-sill and peered into the storeroom. The wide patches of shadow danced as the flame flickered, the whole room quivered like an earthquake in the ruddy glow, then the dangling bunches of garlic, last year's yellowing corn-cobs, piled up sacks of grain, all grew still again and could be vaguely seen for what they were.

'Here's where you sleep.'

Barefoot, the two boys went in across the floor of beaten earth, leaving the light by the window. 'The Padre said we were to wash,' Rico breathed in a whisper. 'I'm sleepy. I'd rather stick my feet out over the edge of the mattress.'

'If the Padre catches you, you'll see what happens. Look at what he did when Biscione started playing up today,' muttered Gosto, under his breath.

'You silly ass! Biscione does it all on purpose. What happened to him? Nothing. Biscione ran off and came to bed. That way he didn't do any more work. Every time Biscione manages to get himself kicked out, we stay and do the work by ourselves. He did the same thing when the garden had to be hoed. Afterwards the Padre forgave him, but meanwhile I did the hoeing. You were in the vineyard, that time.'

Festival Night

Rico shook the lantern to put it out. Its dying flare danced over the three mattresses lined up against the wall. The furthest one was torn, and on it lay Biscione, face downwards with his legs together, his chest bare, his pale arms crossed under his head. He had not moved, not even disturbed by Gosto's muttering or the rustling of the dried leaves of the mattresses. As the shadows gathered, Gosto made the gesture of throwing a stone at him, his mouth distorted in an ugly grimace.

'No!' whispered Rico, and as he spoke the storeroom was plunged into darkness. There came a deep breath or two as they stretched out, creaks and rustles from the mattresses, a grunt and a sigh. Then the outline of the wide open window came into view again, a vague shape in the shadowy gloom.

Through the window, in the chill night air, came the sound of music, now echoing in the distance, now very close at hand, clear, yet faint. It seemed to breathe with the wind, suddenly ceasing, then coming back again mixed with the noise of the grass-hoppers or drowned by a gay voice singing, who knows where. Then the voice died away in the night and the wave of sound was lost among the trees.

'Rico,' Gosto muttered, ' you stink. It makes me sick.'

'You're the one who stinks. I ran round the meadow to wash my feet in the dew.'

'That was no good, Rico. There wasn't any dew by that time.'

'The Padre will scold you tomorrow. You'll see. You're not Biscione, you know.'

'Tomorrow,' said Gosto, his voice muffled against the mattress, 'I'll ask the Padre to let me go bathing in the Piana. He said he'd let me, if I didn't run off on the sly. I know a little lake, cool as a well, where the girls go. Once I saw some of them there, wearing only their shifts. I'll tell

Festival Night

him we're taking the ashes to the rubbish dump, and then we can run to the girls' bathing pool. The Padre lets us go and wash after taking the ashes, so we can stay there as long as we like.'

'How did you manage to see the girls, Gosto? We aren't allowed to.'

'There are rushes growing on the sand by the river. You can get quite close without being seen. You ask the Padre, too. Then he'll let us. You need a good wash, too.'

'Don't be stupid, Gosto. The threshing floor's finished, now. Tomorrow we'll be bringing in the maize. Workmen are coming and we'll all be off to the fields before daybreak. A fine chance that he'll let us go tomorrow! We'll be carrying so many of those baskets that we'll be streaming with sweat inside our shirts. Even Biscione will have to work tomorrow.'

Gosto gave a deep sigh and turned over noisily. The storeroom was alive with tiny sounds, the creaking of wood, gnawing teeth, the flutter of wings. Biscione had not moved.

'Let's go another time, with Biscione,' Rico whispered. Then, after a silence, 'Do the girls always go there?'

'If Biscione comes, too, the Padre's sure to notice it. He was already playing up, today. He's capable of starting to talk to the girls, and then I shan't be able to go there again,' Gosto objected.

'What are the girls like? Can you see them?'

'No, because they keep their shifts on. But you can see their legs. The big ones have legs as white as butter.'

'Biscione saw one of them once with a man, when he went to tread grapes at the Rossi's place. He says they were lying together behind the bushes in the Pratone, towards evening. They were doing what dogs do. He heard the woman laughing.'

'When was that?'

Festival Night

'Last year, at the feast of the Rosary.'

'That was wrong of Biscione. Why didn't he tell the Padre? Are we the only ones who have to make confession?'

'Then the man went away and the woman saw Biscione. She told him people are allowed to embrace in the grass.' Rico's shrill, breathless little voice broke in a stifled snigger.

'Ugh!' replied Gosto, stuffing his mouth against the pillow.

'Biscione gave me a cigarette, once,' Rico went on softly.

'Did you smoke it?'

'Sure.' Again a distant surge of music echoed through the trees. Rico paused until it was drowned by the shrill piping of the crickets, then he repeated, more emphatically. 'Sure. And he told me the Padre doesn't get goitre, simply because he chews tobacco. Look at the schoolmaster: he smokes a pipe and he hasn't got goitre, like you. You ought to smoke, to cure it. I'm going to smoke, so that I shan't get it.'

'But Biscione has never had it.'

'Because he smokes, that's why. He told me that the Padre won't let us smoke, because then we'll both get goitre and no-one will give us work outside the village.'

'But what about women? They don't smoke, and hardly any of them have goitre.'

'It's not the same for women. Besides, once in the main road I saw one go by in a carriage that came from Canelli, and she was smoking.'

There was silence for a moment, then Gosto said, barely forming the words: 'You'll see. He won't get away tonight as he did on Sunday. If the Padre gets to know about it, he won't let him come back in. That's why he was cheeky to the Padre today.'

'Biscione gets out when he likes and he always comes

Festival Night

back,' Rico stoutly protested, ' even if you spy on him as you did on Sunday.'

' But he was going dancing.'

' Ass! D'you think they'd let him go in the dance hall, barefoot? Instead, he went to see the menagerie in the big tent. He says there are so many other things to see, but that's the best of all.'

' Really?'

' There's a woman dressed to look naked, in glittering tights. She waits by the door and calls the people in. Inside there's a lion leaping about in a cage, and the trainer who rattles a pitchfork along the bars to make him turn. He says the lion roars like thunder. Everybody goes to see him. Biscione couldn't go in because it costs ten *soldi*, but he says you can hear everything from outside, even the tamer talking to the lion and the woman when she dances. Even the straw smells fierce, quite different from ours. When the show was closing, Biscione had a chat with the lion-tamer. He says he was wearing top boots and leather arm-bands. He's a Hungarian and knows lions as if they were oxen. He went into a booth for a minute and threw four darts: every one of them hit the bulls-eye. Then, Biscione says, he laughed and talked with the girls in Hungarian, and the woman who looked naked came along in those tights to take him away, and he ran after her with his whip all the way to the caravan where they sleep.'

' Does the woman really wear only tights?' Gosto mumbled under his breath in the silence.

3

There came a louder burst of music and Biscione suddenly raised his head. In the deserted night, that drunken tumult

Festival Night

was the only sound on the wind. He stayed still, his eyes wide open, and soon he could make out the vast walls, the vague shapes of implements, the sacks and the dangling bunches of vegetables. From the next mattress came Gosto's rapid breathing.

Cautiously, Biscione got up and climbed through the window. Outside, the night was clear and cold. He looked up between the star-filled trees to make sure the night was still young. He did not hear the crickets singing. He ran lightly across the courtyard to the little door of the Padre's house. As he ran, he kept one hand firmly pressed against the leg of his trousers.

At the door he looked around, bending his head and straining his ears. In the distance the noise of a crowd was caught by the wind, but the music had ceased. Nothing could be heard, not even the dripping of the pump. He could have wished for the sound of a drunkard in the street, the howl of a dog, anything: instead, the night seemed utterly empty, hostile, making Biscione's ears ring, as if waiting.

A cricket chirruped. Biscione loosened his belt and took out the bill-hook. He brandished it for a moment in the shadow of the wall. The great hooked blade was cold but the smooth horn handle, broken at the tip, was still warm from his trousers. With a laugh he drew it across his cheek and the chill of it made him shiver. Then, silently, he whipped it through the air at the full length of his arm. If the Padre had had a goitre, like Gosto, that blow would have sliced it off. Biscione remembered when he had cut a grass snake in two. What a stroke! And the two pieces went on wriggling. A snarl escaped him.

He pushed the little door. It was shut. 'Bastard! He doesn't trust anyone,' he whispered. He turned and ran to the window. This was open – wide open. Biscione leaned

Festival Night

through it and listened. He could hear no sound from the darkness. The crickets were now in full chorus, but he heard nothing else. 'If the crickets don't wake him, no-one can, as long as they don't start shouting.' Out of the gloom came a faint creak – perhaps a piece of wood in the wind – and the bill-hook slipped from Biscione's hand. Before it reached the ground he caught it by a sudden convulsive effort, then he groaned. Jerking forward, he had hit his forehead on the window-sill. The whole world seemed to crash around him, the night, the stars, the blackness. He fell to his knees under the window, dazed, filled with a presentiment of evil, his breath coming quickly, his spirit cowed.

Nothing moved in the room. 'Oh Lord, grant that he hasn't heard me.' Then he stood up again, listening. He climbed over the sill.

His feet on the cold tiles, he went forward blindly, shutting his eyes to accustom them more quickly to the dark. Suddenly he stopped. Far away, a dog howled in the night. Gripping the bill-hook, he strained his eyes in the gloom. He turned back to the window. Now he could see the first tiles beneath the sill, a chair in the corner, the vague outline of a cupboard. He swung round again: now he could make out the pale shape of the bed. He held his breath and took another step forward. Light blazed out and flooded over him where he stood.

The Padre was sitting up in bed, his hair on end, one foot on the ground, glaring at him with wide-open eyes, his hand still on the light switch. His loose nightshirt was undone, showing his bony leg protruding from the thrown-back bedclothes and reaching for the tiled floor. He pointed his left hand at Biscione, who was hurriedly trying to stuff the bill-hook inside his trousers. 'Assassin! What do you want?'

Festival Night

Biscione was turning his head in every direction, looking for a way to cross the room, jump through the window and escape in the darkness. But he felt the cold steel slipping down his leg and twist itself round his feet.

'You won't get away,' shouted the Padre, jumping out of bed, his white shirt flapping round him, 'you'll never get away as long as I live. Where did you want to break in?' He was on him now, hitting him. Biscione twisted round, trying to bend down. 'Stay where you are! Stay there! Every night we have more thieves. What's the matter with your feet?' Biscione tried to throw himself on the ground, clenching his teeth and bellowing. But the Padre punched him aside, then bent to pick up the tool that had fallen free. 'You rogue! Going round with bill-hooks in the middle of the night! What were you meaning to do with it here? D'you fancy you're an expert already?'

'I wasn't going to burgle anybody,' whined Biscione, clutching the table where he had ended up, very out of breath.

'It's all the same. A bill-hook's for breaking in somewhere or killing someone. There's no one for you to murder now. What did you want in here?'

They stared at each other, dazzled by the harsh light, the Padre suspicious, dishevelled, as if his shirt had been blown on him by the wind; Biscione breathless, limp as the trousers that were trailing on the ground. They stared without a word. Biscione's mouth twisted in a faint ironic sneer. The Padre even had hair growing in the hollow at the base of his throat.

The Padre's eyes flashed at that look. He shook all over as if he had ague. He turned his head this way and that, lost in thought. Then with a scowl he raised his eyes, passed the bill-hook into his left hand and with his right made the sign of a great cross, finding himself in some difficulty as

Festival Night

he tried to put his hands together afterwards. Biscione stood waiting, hanging his head.

'Don't move,' said the Padre quickly. He ran to the window and looked out, then closed it. He went back to the bed to find his underpants. 'Don't move,' he repeated, threateningly. He laid the bill-hook down on the bedside table, hastily dragged his pants on anyhow and then looked around for his cassock. Swiftly he whipped it over his head, emerging with his eyes still on Biscione. The lad had not moved from the table but was now leaning on it watching the Padre's every move, still with the same faint sneer.

'There's nothing to laugh at, you fool,' said the Padre coming over to him, fully dressed. Biscione cringed aside as if to avoid a blow.

'Now kneel down.'

Instead, Biscione straightened up with his hands on the table, still staring at the Padre.

'Kneel!' roared the Padre, raising his fist. 'Down on your knees, you madman! You could have died tonight!'

Biscione let himself slip to the floor, knocking his knees on the tiles. He saw the Padre's knobbly feet, then, as he glanced upwards, his furious eyes glaring down at him.

'I repent, O Lord my God....'
'I repent, O Lord my God....'
'of the dreadful thought I had....'
'of the dreadful thought I had....'
'against my benefactor....'
'against my benefactor....'
'and I thank Thee for having saved me....'
'and I thank Thee for having saved me....'
'in Thine infinite mercy....'
'in Thine infinite mercy....'
'from the death of the soul.'
'from the death of the soul.'

Festival Night

' Now make the sign of the Cross and repeat the act of contrition.'

Putting his hands together at his breast, Biscione bowed his head and began mumbling devoutly under his breath while the Padre stood over him with outstretched arm, repeating the prayer with him. At last, Biscione slowly raised his head and the Padre solemnly traced on his brow the sign of absolution.

' That's better,' he said with a deep sigh of relief. ' Let's hope you'll benefit from it. On Sunday I'll confess you again with the others. Understand? Then you'll make general confession and we shall see what you deserve. You are to recite five *paters, aves* and *glorias* each evening from now until Sunday.'

Biscione had risen and stood tapping his arms with his crossed hands, looking doubtfully at the Padre who was mopping his forehead.

' Vagabond, did you mean to break in here? Don't you know that even to think of it is a mortal sin? Let us thank the Lord for his goodness in saving me, and saving you, too. What on earth's got into you? I hardly recognise you! All because I stopped you smoking?'

Fidgeting restlessly, Biscione let him talk, his eyes growing obstinate as he stared at the covered window. Then he replied, ' On Sunday I shan't be here.'

' What?'

' I told you before, Padre. I'm going away.'

' Where do you want to go?'

' I'll find a job. Anyway, I'm not stopping here.'

' But where will you go, you vagabond? Think of what you've done, and will do! Is this how you repent, how you turn from evil? God can hear you, you wicked boy. If your Padre doesn't keep you, who d'you think will take you? D'you really want to die in a ditch? We begin harvesting

Festival Night

tomorrow morning, and you with mortal sin at your throat? Put it out of your mind, Biscione. There's no need for you to run away. As far as I'm concerned you are forgiven, but God calls you to give an account of yourself and change your way of living.'

'I'm going away because here we are no better than animals.'

'Animals? How?'

'Beasts of burden. Say what you like to Rico and Gosto, in front of anybody, but don't give me that stuff about being a fool and dying of hunger. With the schoolmaster there, too. I work like the others – more than the others – because I'm no fool; but when I've finished, I've finished. I want to relax like the schoolmaster and everybody else; and to smoke if I choose, or go for a walk in the country when my day's work is done, like all workers. I'm sorry about tonight and I won't do it again, but I won't be such a fool as to go on working for someone who doesn't pay me.'

'Biscione,' cried the Padre, 'you repented and you can still think of payment? Is this how you fear God? At your age?'

'I don't want to rob you of anything,' Biscione went on, 'and if I'm young, that's not my fault. I work like anyone else, in working hours, and I've just as much right to be paid.'

'But your food, a place to sleep, what you wear, isn't all that payment enough?'

'No! It's not enough! The day-labourers you employ get their food, too. You give them rough wine as well. We get none. It doesn't cost anything to sleep. And the trousers given us out of charity are worn-out before we get them. That's happened to Rico twice, and he's so short he can cut them off at the knees. No, I'm not satisfied.'

Slowly the Padre walked over and opened the window,

Festival Night

letting a soft breath of night air into the stifling heat of the room. The wavering square of light shone across the courtyard and out into the night. There came from the darkness a confused noise of horse-play and far-off shrieks of laughter.

' Listen, Biscione. You were born in shame; you have no family, no-one. You came from the foundling hospital. It's no good thinking of the schoolmaster. You can't go to school, like gentlemen's sons. You've got a home here, you're learning a trade, there are good examples before your eyes. Why aren't you happy? Why don't you thank God? D'you think you could find work anywhere else, at your age, without our help? Shame is what you'd find, vices and temptations. You've shown what you're capable of already tonight. You might threaten someone and be taken seriously, another time.'

' The world is full of people who threaten and are still respected. When a man gets a pay-packet, temptations don't bother him.'

' Look here, Biscione, to your shame you're not a fool, but even if you'd been born mad the Lord would still have loved you. For men who work in the country it is a good thing to be simple in spirit and never look further than your own cattle, thanking the Lord for that much luck....'

' You're no fool, either, Padre. There are other jobs, away from the land.'

The Padre came closer, his eyes sharp. ' What other jobs?'

' There's a man from the Piena earning four *lire* a day, looking after the horses at the circus in the square. He just gives them a little chaff night and morning, and takes them to the pond. It's already settled. I'm going to Alba with them.'

' Behold the Devil!' roared the Padre, starting back.

Festival Night

' Circus horses, running round and round all day! Going off to Alba! Living like a gipsy! To think of it! And that's where I came from ... They're always on holiday, and what are the consequences? Did they talk you into it? You're a penitent, like me. You repented. Vagabond! You dare to talk of payment? A man gets paid for working, not for going round the streets with music and dancing. Let that suffice! What other miracles did they lead you to expect?'

'You're the one for miracles, Padre. Who mentioned music and dancing?'

'Wretch! Vagabond! Don't you know they're all runaways, delinquents? If you're already so wicked, with the life you lead here, what will you become with people like that?'

The Padre was thoroughly excited, waving his arms and raising his voice above a din that burst out at that moment beyond the trees by the roadside, an uproar of voices shouting and dogs howling. Even Fido had started barking. He was tied by a running tether to a wire near the railings, and the wire hissed as he chased up and down. Instantly the Padre ran to the window and peered out. He muttered harshly for a moment, then turned back to Biscione, solemnly shaking his head.

'This is what that sort of life leads to,' he said in a lower tone, his voice bitter. 'Is this what you're so keen to do? You've got it in you, you have indeed. But take care. Crafty men can be cheated by craftier ones. You wouldn't be the first they've worked to death and thrown penniless into the street when the festival's over.'

'It's hard to get paid anywhere. That's why I'm only asking for a half-day off. Half-pay till the grape harvest, plus board and lodging. Because I'm young. When seed-

Festival Night

time comes we'll go into it again. Free on Sundays, and allowed to go out when the work is not pressing.' Biscione was looking the Padre straight in the face, his hands stuck into his belt over his bare stomach.

The Padre said quickly: 'I'll give you Sunday if you don't draw your pay and take advantage of it at seed-time. However, first we shall hear what the Father Superior says.'

'Sunday without pay is like mass without wine. And the Superior is you. I'm too young to bother about profit. It means that I confess to you on Saturday.'

The Padre pulled at his knuckles. 'Now it's time to sleep, Biscione. We'll talk to the Superior about it. Night isn't the time to go into such things and I cannot . . . .'

'Night or day, what's the odds? It's enough that we've come to terms. It means I can get away. I'll come back at harvest time when you're short-handed and you've hired me by the day. To keep me out of temptation. Is that all right?'

Slowly the Padre went over to pick up the bill-hook from beside his bed, then returned to the table. 'Biscione, you filthy wretch, you deserve to have this round your head.' Holding it out to him, he went on: 'Go to bed, and put this back where it belongs.'

'Of course, Padre,' and he stuck the blade through his belt. Then he turned, looked around, and came back to the table with an air of decision. 'But this is a mass without wine, Padre.'

'What's that?'

Biscione grinned. 'Good bargains are made over a drink.' And he did not move.

'Vagabond of a vagabond!' snorted the Padre. 'At this hour! Don't you trust anyone, you of all people?' But he went to the cupboard and took out a bottle and a glass, then went back to the table and poured the dark wine.

Festival Night

'Pick it up. I'm taking mass tomorrow and it's past midnight.'

While Biscione sipped it, there came another outburst of shouting outside the window and such a din of stones thrown at the iron fence that even Fido's frenzied barking barely drowned it.

4

Seated at a little iron table, the schoolmaster listened to the dance music in the square as it worked up to its final thunderous climax, more vibrant and deafening than ever. The roar of the trombones drowned the shrill clarinets, the cymbals clashed in frenzy, the trumpets joined in a long-drawn-out, ear-splitting squeal. Then suddenly there was silence, except for a low-pitched vibration, as if the voice of the music, having soared to its peak, had sunk down to earth again, humming under its breath.

In the cool night air, mellowed by the fumes of wine, he watched the comings and goings of the customers. It was stifling in the large room and the noise was deafening. The thick curtain of smoke swirled as men shouted to one another, all of them streaming with sweat. Around the tables were groups of carters with their red woollen sashes; old men from the country, their hair over their eyes; flashily dressed young hooligans; all holding glasses, sucking up their drinks with wet lips, banging on the tables, yelling, surrounded by a litter of waste paper and puddles of wine. Outside it was festival night, by God!

In his seat beside the door, the schoolmaster was cooling himself by holding his hand round the little empty beer bottle, leaning against the wall with his usual saturnine smile. Steering a course between the backs of customers in

Festival Night

the half-light came a rough looking barmaid, a tall, raw-boned woman with big hips. As she poured wine from bottles or flasks, her lips twisted contemptuously as if she found the wine, the festival and everything else thoroughly distasteful. Every time she straightened up her hips bounced, and the schoolmaster half-closed his eyes.

Outside the door, where a ruddy light was shed by a lamp hanging from the architrave, a brawl had started between two deep-voiced country bumpkins. They stood there, their laboured insults inaudible above the noise of trumpets, the cries and the interminable trampling of feet, panting like a pair of bullocks. Stubbornly they persisted for a while, undeterred by the uproar around them, until the barmaid went to the door and stormed at them to go somewhere else. There was a silence, except for a wild burst of trumpet music coming from who knows where, then the two yokels pushed the barmaid aside and staggered in, arm in arm, making for a table at the back of the room.

The barmaid stayed by the door for a moment, her hips only a couple of handbreadths away from the schoolmaster's cheek, stretching her neck in the ruddy light, trying to pierce the distant gloom illuminated by swinging acetylene flares. The schoolmaster leaned forwards, too, peering between her hips and the door jamb, until the maid turned to look at him with a frown, croaking ' Excuse me.'

' Let's have more air,' stammered the schoolmaster.

' There's plenty of air,' she retorted, darting away as someone called her.

As the night proceeded, the din outside grew less deafening. Only an occasional burst of music raised its head, enlivening the confusion for a moment before it died away. One by one the flares went out and the crowd thinned in the square. Here and there in the distance, along the roads to the hills, shouting broke out, wavering in the

Festival Night

wind. In the big room there were fewer people, more smoke, more wine fumes and a shriller babble of voices.

The schoolmaster had lit his pipe, wedging it between his sound teeth, and with narrowed eyes was watching everything through the smoke of it. The barmaid had come to the other side of the door and was sitting looking out, one large hand resting on her jutting knees. Now and then she glanced uneasily at her ugly, worn-out shoes. Her face was set in lines of utter weariness.

There came a moment when she broke into a smile. Another woman had appeared in the doorway, clutching to her breast a dark cloak that reached the ground. She was blonde and she looked furious, upset. She hesitated on the threshold and smiled at the barmaid. 'Hullo, Adele,' she said.

Adele twisted her knees aside so that the other could pass between her and the table, to sit in the corner. 'It's over,' sighed the blonde, falling back against the wall with her eyes closed. 'I'm worn out! More tired than a horse.'

Adele gave a thin smile. 'And I'm not, I suppose?' she asked, barely moving her lips. Then she rose to go away but paused at the door, her eyes searching the space outside.

'There's no hurry, Adele. I don't even feel like a glass of milk, tonight. There's a stink everywhere tonight. What a fug, in here! How they shout! And they stink like animals. Those at least can't wash themselves.' As she stretched her legs under the table her rose-pink shoes came into view. The edge of her cloak fell open, revealing the pink tights that covered her body as far as her breasts. Glimpsed thus, with her cloak undone, she looked naked but it was a lifeless, artificial nakedness.

'Still waiting for that fellow, Adele?' she asked casually, staring into mid-air through the smoke.

Adele swung round. 'I wonder why it is that other times

Festival Night

he jumps down from his cart when his day's work is barely over and doesn't get to his feet again. He sits where you're sitting now. Even when I'm dying to get to bed he keeps me here eating and laughing till daybreak. He'd even have me dancing if I listened to him.'

The blonde listened, rubbing her lower lip against her teeth, her chin in the air. She looked resentful.

'... and when San Rocco comes round I don't set eyes on him again. Off he goes in his cart, the sot, calling at every pub in the valley and sleeping under the stars. As long as the festival is on and there's a bench to be had, he doesn't come here, not even to save his life. He'll go and drink anywhere else, but here, no! I? Wait for him? Not likely! But what I'd like to know is, wine's the same everywhere, isn't it? Why doesn't he come here? It would cost him less, too.'

'No man bothers about the cost when he's out to enjoy himself,' the blonde replied slowly, 'and they don't fancy the wine they get at home. They stay away till the morning and then they're not fit to be seen, coming back with a splitting head, whining and moaning. And we're fools enough to give them coffee.'

'I haven't married him yet, so I can't order him about,' retorted Adele, 'but if he comes in here tonight he'll get coffee! I'll bash him over the head with it, the vagabond! In ditches, when he should sleep here with me!' The other barely smiled. 'Believe me,' Adele went on, 'I'm sick of it! Still, perhaps he feels bashful, and that's why he does his drinking at a distance. Once married, he'll no longer be shy.'

The blonde had loosened her cloak and was fanning her thin cheeks with the edge of it. In that dull pink sheath, with her too-red lips pursed, her light hair lifting as she blew, she looked like a picture from a calendar. In every

Festival Night

group in the room, men were eyeing her, putting their heads together and passing remarks. The schoolmaster gazed in the opposite direction, still surreptitiously watching her and listening, discreetly swallowing his saliva.

'For me, it's San Rocco all the year round,' sighed the blonde. 'We're always in ditches or bumping along the roads in a rickety wagon that lets in the rain. At least that carter of yours goes off by himself and you wait for him in peace and comfort. You don't have to trail round after him day and night as I do, with no friends anywhere and no company but two great insolent beasts. All day long they foul themselves and eat, foul themselves and eat. They've got to be cleaned and they've got to be fed, otherwise they'd fall ill and then we shouldn't eat, either. He never thinks of anything but those animals of his. If it rains we must go out and cover up the cage; if we have no money we've got to find some for them; if I had a baby they'd eat that, too . . . .'

The schoolmaster didn't even blink. '. . . yet I'd put up with it all if it wasn't for the stink,' she went on, breathlessly. 'For six years all I've smelt is that stink. And everywhere we go the people stink, too. Blaring music, deafening noise, drunks, people with their mouths wide open, yelling, drinking. If it's summer, they smell of sweat; in winter, they stink of the stable. Some nights I even smell it in bed. He brings it to me. The minute we're shut he rushes off to fill himself with wine and rub shoulders with the crowd. He has a fine time spending the night in ditches till the smell gets into his skin and he stinks worse than the lions . . . .'

Adele had jumped up and run to the door as the iron-rimmed wheels of a cart approached, and the blonde went on, turning to the schoolmaster: 'Some nights I can't understand how I manage to sleep with him. He'd just as soon sleep in the cage. But maybe now I stink, too. What am I in here for, anyway?' Her eyes widened as she looked

Festival Night

around. ' Wine and sweat. Nothing but drunkards. Give me that milk, Adele, I stink too, I stink.'

The schoolmaster knocked out his pipe in the hollow of his hand and mopped his forehead without answering. Adele turned from the door looking dazed, and said to the blonde: ' He's gone past!' Her breath came in a shuddering sigh.

' Who? Oh! Your carter. So you see!'

' There were four of them whipping the horse. Drunk already, and on their way to drink somewhere else.' The blonde took her hand as it lay clenched on the table and said to her calmly: ' Cheer up, Adele. The man I'm married to even left me stuck with the lions this evening, half-way through the show. I had to whip them through their turn myself. I'm furious about it. I felt as if I was beating him and getting my own back for all this filth. Who knows what state he'll be in when he comes back to me in the morning! You women in this part of the country never wash yourselves. Go on, Adele. Get me some milk.'

As Adele sullenly walked away, the schoolmaster cleared his throat and remarked, out of the blue: ' Aren't you hot in those tights?'

The blonde winked at him, opened her cloak and looked down at her breast. ' You want me to go without them?' she replied.

There was a brief silence, then the schoolmaster went on: ' I don't consider that you smell.'

' What d'you know about it?' said the blonde. When Adele came back with the beaker, she asked her sleepily: ' Has this gentleman laid his hands on you?'

Adele looked shocked. The schoolmaster's eyes widened and his mouth dropped open, showing his teeth like a horse. ' That gentleman there?' she answered. ' Why, that's the schoolmaster. He lives with the priest.'

Festival Night

The blonde opened her eyes as she drank, covering her faint smile with the beaker. ' I just wanted to be sure of it,' she said gravely, when she had finished. Then she pulled her cloak around her shoulders and went on: ' If you really want to, sir, let's go where it's cooler. These tights certainly keep me very hot.'

5

The Padre turned off the light and went out into the dark courtyard. Under the trees that hid the street he heard Fido whining, then the vibration of the wire as the animal bumped its head against it. He breathed the dog's name and it shot over to him like a dusky catapult, putting its paws on his stomach and wagging its tail. ' Good Fido,' whispered the Padre. ' The devil's even got into you, tonight. Good dog. On nights like this you should stay at home.' Fido rubbed against his hand, then stretched out its neck frantically whining to be let loose. The Padre pushed down the paws and moved back. ' Good dog,' he said again. ' Keep guard and set a good example.' Fido did his best to follow the retreating shadow, straining at the leash, half strangled; then falling back, struggling to get free and giving vent to a few muffled barks.

The Padre went to the storeroom window and groped for the lantern. He set it on the ground, bent down to light it, then straightened up, holding it at arm's length, suddenly casting its beam into the room and on to the mattresses. The great shadows loomed up and a smell of hay, sewage and sweat hit him full in the face. ' So they didn't wash, the little devils.' In the wavering light the half-naked bodies appeared, yellow and foreshortened. Rico was curled up, fast asleep with his face against the pillow and one elbow

Festival Night

thrust out behind. Gosto, his trousers undone, lay on his back with his face to the ceiling, his mouth open, choking now and then from his swollen, brownish goitre as if it were a breast created to suffocate him. On the end pallet, Biscione lay at full length on his side, still in his trousers, his eyelids tightly screwed up against the light. 'That one sleeps soundly – just as I do myself,' the Padre muttered. For the first time he noticed that Biscione's cheeks showed patches of soft, reddish hair. Or perhaps it was the reflection of the light.

As he stood holding up the lantern, running his eyes over the sacks, the store of corn-cobs, the blades of scythes stacked in the corner, there reached him on the still night air the faint sound of a song from some far-away farm, a gay, deep voice that hardly broke the silence and softly died away in the distance. There, at least, was someone celebrating San Rocco on his own.

Bringing his mind back to the work in hand, the Padre lowered the great lantern and made his way towards the cowshed. Its low wall, white and unbroken, ran out at an angle from the side of the main farm buildings, under the hay-loft. The Padre turned the corner of it, lifted the lantern and pushed the smooth wood of the door. In the solemn darkness everything was quiet. Two oxen were lying comfortably on the straw beyond the ladder, chewing the cud. At the sudden influx of light they twitched their ears, still staring ahead into emptiness, their great muzzles undulating in response to the steady, silent rhythm of their jaws.

The Padre set down the lantern on the low window-sill. Beyond the grating, the circle of light shone over the smooth surface of the threshing floor, darkened and clotted here and there where the newly-spread manure was still damp. At the edge of it, the mulberry trees cast a line of dark shadow.

Festival Night

Pitchfork in hand, the Padre passed the ladder and slapped one of the bullocks on the back. The animal placidly turned his head, his chain jingling. The Padre prodded him with the pitchfork to make him rise. Puffing and blowing the bullock got to his knees, bumped his nose on the manger, then, with a wave of his tail, heaved himself up until his muddy great haunches were level. 'You filthy great beast,' said the Padre. 'You're covered in muck. Worse than the boys.' Planting his bare foot on the ladder, he drove the pitchfork into the sodden straw by the animal's hooves and hoisted up a large black mass of it. Controlling the handle with both hands, he walked over to the barrel at the back of the shed and shook the load into it with a sigh of relief. Then he brought back a forkful of fresh straw, threw it down and spread it under the bullock. Almost before he had finished, the animal dropped to its knees and settled down again, still chewing the cud. All this time the other bullock gazed into the void, chewing placidly.

In the suffocating heat, the Padre went over to the window, put out the lantern and stood looking out through the bars into the darkness. From the dark patches in the pasty mass on the threshing floor rose a stench not yet dispelled by the freshness of the night. Once it had soaked up the dew it could be spread on the land without a single crack, to soften and enrich the soil.

Still restless, the Padre cast a final glance at the faint outline of the bullocks, hardly distinguishable in the shadows, and went over to the big double door. Pulling away the beam that secured it, he slipped outside. He had just stepped forward to test the surface of the paste with his foot, when, by the uncertain starlight, he glimpsed a human figure coming down the sloping side of the dunghill towards the path. 'Who's there?' he exclaimed.

Festival Night

After a moment's silence, the vague shadow replied: 'Nothing to worry about. It's only me.' Jumping down to the threshing floor, trampling over the soft manure before the Padre had time to shout: 'Careful! Watch how you go!' the schoolmaster came across and stood beside him.

'It doesn't matter,' he cried shuffling his feet. 'Mud, dung and dew are the elements of night.'

'It does matter,' the Padre protested. 'You're spoiling what we've prepared with your shoes. Is this a time to be wandering about? I thought you were asleep long ago.'

The schoolmaster looked all around him, breathing through his nose. He raised his face to the dark sky, breathing noisily again. He watched the dim outline of the Padre moving back towards the cowshed window. He heard him strike a match, and in the sudden gleam of it saw him going to the threshing floor, protecting the flickering flame with one hand and holding up his cassock with the other, testing the state of the surface with his bare foot.

'And you? Is it night or morning with you, Padre?' the schoolmaster enquired jauntily, his voice vibrant with good humour.

'You, it seems to me, have been making a night of it' came the grudging reply. The feeble light flickered out and darkness closed around them again, blacker than ever. 'Haven't you been to bed?' the Padre enquired, breathing heavily.

'Too much noise, with all those drunks and festivities; even the crickets were too loud; it was too hot, anyway,' the schoolmaster answered boisterously. 'By the way,' he went on, 'I hadn't noticed that the crickets have stopped and it's almost chilly now. Who'd have thought it!'

'And it's nearly dawn already,' the Padre chimed in.

'Is it possible? How quickly summer nights pass!'

'Especially at San Rocco. The work-people will say the

Festival Night

same when they fall asleep in the furrows tomorrow morning.'

'As for me, I'm not sleepy, but I'm very hungry. I fancy I've discovered that night sharpens all our senses.'

'As to that, it's usual to sleep at night.'

'That's a pity, Padre.'

By now they could both make out the vague shapes of things in the darkness.

As they leaned against the rough stones of the cowshed, the low expanse of the threshing floor lay before them, shadowed on the far side by the wall of the first field, its slopes crowned by black mulberry trees. Beyond the trees, the great jutting hill revealed itself only as a space devoid of stars, a stretch of empty sky. A little eddy of wind whipped up the harsh smell of the night, and set the leaves of the mulberry trees rustling obediently.

'I'll sit here,' said the schoolmaster, 'and wait for the dawn.' He stuffed his pipe in his mouth and leaned back against the pump. 'It can't be all that long, now.'

The Padre was walking backwards and forwards over the threshing floor, intent on testing with his bare feet the persistent dampness of certain patches. 'If the morning sun gets on these puddles,' he muttered between his teeth, 'the surface will crack like glass. Damn those boys! Instead of spreading it out evenly they left lumps in it.' He licked his dirty finger and spat quickly before holding it in the air to test the breeze.

'How peaceful it is tonight,' the schoolmaster remarked through the smoke. 'Don't complain, Padre.'

'That cursed Biscione.'

'Padre, you're always up at dawn. Why have you never told me how beautiful are these hours of night? So mysterious, so tranquil. It's another world. Everything looks different, living a secret life. The strangest things

Festival Night

happen at night. It's a pleasure even to breathe, to be caressed by the darkness, the smells, the silence. One feels a bigger man, for good or evil. It's good to be alone, good to have company. Even this stink is good. It's fresh and warm, it's cheerful, it's human. To think that crimes are committed at night! How stupid the world is! Anything can happen at night.'

'Didn't you know that?'

'All I remember now is what I knew as a boy. But then I was afraid of the dark.'

'Listen, schoolmaster,' said the Padre, planting himself in the middle of the threshing floor. 'It seems to me that the fresh air has gone to your head like wine. Till yesterday I thought you an abstemious man.'

The schoolmaster bent over his pipe for a moment, then laughed hoarsely. 'As a matter of fact,' he muttered, clearing his throat, 'I have been drinking wine; the wine one can drink only at night, the wine of meditation...' He glanced at the other and suddenly went on: 'I'm happy to be alive, Padre.' Looking up again and waving his pipe, he added: 'Have you ever known this happiness?'

'Not on the feast of San Rocco, of all days in the year, and if you asked my opinion, I shouldn't advise you to look for peace and quiet on this particular night. Where the devil did you find them?'

The schoolmaster spat on the ground. 'I didn't look for them. They came to me,' he said slowly, with conviction, and over his face, already flushed in the mist, there passed a smile of pride.

The Padre shrugged his shoulders, then turned his head anxiously to the hill, now standing out black against the pale sky, and sniffed the wind again.

(March 5th – 29th, 1937)

Friends

A young man was standing in the asphalt yard, yelling at the top of his voice to someone on the third floor, where some of the windows were still dark while others were splashes of light: 'Everything's O.K. I'm free now.'

Children were shrieking in the yard and on the stairs. On all six floors, lighted windows gleamed brightly on the iron railings of their little balconies. In a balcony on the third floor stood a woman, still and silent in all that noise and confusion, watching a tall young man in a hat who had rushed down the stairway. The first man, red-haired, red-bearded, with a white kerchief loosely knotted at his throat over an open-necked sports shirt, met the second in the middle of the yard and directed his attention upwards with a jerk of his thumb. The second man looked up and waved goodbye, the woman went back indoors and the two men walked off towards the street.

'What a lot everybody eats,' cried the red-haired one, nicknamed Rosso. 'Nothing but the smell of frying all over the house. The very thought of it makes me sick.'

The other touched his hat to a little fellow in shirt-sleeves, who was sitting astride a wooden chair in the gateway, then asked his companion in a serious tone: 'Have you found a job yet?'

Festival Night

'Listen, Celestino,' Rosso replied, stopping short and gripping him by the sleeve. 'I came to go for a walk with you. I can't go by myself. In a minute I'll have to light a cigarette, I'm so much on edge. Where to go I don't know. I come with you so as to keep my spirits up and you ask me if I've found work. No, I haven't, and I couldn't care less. If you want to know, you bore me stiff. Is it that wife of yours who's made you such a softie? You don't seem like my pal Celestino any more. You're more like my father. You wear a hat like him, too. You'd better watch it! My father uses his belt on his wife.'

Jerking his arm away, Celestino replied: 'If a man resorts to a belt, it means he's no good with his hands. Only cads treat their wives that way. But what's that got to do with Gina? Or with you?'

'Me? ... Nothing. I was just talking. You started wrong. Anyway, you're too touchy.'

'What d'you think you can teach me? All you know about women is what you learned from negresses!'

Rosso raised his arm and slapped Celestino's shoulder. Celestino, still annoyed, stared at him with narrowed eyes, but seeing him smile he relaxed and smiled back. 'Never talk about women,' Rosso exclaimed, 'except after a good dinner. We're good friends. Let's leave your wife out of it. Celestino, Celestino, we're getting old: you stick to your wife, I stick to my short temper. We won't talk about her, nor about whether I've got work or not. Where are we going?'

'For a walk. It's chilly.'

Under the trees of the main road the street-lamps cast patches of light alternating with zones of darkness, and the shadows of the two men seemed to dance along the pavement as they walked. Rosso had lit a cigarette and was

Friends

drawing long puffs at it. Celestino raised his hat to a slim girl who suddenly shot round a corner.

'That girl,' he murmured, 'started working in the shop a year ago. She's already well in with the business manager.'

'To tell the truth, you envy her her career.'

'I? Jealous of her? She's playing a dirty game, not aiming at a career. I wouldn't touch her if she was washed in petrol.'

'Not if she were washed already, but maybe you'd like to wash her! Still, that's your wife's concern. There was a time, when you didn't wear a hat, when you greeted girls very differently. You're not the same man now, Celestino....'

Celestino shrugged his shoulders, and Rosso went on... 'And what an idea! Washing a girl in petrol....'

Celestino turned to look at a gang of kids rushing out from a side road, shrieking and yelling, streaming across the avenue behind them, piling up on a seat and making noises like machine-gun fire, while the smallest boy circled round them, waving his arms and yelling: 'Cops! Look out! Cops!'

Celestino shrugged his shoulders, and Rosso went on: 'Pregnant women get ideas like that! And then set fire to the petrol! It must have been a woman who invented the flame-thrower! Now we're back at your wife again!'

Celestino twisted round and asked in a dry tone: 'Have you found a job?'

Rosso stopped short, scratched his head and looked at his friend, lifting a hand to protect himself. 'What fools we are!' he exclaimed.

'What d'you want us to do,' asked Celestino, 'other than talking about women?'

'There was a time when you enjoyed a pint....'

'Now that's something that Gina really does object to.

Festival Night

She wouldn't say anything about Carmela, but she'd go up in flames if I went home drunk.'

'I wonder what became of Carmela. We were happy, that year.'

'In those days all the girls encouraged us to have a good time with them. That's why I married Gina. Right from our first dance together, she told me that whenever she smells wine on a man's breath she wants to box his ears.'

'Did she box yours?'

'Women get these ideas! Understandable, poor things! It's better to be jealous of another woman than of a pint. Another woman is at least a woman.'

'The real reason,' Rosso said, stopping and taking his cigarette from his mouth, ' was explained to me by a fellow I met in Massawa, where the people understand that sort of thing. They all have several wives, down there. He said that a man who comes home drunk has the same glazed eye, the same besotted look, as when he's been to bed with them. Rivalry! Competition! He says that the Arabs don't understand these things.'

'Now she's expecting a baby, even the smell of it makes her sick.'

'Does she allow you orange-ade?'

Celestino halted with a smile in front of the sloping window of a tobacconist's shop and gestured to his friend to wait for him. 'It's a good thing she'll let you smoke,' Rosso cried.

Rosso waited a while, listening to the noise of a radio blaring through an open window behind the trees, then he mounted the step of the shop and found Celestino, leaning on the counter chatting with the proprietor. 'What are you selling him?' he asked. 'The radio?'

Celestino waved his hand impatiently, said a couple of words to the shop-keeper and turned round with a smile.

Friends

'No need to shout!' he exclaimed. 'I'm just having a look at a set.' They vanished into the back of the shop and in a minute or two the proprietor came back. Rosso was sitting in a corner, lighting another cigarette. 'Are you the one who's been in Africa?'

Lifting his eyes, Rosso gazed at the shop-keeper's plump round face with its huge moustache, and the patch of skin showing through his ragged singlet where his shirt was unbuttoned. 'That's stale news,' he replied.

'I did the other thing.' Then Rosso noticed that the fat man had lost a hand. The old scar was pale against the rounded, thickened stump. 'Is that how you got hold of a tobacco shop?' he replied.

'Got hold of it?' roared the other. 'I pay the rates, the rent and the taxes.' A customer came in, bought a cigar, paid for it and went out. The fat man continued, thrusting his stump into his belt: 'Is it true that in Abyssinia they gave old soldiers the special concession of running a tobacco shop free of rent, rates and taxes for ten years?'

'They even gave them cars for doing the rounds of their customers.'

'Do me a favour and give me a straight answer. I'm asking you if it's true that men mutilated in that campaign were given these concessions?'

'I'm not mutilated.'

'So I see,' replied the other shortly, looking him straight in the face. 'Where were you posted?'

'Somewhere where we got our smokes free.'

At that moment Celestino came into the shop and said a few words under his breath to the proprietor who was eyeing Rosso darkly. Finally he patted him on the shoulder, murmured: 'Top price' and went out pushing his friend in front of him. Once outside, Celestino remarked: 'These little jobs pay for Gina's clothes.'

Festival Night

'You're doing fine,' exclaimed Rosso. 'Cheat your firm and make a bit on the side. Otherwise they'll cheat you. Pity you married Gina. When I was over there I used to say: "Once I'm discharged I'll get away from this heat, draw all my back pay and go into partnership with Celestino." Instead, you pulled a fast one and went into partnership with Gina.'

'Anyway, you've spent all your pay.'

'Down to the last penny. Money you get from the war never lasts long. A man says: "I can stay here," and he starts spending; he makes so many stops on his way home from the army, and the notes simply fly. Then he gets down-hearted; he remembers Pinotto, who washed his feet one day and on the next was crushed on the rocks like a sparrow; he thinks of Celestino who has got married and forgotten all about him; and it's all up. He sings a bit, has a couple of drinks. It's lonely in Naples, especially at night. If you've seen it, you've seen it.'

'Tell me, is it true that after a battle you can smell burned flesh?'

'Don't talk of smells.'

'Did you do any shooting?'

'At birds.'

'Is it true that . . . .'

'You're worse than that fellow with only one hand. Why didn't you come and see for yourself? A nice little trip with your wife. You were sent into the world to travel, weren't you? It's the finest work there is, travelling. When a man has the chance. You ought to take Gina there – the girl who can't bear the smell of a man's breath when he's had a drink. If I had the chance, I'd go back there tomorrow.'

Talking heatedly, they had come to a dark open space. On the far side of it shone a row of wide, well-lighted windows behind a line of potted shrubs. In front stood a

Friends

crowd of idle sight-seers, peering through the leaves and listening to the loud orchestra. 'I never went to the *Paradisio* again,' said Rosso. 'Never went dancing, after that time in Turin. Once, in Naples, I met a girl from Turin in a dance-hall. She didn't even recognise my accent. I was just so much scorched earth, to her. I knew she was from Turin by the way she laughed and said: " Watch out! My man's jealous." They say that down there women are closely guarded, but her man was a rotter. He sent her out dancing and pocketed her tips. The girl gave me the glad eye when I told her where I came from, and when we'd gone round once I wanted to stay, but she said: " Get along with you! Go on! You're not in Africa now. It took the African campaign to get a Turin man to grow a beard ".'

In front of the *Paradisio* they stopped to look inside at the high walls painted pale green and decorated with brightly coloured murals of palm trees, naked negroes, leopards and antelopes. The orchestra, all in black, was blaring away in a niche at the back of the room and the dance floor was crowded with couples absorbed in close embrace. A sergeant in a trim-fitting uniform was crossing the room. The broad windows stood wide open to the cool evening air.

'How it's changed, like me,' exclaimed Rosso. 'This isn't the *Paradisio* any longer. What about Carmela and Lidia and Ginetta? Where do they go dancing now? Don't the local lads come here any more?'

'The atmosphere's quite different, now,' Celestino said. 'We had some high old times here, but that's all over. Try and go in there in shirt-sleeves, as you are now! They'd send for the manager!'

'It's full of people from Naples.'

'No. It's just that life has changed. You mentioned

Festival Night

Lidia. I saw her last winter in a fur coat and I don't think she'd stolen it.'

' I'd like to see M. Berto's face!'

' He's not the boss here now. He's gone to ground somewhere. A man from Rome took over the place and altered it all, even put in a new dance-floor. He had the rooms repainted, advertised in the papers, put on a cashier and doubled the orchestra. People drink bubbly wines and eat in little cubicles. He's spent a lot, but it's paid him. People come in cars.'

' It's the women's fault. If Carmela and Ginetta came back you'd soon see a change in the atmosphere.'

' Try it yourself, with your beard,' Celestino laughed.

Rosso slipped his fingers between his collar and the kerchief and stood hesitating, fingering the material. Then he laughed. ' To think I bought this in Massawa as Indian silk! I'll bet it's rayon! It's already in shreds, like the note I paid for it.'

' Perhaps it's because you don't wash your neck.'

' Neck? Imagine me washing my neck, with the sort of life I lead! Down in Africa, a beard and a kerchief marked a man as a sultan.'

' With that tanned face of yours you look like the Negus of Abyssinia himself!'

' If only I had the money he has!'

' Try and get it from him!'

Rosso's eyes wandered along the green shrubs to the corner of the square and the line of gleaming cars parked there. ' So to dance with a Turin girl I'll have to go to Naples? This isn't the *Paradisio*! It's all very well for you to grin! You've got a wife.'

' Cheer up! They've changed its name. It's not the *Paradisio* any longer. It's called *Nuovo Fiore*.' He took Rosso's arm and went on: ' Come on, Milio. They'll make

Friends

us pay if we stop here much longer.' Rosso allowed himself to be led away from the square into a long road where the street lamps were few and far between. He drew the last puffs from the stub of his cigarette, almost burning his fingers, and threw away the end. ' Aren't you smoking tonight?' he asked Celestino.

' Half a cigar, perhaps, when I'm sitting down quietly. It's more healthy, and it's cheaper.'

' A man who's got money can make savings.' Rosso had been dragging his feet on the pavement. Now he stopped short, raised his head and asked: ' Where shall we finish the evening?'

' Let's get a breath of air. I never go out.'

' I've been wandering round pavements ever since this morning. The next café we come to, I'm putting my feet under the table. What d'you say?'

' All right. Just for a minute.'

On they went. The road seemed endless and they did not meet a soul. Now and then a car swished quietly past, its headlights streaming over their shoulders, sending their shadows dancing and picking out every stone. Then the darkness closed in behind them again, the red glow fading to black. Celestino remarked: ' With all the cafés there are in the centre, why are we making for the outskirts? D'you want to end up in the fields?'

' There isn't even a tram. Here's a side road. Still, it's safer to turn back. If the worst comes to the worst we can always go to the *Paradisio*. There'll be something worth drinking, there. Strange, how much bigger Turin seems at night.'

When they reached the square they scarcely glanced at the streaming lights shining green on the row of shrubs, but made their way to a narrow alley in the far corner where they could hear the clang of a nearby tram. ' Good!' Rosso

Festival Night

said. 'We're back in Turin again. Haven't you got anything to smoke? Have half of mine? Still, if I break it again there won't be any left. Never mind. We're sure to find a cigar end by this corner.'

On the corner they discovered a tiny bar with a little garden behind a wistaria-covered trellis, lit by a small unshaded electric bulb hanging like a fruit. They sat down on a couple of iron seats by a rickety table.

At the next table sat a young woman, a workman and a young baby. The baby was drinking from a beaker, holding it with both hands. A grey-haired woman came up, looking doubtfully at Rosso's great kerchief.

'Is this a café?' asked Celestino.

'Who cares?' Rosso replied. 'You've got to have a drink with me. I've still got two *lire*, and they'll both go on wine. Don't you like wine any more? Let's have a pint!' The woman went away. Celestino grimaced as he looked round at the company. 'I'm not the one who doesn't like it, you know.'

'But that's just it,' said Rosso. 'If you like it, that's enough! What the devil! Look how the kid's sucking it up! He's losing no time.'

At that moment the child took the beaker from his lips and gazed solemnly around with two enormous eyes, getting his breath back with a gasp. Catching Rosso's eye, he choked and coughed so hard that the old workman leaned over and patted him on the back. The wine arrived and the woman poured it out. Rosso took a deep draught and watched Celestino lifting his own glass to his lips.

'Damn!' he said. 'The wine's been watered. But at least we're drinking it in our own home town. D'you know, in Africa we had a thirst for water...? This isn't too bad. I like it.'

'I can drink it, myself,' said Celestino.

Friends

' Then drink up.'

Celestino took his half-cigar from his waistcoat pocket, felt it gently, leaned forward into the light and carefully put a match to it. After pulling at it a moment he waved it between two fingers and planted his elbow on the table, raising his glass with his other hand and taking another sip.

' Good health!' cried Rosso, draining his own glass. ' Mine's empty. Let me refill yours, too.'

Celestino put his hand over the top of his glass. Rosso filled his own to the brim, then tried to top up Celestino's by force. Celestino pushed his arm aside and a splash of wine fell on the table. ' Careful!' he muttered.

' Ah! You don't like to see it wasted,' Rosso remarked.

' I don't like us to look like a couple of drunkards.'

' No fear,' said Rosso, peering at him through narrowed eyes. ' It would be fine, though. Drink up.'

Celestino gulped down half his wine. The glass was at once refilled.

Rosso planted both elbows on the table and stared at his friend. ' This wine is like Turin,' he began. ' There's more of the south in it than in Piedmont wine. Still, it's warming, that's the main thing. Would you believe that the southerners, when you live with them, are much the same as us? Rotters are rotters wherever you find them, but the right sort are so friendly you wouldn't believe it. You've got to learn how to tell the good from the bad, though. They all talk the same queer lingo . . . .'

' At my firm we've got two Sicilians, the manager and the secretary. Two years ago, they had to stay in bed if they wanted their trousers pressed. Now they've each got a car . . . .'

' What of it? Any man can get on when he's in a job. The trouble is finding work. I like them best when they're doing nothing. They know, better than any, how to be idle.

Festival Night

Even at home they're like that, but you ought to see them when they've been posted overseas and have just arrived. The first thing they do is go for a walk.'

Rosso sipped his wine and gestured to his friend to do the same. Celestino, his eyes half-closed, drank a mouthful without moving. '... and when work is short they don't fuss about it, as we do. Not even when they have a family. They don't go looking for work. They go for a walk. A negro, on the other hand, if you leave him alone he sits down on the ground. Negroes drink....'

' They must be fools. I've never heard of a negro who had learned to manage a machine.'

'... yet, for all the wine they've got there, Neapolitans don't drink it. They're grand company and all that, but they prefer aniseed. I could never understand them.' He moistened his lips and glared ironically at his companion. ' What are you doing? Acting the Neapolitan? Drink up.'

' Let me smoke,' Celestino protested. Rosso sniggered. ' Drink, I tell you. It's not allowed...' Celestino shrugged his shoulders. Rosso drained his glass and turned to refill it.

' They've got some good wines,' he went on, putting his elbows on the table again, ' twenty degrees proof is nothing. I once drank some that was the colour of coffee, so strong that it left your mouth dry. Not like this thin stuff. If it hadn't a bit of the south in it... Drink up. You can say that for once you resisted the wine cask. This is just water.'

' What's that palm wine like?' Celestino enquired.

' I never saw any. It must be something like elbow grease. But, now I come to think about it, the negroes drink it like so many monkeys.'

' What sort of wine can you get there?'

' All the negroes want is something with a strong smell and they gulp it down. They'll even drink petrol.'

Friends

Rosso pushed a glass, filled to the brim, against Celestino's hand with a glance of invitation. Celestino lowered his head and drank from the overflowing edge pushing his lips forward.

In came two soldiers wearing grey-green battle dress, chasing each other into the corner like a couple of boys. Celestino eyed them casually through the smoke of his cigar, then his glance rested on the table where the three were still sitting. The baby had dropped off to sleep with his head on his arm beside the bottle; the workman was staring at nothing, rocking himself backwards and forwards in his chair with his hands in his pockets; the woman was picking at the crumbs and scraps of food littering the table among the empty paper bags. Rosso called the landlady: ' My bill, please.'

' You bought cigarettes, I'll pay.'

' I tell you I'm paying.'

' You aren't a millionaire.'

' But I haven't a wife to keep.' The landlady stood waiting. Celestino held out two *lire*. ' All right, then,' said Rosso. ' I'll pay for another. Landlady, a pint bottle.'

Celestino tried to get up, but Rosso held him by the sleeve with a pleading look. ' What have you drunk? Nothing. Are you afried of Gina?'

' It's nothing to do with Gina. I just don't want to make a pig of myself. I've got to work tomorrow.'

' Stay for a friend, Celestino. You can keep awake every now and then, even when you do make a pig of yourself. Just keep me company. I'm alone all day.' Celestino sat down again. ' . . . And finish the bottle. We're getting along all right now. It's not too bad.'

Celestino did not drink. Instead he puffed nervously at the stub of his cigar. The wine arrived. Rosso paid for it hastily, poured out a glass for his companion, then refilled

Festival Night

his own, smacked his lips and raised his elbow. ' You'll never get work,' Celestino exclaimed through clenched teeth.

' Ah,' replied Rosso, with a glint of malice in his eyes, ' I'm working this evening, only it's worse than navvying. My throat's rusty. I haven't had a drink for a month, because I must smoke. I've nothing left to pawn except this kerchief. What'll you give me for it?'

' A kick in the pants, and you can keep the thing. You've forgotten your own trade, that's what's the matter with you.'

' I messed about with lorries and cars over there, more than I ever did before. D'you really want to know what's the matter with me? I've never forgotten anything; it's you and the people I used to know, who've forgotten me. That's the whole story ... Have another drink.'

Celestino threw away his cigar stub and moistened his lips. ' Get on with it,' stormed Rosso, seizing his elbow and leaning over him. ' You've forgotten how to drink.'

' Swine,' jeered Celestino, suddenly pulling away as the wine spilled over.

' No fear. Here's health ...' and Rosso drank the toast.

Celestino wiped away the splashes from his clothes. ' You must think the war's still on,' he muttered. ' It's plain you've been with Neapolitans, you're so free with your hands.'

' Leave the war alone. You don't even know the smell of it. All you did in the war was operate a radio ... Come on ... no offence ... let's drink on it.'

Celestino did not drink. Rosso put down his glass and went on: ' A fine thing, war. A man no longer thinks of anything. Later, he thinks of the danger. He lives a day at a time. You have your job, all the rest have theirs. The only thing to be afraid of is getting lost. I remember a fellow at Djema driving round on his axles with his helmet on his

Friends

neck, filthy with sweat like a cyclist, who stopped me and cried: ' Where's my lot gone? Holy Mother of God, tell me where's my lot?' He'd only lost his column, but imagine what it's like to be lost in the open country, alone among all those trees like so many bundles of dry sticks. Who's coming to look for you then? You're forgotten, and above you fly the vultures.'

Rosso bent down, picked up the stub his friend had thrown down and lit it, burning his lips. He blew out the smoke and leaned on his elbows again, his eyes fixed on Celestino. ' I was lost myself, once,' he suddenly continued, talking as if he were alone. ' We were going back to Diredawa. The rains had started. Such great black clouds I'd never seen before. The sky seems wider, there. Late one afternoon I left camp for a bit of a walk in a flat muddy field. It looked like one of our fields after the grape harvest and it stank of corruption. The rain caught me outside the native village, coming down cats and dogs. I made for the first hut I could see, because I couldn't tell where the sky ended and the earth began. A man could have drowned. Inside were bundles of rags and eyes like cats. That was all I could see, it was so dark, but those blacks were watching me. Outside it was raining to split open the earth itself; I watched the splashes dancing in front of the door. I was thinking: " They'll stick a knife in my back here and now in revenge for the war." I stayed there I don't know how long, leaning against the door with my back to all that filth, bayonet in hand, ready to leap out. I didn't even notice the smell, I tell you.'

' And they didn't do anything to you after all?'

' What d'you think they were likely to do? They were afraid of me. But it taught me that to wage war men should keep together. To kill a man, if you're alone, is sheer madness.'

Festival Night

'Have you done any killing yourself?' asked Celestino, rising to his feet.

'I don't know. Nobody knows. I've seen plenty of dead bodies, that's certain.'

'The rules of war. Shall we go?'

Rosso remained seated, his head raised, his thoughts far away. 'Don't you want us to finish the wine?' he stammered, picking up his glass.

'Leave it, for all I care.'

'Keep me company a little longer, Celestino. You've drunk so little! Gina wont say anything to you. She knows well enough that you're with me.'

'But that's just it,' said the other with a wry smile. 'It's because I'm with you that Gina's waiting up for me.'

'Does it bore you if I drink and if I talk about Africa? God! I was there, wasn't I? You asked me, anyway. You don't talk about anything, you don't. Tell me about Gina, then. When's the baby due? Finish your drink.'

Rosso emptied his glass and with a shaky hand refilled it with what was left in the bottle. 'Listen,' he cried to Celestino who was edging away under the pergola. 'I meant to make you drunk tonight, then I thought: No. He's in a job, and he's got a baby coming. Better not. But stay and keep me company.'

'You're a swine, Milio. Either come away now or stay here by yourself.'

'No! I won't come,' Rosso cried. 'It's either me or Gina. I haven't come back from Africa to take orders from another man's wife. If you're not free to have a pint when you like, you're no longer my pal Celestino.... Stay and drink here, you fool.... The negroes have got more sense than you have.' But Celestino had gone.

(May 8th – 14th, 1937)

Gaol Birds

1

Not even one of the three prisoners could hear the sound of the sea. It was as smooth as oil, that day, and all of them lay on their camp beds with half-shut eyes as if they were drifting away to oblivion. Noise and voices from the street could be heard in the cell, bringing the atmosphere of sunshine, sand and torrid sea inside those thick walls.

A shadowy mass of large wooden crates had been piled up outside the two barred windows. High up, two gaps between them allowed prisoners to glimpse a narrow, lozenge-shaped patch of pale sky; lower down, little pinpoints of light shone through holes and cracks in the old wood. The density of the shadow testified to the fierce heat of the sun outside.

'The train's coming,' cried Nanni, jumping off the bed on his bare feet. The other two did not move. Nanni, holding up his trousers, ran to the window, strained his ears towards the sky outside, then turned to the other window. There was the clatter of a tin, ending in a splash. Nanni gave a cry and bent down.

'Look at him! The swine! I ought to make you lick it up,' shouted the fair-haired man, nicknamed Biondo, sitting up on his bed.

Nanni was hopping about, holding his toe. 'Who left the

Festival Night

can around?' he gasped. 'Don't blame me! I'm lamed for life! Talk to the ice-cream man.'

Biondo glanced at the tin pot that Nanni had quickly set upright again, then turned over on his bed and stretched himself, arching his chest in its red singlet until his rib-cage creaked. The third man, all in white, lay at full length with shoes on his feet and his grey beard in the air. As the other two fell silent he asked: 'Why's this boy so crazy about the train? Every day at this time he gets restless. It's not natural. If he doesn't learn to settle down quietly in prison, where will he learn?'

Biondo sniggered: 'When a fellow has a guilty conscience he thinks every train has come for him. They'll clap hand-cuffs on him and put him on a train. He'll take a trip to the police court and find himself in the dock with a couple of policeman. Then they'll read out his sentence – so many years hard labour! Look what a face he's making! They'll shave all your hair off, Nanni, put you in sackcloth, fix chains to your feet. How many chickens did you steal, Nanni?'

'I stole an ass like you.'

Biondo gleefully kicked up his heels, and his loose sandal shot off his toes to land on the old man's bed. 'Tell me, ice-cream man,' he said gaily, settling his hands behind his neck and crossing his legs, 'will they charge you with selling fags again?'

'A man can't even get a bit of sleep here any more,' stormed the old man, wandering over towards the door.

'Why didn't you bring along your little cart with your shop on it?' Biondo went on. 'For the six days you're doing we could have enjoyed ourselves. You'd have had your old woman, I'd have iced lemon and Nanni there could have cured these fits of his with ice-cream. Look how strung up he is!'

Gaol Birds

Nanni was still clinging tightly to the bars, conscious of the burning heat of the wall through his thick serge clothing. His eyes were fixed on a shining crack in the crate outside, but he saw nothing. His ears were strained to catch every sound. Holiday-makers, who had wandered over to the station to enjoy the shade and watch the train go by, were strolling back to the beach – white-suited men, bare-headed women in sandals, shouting boys, crying babies, laughing girls. Nanni saw nothing: he tried to imagine what it was like, the road outside the prison leading down to the sea, but he didn't even know whether there were any trees or houses or flowerbeds. When they brought him in he hadn't thought to look.

Nanni turned round, streaming with sweat from having stood so long at the window. A noise was heard just outside the door, the sound of voices and a shuffling of feet. Even Biondo raised himself on his elbow and looked anxiously around. The voices echoed in the passage. As a louder tone rang out, the ice-cream man thrust out his beard in irritation and twisted round towards the other two. They were staring each other in the face. ' Oh, Biondo,' he laughed, ' Perhaps you're the one who's going on that trip. Or Nanni? It's a bit of good luck for whoever has to go. He'll travel in the cool and stay cool when he gets there. State prisons aren't like these provincial guard-houses!'

Biondo started up from his bed with a curse. ' Blood of Mary! A man can't get a bit of peace even in prison.'

Nanni, his eyes on the door, remarked softly: ' The train's a long way off by now. It's somebody coming, not going.'

The noise continued. Someone said goodnight and went away. They heard Ciccia talking and giving orders, the sound of water splashing into a basin, the gasps and grunts of a man washing himself.

' Who on earth can be arriving by train at this dead end?'

Festival Night

said Biondo. 'If you ask me, they've come to trim that fool's beard.'

'Nanni hasn't even got a beard yet,' the old man replied.

'He'll have time to grow one in prison.'

'I expect it's someone else they've arrested – from a village where they don't stop at the first man to be killed.'

A key grated in the lock, the bolt shot back and Ciccia appeared, walking sideways and pushing the door open with his buttocks. Nanni stared at the doorway, bright in contrast with the dusk inside.

'There isn't anywhere else, your reverence. I'll put you in here for now,' Ciccia mumbled through his moustaches. 'You won't have a bed to sleep on, but surely to goodness someone will move over... just for one night.'

In the sudden draught there appeared on the threshold a dark man in a dirty grey jacket much too small for him. His face was gaunt, his eyelids drooped from exhaustion and his tired eyes glittered as he looked around.

'Make yourself at home, your reverence. There aren't any more beds. One of these chaps will have to let you have his... the youngest... Nanni. We'll see, later on... Now I must see about getting something to drink... we're all thirsty. Now you others, behave yourselves. No foul talk. The reverend's listening to you... Have the goodness....'

The door closed again. The man with the fleshless face came forward a step or two and raised his hand. 'I greet you all,' he said quietly. Biondo had risen, shouldered past him, and was now looking him full in the face. The ice-cream man was standing, too, and smoothing his beard.

'You're a priest in disguise, I suppose?' Biondo burst out.

'Yes, I am a priest,' replied the other, not moving.

Biondo glared at him, then threw himself down on his bed. 'And, pardon me, what have you come here for?'

Gaol Birds

'Stop that! Don't bother him. It's none of our business,' the ice-cream man broke in. 'Shut up, you gutter-snipe. The reverend came by train? Like a turkish bath, eh?'

'My sons, you must excuse me,' said the priest screwing up his eyes. 'I'm still blinded by the bright sunshine outside and I can't see you very well. I hope I'm not disturbing you. I shall be gone first thing in the morning.'

'And where are you going?' Biondo asked.

'They're taking me to the islands to be interned.'

'Even priests?'

'Why not?' said the ice-cream man. 'Justice concerns everybody.'

'Internment? What can you have done to be interned?'

'When they can't put a man in prison,' the ice-cream man explained, 'they send him to an internment camp.'

By now the priest's eyes were almost shut. Nanni, who was nearest him, noticed that his cheeks were darkened by a three-day beard, and though his eyelids were weighed down with weariness his eyes had a vigorous gleam.

'And this one, who hasn't spoken? Why, he's still a boy!' exclaimed the priest in consternation.

'Nanni's the one for chickens,' Biondo explained. 'He got caught in a trap the night before last.'

'You, a thief! Must I believe it? But wasn't your mamma looking after you? Stealing other people's property!'

'Look here, reverend,' said the ice-cream man. 'You're right, of course. I'm not sticking up for Nanni. He deserves what he's got, and more. But with a family like that, why pick on the boy? Let's be fair. They all had a go at those chickens.'

Nanni backed away, his eyes blinded by tears, and bumped his shoulders against the wall in silence. When his storm of passion had spent itself he turned round to see the old grey-beard sitting beside the priest on a camp bed.

Festival Night

The priest had his eyes bent on the ground. A shirt with a frayed white collar encircled his neck. He had no tie. His hands were resting on the heavy black cloth that covered his knees and his short sleeves left his forearms bare. Nanni suddenly noticed that the priest was furtively rubbing his wrists. Both men were looking down.

' Did you travel here in handcuffs?' asked Biondo.

Once more the bolt shot back and Ciccia reappeared, carrying a loaf in one hand and under his arm a few covers which he put down on the stool. Nanni saw his eyes shining.

' Ciccia,' said Biondo, ' you'll at least give the reverend a taste of that thin wine you drink yourself when there's nobody else about.'

' Sure! And why not to you all! Why not! This isn't exactly a tavern. Open and shut, open and shut. They all give orders as if they were fine gentlemen. I'm not exactly a jailer. I'm not talking to you, reverend, this doesn't concern you. I'm talking to these oafs here. And they still call us " executioners " ... Now, how are you getting on? Bad company, eh? However you like to look at it, we're in prison. Has anyone offered you his bed yet?' We'll wait...'

He was on his way out when Biondo called after him: ' The peephole, Ciccia. The peephole for his reverence...' Ciccia quickly came back, looking confused and sucking his moustaches. ' I mustn't get in a muddle,' he muttered. ' I was looking for the covers and they're here already.' He drew up the stool and sat down on it with a sigh, blocking the doorway with his shoulders. ' There's no place for you and no peace for me,' he went on, looking at the priest, ' even the murderer is grumbling. These fine wool covers are not good enough for him. Yes, ever since yesterday we've had an assassin here. All the morning he was doing nothing but call for water; he didn't even want to drown himself. That would have been better for him and for everyone else.'

The priest, who had been listening with bowed head, suddenly raised his eyes. ' Gentlemen,' he said, putting his hands together, ' this man is in a worse position than either of us here. Where is he? Is he asking for a priest?'

' He's probably still furious that he was caught,' said Biondo.

' But what did he do? Who is he?' the priest persisted.

' Before yesterday, no-one knew who he was,' said Ciccia. ' He's one of those country bumpkins from the lower slopes of the mountains. It seems he's been working at La Spezia. As for the crime, three knife wounds in the victim's stomach ... women's gossip ... we don't really know. But he must have been pretty drunk because he hasn't eaten a thing all day. All he's asked for is water, and he's not the sort to suffer from fever ... Have you given the reverend any fresh water?'

' Is he a young man, then?'

' It seems he was due to be called up this year. There were lots of things he wouldn't tell, even to the sergeant: he'll tell them at La Spezia ....'

Nanni saw the priest leap to his feet and stride over to the window, he barely had time to bend down to push the tin pot out of the way under a bed, splashing its contents over his feet as he did so. Hardly noticing him, the priest paced backwards and forwards, followed by the eyes of everyone present. Up and down he went, up and down, his folded arms clutching his elbows against his chest, his lips quivering, his head bowed. They all stared at his tonsure, until the ice-cream man broke the silence, turning to Ciccia: ' If he can prove he was drunk when he killed that man, he may get away with twelve years or so.'

Festival Night

The priest faced Ciccia and asked: 'But is he alone in the world? Hasn't anybody visited him?'

Ciccia was bewildered. He winked, looked up and replied: 'It's a fine thing to talk of visiting him. He'll get justice, when the time comes.'

'But hasn't his family come? Aren't there any women at home? The poor fellow needs help desperately. Doesn't the parish priest visit the prison?'

The ice-cream man and Ciccia replied in unison: 'He can't, without special permission.' Ciccia went on: 'The women will come, worse luck. They stick themselves outside the doors with their babies in their arms and a man can't move a step or they're under his feet. Once the inspector....'

'But the parish priest? Doesn't he come? It's his duty.'

Ciccia thrust out his lips: 'I've never seen him.'

Biondo was stretched out on the bed, nibbling a piece of bread. 'At La Spezia,' he said, 'there was a friar who heard my friend's confession. But La Spezia is a different city.'

In a state of great agitation the priest lowered his eyes to Ciccia's feet. Nanni had the impression that he wanted to spit. His thin cheeks turned red. Then with an effort he swallowed, and raised his chin. Ciccia was watching him, and winked at the ice-cream man. Wearily he rose from the stool, his bunch of keys jingling. He said to the priest: 'Confess these lads, reverend. It's not often they see a priest. Hear their confessions. As for that other one I'll have to confess him myself. Orders are orders. I'll come back again with the water.'

He had scarcely gone out and hung the chain over the spyhole when Biondo leaped from his bed and threw his crust of bread at the door. 'Rotter!' he exclaimed. 'Water for us and wine for him. I suppose it's no good talking to

Gaol Birds

him, ice-cream man, in spite of the cigars he pinches from you?'

At that moment a door slammed; footsteps ran past; there was inarticulate shout and a jangling of keys. The priest had seated himself on the bed again, staring down at the flagstones between his knees, lost in thought. Nanni saw Biondo run to the door and give a shout of excitement at something he saw outside. Ciccia's voice could be heard in violent protest. Then, suddenly, another yell by the door made Biondo fall back and slam the peephole shut. They were locked in.

2

To Rocco's amazement, the door of his cell was not fastened. It did not even creak as he pushed it open. The passage beyond was full of light and there was not a soul in sight. Between the railings he could see the shining cobblestones of the street, only a step or two away.

The key of the main gate was in the lock. Rocco turned it, cautiously pulled it towards him and tip-toed through the entrance. Behind one of the barred doors a voice rose in excitement and with one bound Rocco shot into the street.

At the end of the narrow road the corner of a building stood out against the sky. That must be the barracks of the *carabinieri*. Rocco crept past it on the opposite side, hunching his shoulders, trying to accustom his eyes to the dazzling glare, ready to run forward or go back. Every second he expected a burst of firing.

He reached the side turning. Not a soul to be seen. Sounds reached him from the beach – the hum of a crowd, bells in the distance, snatches of music. A light breeze

Festival Night

fanned his neck and he raised his head, savouring the air of freedom. He saw a clump of bright green leaves on an old red wall, and beyond it a stretch of pale, quiet sky.

All along the street he was watched by an endless row of windows, their blinds lowered against the heat. He crept along close to the walls and came to a little footpath used by bathers going to or from the beach. Blindly, Rocco dived into it, bumping into a fat woman who was coming up. She wore shabby sandals on her great bare feet and was dragging a sunburned little girl along behind her. She nudged Rocco sharply with her elbow and he jumped aside without looking up or listening to what she said. A little further on stood a large grey car, blocking the way and sounding its horn. No one could get by. Rocco rushed wildly in the other direction and did not stop until he reached the house where Petro lived. He opened the street-door quietly, peered into the cool shadows of the passage, rushed up the stairs and knocked at Petro's apartment, his heart in his mouth.

A little girl came to open the door, her face white in the gloom. Petro wasn't at home, she said. What did he want? Rocco patted her cheek and went in, pushing the door shut with his shoulders. The child followed him into the tiny kitchen. 'What do you want?' she asked again.

'I want Petro. I've come all the way from La Spezia. Look how I'm sweating! I'm wet through! Why isn't Petro here?'

Half frightened, half pert, the child stared at him and said: 'Are you the man they arrested?'

Rocco's sweat froze on him. 'What d'you know about it?'

'Petro told us this morning. You're Rocco! I know by your little moustache! Whatever would mummie say if she

Gaol Birds

saw you! It's lucky she's gone to Grandma's to help with the flower-picking.'

' So Petro's not in?'

' Petro's working at the Neptune. Why don't you go and look for him on the beach?'

' What did Petro say?'

' Then you really are Rocco. You haven't come from La Spezia after all. You've been in prison.'

' What did Petro say?'

' He only said they'd arrested you, but mother's been grumbling all the morning that Petro's friends were the wrong sort; she'd always known it, and the same thing would happen to Petro, too, if he went on wasting his time at La Spezia instead of working. But surely they wouldn't arrest Petro, would they?'

' Listen. They haven't arrested me, either,' Rocco replied, looking her straight in the face. ' As you see, I'm free. I only want to talk to Petro.'

' Then you'd better go and find him,' the child retorted, running to open the door.

' No,' Rocco cried, darting after her. ' I'm not in any hurry. I'll wait. When will he be back?'

' When it begins to get dark. They shut the place then.'

Rocco sat down by the window, where the last rays of the setting sun slanted through the dusty air. He pulled one of the shutters across and hid behind it, as if he were still behind bars. Thus concealed, all he could see was a patch of sky, but by leaning forward a little he could make out, through the luminous haze, the dry, flowery slopes of the steep high cliff beyond the beach. The little girl had gone back to her work at the table and was vigorously pounding a mass of greenstuff with a crescent shaped chopper. Now and then she turned to shake a sizzling frying pan over the pungent smoke of the fire.

Festival Night

Rocco felt for a cigarette. He hadn't one. He took off his thick jacket, leaned his chin on his hands and sat staring at the sky. Slowly the quivering heat of the sun died down and the air grew clearer. Suddenly he shivered, looking down at the floor, wild-eyed. He heard the child ask: ' You aren't ill, are you?'

' Is there a moon tonight?' he said.

' Oh, yes. We're going out in the boat with the fishermen. Are you coming too?'

Rocco smiled, putting a finger to his lips to silence her. The room was nearly dark now. The little girl went out and brought back a heavy oil lamp, carrying it carefully in both hands. Before she could light it they heard a knock. Hastily she put the lamp down and ran to open the door. Rocco looked up, his heart in his mouth. The child cried: ' It's Rocco! Rocco's here!' and Petro rushed in. He had on a dark singlet and his arms were bare. Rocco had jumped to his feet. In the gloom he could hardly see Petro's face. ' I've come to supper,' he stammered.

' Did they let you out?'

' I found the door open.'

' But did they release you? Are you free?' Petro gasped.

' Is it likely they'd release anyone? I found the door open so I walked out.'

' Did you really murder that fellow, then? You've escaped?'

' Why shouldn't I kill him? Of course I did. I rather wish I hadn't, so that I could do it again! Are you like all the rest? You blame me, too?'

The little girl stood looking up at them, listening. Petro swung round and shouted at her: ' Light the lamp, Mina, and get out of here.'

She obeyed, and Rocco jumped up to close the other shutter as the bright light flooded the little kitchen. Mina

Gaol Birds

carefully turned down the wick. ' Off you go!' Petro cried.

As she went, Petro kept his eyes fixed on the wall. In bold letters across his navy blue singlet was the name "Neptune". His jaws were clenched, his looks as wild as if he himself were Rocco. ' Did anyone see you come in here?' he asked sharply with a break in his voice.

' No. I got away without anybody seeing.'

' Why did you come here?'

' Where should I go? I don't know anybody else. It was broad daylight, but I'll get away tonight.'

' Keep your voice down. How could a man escape in daylight! Did you break the bars?'

' It's easy to see you've never been in prison,' Rocco grinned. ' The bars are iron. I just went through the door. That old fool with the moustaches must have thought he'd locked me in, but he shot the bolt outside the staple. Don't worry. I'll be on my way tonight.'

Mina's shrill little voice piped up outside the door: ' The sauce is burning.' She ran across to the stove.

Petro edged round the table, seeing nothing. Rocco was sitting down again with his back to the window. Neither spoke while the little girl busied herself over a saucepan. The noises from the street sounded faint and far away.

Rocco asked: ' Got a cigarette?'

' Is Rocco staying to supper?' Mina enquired. Petro made no reply. With the cigarette between his lips, Rocco leaned forward to light it at the match Petro was holding, and noticed how the other's hand was trembling. Petro shook out the tiny flame, exaggerating the gesture in the hope of concealing his agitation. Both men remained silent a while longer. Mina set plates on the table.

' Who's this woman?' Petro burst out.

' What woman?'

' Everyone knows you kept going to that boarding house

Festival Night

because of a woman. You were all over her! It's plain enough you didn't go there just to watch her blow her nose!'

Rocco's face was tense as he looked up. Mina's eyes dropped to the plates. 'If nobody knows any more than that, so much the better,' Rocco replied in a low voice. 'No one must know. I mean that, whichever way it goes. Is there a moon tonight?'

'What's the moon got to do with it?'

'With women it makes a lot of difference. It suits them, somehow. Is it very bright, these nights?'

'Why?'

'Because I've got to go out, you fool, and if it's moonlight they can catch me.' Rocco lowered his voice at the last few words. Mina was still gazing at him, fascinated.

'I really don't know what you can do,' Petro sounded at his wits' end. 'As for getting on board a boat, you know perfectly well that's quite impossible.'

'I know,' Rocco replied softly.

'D'you want to get back to the mountain where you came from?'

'Too far away. No good, anyway. That's the first place they'll go to look for me.'

'Then why bother to escape? You should have thought of that first. In here, you'd die like a rat. Is that what you want?'

'I'd die like a cat, instead!' Rocco's lips twisted in an ugly grin.

Mina placed some red peppers and ripe tomatoes on the table, lifting them dripping wet from a bucket. At a brusque gesture from Petro, Rocco pulled his chair up to the table, finishing his cigarette while Petro sliced a tomato and impatiently asked the child for some oil. She brought oil and salt, avoiding Rocco's eyes, then turned back to the stove to flour some fish.

Gaol Birds

' So your mamma is out?' Rocco said to her, stubbing out his cigarette. ' You manage very well without her, I can see . . .' He turned to Petro: ' What do they pay you at the Neptune?'

' Just chicken feed. Get on with your supper.'

' You don't get tomatoes when you're inside,' Rocco remarked with his mouth full, ' and it's as hot as hell. So it is in here,' he went on, turning to the window. ' It's as bad as being in prison.'

' Open the shutters, Mina,' Petro told her, ' or we'll melt. Not too much though. We don't want anyone to look in.' The street noises sounded clearer now, and the two men ate in silence. Mina took the spluttering fish from the pan, put the dish on the table and sat down on the vacant side.

' I just can't understand how anyone could do such a stupid thing for the sake of a woman,' Petro began, chewing steadily.

' Look here! You knew me pretty well at La Spezia,' Rocco interrupted him. ' I come from the mountain, but I'm no fool. Who was it warned you to be careful when you were acting the goat with that little strumpet Rosa? She was out for all she could get. And who told you . . .?' He broke off and glanced at Mina, who was sitting with her elbows on the table, listening attentively. ' I was the one who understood women then, wasn't I? So mind your own business. I had my reasons.'

' Did you love her?'

Rocco made no reply.

' You wanted to marry her?'

' If I had loved her, she's the one I'd have killed,' said Rocco, tight-lipped.

Petro looked up from his plate, noticed Mina and shouted at her: ' What are you doing here? Get along outside.'

Festival Night

'Let her have her supper,' Rocco said. 'She'd better stay ... as long as I'm here.'

The child had jumped back, but now she glanced at him timidly. Rocco smiled at her. Her grave manner did not change, but her look grew pleading.

Petro hastily finished eating, jumped to his feet and started pacing up and down the room. 'You must have been drunk, then,' he began in a tone of conviction. 'Whatever made you do such a dreadful thing? You say yourself that she didn't matter to you....'

Slowly, Rocco also stood up. 'I'll be going,' he said quietly. 'It's dark now.'

'If you didn't want to marry her, what was the sense of it? Why bother?... Mina, it's time we were off to the beach. The fishermen are waiting for us. Are you ready yet?'

Mina nodded her chin up and down, her wide eyes fixed on Petro. 'Petro's coming with you,' Rocco reassured her. 'I must go now, Petro.'

Petro stood looking embarrassed, his eyes cast down. 'And where will you go?' he murmured. 'If they catch sight of you....'

'Don't worry. I'll be gone in a minute... and I shan't come back. Have you got a dark singlet you could let me have? I'll leave you my shirt and jacket.' Petro hesitated and Rocco went on: 'Just so that they won't recognise me... I'll leave my jacket...'

'Rot!' Petro exclaimed. 'I don't want your jacket. Between ourselves, it's not for the value of it, but suppose they catch you with my singlet? You know they always ferret out everything. Who d'you think is going to see you in the dark?'

Rocco picked up his jacket, threw it over his shoulders and looked around the room. He went over to the table and

Gaol Birds

picked up a small loaf. ' You'll give me this?' he asked, and stuffed it into his coat pocket. ' Is the road clear? I'm ready now.'

As Petro turned towards the door, Rocco quickly picked up a knife from the table and slipped it into his pocket. Encountering Mina's astonished eyes he smiled at her and said: ' 'Bye, Mina. Don't ever tell anyone I came to see you.' Then he followed Petro outside.

Neither spoke as they groped their way downstairs. When they reached the street door, Petro leaned out into the hot night air and whispered: ' This pavement's in shadow. The moon's already shining on the other side of the street. See? Wait! Someone's coming.'

Rocco, concealed behind the door, remarked in a low voice: ' To think that in a couple of years your little sister will be a woman, too!'

' Quick!' said Petro. ' Now! Keep close to the wall.'

Rocco shot out into the darkness.

3

' I'm the ice-cream seller,' said the old man in white. ' This is a bit of bad luck for us, you know, reverend. I was given six days in gaol instead of a fine that the magistrate was good enough to impose on me because of some milk I used . . . .'

' Tell us how it is they never confiscate your little cart,' Biondo interrupted.

' That's simple enough. It belongs to my wife. As a matter of fact, so do I, this poor delinquent, yours truly.'

The prison cell was stifling; a wave of intense heat was coming not from the setting sun but from the very stones of the wall and the air itself. The priest felt it full on his face

Festival Night

and could hardly breathe for the smell of the sun-baked walls and the concentrated stench of human acidity. Nanni was still watching him closely as he stood motionless in the heavy atmosphere.

'Don't you ever get the sea air here?' he asked the old man.

'Sea air? For prisoners? What a joke! They even rob us of the breeze the good God sends from the land.'

'We're like capons in a coop,' laughed Biondo, 'only we live on short rations and capons don't.' The others saw his taut face and sweaty skin shining as he winked and showed his teeth in a smile. The priest raised his head with an effort and looked at him.

The old man enquired: 'You don't live by the sea?'

'I come from Alexandria. I live in the country.'

'And... did they make you a bourgeois?' Even Nanni on his bed was listening with close attention.

'It's as God wills,' the priest said. 'It would cause a scandal... my calling....'

'But you're still a priest, aren't you?'

'Of course,' he replied, looking round at them all. 'Ordination is like Holy Baptism: a priest is a priest before God, no matter what happens; just as a man who becomes a Christian must answer to God for his faith, whatever happens, and especially if he has relapsed. Never believe that any sin can cut us off from God. That is a most grave error, the sin of Judas.' Biondo stood slouching carelessly against the wall, listening with a sneer. The priest went on: '... We must remember that His mercy is infinite, and it is precisely when we have offended Him, sinned most bestially, that he stretches out His arm to us.' Biondo still listened, jeering openly. The priest could just see Nanni in the darkness, and felt the old man breathing on his shoulder. He lowered his eyes and continued: 'Whatever

Gaol Birds

happens, we must always forgive others as the Lord forgives us; and forgive ourselves in others because evil exists in every man's heart, and no matter what happens, what injustice, it is always our own fault before anyone else's.'

'By your accent I take it you're from Piedmont,' Biondo said. Swinging round towards the boy he went on: 'Hi, Nanni! Aren't you going to sweep up tonight, with the reverend here?'

Nanni jumped up and bent swiftly over the black flagstones, both arms busy. The old man leaned forward from his bed and asked in a confidential tone: 'How ever did you land up here, reverend? People working against you?'

The priest scanned that dark and wrinkled face with its two little grey eyes glittering behind a fringe of hair, but did not answer.

'A word too many?' the other persisted.

The priest saw the two boys watching him; Biondo was just taking his lips from the water pitcher. He replied in a low voice, without hesitation: 'I was wrong in what I said and did. Whatever happens to me, I deserve it.'

'Sure,' the old man answered, 'they can always put a man in the wrong. But you can defend yourself. Why don't you? A statement to someone....'

'What about us learning to hold a pen? Eh, ice-cream?' Biondo broke in.

'You shut up, you scum! In my day they didn't teach us to read and write, but to stay in a job. The likes of you, knowing how to read!'

The priest heard their voices drumming on his temples in the close-shut stillness. No distant sounds from outside reached them there, though beyond the black beams of the door there was still air and light.

'Take it from me,' the old man said, 'if a man breaks the law they put him in gaol. You're not in gaol, so you

Festival Night

haven't broken the law. You'll have offended somebody or other.'

'I wish I could tell you something better,' the priest answered, 'and with more authority. I only hope you won't imagine some scandal or other from what I've said or how I seem to you. I know that nobody in prison is ever guilty; it's always a mistake; but I know too, that no man lives innocently. We are poor men, sinners; you may think you have good reason to sin, but listen to me. If I tell you I deserve whatever happens to me, it's not through false pride or humility; nor in the sense that we all deserve what happens to us because we are sinners....'

'But what have you done, anyway?' Biondo interrupted him.

'A wicked and a stupid thing, lad. I murmured against one of my superiors because I thought he was unjust.'

Nanni and Biondo, pale in the darkness, looked at one another. 'And so....'

The priest was no longer conscious of the sweat that streamed from him. 'You see,' he exclaimed in an agitated voice, 'I want to make it clear that he really was unjust; that the persecution I have suffered was undeserved. I had the right to take up the matter with him, to call in others to help me, to write statements. Then one of two things could happen; either those statements were false, in which case there was nothing to discuss; or they were true, and equally offensive to that authority which, remember, has every right to demand my death. When it commands it is obeyed, and suffers even graver scandals.'

'Now, Biondo, you stay quiet,' the old man began, deep in thought. 'I know it isn't all that easy to make statements in writing, especially when the ecclesiastical courts are concerned. But will you explain to me what the devil's happened here? You came here with a police guard, didn't

Gaol Birds

you? In handcuffs! What had that to do with your superiors?'

The priest stared down at the paving stones in the darkness. 'This is the consequence of every evil action,' he said softly. 'Learn from this how every protest can become a fount of evil, every reckless resentment, even in defence of justice itself. I have been banished from my parish, but my people there believed I was right. There have been quarrels, riots in my name, and the blame for them rightly falls upon me, though God knows I would have prevented them if I could.'

'Riots?' That was Nanni's voice.

'Blood of the Madonna!' Biondo exclaimed. 'They fought for you, and you complain?'

Suddenly, beyond the outside door, the barred gate slammed with a resounding clang. In the silence that followed, breathless voices broke into a confused hubbub close under the window. Someone walked into the passage. The face of the old man, the only one still visible in the gloom, shrank back with a sigh. 'What's happening, reverend? They're leaving us in the dark tonight.'

Nanni said: 'That's Ciccia.'

'Hi, Biondo,' exclaimed the old man, 'find out when he's coming to bring us some water and light the lamp. Remember that shout he gave? I wonder what happened?'

'Somebody stole his keys, I expect,' Biondo replied with a grin as he ran to the door.

He started banging on the cell-door and shouting complaints. The outside door creaked and the spy-hole opened, letting in a beam of light. 'What's happening in there?' shouted Ciccia.

'What's happening to you? You slam the door in our faces and leave us here in the dark with no water. We're suffocating in here! Do your job!'

Festival Night

The outside door slammed. Biondo turned to the others and said: ' There was a smell of fried fish outside by the railings ... made me long for a café ....'

The cell-door was unlocked; it swung open, letting in a wave of luminous air, and there was Ciccia with the pitcher. He put it down without a word. He looked worried and depressed; even his moustache was drooping and his eyes were evasive. He turned and went out, refixing the chain. A dim, yellowish light from the ceiling flooded the cell. The prisoners stood looking at one another. Ciccia reappeared. ' Have you got a bed ready for his reverence?' he asked sharply.

' Not yet,' Nanni faltered, standing in the light and looking round for the blankets.

' Then never mind. You come with me, reverend. There's a better bed already made up for you.'

' For me?'

' That's right. You shall sleep in a bunk by yourself. Keeping more than three in here isn't sanitary.'

' Oh, why are you taking him away?' cried the old man. ' We were just getting to know each other.'

' He won't lose anything by getting away from you. Look at that heap of muck!'

' And where the devil do you expect us to put it,' Biondo asked. ' Any room for it in your house?'

' I was waiting for the light,' Nanni said, ' so as to clean up.'

' A cell's come vacant. The assassin's gone off,' Ciccia mumbled.

' Have they betrayed him already?' the old man cried.

' He betrayed himself: he's gone.'

' Dead?' asked the priest.

' Gone, by God! Escaped! Slipped off! Don't make me swear. It's not my fault. God shouldn't allow such things!'

Gaol Birds

His eyes glistened and his moustaches quivered. He shot a dirty look at the other three and gave a groan that was almost a belch. The priest, standing lost in thought, opened his mouth to say something when Ciccia interrupted him. ' Come on up. Say goodbye to them tomorrow. These aren't going to escape and I've no time to waste.'

The old man grinned at him without rising from his bed; Nanni watched him without moving; but Biondo followed him to the door. ' Pray that they don't catch that prisoner again tonight, reverend, or you'll have to come back with us. So long!'

' If only they do catch him, I'll stick him in the cellar,' said Ciccia, shutting the door.

' Don't forget the wine,' Biondo chuckled under his breath.

Ciccia was still fumbling at the door of the next cell and peering at the ground. ' ... They'll haul me up before the Board of Enquiry, and I'll be for it. All they want is somebody to blame. Justice! They ought to be out hunting for the murderer. Instead, they pick on the gaoler. Did I commit the crime? That's the law for you. Is it on our side or the criminal's? That's what I want to know! They give us starvation pay! Just look at these locks! Flimsy cells you can't open or shut properly. They'll put prisoners in a beach-hut, next, you'll see, and still hold us responsible. Men handy with knives, too, and they expect us to control them. Three times I brought him water – couldn't have done more if he'd been my own son – I should have let him split his throat. They'd ruin an honest man just for turning his head a minute. And what good does that do? Murdering, escaping, it's all the same to these chaps, as long as it's against the law.'

The door was open now, but Ciccia still stood there irritably twisting the key in the heavy lock, shooting the

Festival Night

bolt in and out. ' He'll have gone to look for his own people again,' the priest said, rousing himself to reply.

' The sergeant's there already, waiting for him to get home. But why should he want to go back? A man who'd escape has no fellow-feelings. Wherever he goes he must stay in hiding. He'll take to the woods; he can't escape; and when he's brought back by a troop of *carabinieri* he'll look like a wild animal, famished and scratched to bits. All my peace of mind destroyed for nothing. It's happened before. They'll find out whether it was my fault or not.' He held the door open and added: ' Unless he puts up a fight and they have to shoot him down.'

Against the broken plaster of the wall stood a camp bed with a crumpled, sweat-stained sheet; there was a streak of water on the floor and a pot-bellied pitcher on the stool. The air was lifeless, sultry, oppressive. A little brown loaf left on the pillow looked like a heap of filth.

Ciccia made a lot of noise outside the door, turning the key backwards and forwards several times, but at last he stopped and the sound of his heavy steps died away in the distance. The priest halted in the middle of the cell and shuddered. Slowly he looked around, scrutinising all those objects one by one with the light beating down upon them under the bare walls and the gleaming bars. He went to the bed, lifted the coarse bread with both hands and placed it on the pitcher. He turned back to the bed, leaned one hand on it and sank to his knees. Then he made the sign of the cross, hid his face in his hands and bowed his head down on the edge of the bed.

4

Rocco clambered up the path between the olive trees that flanked the villa. In the moonlight he could hardly tell the trees from their shadows. When he reached the height where the precipitous sea-cliff was concealed by the foliage, Rocco slackened his pace. His eyes widened as he saw the yellow gleam of headlights, and he felt his sweat turn cold in the night air.

He turned and ran down the bank towards the dark house. He fancied he could hear voices laughing in the garden beyond the villa; there was no light in the kitchen or in Concia's room; everyone was out by the gate. Brushing past the clump of black olive trees he turned the corner of the house and peered through the shadowy bushes in the garden. A car stood by the gate, its headlights casting a beam of greater brilliance across the shrubs that shimmered under the moon.

Rocco could distinguish the happy faces of girls and young men dressed in white; one or two boys running about in the light and shouting; and there, standing by the car holding something out to the occupants, was Concia. There was Concia. Rocco leaned back against a tree-trunk, taking deep breaths of the lovely perfume of the garden that had basked in the sun all day.

At last, Concia's employers and their friends were all in the car; the headlights swung over the garden and across the sky; then they were gone. The diminishing sound of the engine echoed in Rocco's ears. Concia, too, seemed to be listening as she stood there. The pale moonlight had resumed its sway over the garden. Suddenly Concia darted back and was on the steps of the villa before Rocco could move into the light. Indeed, he was so absorbed in watching her that he hardly thought of moving, she ran so lightly, holding her head high, never even glancing down at her long legs as they mounted the steps. Now she had vanished.

Hastily, Rocco slipped back through the olive grove behind the villa and came out into the moonlight. Almost

Festival Night

at once a light was turned on in a room on the ground floor. Rocco leaned against the wall, trembling, hardly managing to refrain from whistling. He was on the point of walking boldly into the kitchen when the door at the back of the room opened and Concia was standing in the doorway, feeling for the switch. 'Don't put on the light, Concia,' said Rocco, leaping forward to seize her in his arms. She jerked herself free with a gasp of terror. Rocco repeated: 'Don't put on the light. You heard me. Come over here.' She resisted as he pulled her to the middle of the kitchen.

'You're hurting me,' she panted.

'I know,' Rocco murmured.

All at once she stopped struggling and let her arm lie limply in his grip. Breathlessly they looked at each other. The profile of Concia's dark head was dimly outlined against the half-light of the outside door. Rocco could guess at her quivering nose, her teeth, her wide frightened eyes. He heard her draw a deep breath that raised her shoulders. His hand gripped her sweaty wrist.

Concia tried to twist herself free, but he was too strong for her. Using his knees and elbows, Rocco pushed her over against the wall near the door. She hit him and he moved back a little, without letting go of her wrist. Concia leaned against him, trying to cling to him, but another thrust of his knee drove her back against the wall.

'Forgive me, Rocco,' she moaned, sliding her free arm round his neck. He made no reply and took hold of her arm to pull it away. Concia raised it and slapped his face. They fought in silence. Rocco hurled her to the wall and jammed her there with the weight of his whole body. Through his flaring nostrils he smelt her strong odour.

Concia gave an ear-splitting shriek. 'Shut up!' panted Rocco, stopping her mouth with his hand. 'Shut up, you harlot. No-one can hear you.' Concia bit his fist and clung limply to him once more. 'Quiet!' Rocco said, moving away. ' Quiet, or I'll slit your throat!'

Concia's final scream stopped short in mid-air, and again they stood staring each other in the face, the sudden silence disturbed by their rapid breathing.

' If anyone heard...' Rocco stammered.

' D'you think you can frighten me?' Concia whispered, her voice trembling.

' If anyone heard....'

Outside the crickets were chirruping and the moon was shining further over the flagstones of the threshold, leaving a deeper shadow across the wall where they stood. Rocco let go Concia's arm and placed himself between her and the door. If anyone did come, one leap would be enough. In the wedge of shadow, the long white strip of shirt between the edges of his coat could be faintly seen, but not his legs or his face.

No one came. Concia, motionless against the wall started hiccuping from nervous tension. Rocco felt a warm drop, like a tear, slipping down his cheek and wiped it away with his hand. It was blood. ' You've scratched me,' he muttered.

Concia gave an uneasy laugh. ' Your own fault,' she said. ' Do they know you're here?'

'Who'd be likely to know that... D'you know where I've come from?'

' They told me they'd put you in prison. What have you done? Beaten up somebody?'

Rocco peered into the shadow. ' Come over here, quick,' he said. As Concia moved forward he took her arm and pulled her to the door in the moonlight. Now he could see her dark face, the whites of her eyes and a smile that showed her teeth. Her smile grew more coaxing and she half-closed her eyes. Rocco dropped her arm and took her face between his two hands. He felt the trembling of her

Festival Night

body, saw her eyes widen; then she looked down and put her arms around his neck, pressing herself against him. His knee pushed her away, but he still held her face in his hands.

'You're falser than Judas,' he breathed. 'I had to see your face again and know you for what you are. That Genoese friend of yours, I slit his throat for you and you know it... D'you think that'll do you any good this time?'

'Kiss me... you coward,' Concia moaned, her eyes closed.

With his mouth close against hers, Rocco said again: 'I cut his throat and you know it.' But Concia still clung around his neck and held him close, kissing him, biting him. 'Fool,' she said: 'What a fool you are! Why don't you take me?'

Rocco suddenly seized her by the waist, roughly, like a madman. Concia hung on his neck covering him with kisses, sobbing with emotion. Rocco lifted her in his arms. Blindly, gropingly, he crossed the kitchen, opened the door, bumped into the wall and carried her upstairs. Without a word he flung open the door of her room and they threw themselves on the bed. When Concia stretched out her bare arm to put out the light, then turned on her other side, Rocco sat up in bed and blinked his eyes in the dark. Little by little, through the open window, he could make out the hillside where the olives grew, pale in the moonlight, but the window-sill was black. He moved his leg a little and Concia started up. 'It's late,' he murmured. She said nothing.

Then he jumped out of bed and heard Concia make a movement, quickly suppressed. He leaned over in the darkness, feeling for his trousers on the cold tiled floor. As he slipped them on, his hand discovered a great rent in them between the legs. Quickly he glanced at the bed, where

Gaol Birds

Concia lay motionless. He could scarcely see the outline of her body in the gloom. He went over to the window, and knew from her breathing that she had turned her head to follow his movement.

'Stop that,' he said in a fury. 'I know very well you're not asleep.'

Concia gave a long sigh, stirred, then sat up in the darkness. 'I was drowsing, Rocco: what's the matter?' she murmured with a yawn.

'You're more treacherous than a cat, but it's not worth bothering about. Who taught you that trick? Your customers?'

'Why humiliate me so?' Concia whimpered.

Rocco turned to the window. 'Look here,' he said dryly. He held up the knife. 'Take a good look at it. I was going to give it you in the neck. You knew it, too. But it's not worth the trouble. Watch.' He took the point between his fingers and threw it shining high in the air among the olives. He strained his ears to hear it fall, but the leaves were rustling and he could catch no other sound.

Concia had not moved. 'Get dressed, damn you! Cover those breasts. You should be ashamed even to let the air touch them.'

Concia jumped from the bed. 'If they hear you Rocco...' Staggering slightly she went to the window, where Rocco was staring down at the ground. Raising her arms as to balance herself, she swung round to look at him then silently moved back to the bed and sat on the edge. 'Rocco,' she murmured, 'why did you want to kill me?' Rocco did not answer, and she went on: 'Wasn't one murder enough for you? You wanted to make it a pair?' Rocco gritted his teeth. 'I'm serious,' she continued. 'First, your things need mending; they'll be all right. But unless

Festival Night

you come back to bed I won't do them. Answer me. D'you think this house is a cinema show?'

'That'll do, Concia,' Rocco replied in a strangled voice. 'You know I saw you. I saw him too, from the woods, putting on his coat by this window. If it hadn't been for your old mother I'd have climbed up and strangled you then and there.'

'And then you killed this fellow... who did you say he was? Sure; men come and put on their jackets by my window, so....'

'Concia, it's nothing to laugh at. He told me. I made him spit it out and he boasted....'

'And you killed a man, just for that? I never even saw the poor chap, but may God forgive him.' Concia felt over the bed for her dress, held it up in front of her and crossed herself. Rocco's eyes followed the gesture of her pale hand. In a low voice he faltered: 'I forgive him, too. He wasn't to blame. He didn't know you.'

'It's cold, Rocco,' Concia said lightly, slipping on her dress. Barefoot, she walked round the bed tucking in the sheet. Rocco was leaning on the window-sill, the muscles round his heart still quivering. Hesitantly he asked: 'Haven't you something to smoke?'

Concia raised her head. 'Why ever didn't I think of that?' She ran over to a little cabinet and felt inside it. In the light of the match his face looked bewildered and the whites of his eyes shone. She stood for a moment, enjoying the caress of the smoke. Rocco drew back. 'They're foreigners...' he muttered.

'They're from the Civil Engineer's department...' Concia laughed.

'When's the car coming back?'

'Oh, sure! The car. It'll be almost morning when they get

Gaol Birds

back, but you must be gone by then. Won't you even let Concia get a little sleep?'

Roughly, Rocco pushed her away and flung the cigarette through the window. 'You know they're hunting me to my death. You know I must go back to prison. And all you feel is fear. Why do you laugh like that?'

The corners of her red mouth dropped. 'I'm not laughing,' she said.

'You're just afraid, and you're keeping me company because you daren't run away. Because you were fooling from the start and you're fooling now! Tonight you've been false to him, too. You're the one who should die.'

Concia gasped and Rocco raised his fist. 'You're laughing, damn you, and in the very room where you seduced us both. One man in prison and another underground. Talk about the cinema! You've been play-acting in this room, always.'

Concia burst into tears, covering her face with her hands.

'Don't whine or choke yourself,' Rocco roared. 'Don't try that on with me. Anyone who really weeps, weeps alone. Tomorrow you'll be back with all the others. But remember, always, that you're the one who killed him.'

'But I love you,' Concia whimpered.

'Don't say such things,' Rocco shouted. 'If the other fellow came back, he'd be the one.'

Concia moved in the darkness and glided gently up to him. Softly she said, without looking up: 'Rocco, stay here ... in hiding ... here with me ....'

Rocco said nothing, but turned his head towards the window. 'Won't you stay with me, Rocco?' she pleaded, clinging to his side, her lips seeking his. He twisted his face away and looked out at the black olives under the cloudless sky.

'The moon has set, now,' she whispered. 'They didn't

see you climb up here?... If you could stay, Rocco... we could be together every night, just we two, and you could punish me... Don't you want to punish me any more?'

Rocco pushed aside the mouth that sought his cheek, and suddenly Concia reared her head. 'Wretch! Why treat a woman like this? If you don't want me, get out of here! Get out at once! Run away as far as you can, but don't treat me like this just because I'm a servant!' Her shrill voice re-echoed from the trees.

Rocco picked up the jacket he had thrown across the window-sill, and, pushing Concia out of his way, he walked heavily across the room without a word. When he reached the door he looked round to see her white face. He saw her dark outline against the window and knew that she was looking at him in desperation.

'You don't realise how false you are,' he said calmly, and went out into the dark.

5

Ciccia came out into the cold air, looking up with dull eyes. There was nothing to see in heaven or earth, and no-one was coming from the barracks. At that hour even the sea was still, the lucky fishes sleeping peacefully below the surface of the water.

Ciccia went in and switched off the light in the cell. Everyone there was fast asleep. It was already daylight outside the door, and the start of another lovely day. Ciccia carried his seat to the railing and sat down with a sigh. His back was aching and the dawn brought no humidity. He put his head outside the gate, but there was no-one in the street.

He was dozing, when suddenly a voice roused him. It

was his son, Cicciotto, coming back alone. ' In the woods, nothing. Have any others escaped?' He was laughing, but Ciccia gave him a black look. ' We've been as far as Torre, Dad. But the man in charge of the point there told me that they'll soon catch him. It's only a question of time. If nobody says anything, and they catch him today, the sergeant needn't put in a report. But they've got to find him.'

' Is the sergeant back?'

' It takes six hours just to get up there. If they've found him already, he'll be back this morning. However, the point official told me that he hasn't gone back home, as far as he knows. They'll have to find out who the woman was. Sure enough, that's where he's gone; to hide, or to take it out on her. Unless there's some other girl he knows.'

Ciccia was deep in thought, his moustaches quivering. 'They're strumpets, the whole lot of them, doing such things and keeping it dark. If she were my daughter . . . .'

Mopping the sweat from his brow, Cicciotto remarked: ' In my opinion he's still in the neighbourhood and someone's hiding him. The moon was very bright, last night. I was out with Melo and the constables and we inspected everyone in the streets. It was so clear that from Torre we could see the waves breaking on the shore.'

' That's only playing with the job,' Ciccia said. ' You could have done all that by yourself . . . .'

' If the sergeant comes back empty-handed, we'll have to send word all along the coast. Then we'll be sure to catch him, even if he's still somewhere handy.'

' Sure, and once La Spezia knows about it, I'll be for it.'

' As long as they catch him, they won't do anything to you, Dad. I suppose he really did go through the door?'

Ciccia muffled a groan. ' It was wide open when I found it, like this gate is now. He'd have been a fool not to walk

Festival Night

out.' He waved his bunch of keys. ' With the sort of ironwork the governor gives us, you couldn't even keep the garden gate shut, if there were a garden . . . .'

' Tell me, Dad, have you got your flask here?' Ciccia looked at him suspiciously. ' No? Never mind. I'll go home and get a meal. But I was saying it would be better, if they do have an enquiry, to hold it somewhere else. They'd say you'd been drinking, that's certain.'

Ciccia sucked the ends of his moustaches and gestured to show he understood. Cicciotto was stamping his feet to shake off the lumps of soil that had stuck to his boots on his way back from the search of the marshes. Suddenly he looked up and said: ' Is it possible he didn't touch the lock? The man at the checkpoint says that everything depends on that, when they hold your enquiry. If he had forced it, they couldn't blame you at all, nor him, either, because the law's always on their side.'

Ciccia opened one eye and gave him a sidelong glance.
' Anyway, show them that lock,' Cicciotto finally advised. Then he stopped by the cell-door and leaned forward. ' Is it shut?' he asked.

' Yes. That priest's in there . . . the one going to the internment camp . . . He'll be gone again by five o'clock. I put him in here because it was empty . . . .'

Cicciotto's face grew blank with amazement as he listened. ' Has the sergeant inspected it?'

' Yes . . . No, he only came to the railings. The authorities will inspect it today . . . .'

' You should have called me over here last night, Dad. Can't you move that priest out for a minute? I'll go and get an iron bar.'

Awakened so hastily, the priest started up in alarm. He was fully dressed except for his coat. God! what a gaolbird's beard he had! ' Quick, reverend. You can say your

Gaol Birds

prayers later.' Helping him, pushing him, Ciccia took him to the other cell, opened it swiftly and thrust him inside, into the warm dark.

'You already know one another. Stay quiet. It's only for a moment....' He locked the door and went back to the other cell. Sure enough, a couple of blows would do it. Why doesn't Cicciotto come back?

He began probing the lock with another key. The lever and the wards moved a little, that was all. He would have to take the lock right off. He put in the proper key, and in two shakes the bolt slid out, solid as iron. It was iron. Not even a sledgehammer would have broken it. He turned the key back and the bolt vanished.

Cicciotto was back now, out of breath and carrying a tool box. His foot slipped in the entrance and the box fell to the ground. 'Quick you slacker! Any minute the *carabinieri* will come for the priest. When's the train?'

Ciccia fumbled a few minutes more, gritting his teeth and breaking a screwdriver. He groaned and kicked the toolbox.

'Give it here, Dad. I'll try.'

'Locks for strong-rooms, that's what they are. Even the man who made them couldn't... It's the only money they willingly spend....'

'Who's that talking?'

'I've put the priest in with the ice-cream man and the others. It's all right.'

Cicciotto slipped a plain hook into the keyhole and cautiously worked it about, feeling for the spring that worked the mechanism. 'No need to smash it,' he said, his lips barely moving. 'Just so that it doesn't shut, but looks shut. Don't forget that fellow didn't have any hammers. Now...' He stopped a moment, pressing gently and half-closing his eyes. 'I think it's giving...' he said.

Festival Night

' Give it here, you good-for-nothing. Let's break it. It only means he must have had a nail in his pocket and the sergeant overlooked it. I'm not obliged to hang around here all day. He'll have broken it while I was out.'

' Suppose he had filled up the hole in the wall where the bolt slides in? You turned the key and thought the door was locked, but it wasn't.'

' You don't know what prison's like, you don't. When d'you think he could have filled the hole? The bolt was in it, all the time he was in here.'

' Got it!' Cicciotto exclaimed, still bending over the lock, working on it. ' I felt the spring give. Bring the hammer.'

Ciccia swung the hammer round his neck and Cicciotto stretched out his hand to grasp it. Then he dealt a heavy blow on the screwdriver he had wedged in the keyhole. The screwdriver dropped to the ground.

' Fool! The point is still inside.'

' What's the odds?' said Cicciotto, straightening up. ' Try the key.'

In fear and trembling, Ciccia put in the key and turned it while they both stood silent. He tried it this way and that, but nothing moved. Then something jingled inside the case but the bolt no longer came out. He wiped away his sweat. ' Now they can come,' he said in a fury. ' That's O.K.'

' The best of it is, they can't put it on his charge sheet. It's agreed he meant to escape. They'd charge you with it, though, if they knew you'd broken the spring.'

' I didn't break anything! What did I break? ... It was you, you fool. Take away that toolbox.'

Ciccio tried the key again, the tip of his tongue between his teeth, then he picked up the tools and went off. Ciccia turned the key again, standing in the doorway. The door remained unlocked. No-one would ever have noticed it, naturally. Twirling his moustaches in high good humour he

Gaol Birds

went to the other cell and lowered the shutter covering the peephole. Inside a voice was speaking slowly. Ciccia leaned down and called: 'Hold yourself in readiness, reverend. Any minute now, you'll be off.' Then he closed the peephole.

Cicciotto reappeared on the front step. 'The *carabinieri* are coming, Dad,' he said, then ran off, bent double to avoid being seen. Ciccia gazed round unconcernedly at the open door and the cool pavement. He heard footsteps; saw men in heavy boots and thick uniforms of black and red, their berets worn aslant. 'Up and about already, you chaps?' he greeted them.

That stocky fellow with a hair-brush moustache still had his eyes shut. He tipped his beret with a flick of his finger and gave a sour smile. 'D'you have fun and games like this every night?' he asked irritably. 'We were lucky to stay in barracks. The police chief even wanted us to turn out! Us! That 'ud be a laugh! We're *carabinieri*. We don't belong to the regular force.'

The second man stood waiting by the main door. Ciccia looked back as he went towards the cell and asked: 'No-one's come back yet?'

He tried to look disappointed about it as he selected the key. 'There are exceptional cases,' he remarked. ''Tisn't every man who can force a door. Had a bathe this morning?'

'In sweat,' grumbled the man in charge, running his hand round inside his collar. 'It's a wretched beach. More pebbles than water.'

'Full of mosquitoes and loose women,' added the surly fellow by the door.

'Hand over that priest, will you?' said the little man impatiently. 'We mustn't miss the train.'

Ciccia unlocked the cell-door and called the priest.

Festival Night

Biondo and Nanni crowded round him, saying goodbye. Biondo shook him by the hand, crying: 'Good luck, reverend. Don't forget us prisoners,' as the priest came out backwards.

'Be quick!' Ciccia urged. 'Get back, you others.' He pushed Nanni inside and shut the door. There was a sound of tramping feet, then silence. While Ciccia was filling up the exit permit, the priest folded his hands in prayer, then went over to the first guard. The second one at the gate came closer too.

'Is there any news of the young fellow who escaped?'

'Not yet, reverend. It's a question of time. He's not one who'd get by because of his honest face. If he does get clear, though, and commit any more stupid crimes, our friend the door-keeper here will be in trouble....'

Ciccia raised his head. 'When a man's done his duty....'

'You call it doing your duty, letting him escape?' said the *carabiniere* dryly.

Ciccia lost the thread of his thought. He saw the other *carabiniere*, the solemn-faced one, start to grin, so he bent his head again and swallowed what he meant to say. The priest stood quietly in the middle of the room, his coat unbuttoned, his loose heavy trousers sagging over his shoes.

'D'you feel refreshed, now, reverend?' asked the first *carabiniere*. 'Then excuse me...' He turned to his companion who came forward, fumbling in the pouch slung round his shoulder.

Ciccia watched the priest's hands extended, crossed and wedged under the teeth of the hand-cuffs. The officer's swift fingers made sure the wrists were firmly gripped, then he clicked the padlock shut. The priest raised his head again. 'Regulations,' said the one with the moustache, thrusting out his lower lip. 'Ah! Your cap. Where is it?' He found

Gaol Birds

the cap crumpled on a stool and put it on the priest's head himself.

Ciccia stood up and offered his pen to the *carabiniere*. While he was signing, there came the sound of a car stopping outside. ' At least they're punctual round here,' he muttered. ' Well, then, look after yourself; take a tip from me; in a pub, leave after the last round, not the first.'

They went out. The car moved off. From the doorstep, Ciccia watched the flowery slopes above the wall brightening to gold in the warm light. The new day was beginning with doors banging, children crying, voices calling to one another. The rattle of a cart made the air quiver. There was nobody about.

Ciccia went back in, fastened the gate and wandered slowly off to the cupboard. Stealthily he opened it and took out the flask, clearing his throat.

The musty smell of yesterday's wine was still clinging to the dirty glass. He poured and drank slowly, looking up now and then. He heard someone banging on the railings. Against the light he did not at once recognise the fugitive who stood there with his jacket over his shoulders, staring into the room. Then, stupefied with shock, he dropped the glass. But all the other said was: ' You can go on drinking. I know the way.'

(20th June – 7th July 1937)

Suicides

There are days when the city where I live wakes in the morning with a strange look. The people in the streets, the traffic, the trees – everything seems familiar but as if seen with new eyes, like those moments when one looks in the mirror and asks oneself: 'Who is that man?' For me, those are the only days in the whole year that I really enjoy.

On such mornings I get away from the office a little early, if I can, and go down into the streets to mix with the crowd, staring unreservedly at everyone who goes by. One or two of them, I imagine, may stare at me in the same way, for in moments like this I really do feel a self-confidence that makes me quite a different man.

I am convinced that never in my whole life shall I have anything more precious than the revelation of how I can derive pleasure from these moments. One way of prolonging them that I have sometimes found successful is to sit in a modern-style café with wide, clear windows, and from that vantage point to savour the bustle on the pavements and in the streets, the whirl of colour, the babble of voices, and the inner calm that controls all this movement.

For some years, now, I have suffered from delusions and the bitterest remorse, yet I can affirm that my dearest wish is only for this peace, this serenity. I am not made for

Suicides

storms and struggles: and if, on certain mornings, I go down full of zest for a walk around the streets, and my past seems a perfidy, I repeat that I ask nothing more of life than being allowed to watch.

Yet even this simple pleasure sometimes leaves me with the bitter after-taste one normally associates with a drug. Long ago I realised how essential astuteness is to living, and before being astute with others one must be astute with oneself. I envy those people who, before doing something wicked or grossly unfair, or even merely satisfying a selfish whim, manage to pre-arrange a chain of circumstances to make their action seem justifiable, even to their own consciences. Women are especially clever at this. I have no great vices, (unless, indeed, my timorous shrinking from life's battle and my quest for serenity in solitude are the worst vices of all), but nevertheless I know how to be astute with myself and keep my self-control when I enjoy what little pleasure life allows me.

Sometimes I actually stop short in the street, look around me and wonder what right I have to enjoy such self-confidence. This frequently happens when I go out more often than usual. Not that I steal the time from my work; I maintain myself decently and support my niece at boarding school. (She is alone in the world and passes for my niece, but the old woman who calls herself my mother will not have her in the house). What I wonder is whether I am not being ridiculous when I stroll about so blissfully, staring at people; ridiculous and offensive. I sometimes think such pleasure is more than I deserve.

Or else, as happened the other morning, I may be sitting in a café and find myself watching some intriguing scene that first attracts my attention because the people taking part in it are so normal. Such an incident is quite enough to make me relapse into a guilt-stricken sense of loneliness,

Festival Night

a prey to so many desolate memories. The more they recede into the past, the more does their unchanging life reveal their subtle, terrifying significance.

I watched five minutes of byplay between the young girl at the cash-desk and a customer in a light-coloured overcoat, who had a friend with him. The young man explained that the cashier owed him change from a hundred *lire* note. He banged on the desk, pretending to search his wallet and pockets. 'That's not the way to treat clients, my girl,' he said, winking at his embarrassed friend. The girl laughed, and the fellow invented a tale of the trips they would have taken together, with that hundred *lire*, up and down in the lift at the public convenience. With muffled bursts of laughter, they decided they would deposit those few *soldi* at the bank – when they got them.

'Goodbye, my girl,' he called as he finally went out. 'Think of me tonight.' The cashier, laughing and excited, said to the waitress: 'What a man!'

I had noticed that cashier on other mornings, and sometimes I smiled without looking at her, in a moment of forgetfulness. But my peace of mind is too fleeting; based on nothing. My customary remorse comes over me.

We are all dirty-minded in that way, but some of us can be genial about it, smiling and making others smile. Others keep it to themselves, letting it create a void inside them. After all, the first way is not so stupid as the second.

It is on mornings like this that I am surprised by the thought – and every time it strikes me afresh – that all I am really guilty of in life is stupidity. Others perhaps can do something wicked deliberately, with complete self-assurance, interesting themselves in their victim and in the game – and I suspect that a life spent in that way may give a great deal of satisfaction; as for me, all I have ever done is to suffer from a vast, inept lack of confidence, and to

Suicides

react against other people, when I come into contact with them, with stupid cruelty. That is why – and there's no remedy for it – it only needs a few moments of remorse and loneliness to overcome me, and my thoughts go back to Carlotta.

It's more than a year since she died, and by now I know all the ways in which the memory of her can take me by surprise. If I want to, I can even recognise the state of mind that initiates her reappearance and with a great effort distract myself. But I do not always want to. Even now, that remorse offers me dark angles to explore, new points that I scrutinize with the same anxiety and terror that I felt a year ago. I have been so true to her in my tortuous fashion that every one of those far-off days appears to my memory not as something fixed and unchangeable, but as an elusive impression that is to me as real as today.

Not that Carlotta had any mystery about her. She was, on the contrary, one of those women who are too simple, poor things, and grow worried if, for a moment, they stop being absolutely sincere and attempt a subterfuge or a touch of coquetry. But since they are simple, no-one notices them. I have never understood how she could bear to earn her living working at a cash desk. She would have made an ideal sister.

What I still haven't fathomed, even today, is the way I felt about her, the restraint I had then. What, for instance, can I say about the evening when Carlotta had put on a velvet dress – an old one – to receive me in her little two-roomed appartment? I said I would have preferred her in a bathing costume. It was one of the first times I had called on her and I hadn't even kissed her yet.

However, Carlotta gave me a timid smile, went off into the other room and reappeared – incredibly – in a bathing costume. That was the evening when I kissed her for the

Festival Night

first time and threw her down on the divan, but as soon as our lovemaking was finished I told her I always preferred to be alone afterwards and I went away. For three days I did not let her set eyes on me, and when I went back I addressed her formally in the third person.

So began a ridiculous love-affair, made up of timid confidences on her part and an occasional word or two on mine. Once, without thinking, I used the intimate *'tu'* as I spoke to her, but Carlotta did not respond. Then I asked if she had made it up with her husband. Carlotta answered tearfully, ' He never treated me the way you do.'

It was easy to make her lean her head on my breast while I caressed her and told her I loved her. Lonely as I was, why shouldn't I make love to that quasi-widow? And Carlotta gave in, softly confessing that she'd loved me from the first moment and thought I was an extraordinary man, but I had caused her a lot of unhappiness in the short time we had known each other; she didn't know why, but all the men treated her like that.

' When one is hot and one is cold,' I smiled with my lips in her hair, ' love will last.'

Carlotta was pale; her enormous eyes often looked tired and strained. Her body was pale, too. That night, in the darkness of her room, she asked me if I had left her, that other time, because her body did not please me.

But I had no pity on her this time, either, and in the middle of the night I dressed myself and told her, without offering any excuses, that I had to get moving and go out. Carlotta wanted to go with me. ' No,' I said. ' I like to be alone,' and I left her with a kiss.

Suicides

2

When I knew Carlotta, I was just recovering from a bitter blow that almost cost me my life; and I felt a grim amusement in going back through the deserted streets, fleeing from the one who loved me. It had so long been my lot to spend my nights and days humiliated and infuriated by a woman's caprice.

I am convinced, now, that no passion is powerful enough to change a man's true nature. Even the fear of death cannot alter his fundamental characteristics. Once the climax of passion is over one becomes again what one was before – honest man or rogue, father of a family or a mere boy – and lives one's own daily life. Or, rather, in the crisis one sees one's own true nature. It horrifies us, and normality disgusts us. The insult to us is so atrocious that we would rather be dead, but there is no-one to accuse us except ourselves. It is to that woman that I owe my present condition, reduced to a daily job with no scope and no hope of forging a closer link with the world at large, disliked by the next man, disliked by my mother whom I support, and by my 'niece' whom I do not love. I owe it all to her. But would things have turned out differently with any other woman? Another, I mean, who would be capable of humiliating me as my nature demands?

Anyway, that was the thought that came to me whenever I had done something wrong, something that woman I loved could call faithless, and it gave me some comfort. At a certain stage of suffering we inevitably think we are suffering unjustly; it is a natural anaesthetic; it restores our energies, makes life as entertaining as we could possibly wish, fills us with a sense of our own importance in the face of things in general, flatters us. I have experienced it, and I could have wished that the injustice, the ingratitude, had

Festival Night

been even more flagrant. In those long days and nights of anguish, I was conscious of a vague, secret awareness, like an atmosphere or a radiation. I remember my stunned amazement that it could have happened; that that woman was only a woman after all; that the delirium, the agony, the sighs, words, actions, even I myself, could all have turned out as they did.

So, having been treated unjustly, I revenged myself, not on the guilty one but on another woman, as happens in this world.

When I left Carlotta's apartment at night, after indulging my passion to the full, my mind was at ease. It pleased me to wander about by myself, feeling free to enjoy walking down that long avenue, vaguely recalling the sensations and the thoughts of my youth. I have always loved the simple pattern of the night. Street lamps alternating with zones of darkness evoke my most cherished flights of fancy, colouring and heightening them by the contrasts they present. Here I could give free play to the dull resentment I felt towards Carlotta because of her meekness and her lust, unhampered by the restraint I imposed on such thoughts, out of pity, while I was actually with her.

But I was no longer young. I tried to cut myself loose from Carlotta by reviewing in detail her body and her caresses, dispassionately. It seemed to me that, separated from her husband as she was, still young and childless, she might well fancy she had the right to turn to me as a refuge. But, poor girl, as a lover she was too naive. Perhaps that was really why her husband was false to her.

I remember one evening when we were strolling arm in arm through the streets in the dusk on our way back from the cinema. Carlotta said: ' I'm so happy. It's nice to go to the cinema with you.'

' Did you ever go with your husband?'

Suicides

Carlotta smiled: 'Are you jealous?'

I shrugged. 'What difference does it make?'

'I'm tired,' she said, clinging to my arm. 'This useless chain that binds us is ruining my life and his, too, and compels me to bear a name that has done me nothing but harm. It should be possible to get a divorce, at least when there are no children.'

I felt affectionate that evening, from our long, warm contact and my rising desire. 'Have you any scruples about it?' I asked.

'Oh, my dear,' Carlotta sighed. 'Why aren't you always as nice as you are tonight? Think... If I could get a divorce....'

I said nothing. At one time, when she spoke to me of divorce I was shattered and exclaimed: 'Please yourself. You're the best judge of that. Do what you like, and I'll bet you'll be awarded alimony, too, if it's true that he was unfaithful to you.'

'I have never wanted anything,' Carlotta replied. 'Since that day I've been working,' and she looked at me. 'Now I've got you, I should think that I wasn't being fair to you if I took money from him.'

That evening after the cinema, I closed her mouth with a kiss. Then I took her to the station café and gave her a couple of drinks. In the dim light from the windows we sat in a corner like a pair of lovers. I had several drinks myself and said to her, out loud, 'Carlotta, let's get ourselves a child, tonight, shall we?'

People glanced at us as Carlotta, laughing and blushing, put her hand over my mouth.

I talked and talked. Carlotta spoke about the film, saying all sorts of silly things, passionately comparing us to the characters in the drama. I went on drinking, knowing that was the only way to make me feel loving towards Carlotta.

Festival Night

The cold air outside revived us and we ran to her home. I stayed with her all that night, and when I woke in the morning I felt her beside me, rumpled and drowsy. She stretched out her arms to embrace me and I did not repulse her. When I got up, though, my head was aching. I felt irritated by Carlotta's air of happiness as she prepared coffee for me, humming to herself. We both had to go out, but remembering the concierge she sent me on first, after kissing and hugging me behind the door.

My most vivid recollection of that awakening is of the trees in the street outside, their boughs stiff and dripping in the fog beyond the bedroom curtains. After all that warmth and affection inside, the keen air waiting for me out of doors stimulated my blood; only I would have rather stayed by myself, smoking and thinking, conjuring up a very different awakening and a different companion.

On these occasions Carlotta drew from me a tenderness that I reproached myself for, the moment I was alone again. I spent frenzied moments trying to purge my mind and free myself from even the faintest memory of her. Again I promised myself to be firmer, harsher, a promise I kept only too well. It must be clear that we made love out of boredom, lust, for any reason except the only one she tried to delude herself existed. It irritated me to recall her serene, blissful look after love-making. It made me furious to see it on her face, while the only woman from whom I wanted it had never given it to me.

'If you take me as I am, all right,' I told her once, ' but get it out of your head that you can be part of my life.'

'Don't you love me?' Carlotta faltered.

' The little love I was capable of, I burned up when I was young.'

But sometimes I grew angry at having admitted, out of shame or lust, that I loved her at all.

Suicides

Carlotta tried to smile: 'We are good friends, at least?'

'Listen,' I told her seriously, 'that sort of nonsense makes me sick: we are a man and a woman who bore each other, but we get on all right in bed ....'

'Oh, that, yes!' she cried, clutching my arm and hiding her face. 'I like it, I like it!'

'... and there's no more to it than that.'

One such conversation, in which it seemed to me I had been weak, was enough to make me avoid her. If she telephoned me at the office from her café, I replied that I was busy. The first time this happened, Carlotta tried to take offence. Then I made her spend an evening of anguish by sitting coldly beside her on the divan. The shaded table lamp threw a white light over her knees, and from where I sat in the shadow I could feel the barely restrained passion of her glances. The tension was almost unbearable, and I myself broke it by remarking: 'You should thank me, Signora: you will remember this session, perhaps more than many others.'

Carlotta did not move, and I went on: 'You'd like to murder me, Signora? Why not? But if you think you can act the lady with me, you're wasting your time. As for whims and fancies, I can produce those for myself.' Carlotta was panting. 'Not even a bathing costume,' I told her, 'will be any use to you tonight.'

Carlotta leapt in front of me and I saw her dark head flash through the white light like a missile. I threw out my hands to ward her off, but she collapsed at my knees, weeping. I patted her on the head two or three times and rose to my feet. 'I ought to cry, too, Carlotta, but I know it's no use. All you are feeling now, I've felt myself. I wanted to kill myself, but I lacked the courage. Here's the joke: one who is weak enough to think of suicide is too weak to do it ... So get up, Carlotta, you'll be all right.'

Festival Night

'Don't treat me like this,' she sobbed.

'I'm not hurting you. And you know I like to be alone. If you let me go off by myself, I come back. Otherwise we shan't see each other again. Listen! Would you like me to love you?' She looked up, her face transfigured. 'Then stop loving me. There's no other way. "It's the hare that makes the hunter".'

Scenes like that shook Carlotta to her very roots, so much so that she thought of leaving me. (After all, didn't they show that our temperaments were basically similar?) Carlotta was fundamentally simple – too simple. She was incapable of realising this clearly, but certainly she felt it. She tried – poor, hapless creature – to mollify me by treating it lightly. 'Such is life,' she would say sometimes, and 'Poor little me.'

If she had thrown me over then, and stuck to it, I think I should have felt a little hurt. But Carlotta could not reject me. If I missed two evenings in a row, I found her with swollen eyes; and if sometimes, out of pity or tenderness, I stopped at the café and asked her to come out, she would jump up eagerly, confused and blushing, even pretty.

My bitterness did not trouble her; what did hurt her was any restraint, any resentment, that our intimacy tended to create in me. Since I did not love her, it seemed to me monstrous that she should have even the slightest claim on me. There were days when it made me shudder to address her as an intimate friend, an equal. I felt degraded. What was this woman to me, that she should take my arm?

To offset that mood, there were days when I felt reborn; times when I could leave work and walk in the fresh sunlight through the shining streets, free of her and of anything else, my body satisfied, my old griefs lulled to rest, eager to see, to savour, to feel as I did when I was young. The fact that Carlotta was suffering for love of me softened

Suicides

and alleviated my own by-gone sorrows, made me feel rather remote from them and from the mocking world. Away from her I found myself again, unharmed and more experienced. She was the sponge that had wiped me clean again. I often thought of her.

3

Some evenings when I talked and talked, absorbed in the game, I forgot my bitterness and became a boy again.

'Carlotta,' I would say, 'How are you off for lovers? It's a long time since I've been one of them, but, after all, that's the best way. If all goes well, one enjoys it; if badly, one hopes for better luck next time. They taught me to live a day at a time. How does that suit you, Carlotta?' She laughed and shook her head. 'And then,' I went on 'they inspire such fine thoughts! The man we love – who couldn't care less – will never be as happy as we are. Unless...', and I smiled, ' he goes to bed with some other woman and gets his own back that way.' Carlotta frowned. 'Love's a fine thing,' I concluded, ' and nobody can escape it.'

Carlotta served me as an audience. I talked on my own account, on those evenings, the best kind of talk. 'There's love,' I said, ' and there's betrayal. To enjoy love to the full, it must also be a betrayal. That's a thing boys do not understand. You women learn it more quickly. Did you betray your husband?' Carlotta blushed and tried to smile.

'We boys were more stupid. We fell nobly in love with an actress or a girl-friend and devoted all our finest thoughts to her. Only we forgot to tell her about them. As far as I know, every girl of our age was already well aware that love is a problem of astuteness. It seems impossible, but boys go to the licensed brothels and conclude from that

Festival Night

that the women outside are different. What did you do when you were sixteen, Carlotta?'

But Carlotta was thinking on different lines. Before she said a word, her eyes told me that I belonged to her. I hated the firm, possessive care for me that radiated from the look she gave me.

'What were you doing at sixteen?' I repeated, looking at the ground.

'Nothing,' she replied gravely. I knew what she was thinking.

Then she asked my pardon, called herself a poor little thing, said she realised she had no right, but the gleam in her eyes was enough for me. 'You're stupid, you know,' I told her. 'As far as I'm concerned, your husband could have you back,' and I went away feeling relieved.

The next day but one, she phoned me timidly at the office and I replied curtly. In the evening we saw each other again.

Carlotta was amused when I told her about my schoolgirl niece, and shook her head incredulously when I said I would rather have sent my mother away to school and lived with the child. She imagined us as two beings living apart, pretending to be uncle and niece, but in reality sharing a whole world of absorbing secrets. She asked me scornfully if the girl wasn't really my daughter.

'Of course. She was born when I was sixteen. And she would be blonde, just to spite me. How can one manage to be born blonde? To me, fair-haired people are just animals, like monkeys or lions, as if they were always in the sun.'

Carlotta remarked: 'I was blonde, as a baby.'

'I was bald,' I replied.

In those last days I grew mildly curious about Carlotta's past, sometimes forgetting what she had already told me. I scanned her as one scans the gossip columns in the daily

Suicides

papers. I amused myself by puzzling her, asking her cruel questions and answering them myself. In reality, I was just listening to my own voice.

But Carlotta had understood me. ' Tell me about yourself,' she would say on some evenings, squeezing my arm. She knew that to make me talk about myself was the only way of keeping me as her friend.

' Have I ever told you, Carlotta,' I said to her one night, ' that a man killed himself because of me?' She looked at me, half smiling, half dismayed.

' It's nothing much to laugh at,' I went on. ' We died together, but he stayed that way. The dreams of youth . . .' (That's strange, I thought. I've never told anyone about it; and now I'm telling Carlotta.) ' He was a friend of mine, a fine, fair-haired chap. He really did look like a lion. You girls never make friendships like that. You're already too jealous, even at that age. We went to school together, and always saw each other in the evenings. We talked filth, as boys do, but we were both in love with a lady. She must be living still. She was our first love, Carlotta. We spent our evening discussing love and death. No lover has ever been more certain of being understood by his friend than we were. Jean - that was his name - had a haughty sadness that put me to shame. All by himself he created the melancholy that pervaded those evenings we spent walking round in the fog. We had never believed one could suffer so much . . . .'

' Were you in love with her, too?'

' Jean was more unhappy than I was, and that troubled me. In the end I had the idea that we could kill ourselves and I told him about it. He thought it was a fine plan – he who was usually just a dreamer. We had only one revolver and we went into the hills to try it out in case it wouldn't work. Jean was the one who fired it. He had always been

Festival Night

the leader in any adventure – indeed, I believe that if he hadn't fallen in love with that beautiful girl, I shouldn't have done so, either. We fired the gun – it was winter-time, and we were in a deserted lane half-way up the hillside – and I was still dazed by the violence of the explosion when Jean put the barrel into his mouth and said: " This is how they do it!" The gun went off and killed him.' Carlotta stared at me, shocked and terrified. ' I did not know what to do,' I said, ' and I ran away.'

That evening Carlotta asked me: ' Did you really love that woman?'

' What woman? I loved Jean. I've already told you so.'

' And did you feel like killing yourself, too?'

' Sure, I did. It would have been a silly thing to do, but it was terribly cowardly not to. I wish I had, sometimes.'

Carlotta often recalled that story and talked to me about Jean as if she had known him. She made me describe him and asked me what I was like then. ' Did you keep the revolver? Not to kill yourself, you know. Haven't you ever thought of killing yourself since?' She looked keenly at me as she spoke.

' Every time a man is in love he thinks of it.'

Carlotta did not even smile. ' D'you still think of it?'

' I think about Jean, sometimes.'

4

Carlotta put me to a lot of trouble at lunch-times. Going to and from my office I had to pass the windows of her café, and hide myself to avoid having to go in and cheer her up a bit. I did not go home at mid-day and I was only too glad to spend that little hour alone in some restaurant or other, smoking with my eyes half shut. Now and then I

Suicides

caught a glimpse of Carlotta perched on her stool, mechanically tearing off counterfoils, nodding, smiling or frowning, sometimes sharing a joke with a customer.

She was there from seven in the morning until four in the afternoon. She wore blue. They paid her four hundred and eighty *lire* a month, and Carlotta was quite happy to spend it all at once. For lunch she had a glass of milk, without leaving her desk. The job would have been easy enough, she used to tell me, if it hadn't been for the slamming of the door every time customers came in or went out. There were times when she felt it was battering on her brain.

After that, I shut the door carefully when I went into the café. When she was with me, Carlotta would try to describe to me those little scenes with the customers, but she couldn't manage to talk as I did, just as she failed to shock me with her suggestive hints about offers made to her by some lecherous old man or other.

' Get off with anybody you like,' I told her, ' only make sure I don't see him. Entertain him on the odd days. And watch out for V.D.'

Carlotta gave a wry grimace. For some days she had had something on her mind. ' In love again, Carlotta?' I asked her one evening, and she looked at me like a whipped dog. I began to lose patience with her, as I had before. The way her eyes shone in the darkness of her little room, the way she kept squeezing my hand, made me burn with anger. I was always afraid of getting too involved with her. I hated the very thought of it.

I grew sullen and boorish. But Carlotta no longer accepted my outbursts of bad temper with the submissive distress she used to show. She would stay quietly watching me, and sometimes she would gently withdraw from the caress I tried to give her to show I was sorry.

That pleased me even less. I found it repugnant to have

Festival Night

to court her before I could possess her. The change did not come about suddenly, though. Carlotta would say: 'I've got a headache... That door! Let's be good tonight. Talk to me.'

When I realised that Carlotta was doing it intentionally, feeling humiliated and dredging up pangs of remorse, I stopped having those violent outbursts. I simply played her false. I started seeing again a woman I had known before, on those dreary evenings when, after visiting a brothel, I would sit and rest in some wretched café, feeling neither happy nor sad, just dazed. To me that seemed fair enough: either one accepts love with all its hazards or turns to the only other thing left – prostitution.

I thought Carlotta was pretending to be jealous and I laughed at her. She suffered, but she was too simple to turn her grief to good account. Instead, as happens to anyone who genuinely suffers, she lost her good looks. I was sorry about that, but I felt I should have to leave her.

Carlotta saw the blow coming. One night when we were in bed and I instinctively avoided any conversation, she suddenly pushed me away and curled herself up against the wall.

'What's the matter?' I asked crossly.

'If I were to disappear tomorrow,' she said, suddenly turning round, 'would it matter at all to you?'

'I don't know,' I stammered.

'And if I betrayed you?'

'All life is a betrayal.'

'And if I went back to my husband?' She meant what she said. I shrugged my shoulders. 'I am a poor woman,' she went on, 'and I'm incapable of betraying you. I've seen my husband.'

'How?'

'He came to the café.'

Suicides

'Didn't he skip off to Algeria, then?'

'I don't know,' Carlotta replied. 'I saw him at the café.'

Perhaps she didn't mean to tell me, but it slipped out that her husband was with a woman in a fur coat. 'Then you didn't get a chance to talk?' I asked.

Carlotta hesitated: 'He came back the next day but one. He talked to me and brought me home.'

I must admit I felt uneasy. 'Here?' I asked softly.

Carlotta clung to me with her whole body. 'But I love you,' she murmured. 'Don't imagine....'

'Here?' I said again.

'It was nothing, dear. He talked to me about his business. Only, seeing him again, I realised how much I love you, and I wouldn't go back to him no matter how much he begged me.'

'He did beg you, then?'

'No, but he told me that if he had to marry again, he'd marry me.'

'Have you seen him since?'

'He came back to the café with that woman....'

That was the last time I spent the night with Carlotta. Without saying goodbye to her, without regrets, I stopped running after her or meeting her at home. I left it to her to telephone me and wait for me in the café, not every evening, but now and then. Carlotta came every time, devouring me with her eyes. Her voice trembled as we parted.

'I've never seen him since,' she whispered one evening.

'You're doing the wrong thing,' I replied. 'You ought to try and get him back.'

It irritated me that she regretted leaving her husband, as beyond all doubt she did. It also annoyed me that she had hoped to bind me closer to her by talking like that. Such futile love was not worth Carlotta's remorse or my own risk.

Festival Night

One evening I phoned her to say I would drop in and see her. She seemed incredulous and uneasy as she opened the door to me. I looked around apprehensively. She was wearing her velvet dress. I remember she had a cold and kept pulling at her handkerchief, dabbing her red nose.

I saw at once that she understood. She was quiet and docile, responding to all I said with timid glances. She let me go on talking, watching me furtively over her handkerchief. Then she stood up, came over to me and leaned against my face; I had to kiss her.

'Aren't you coming to bed?' she whispered in her usual voice.

I went to bed, and all the time I found her face objectionable, damp and inflamed as it was from her cold. At midnight I jumped out of bed and started dressing. Carlotta switched on the light and looked at me a moment. Then she put it out and said to me: 'All right then, go.' Puzzled and embarrassed, I stumbled out.

For days after that, I feared a telephone call, but nothing disturbed me. Week after week I worked in peace. Then one evening I was seized with desire for Carlotta, but shame helped me to withstand it. Yet I knew that if I had knocked on her door, I should have brought happiness. That certainty I have always had.

I did not yield, but a day or two later I passed in front of her café. There was a blonde at the cash-desk. She must have changed her hours. But I didn't see her in the evening, either. I thought she might be ill, or that her husband had taken her back. That idea displeased me.

But my legs shook under me when the concierge at the street door stared at me with her hard eyes and told me bluntly that a month ago they had found her dead in bed, with the gas turned on.

(1st – 3rd January, 1938)

The Villa on the Hill

Once again I climbed the road up the hill. As in the old days, every turn in the steep ascent revealed a fresh sweep of green slopes and old walls rising higher and higher, but now these scarcely seemed real to me. I had lived far away from them for so long, hardly ever thinking of them except in a momentary day-dream, that their actual physical existence meant no more to me than a symbol of the past.

But the evening breeze and the smell of the earth, these were no symbols. In them I rediscovered the very atmosphere of my youth. I had never forgotten them. So many times, in distant lands or city streets, a breath of air had brought back to me the savour of other days.

The voice on the telephone was not a symbol, either. It had made me jump, it sounded so clearly in my ear, so exactly as I remembered it. Probably Ginia had changed more than her voice. Our voices and the smell of our bodies change less than anything else about us. But I shouldn't, I think, have recognised Ginia by her smell or even by her perfume.

I paused by a railing that had not been there in my day, trying to recapture the old feeling of adventure by looking down at the swift little torrent. How often my wandering

Festival Night

footsteps had been halted by its chill breath. Suddenly, with a flurry of stones, a fair-haired young fellow with his coat slung over his shoulder emerged from the half-dried river bed and clambered up to the level of the road. Instinctively I stepped back politely as he swung his legs over the railing and jumped down. Barely glancing at me he gave an off-hand smile as if his thoughts were far away. 'Good evening,' I remarked, casually.

'Good evening,' he hastily replied, then bent his head and hurried on up the road. He disappeared past the first corner and I thought no more about him. I looked around me, trying to recognise the place. From what I remembered of the hill, and from my calculations of the house numbers, I still had a long way to go, past the inn where the lime trees grew, and the great deserted park where in June wild strawberries appeared amongst the thick grass. Whatever gave Ginia the idea of coming to live up here? I wondered if she still remembered how greedily we used to gobble up that fruit, or was she too grown-up for that, now?

My mind was dominated by the thought of seeing her again, but I was quite at ease. I am one of those men who enjoy solitude, especially when I know I won't have to endure it for long, and, alone as I was on that road of the past, my memories swarmed about me. Was I really that boy of long ago? Whom would I meet, that evening? I looked at the torrent and the railings of the scattered villas; and as I walked along the asphalt road I seemed to be trampling down a secret sadness, almost a presentiment. But only the dark outlines of the ancient trees were melancholy, not the breeze or the solitude.

So I came to another bend in the road and saw in the distance the same young fellow I had seen earlier, perched on a low wall. There he sat, smoking a cigarette and looking at the sky, clear with the onset of dusk. As I drew

The Villa on the Hill

nearer I had the impression that he was extraordinarily young for his lanky height. He had one foot on the ground and the other on the wall.

When I asked if he could direct me to the villa, he removed his cigarette and pointed to a fence only a few yards away. ' I'm going there, too. It's just here.'

The gate was close by, revealing a steep, narrow flight of steps that led up to a flower-filled terrace. The red roof of the villa could be seen through the trees, and from somewhere in that direction came the chatter of people enjoying a party.

The boy had not moved. He still sat there, smoking and looking at the sky. I don't know why, but I stood waiting for him by the gate. Slowly he finished his cigarette, then jumped to his feet and with a smile followed me through the little gateway.

' One can't be alone for a moment,' said Ginia, taking me on to the terrace and shutting the door with her shoulder. There was a gleaming table, set for seven or eight guests, and in the cool evening it gathered to itself all the light in the sky. ' It's like being on a lake,' I remarked. Ginia threw herself down on a garden seat and tenderly looked me up and down. From below came the sound of voices and a crunching of gravel.

We talked at great length, eagerly. I was aware of a sadness in Ginia that I could not fathom, and I fell silent, devoting myself to watching her. She was still the same. Her strong face was marked by her first wrinkles, but they had not lessened her beauty. At last she smiled and glanced around. ' They're looking for me, down there,' she said.

' Has your husband arrived?'

Festival Night

Ginia smiled again. 'Not he! He knows we have a lot of things to talk about.'

'We should never finish,' I replied. 'But it all boils down to this: are you still in love?'

Ginia bent her head, leaving me uncertain. Then she said: 'Heaven be praised, yes.'

'Then everything's all right.'

'Shall we go down?' she suggested, rising to her feet. She was wearing a simple gown, white as the cloth that covered the table.

As we went down, I asked her: 'These people, are they your friends or your husband's?'

'We pooled them when we married, as one does with books... that one doesn't read any more.'

'What about new acquisitions?' I asked, pointedly.

'Oh... those....'

We came out into the dusk of the garden, where I was introduced to a few of the guests. They all asked Ginia about her husband, but she parried their questions lightly and invited me to sit in one of the wickerwork armchairs. The fair-haired boy appeared from a side path.

Facing me sat an angular woman with her legs apart. 'Ginia has told me a lot about you,' she suddenly said to me in a confidential tone. In the growing dusk she leaned forward, narrowing her eyes to see me better. Then she sank back into her chair.

'Ginia is an extraordinary woman,' she went on. 'She has the vitality of a teen-ager and an exceptional zest for living. When she talks of something that happened in the past, one seems to feel her enjoying it with her whole body. I always remember the time she described her delight when she went bathing as a child. How do you think she looks, after so many years?'

'Very well.'

The Villa on the Hill

' I'm glad. She seemed a little tired, to me; preoccupied. Perhaps she needs a change, something to distract her. But the pleasure of seeing an old friend again – young, too – will act like a tonic. Do you know her husband?'

' No.'

' You'll meet him. But how late he is! Still, husbands are always late, aren't they?' She gave a harsh, brittle laugh and I closed my eyes in the gloom, resting my chin on my clasped hands. The raucous voice went on: ' He's an interesting man, Paul. Serious, perhaps too serious for Ginia. He's just the opposite of her. Ginia has remained a child, outwardly. Paul lives even more intensely, perhaps, than she does, but he watches himself, never lets it show. Ginia, on the other hand, is transparent as crystal – a delightful crystal. But how silly of me! You know her better than I do!'

At that moment, someone in the house switched on the big lantern above us and in the sudden blaze of light I saw her thin, olive-skinned face and mocking eyes. The light was greeted with exclamations of approval and the conversation became general.

Another cheer heralded the arrival of Ginia's husband. Wearing white flannels he emerged from the flight of steps arm in arm with Ginia and followed by the young man. He was tall, stern-faced, and he went round greeting all the guests with a faint smile, making no apology for his lateness. He shook my hand carelessly and begged us all to sit down. The young fellow had remained behind in the patch of shadow.

The husband went off with Ginia to dress for dinner. Another man got up and went into the house. Soon I found myself alone in the circle of chairs, but I could hear the boy breathing in the shadows.

Festival Night

'Everyone seems to do just as he likes, here,' I remarked quietly in a friendly tone.

'Ginia will come back to call you,' he answered, coming forward into the light and standing uncertainly on the gravel. Now that his face was illuminated it no longer seemed so young and smooth. It bore a trace of suffering out of harmony with his eyes.

'Feeling depressed?' I asked.

'Excuse me...' he said softly. At that moment Ginia appeared at the door and came towards us.

When dinner was over, someone put out the light because of the swarm of mosquitoes, and we stayed sitting on the terrace among the dark tree-tops. A lady had caught cold, so Ginia and Ada went inside with her and for a while no-one spoke.

'The pavements were like a furnace, today,' said a deep voice from the far end of the table.

Two or three were smoking, and the tiny red points shone like glow-worms. I sipped my coffee as though I had not heard. At last another voice – from the vague outline of Ginia's husband – replied: 'The worst is over.'

Then a voice I knew well: 'Haven't you ever been up here before, really?'

'I know these roads,' I answered in the dark. 'I tramped all over them when I was your age. I didn't go down into the torrents, but I risked rolling into them several times. Then I lost sight of them.'

'Did you know Ginia then?'

'Let's get this straight. The hill was one thing, Ginia quite another. Still, I think she enjoyed our little suppers at the inn as much as the rest of us did.'

The Villa on the Hill

The husband suddenly remarked: 'To hear Ginia talk, you all ran wild like a pack of wolves.'

The maid came and spoke in his ear. The husband asked us to excuse him and followed her out, unconcernedly. There remained two elderly gentlemen and a young girl talking together at the bottom of the table, and my young friend, who walked restlessly up and down for a moment, then leaned on the railing.

My eyelids drooped and I hung my head. The time went by unnoticed. Then I heard the young man's voice again, very close to me this time, bitter and mocking. I stood up and took him by the arm. 'Shall we go and look for the others?' I suggested.

Instead, he led me over to the edge of the terrace. Far below us, in the valley, lay a great sweep of the shining city, quivering like a lake. For a little while we stood there, leaning on the railing. I said: 'Tell me the truth. You come up here every evening, don't you?'

'I'm fed up,' he said softly. 'Utterly sick of it all. Tell me! How did you manage to enjoy being young in a place like this?'

'You discover the answer to things like that when they're over. Just go ahead and don't think about it.' He made no reply. 'The hill doesn't suit you?' I continued. 'Try living down there....'

He still said nothing, and spat quietly on the gravel. Then he asked abruptly: 'What's it like in Sicily?'

'For a man like you, very good.'

'That stupid Ada!' he exclaimed under his breath. 'Did you notice how interested she is in you and Ginia?'

'All women are like that....'

At that moment, one of the two old gentlemen joined us and mentioned he was getting anxious about his wife. 'Let's go and look for her.'

Festival Night

We met her at the door with Ginia's husband. 'I'm all right,' she said. ' But Ginia's been taken ill.'

'It's nothing, nothing at all,' said the husband. 'Just indigestion.'

Murmurs of concern broke out. The boy started forward in great agitation, but the husband seized his wrist and drew him back. ' Where d'you think you're going? They'll be back in a minute.'

We sat down again and several started talking. The lady explained in a weak voice that she'd been overcome by the sudden cold after the heat of the day. The husband said calmly: ' Pray don't mention it. No trouble at all.' The boy had not sat down: he was pacing restlessly to and fro.

' Shall we smoke?'

At last the door opened and Ada reappeared, gloomy and cynical. Beside her came Ginia. She was pale and seemed dazed.

I could have wished I was somewhere else. Luckily the darkness isolated me, as it did all the others sitting on the terrace. Even the white clothes of Ginia and her husband were no longer visible. Someone spoke, above the chirping of the crickets. Then Ada started talking.

Why had I come up here?

After a long, long time, one of the old men complained about the mosquitoes and we spoke of going inside. ' It's a pity to turn one's back on a view like this.'

But we all rose and began to file down the steps. I brought up the rear and Ginia came over to my side. The sound of shuffling feet almost drowned her voice as she said: ' Poor devil! Are you bored?'

' Not particularly. Is this how things always are?'

The Villa on the Hill

'More or less.' Suddenly she squeezed my arm and whispered in my ear: 'Talk with that boy. Don't leave him alone even for a moment.'

Below, the elderly men and Signor Paul were sitting in the room, while the ladies were strolling round the garden. I paused a moment by the radio – they were all fumbling with it – then turned back. Just as I was about to set foot on a gravel path I bumped into Ada coming in from the darkness. I noticed her firm step. 'Where is Ginia?' I asked.

'Consoling herself with youth,' she replied sharply. 'Have you seen what's going on?'

'What?'

'You must know!'

'What?'

'Things one mustn't talk about. But there! That's why people marry.' Her voice was derisive, more bitter than ever. 'Up you go! Give her your congratulations! She's waiting for you. Tell her she looks like a little girl again!'

I went inside. I had no wish to seek out anyone and I sat down, gazing into the black trees.

Then, out of the darkness, came Ginia and the boy, arm in arm. They stopped suddenly and Ginia gave me a smile. They sat down in the garden chairs and I joined them. The music of the radio came softly from the room, without disturbing the silence of the night. The blonde young girl came running out and stopped short on the gravel, seeing us sitting there in a circle.

I did not look at Ginia. I did not want to see her pleading glance. I rested my chin on my hands. 'Are you still counting on making that trip?' I was speaking to the boy, but it was Ginia who replied: 'It's so dull here, some days, that it really does make one want to jump on a train.'

'Just an illusion – like any other.'

The boy burst out: 'He's quite right, you know. In

Festival Night

certain circumstances it's even a cowardly thing to do. People talk about drunkards, but anyone who won't shoulder a liability is just as bad.'

'Spending the summer on the hill doesn't seem to me much of a liability,' said Ginia with a smile.

'May I join you?' the young girl broke in as she sat down. 'How are you feeling, Signora?'

In the silence that followed, we listened to the faint sound of the radio until it died away A light breeze had sprung up.

'Will you have a drink?' Ginia asked, rising to her feet. When she came back with the tray we were still sitting in silence. The blonde girl looked at us uneasily. Ginia began to pour out our drinks. 'Taking us by and large, we're all fond of a drink,' she quipped.

The blonde laughed aloud. The boy started to his feet. 'I want to talk to your husband, Ginia,' he said gently.

Coolly, Ginia put down her glass and stared at him. For some seconds they looked each other full in the face. 'Come on then,' she said dryly. 'We'll both talk to him. Let's go.'

The boy turned red and smiled scornfully. Then he moved to Ginia's side, but when they reached the doorway he squeezed her arm and left her, rushing off between the flowerbeds into the darkness.

Ginia was weeping. Her face was all red and crumpled like a baby's. I had never seen her weep. I let go her arm and made her sit down facing me, closing the door. When the silence became unbearable, it was Ginia who raised her great eyes to mine. 'As you see, I'm growing old,' she said with a smile. 'Where can that boy have gone?' I looked at her without replying, and she went on: ' He's so naive. Not even capable of standing up for himself.'

' Should he have?'

' It seems so. Usually these single-minded people are keener on their rights than the rest of us are. They're capable of anything. But they don't know how to get to the root of a problem.'

' Do you wish he had done that?'

' It was better perhaps....'

' Does he know... about you?'

She nodded gravely.

' Is that what upset him?'

Ginia leaned forward, her chin on her hand. ' I think I was his first love,' her lips twisted as she spoke, ' and there's nothing more dangerous.'

Her reddened nostrils quivered strongly. She still looked bravely at me and her eyes were clear again, but she lowered them. Then she came to her feet and walked to and fro. ' Did you expect to be a father, when you were twenty?'

The door opened, and accompanied by a burst of music Ginia's husband came in. He closed it behind him, and in silence came over towards us. To Ginia he said: ' I was anxious. How are you?'

She pouted jokingly: ' We've been having a good cry together.'

He took her hand, turned it over and pressed the palm to his lips. They both stood side by side, looking at me, and the husband said: ' You must excuse me, but I'm uneasy about her.'

' Babies must be taken seriously,' Ginia said.

' Exactly.'

Amid congratulations we re-entered the drawing-room. I felt a need to be alone and I tried to catch Ginia's eye to get her permission. Ginia shrugged her shoulders, then had

Festival Night

to answer something Ada had said, so I went out on to the steps. I saw the young girl's blonde head; she was still sitting where we had left her, staring at an empty chair, deep in thought. I turned away and wandered into the darkness.

I was vaguely hoping to meet the young fellow, and pushed on as far as a little glade under a lime tree. Beyond rose the shoulder of the hill, high and black. The crickets were shrill, but no human sound reached me except, faintly, a voice on the radio.

I tried to accustom myself to the idea that the youth had fled. The cool night, the fragrance of the trees, a vision of Ginia, brought me no peace. No longer did they blend to form an intimate memory. Instead, they gnawed at my very heart, unsettling, bewildering, like things in which I had no part. I was thinking, too, that in this glade, in front of that hill, Ginia and my young friend must have strolled together many a time.

I found him again, sitting where the girl had been, with his back to the light. He was alone and seemed to be absorbed in listening to Ada's voice coming from the room. As I paused I caught a few words. Ada was joking loudly. I sat facing the light and the boy saw me, but did not speak. I looked at him calmly, saying nothing.

For a moment I thought back to our meeting by the low wall, when he had smiled at me unexpectedly as he stubbed out his cigarette. But he was not smoking or smiling this time. ' You're seeking solitude, too?' he asked.

I did not answer, just looked at him.

' . . . Not only away from everybody, but really alone, you understand? Away from jostling feet and curious eyes. You can tell Ginia that. I shall stay alone. Reassure her.' His voice sounded hoarse, but it did not ring true.

' Why did you come back to tell me that?' I asked.

The Villa on the Hill

He was silent for a moment, then he said: 'You can't understand. I wanted to say it to Ginia, but that won't do. You're her friend, you tell her! I must get away...' He was standing, now.

'I shan't tell her anything,' I said.

'Why not?'

'Because it seems to me you're exaggerating.'

Those scornful eyes of his were fixed on my face, but he was trembling.

'Go to Ginia,' I went on calmly, 'treat her as an equal and tell her what you have in mind. You'll see that Ginia is a sensible woman, and you'll manage to get out of it. All the rest does not count.'

'The rest is what does count,' the youth faltered. 'Ginia won't turn back. She's not a fool. Even I, who am talking to you, don't know the truth.'

My eyes wandered to the tracery thrown on the gravel by the shadows of the wistaria. My temples were throbbing painfully.

'I'm going away,' said the boy, 'without saying goodbye to anyone. That way, I shan't come back. I implore you to talk to Ginia...' His light footsteps died away on the gravel.

When I went back inside, I found the guests preparing to depart. While the ladies went upstairs to get ready, Ginia's husband invited me to come back some afternoon. Ginia would be alone then, because of the heat, and would gladly have a chat with me about old times. I presented the young fellow's apologies for his informal departure, but he laughed and said: 'He often disappears like that to wander about by himself, and at his age, who can blame him?'

As we trooped through the garden towards the gate, Ginia shook my hand and whispered: 'Come back soon. Don't leave me all alone.' Her husband was walking on

Festival Night

ahead, between the blonde and the old lady. At the gate, Ada shook hands with him firmly, threw her arms around Ginia and kissed her.

We fell into two groups. In front, the lady and the two elderly gentlemen; behind them, I walked between Ada and the young blonde girl. The dark outline of the trees was lost in the gloom. The deep awareness of earth and night reigned alone, under the stars. I walked unheeding, barely replying to the conversation, longing for the moment when I should be alone again.

(28th June – 24th July 1938)

The Cornfield

As long as the season was still young, no one paid any attention to those tender green shoots, though they were taller than usual, but as the hours of twilight lengthened and people strolled along the roads to enjoy the cool evening air, everyone noticed the growing corn. It would have grown still higher, yellow and rustling, with a poppy or two here and there, and one fine day the old man would have wanted to reap it, make it into sheaves and talk about it in the streets and the shops. Perhaps he would have tried to sell it.

Amalia noticed a group of lads crowding round the seat by the roadside, just where the factory wall ended and the strip of field began, in front of the house. She watched them anxiously. In a way she was ashamed of the corn, yet when it was green, as it was now, it gave her a surge of hope for something she could not have explained. But the lads only looked at it for a while, then went away.

One evening, while the factory workers who lived in the last houses before the boundary were cycling past, Amalia came home carrying her hat, holding her head high so as not to see the green stalks. She ate hastily, not noticing the broken crockery or the dirty litter strewn around the kitchen. She ate what there was; to her it was unimportant;

Festival Night

so were her mother's worn-out shoes and the old man's unbuttoned trousers or the way he wiped his mouth on the back of his hand. Her only concern was to be quick so that she could get away and not have to listen to the old man going on again about his corn and grumbling that the manure had not fertilized it properly.

Still hatless, she went out into the dusk, hurrying away from the house because she did not want Tosca to call for her there. Humming to herself, she made her way to the end of the road where the trees began again, and looked up to see if there was a light in Tosca's apartment. The avenue was full of children, playing and shrieking as long as there was a scrap of daylight left. Amalia stopped by the mirror at the American Bar to put on fresh lipstick and rearrange her fringe of hair. In the greenish reflection her eyes looked deep-set and cruel.

Tosca had once told her she envied their isolated hovel. All Tosca had in mind was the convenience of not having to do the stairs. For Tosca, Sunday was a grand day, especially when she could go and picnic in the fields. Her idea of bliss was to spend the whole day picking grapes.

Someone stared at her. It was Tosca's brother, Tonino. Amalia had once told him plainly she disliked him. She could not stand his ugly, pasty face and spiteful eyes or his great dangling hands with their bitten nails. This time he smiled and muttered something complimentary without moving out of her way.

'Shall I go first, or will you?' she asked, infusing a little sweetness into her answering smile.

'If you put it like that, I'll follow you,' Tonino replied, holding out his hand.

'I'm waiting for Tosca.'

'I'm not,' he shrugged. Amalia stamped her foot impatiently, but Tonino laughed at her, looking pleased with

The Cornfield

himself. Fuming, Amalia turned her back on him and sauntered away.

When she had left him behind she wandered up the avenue alone under the shade of the trees. Everywhere the stink of frying was blending with the dusty smell of the street, but through it all she could feel the cool evening breeze and it pleased her. The clatter of a tram in the distance pleased her, too.

Later in the evening, Amalia inspected the panels of photographs under the red lights outside the cinema and made a face. Tosca was not keen on going in, either, so they strolled around and eventually paused in front of the pleasure gardens called the *Giardino*.

'I'll see if there's anyone inside that we know,' Tosca said. A hand waved at them from a little group sitting just inside the fence. 'Come on!' Tosca cried. 'There's Gianni.'

'We haven't even got hats on,' Amalia protested.

'What odds? Some girls take them off, anyway. Come on!'

Gianni was there, so was Tonino, so were all the young factory workers in the district, drinking beer instead of dancing. There were only a few couples on the dance floor – a square of asphalt between the trees – but the band played all the louder. It was cool under the trees.

Amalia refused beer and asked for coffee. She was furious because she had on the old shoes she wore to work, and when there are only a few couples dancing, people notice a girl's legs. She saw one girl in a white dress without stockings, as if it were summer already. She could see one couple at a table in the shadows. The man had a moustache and looked a sporting type. Perhaps he was the owner of the car outside. The girl was clinging to his arm and talking to him; a typist, probably, judging from her painted fingernails.

Festival Night

Tonino asked her, in his sarcastic voice, if she would like to dance.

'Not now. I'm tired,' she replied.

Tosca and Gianni were already on the dance floor. The other fellows – mechanics and apprentices, apparently – had stopped talking and were sniggering between themselves. Obviously she and Tosca had interrupted their conversation. Amalia looked at them, her face expressionless. Tonino said: ' You needn't stop what you were saying. The young lady isn't from Turin.'

A cross-eyed idiot whom Amalia did not know asked: ' Really? Where from, then?'

Another fellow remarked, shaking his head: ' A woman's a woman, wherever she comes from.' But that cross-eyed fool kept on at her until Tonino said solemnly, in an affected voice: ' We're agricultural workers, we are. Fed up with planting cabbages, so we've emigrated. Now where would our little village be, I wonder?'

Amalia pretended not to hear, but she knew he was getting at her and she felt herself sweating. For a moment her heart was louder than the band. Tonino went on: ' We're a proud lot, in our village. Won't have anything to do with people who don't work in the fields with us . . . .'

A tall curly-haired fellow came towards them, his jacket over his arm. One of the group waved and called to him. He wore a white pullover and his sunburned arms were bare. The cross-eyed chap smiled, addressing him as Remo.

Amalia sat there, looking down, while they exchanged greetings and a joke or two. Then she heard this Remo say to the others: ' Is she free?'

The orchestra started up again and Amalia jumped to her feet, throwing him a smile. They strode towards the asphalt dance floor.

The Cornfield

Before putting his arm around her he squeezed her hand, then gripped her closely by the waist, his right hand exploring the firmness of her spine. Amalia relaxed against him, and was surprised when a little later he asked her in a low voice where she came from. She gave him an astonished smile and they said no more. When the dance was over they looked at each other for a moment. Then she said: ' You'd better put your jacket on again. It's cold.'

They walked past the couples who were still standing there, made their way to the gate and went out into the shadows of the avenue. Her companion had flung his jacket over his shoulders, his long, unhurried strides keeping him abreast of her. He did not speak, leaving the problem of conversation to her. For a moment or two, Amalia forgot he was with her, then she took herself in hand and remarked: ' I've had enough of those four ignorant fools.'

The other looked at her, then murmured: ' They're fools, all right. Don't understand a thing. What's your name?' and he took her arm.

Once again Amalia felt the same amorous squeeze as before, and gently moved his hand away. ' Let's just go on walking,' she said softly, but by the time they had reached the metalled road between the houses and the dark fields, Amalia was clinging to his elbow, listening to him telling her about last year's great race, when he and the other leading cyclists had passed the boundary line at that very spot. Amalia vaguely remembered a Sunday of shouting and uproar, and a whole flood of cyclists hunched over their handle-bars, all quite unrecognisable. Amalia had never heard the winner's name, but her companion was certainly a good dancer. She liked the way he had not boasted, saying he was riding as one of a team. ' And what are you doing now?' she asked.

He was training for a race on the Riviera. Amalia's heart

Festival Night

began to beat faster, for this meant he was an important contestant. 'The Riviera? Really?' she said.

Remo never smiled. Even in the darkness Amalia had noticed that he did not smile, not even when he stroked her thigh and told her she was a pretty girl. 'All over the Riviera?' she enquired.

Remo told her that races were won in training, and that roads were all the same. Amalia felt a longing to see him with his thighs bare. They must be very strong and well developed. She asked if he had any photographs.

Still grasping her arm, Remo suggested: 'Shall we go into the field?' They sat down in the grass, and Amalia asked when he would be going to the Riviera? Had he been there before? Remo murmured something as he ran his hand up her leg, slipped the other arm round her neck and held her close against him, kissing her. Amalia started to her feet. Remo, still squatting on the grass, looked up at her. 'But...' Amalia stammered, 'we hardly know each other.'

Remo stretched out his arm to seize her by the ankle, but Amalia jumped back, clearing the ditch by the bank. Far away, under the street lamp, she saw a man cycling past. Remo, still sitting in the field, cried: 'Come here, you fool! It's night-time, isn't it?'

'No! No!' Amalia cried, her heart in her mouth. 'We're not dogs.'

Cursing, Remo jumped up. Amalia ran lightly and managed to reach the street lamp. Remo followed her with great strides, but Amalia had slowed to a walk and turned aside along the pavement.

The Cornfield

Amalia slept on a sofa in the kitchen. Her mirror and little boxes were on the chest-of-drawers in the other room where her father and mother slept. She went home only to eat and sleep. Now that the corn in front of the door was growing taller, she didn't stay at home even on Sunday mornings. The walls of the two-roomed hovel were peeling, but solidly built. The place looked like an old tavern. Amalia heartily wished the factory owners would take over the hut and the bit of land and level the lot. But her father seemed to feel secure enough, since he had sown the field.

At night, any noise outside could be heard through the door; the voices of occasional passers-by, a dog barking in the distance, the trains. With the dawn came the creaking of carts. Sometimes, but not often, the hum and swirl of a car.

This was the hut that Tosca considered more convenient than her third-floor apartment. Tosca wasn't one to go and sit in a field with a cyclist. She wouldn't even have gone there with Gianni. She was born in the town. But she would have made love in a cinema, or on a Sunday out in the country.

Amalia had done it herself in the vineyard when she was a child, but wouldn't sink to that any longer. What was the point of getting a job in the town and living her own life, if she was going to have a roll in the fields like some country wench? Anyway, love-making wasn't all that much fun, and to do it like that was disgusting. Knowing when to give way was what made her different from girls like Tosca, who would lie with any workman for the sake of a ticket to a show or a day out.

'All men are equal,' Amalia thought to herself, ' but one man isn't the same as another. That cyclist was rather nice, even if he did go off swearing in the end.' She'd have liked to ask Tosca about him. Tosca could have asked Tonino, who would have asked the others. But she was afraid they'd

Festival Night

gossip and laugh at her. One evening she was just about to go into the *Giardino* when she saw a crowd of young fellows inside with Tonino in the middle of them, so she stayed outside, craning her neck, looking among the trees in the hope of seeing the curly-headed cyclist. There he was, wearing a polo-necked sweater, arguing with somebody and red in the face.

The very next day – it was a cold, cloudy morning – Amalia was washing herself in the dark corner of the kitchen when she glanced through the window and saw a tall man with bare legs, wearing a sweater and a white beret, leaning on a bicycle, his chin raised as he surveyed the place. It was Remo.

When Amalia went out, she kept her head down, adjusting her hat. Four steps took her along the path through the corn and into the road. She walked on without looking round, and suddenly Remo was there beside her, his bicycle clicking as he wheeled it along with one hand. He had the tanned thighs of an athlete, softened by a light covering of fair hair. Amalia was silently cursing herself for having let him pick her up at home.

'Going to work?' Remo asked quietly as they walked along.

Amalia eyed him crossly, not knowing what to say. Suddenly she snapped: 'Are you doing your training?' Then she stopped walking. At a corner in the distance, a crowd of girls and workmen waited in front of the entrance to a factory. On the chill air rose the blast of the works siren, long, discordant, imperious. 'Who told you where I live?' she asked.

'No one. I go along that way every morning,' he said, 'with my little bike. You're working today?'

'I'm in a hurry.'

'I'll call for you tonight.'

The Cornfield

'Tonight I'm going to the theatre.'

Remo did not seem surprised. 'By yourself?' he asked. 'Then I'll come, too.'

'Don't call for me,' Amalia said. 'I'll be outside the *Giardino.*'

That evening they went to the cinema instead – the one at the town centre, because Amalia told him she was sick of seeing the same old faces round her. Remo put on his jacket before they climbed on the tram. They stayed quiet in the cinema, because she stopped him and said teasingly that there was a time for everything. The film, viewed from a comfortable red arm-chair, interested her so much that if he had started anything she would have been really annoyed.

On their way back they stopped at a café, and Amalia got him to talk about the race on the Riviera. He told her about the sea, the bathers, the palm-trees. She asked if he had ever been abroad before, wanted to hear all about his past and his plans if he won the race.

Remo talked readily enough about his bicycle and his races, but had very little to say about anything else. Every now and then he tried to let his hand stray and Amalia had to slap his fingers, blushing at the vivacity of the gesture.

She would not allow him to escort her as far as the cornfield. She shook hands when she left him and Remo stayed in the middle of the road, tall and a trifle round-shouldered, watching her go into the distance.

Now the dog-days had come with their scorching heat, and the old man was fussing round the field all the time. When Amalia came home from work she nearly always found him there in front of the house, testing the weight of the ears with his hand, grubbing up weeds, then straightening up, his face radiant in the shade of his tattered old straw hat, looking as if he had changed into one of his own cornstalks. He would stop passers-by for a chat. Luckily, his traditional reserve kept him from telling the whole town his piffling little hopes and plans.

But he discussed them eagerly with her mother, making all sorts of calculations. He already saw himself as the owner of that couple of handfuls of land. Amalia would have given up her bottle of Cologne, if only the men who owned the factory next door would have turned them out of the cottage. Instead, her father kept on working harder than ever, going round the place several times at night and sometimes staying out until morning, so that the owners should see him there with his little lamp on his belt when they came to pick up the keys.

How was it possible that his earthy, sour-smelling body, raised between the furrow and the cowshed, could be the same flesh as her own? Amalia shuddered, thinking how he and her mother had come together – her down-at-heel mother, he with his bearded, cigarette-stained mouth on her mother's bloodless body – to bring her into the world. When Amalia washed herself, shut up in the kitchen, standing in the wash-tub, she felt she was scouring off the taint of the land and the vineyard.

Looking through the window one morning she saw her father and Remo talking together, Remo standing by his bicycle. She quarrelled violently with Remo about it and that night she did not go to meet him as arranged. Instead, the moment she had finished her supper, she ran over to Tosca's place, so that he wouldn't catch her at home if he came to the hut.

She found Tosca eating salad. Tonino was shaving. She sat down at the table facing Tosca. Tonino said he could see her in the mirror.

'You're lucky, you two,' Amalia said, 'to be by your-

The Cornfield

selves like this. All you earn is your own, and if you don't like the place you can move.'

'Why don't you make a third?' Tonino asked. 'I'd stay here.'

Tosca went on eating, looking keenly at Amalia. 'Oh, you!' she said to Tonino. 'Everybody gets fed up with their life,' she went on. 'I wish I'd been born in the country like you, Amalia. At least you're not shut in all day and if you're tired you can always lie down in the shade.'

Tonino started singing: 'Back to your village....'

Amalia smiled as she looked at the salad. 'It's not all that easy: there's more work to do than there is here and nobody gives you a word of thanks. The pigs have a fine time, but not the one who looks after them. It's worse than being a servant.'

'At least you get cyclists there,' Tonino cried, half turning round, his mouth twisted under his up-turned hand.

Remo made it up with Amalia, letting her see he understood that she didn't want him coming to the house. Instead, he waited for her outside the *Giardino*. Amalia smiled as she saw him coming towards her to seize her eagerly by the wrist. Still, it hurt her a little to meet his penitent eyes as he looked down at her. Joking with Tosca at the factory, one day, she told her: 'If only he'd say a word or two!'

Remo quickly understood, too, that when they were together she didn't want to see around them faces from her own neighbourhood, so one Sunday he took her to a fashionable swimming pool where there was a string of cars outside.

They sat on the cool mosaic with their feet in the green-tinted water and smoked a cigarette. Amalia watched the bathers, envying the slim lines of their flanks, their supple

Festival Night

spines. In her own tight costume she thought she looked plump but well built. She knew that sunbathing enhanced the attractive contrast between her skin and her hair, and a headscarf could do a lot for her. She noticed that few of the men were as well developed as Remo, and for the first time she felt a thrill in her blood as she looked at him.

Lying at full length on the sand with her eyes half shut, she thought the sun seemed more glorious, more marvellous, than on other days. Could this be the same sun that used to scorch her calves and the back of her neck as a child in the fields? Remo, stretched beside her, asked in a whisper if they could have supper together that evening. Amalia nodded without speaking.

They ended up in a room where they were served by waiters in white jackets. Amalia felt stiff after her day in the open air, and jokingly asked Remo if his training would have suffered. For the first time he laughed, revealing his teeth. ' Training gives one more strength, not less,' he told her. That day he was wearing a sports shirt and a fancy handkerchief.

' I'm a poor country girl,' Amalia babbled as she drank her iced white wine. ' You've seen where I live, haven't you? My father planted corn all round the house, as if it were a shed. If you really love me you ought to set fire to the place. At the very least, burn the corn, root it out, so that I never set eyes on it again . . . .'

She was laughing as Remo carried her bodily up the stairs of his home to an attic under the roof. He had the key of it, and kept her there till three in the morning.

In the days that followed, Amalia grew to hate that attic, the canvas camp-bed and the slanting beam that hit her head unless she was very careful. In spite of their new

The Cornfield

intimacy, Remo was no more talkative than before.

He answered crossly when Amalia remarked how nice it would be to go to the Riviera together and have a fine room and stroll on the beach. It worried her to think he was exhausting his body too much just before the race, but she knew she must bind him to her, increase his passion for her, and anyway it wouldn't have done any good to refuse him now. Instead, she must make him so used to having her that he couldn't do without her. The more so because now she, too, spent the nights in a sweat of desire. She found peace only in those thrilling moments when Remo was taking her to the attic.

One Sunday she went to Fontana Fredda on the back of a motorbike, clinging tightly to his back. There was a meeting of competitors from the whole area. Once she grew accustomed to the trick of balancing, Amalia glanced sideways at the fields flying past them. Looking at them like that made her feel happy. On their way back at sunset, facing the golden brilliance, she pressed her cheek against Remo's solid, leather-covered back, almost closing her eyes to shut out the dazzle from the roadside trees.

At Fontana Fredda, Remo talked with a man in a white suit who spoke to him like an old friend and slapped him on the shoulder. He was a Federation Technician. The following morning, Remo intensified his training and decided with Amalia that they would stop indulging in irregularities. In the evening they met for a beer or went to the cinema. Again Amalia asked if she couldn't go to the Riviera with him on the Sunday of the race, but Remo said no.

Gradually she saw him less and less – just for a moment before supper – because immediately afterwards Remo went to bed, so as to be up at dawn. His mind was full of the race and he said less than ever.

Festival Night

Meanwhile, the grain was swelling and turning yellow. Sparse as it was, it still waved waist-high in front of the house and the old man never left it except at night. Already, many boys had had their ears boxed for throwing stones among the corn. When Amalia went out in the morning she was ashamed to be seen.

One night when she was coming out of the cinema, all alone, she had a sudden longing to go along the road where they used to meet, so she made her way to the *Giardino*. She heard the orchestra when she was still some distance away; only as she drew nearer could she enjoy the cool shade of those trees. She halted behind the fence and looked at the crowded dance floor and the little tables; she saw the workmen sitting there. One was just coming back with Tosca, after a dance. She saw Tonino, laughing, and she saw Remo. Remo who had gone to bed three hours ago.

She felt her heart contract, and she fought down the urge to go in. After all, he wasn't even dancing. Why had he lied? He had no need to, he spoke so little. Perhaps he had felt thirsty and come down for a chat with his friends. But once the day of the race was over, she would never leave him. He meant too much to her.

If she hadn't dreaded being seen by Tonino and the others, she might still have gone in, but instead she walked on in a fury and reached home without even glancing at the rustling corn. If only that day of the race would come quickly and be over!

In the dead of night she was awakened by footsteps outside the door and the sound of heavy breathing. A dog, perhaps? Or a drunk? Terror and uncertainty kept her trembling on the sofa, her eyes starting open as she heard a coming and going, a creaking. Could it be the wind? Her heart felt numb with horror and shame at having to sleep in a low kitchen like a peasant girl, behind a door by the

The Cornfield

road, at the mercy of every passer-by; at having to keep the window bolted, even in June, for fear someone might climb in; at being alone, and knowing that Remo, too, had played her false. She was terrified in case the door was not properly shut; even worse was her dread of anyone seeing the sink in the corner with its constant dripping. She screwed up her eyes and tried to sleep.

It had not been a windy night, that much was certain. The sun was not yet up, but already the heat was oppressive. Amalia, drying herself in front of the window, saw the strip of corn all battered down and ruined. She could see the seat by the roadside, now; only yesterday it had been hidden by the yellow-green stalks.

Amalia was at the door when she heard her mother's scream at the window. They both jumped among the furrows – Amalia already had her hat on – and saw how the stalks were broken, crushed and strewn over the bare earth. A few ears were shedding their grains. A workman cycling past turned to look.

The old woman, still barefoot, was clutching her cheek with her hand, holding her elbow. 'This time your father'll murder us,' she said hoarsely.

Amalia shrugged her shoulders. She bent down and ran her hand once again through the stalks lying on the whitish soil. 'What d'you expect him to say? It must have been a drunk. Doesn't he ever get drunk himself?'

She went off, feeling sorry to leave her mother groaning there alone. She walked quickly, because groups of workmen were now hurrying past on their bicycles. Suddenly she remembered what she had said to Remo when she was drunk.

She went home again at mid-day, not letting Tosca come

Festival Night

with her. From a distance the hovel looked the same. Her heart began beating painfully when she saw the devastated strip. The door looked almost naked. 'Where's papa?' she cried.

The old woman was blowing the fire and looking inside the oven. 'He's gone to give notice to the factory owners. He says they did it themselves, so as to take the land away from him. He wants to go back to the village and die of hunger. Are you sure you didn't hear anything last night?'

'All this fuss for a couple of sheaves of corn, if that much. The seed cost more.'

'Go and tell that to him. You've been to work this morning?'

'He's coming back?'

'He's been back twice already. He doesn't know where to go, any more. How could you possibly not have heard something?'

When her father came back, Amalia dodged the blows, keeping her hat on and putting her gloves on the table. The old man's face was scarlet when he came in, but little by little it grew pale, limp and frightened. He went outside to rake around and came back with great tears welling from his eyes. He spilled his soup on the table. The old woman said nothing.

'Going to the factory today?' he asked suddenly. Amalia lowered her eyes to her plate. 'Work!' he went on. 'Work for those beasts! Run and join the queue! Work to fatten them! They need people like you! They make you work all day and they pay you at night. Old woman, where have you put the hoe?'

Amalia got away half-way through the meal, to stop herself from screaming. She wandered round the deserted streets in the hot sun, biting her lips and looking up whenever a tram went by the end of the road. Suddenly a cyclist

The Cornfield

shot past her, bare-legged and covered with dust. It was not Remo.

At the factory entrance, Amalia asked Tosca if she could spend the evening with her. They went shopping to buy a loaf, then they climbed the filthy stairs together and sat down in the kitchen to recover their breath. Tosca started on her housework. Tonino came home and greeted her with a meaningful nod. Amalia gave him an absent-minded smile.

While Tosca prepared the salad on the balcony, Amalia got up and began undoing a box of eggs. Tonino, who was washing himself behind a partition, said lightly: 'Aren't you even going to thank me?' His eyes and untidy hair appeared above the wooden rail. 'Don't you know I've done you a favour?'

Amalia raised her eyes. 'And if you want any grape-picking done this year, I'll be there,' Tonino concluded, coming into the kitchen rubbing his shoulder. He looked at her with a smile and his eyes grew sharp. 'They told me you wanted to see that corn cut before you could go cycling. Aren't you going to thank me?'

Amalia, leaning on the table, couldn't take it in all at once. Then her cheeks flamed and her breath died in her throat. She leapt to the door, opened it and rushed downstairs. As she walked she hid her face, twisted with weeping, so as not to be recognised, and the shrill cries of the children reached her as from a remote distance, dulled to a faint buzzing. When she reached home she let the old man go on nagging her for a little while. Even after it was dark, he was still persisting that he couldn't make out why she hadn't heard anything from the kitchen.

(26th July – 2nd August, 1938)

Summer Storm

INTRODUCTION

This second series of short stories by Cesare Pavese has, like the first,[1] been selected from manuscripts found among his papers after his death in 1950. He had included a few of them in his volume of stories, *Feria d'Agosto*, published in 1946, but the majority were unknown to his public until they appeared posthumously in 1960.[2]

In choosing which stories to include in this English translation, it seemed pertinent to select those which showed most clearly the effect on his work of Pavese's boyhood and adolescence; and the gradual development of his most trenchant characteristics as a writer of fiction.

Pavese's father, an official in the Court of Justice in Turin, came of a family of peasant farmers. In 1908, Cesare was born in a farmhouse his father had inherited in the village of San Stefano Belbo, in Piedmont, and returned there to spend the summer months every year until, in 1918, his widowed mother had to sell that property. Later she bought a small villa in the hills behind Realgie, and the young Cesare Pavese's experiences in these poor, sparsely populated country districts is reflected in the stories 'First Love' and 'The Name', both written in the

[1] *Festival Night*
[2] *I Racconti di Cesare Pavese* (Einaudi, 1960)

Introduction

first person as a young boy's own account of events in such areas.

During his final years as a student in the University of Turin, Pavese spent his long vacations working hard on his studies of American literature, particularly on preparing his outstanding translation of *Moby Dick*, published in 1932. Almost his sole relaxation during this period was exploring the River Po, rowing or swimming there every day, walking along its banks and getting to know the people who earned their living there, the ferrymen, owners of landing-stages where pleasure boats could be hired, café proprietors and their customers, all the busy, summertime life of the great river which he portrayed in 'Summer Storm' and 'The Leather Jacket'. He himself spent long days of solitary contemplation among the willows on the banks of the Sangone, as Corradino does in 'The Family', and enjoyed the same occasional visits to gay evenings of open-air dancing and variety entertainment in Turin's popular 'Park'.

Young though he still was – not yet thirty – Cesare Pavese was already strongly affected by trends of thought that were to become characteristic of all his later work; his awareness of classical mythology, here hinted at in 'The Name', which he brought to full flower in his *Dialogues with Leuco*; his peasant-like, 'earthy' unquestioning acceptance of birth, mating, bloodshed and death, in 'First Love', and the theme of his novel *The Harvesters*; his deep conviction, expressed in 'Freewill' and again in 'The Family', that the whole of a man's future stems relentlessly from his childhood experiences; that a man's reaction to life's problems will always be the same; that, like a bridge, he can carry a certain, pre-determined load and no more.

Even in these early stories, Pavese clearly shows his distrust of women, whom he generally portrays as self-centred, 'treacherous and cruel as the sea'. Nora, in 'The

Introduction

Leather Jacket', Ernesta in 'The Family', and the prostitute, Mina, in 'The Idol', are typical of all Pavese's women characters. His distrust, even hatred, of women may have been due partly to his mother's harshness to him as a child, partly to an unhappy love affair while he was still a student, though the primary cause lay almost certainly in his own nature. But, whatever the reason, to him women were the root of all men's suffering and in writing of them he shows no gentleness or pity, even for the girl who dies so terribly in 'Summer Storm'. Oddly enough, Pavese was quite unaware that his attitude in this respect was open to question. In his diary he noted on 24th November, 1949, after discussing some of his work with a close friend: 'D . . . remarked that my women characters are all whores and this amazed her. What amazes me is that it is so! I never gave it a thought!'

But Pavese's pity for the sufferings of men is deep and sincere; no one can doubt his quick perception of pain and his sympathetic portrayal of it in 'The Evil Eye', 'The Beggars', and 'The Leather Jacket'. It is the theme above all others that pervades his work and reveals his love for his fellow men, his realization of the mental anguish they often conceal beneath a mask of indifference. This is the outstanding quality in Pavese's work. In his diary for 28th January, 1938, when these early stories were being written, he made a comment that could stand for all he ever wrote: 'Morality is not enough. The only creed worthy of respect is compassion, charity towards our fellow man. The teaching of Christ and Dostoievsky. All the rest is nonsense'.

A. E. M.

The Evil Eye

One day I heard the girl at the cash-desk remarking: 'See? He looks quite sick! Revolting!' I looked round in astonishment. They were indeed talking about a work-mate of mine who was coming slowly up the stairs with an armful of books. As I turned, all I could see was his bald head outlined against the floor. It was followed by his stooping shoulders, his long, grey overall, and Berto came over to the counter to put down the untidy pile of books he had been clutching against his chest. His face had a look of agonized tension, like a man trying hard not to weep, and his eyes seemed strangely deep-set, glinting beneath their lids like water in a well.

'One good thing, he's not married,' the head-clerk murmured to the cashier, whose mouth was still twisted with scorn. She noticed I was listening and beckoned to me. I bent my head beside theirs and suddenly felt as I sometimes did when I left the shop on a light evening to find the heady warmth of spring all around me. I had never been so close to this girl before. She was far beyond the reach of a mere errand-boy like me. 'Does he still have that look on his face when he's in the shop?' the clerk asked me suspiciously.

'But, sir, he can't help his face,' I answered.

'You're a bright boy,' he went on. 'Doesn't he say what's

Summer Storm

the matter with him? Tell you his troubles? A man can't be allowed to look at people like that without some good reason.'

'One of these days I'll make a complaint,' said the cashier.

'If the shop caught fire or one of us were to get the sack,' the clerk remarked in a worried tone, 'I'd say he's a man with the evil eye. But I'm not superstitious. What d'you say, Gigi?'

'Whenever he goes past me he makes me shudder,' the cashier whispered. 'I get an awful feeling he's a gaolbird.'

'There's his age, too. He must be in his forties.'

I had never had any such suspicions about him myself. I was very young at the time and not given to studying other men's faces, still less the face of 'Silent Berto'. I saw very little of him since I was cycling round all day delivering orders. If I had to spend an hour or two in the storerooms now and then, unpacking parcels or looking for volumes wanted by the shop-assistants, any view I had of Berto was nearly always from the back as he faced the book-shelves, scrutinizing them carefully with his head on one side. Sometimes he would dart quickly past me like a shadow, glancing at me without speaking. If I needed to ask him anything he would turn and attend to me at once. An oldish man he seemed to me, impotent perhaps. One rainy day when I got back drenched to the skin he gave me a half-smile, widening his mouth and crinkling those deep-set eyes of his.

True enough, as the girl at the cash desk said, he looked a sick man. But the unchanging expression indelibly stamped upon his face made him look like a sick man in a photograph; there was even the sickly yellow appearance of old photographs around him as he worked in the feeble glimmer of the economical electric bulb. But still he never complained of the proprietor's stingy ways, though the poor light gave all the rest of us a splitting headache when we tried to read the titles on the upper shelves. He simply

The Evil Eye

kept on straining his naked eyes, making them water as if filled with tears. One evening, after almost blinding myself trying to find a book down in a corner, I cursed the whole show and lit a candle. Berto rushed over and blew it out, full of indignation and protesting about the risk of fire.

It was the evening after I had learned that my fellow-employees considered him disgusting, so I had a good look at Berto myself and thought he was quite repulsive. I couldn't bear to look at his bare skull, his mouth pulled down at the corners in a perpetual grimace, his skin all wrinkled and drawn as if some fever had burned itself out in his very bones, or perhaps his spirit. 'What's the matter with you?' I cried as I rose to my feet. 'Got a pain in your guts?'

Berto answered in that quiet voice of his – it seemed incapable of any warmth – explaining that as far as he was concerned he'd have been only too pleased even to smoke in the store, but the boss had given him strict orders and he couldn't go against them. I burst out laughing and told him I meant a real illness, colic for instance, gastritis or some bowel trouble. 'Or have you got V.D.?' I asked.

'I had it when I was your age,' Berto replied after some hesitation. 'It's a frightful thing. I got over it all right, though.'

'And what's the matter with you now?'

'Now?' His face went white, surprise and shock masking his normal look of tension. He dropped his eyes. 'There's nothing wrong with me,' he said. 'Why? Do I look ill?' He was perfectly serious.

'You look like the dead,' I told him. 'That's what's the matter with you. Do they give you a rough time at home?'

Berto's animation vanished. 'I live by myself, my boy,' he said quietly, 'and it's a long time since anyone treated me badly. Perhaps I've caught a chill. I'm getting on, anyway. I expect that's why I've got this ugly, waxy look.'

Summer Storm

He took my questions so seriously and answered them with such apathy that I could not go on. It was like walking through sand – hard-going without much progress. One thing was certain, though. He was not lying. Besides, as I studied his face a little longer, I saw nothing about it to suggest he was ill. Only some poignant suffering, long endured, could have twisted his mouth like that and made his eyes so sunken. And then, what sick man fails to jump at a chance to talk about his complaints? Berto's look was more like the utter desolation one sees on the face of a spoilt child on the point of bursting into tears. I even began to feel uneasy myself when I was with him. How was it I'd never noticed it before?

Next day, when I had to slip upstairs for a parcel that was due in, I chose a moment when two customers – dry old sticks – had buttonholed the boss about something or other and I went over to the head-clerk.

'Apparently he's not ill at all,' I whispered, rather proud to be on such confidential terms with him.

'What's that? Who?' he snapped at me.

'Berto,' I said, taken aback.

'What the devil! It's your fault if orders get behind. What are you doing up here anyway, always under everybody's feet?'

I got away as best I could. But at lunchtime the cashier called to me kindly as she was putting on her hat in the corridor, and asked me if I couldn't carry up the books myself. 'You're so much smarter, Gigi,' she said. 'Only people who look pleasant should be allowed in the shop. How can anyone put up with that old fool?' With a shudder she added: 'I even see him at night, like a ghost in the dark!'

I told her I'd gladly serve in the shop myself, but when I was out on errands it was Berto's job. Louisa went off smiling. She was such a pretty girl.

The Evil Eye

For several days after the episode of the candle I saw little of my friend. We spoke to each other now when we met at the shop-door, and I was often conscious of his eyes on my back. When I turned to meet them they would give me a painful smile. This grimace of his frightened me, gave me a feeling of almost physical discomfort. Always, below the surface, there was that lurking anguish, the pitiful loneliness of his eyes. What must the colours of the world look like, seen through those eyes?

One evening we left work together. It was already dark, with a hint of snow in the wind that I found exhilarating. I asked Berto to come and have a drink with me. I remember that, as we turned the corner, Berto looked up at the great palace of the Central with its rows of lighted windows against the night sky. After a moment's pause he remarked: 'What a lot of people still working! They'll be there all night!'

'And what do you do in the evenings?'

'I go to bed and read. That's the only pleasure I get.'

What he probably read I knew already. Some days previously I had noticed that almost every evening as he left the shop he was stuffing some book or other into the inside pocket of his overcoat. Next morning, furtively but punctiliously, he would put it back. Sometimes it was a history book, more often a novel. I had an idea that the cashier did the same thing, anyway.

At the café I had a glass of wine. Berto asked for coffee. My drink warmed my blood a little and I forgot my uneasiness in his presence. Instead, I talked to him about my plans, how I meant to become head-clerk one day and that in the meantime I'd very much like to get off with the cashier.

Berto listened with his usual long-suffering half-smile. You might even rise to be the boss. Leave the cashier alone. 'You're young,' he told me. 'You've got plenty of time.

Summer Storm

When all's said and done, all a woman can give you is children. You've got all the time in the world ahead of you. What you should be thinking of now is earning a good living.'

'And what have women given you?' I asked him.

Berto's eyes wrinkled as if he meant to smile. 'Nothing,' he said gravely, 'Nothing. You must understand that, Gigi. They do harm to a lot of men. You should realize that there is only one woman really right for each man, and he doesn't always find her.'

'Only one?' I said, thoughtfully.

'Perhaps we're not being fair,' Berto continued. 'It's the same for women as for us. What do we give to women? Many men treat them badly.'

'I don't,' I said.

In short, all that evening Berto's face was, for me, veiled in a mist. I even shook hands with him when we parted. But already, as I dropped off to sleep that night, I was conscious of a vague uneasiness at having been so frank and open, watched by his dead eyes. Towards morning I remembered with a shock just where I had seen an agonized look like his. It was on my own face, reflected in a windowpane, when I was a boy and my father had chased me out of the house, yelling at me and throwing stones. Later, when I had found myself a job, I was allowed back, but I still trembled whenever I recalled how I felt then. Of all the thoughts that ran through my mind at that time, the most cheerful one was to throw myself in the river. Berto had exactly the look of a man who had done so and was still weeping over it. Always, from morning to night.

Next day there were new deliveries to carry up to the shop and the two of us went up and down the stairs with great armfuls of books, supervised by the head-clerk. All the morning that fellow got more and more irritable and

The Evil Eye

he made a special point of picking on Berto whenever he had a chance. I filed past without saying anything, and noticed that, as soon as the poor old chap appeared, one of the clerks near the cash-desk would put his hand in his trouser pocket and rub himself hard, making some remark to the fair Louisa. She giggled and glared spitefully at Berto as he staggered past with his load. Every now and again the boss would poke his head out of his little office and then withdraw it, satisfied with our progress.

Towards midday there was a slight breathing space and the head-clerk called me over to give me orders about the afternoon's deliveries.

'Berto's a good man, you know,' I had the cheek to say. 'His wife must have left him, I think.'

The head-clerk stared at me. 'Who cares who has left him? He doesn't treat books properly, that's the point.'

'When he checks through them to cut the pages, he never makes a slip,' I said.

'Does he read them? When?'

I bit my tongue. 'I don't know . . . Down in the stockroom . . . just a glance when he has a free moment. I read a bit myself, too.'

'What? So we assistants read when we should be selling! That's why you never come when you're called! Let that be the last time!'

'Oh, no, sir. I was wrong. Berto doesn't waste time, and I don't suppose I've read three pages in two months. It's just that he told me he's fond of reading, that's all.'

'He doesn't buy any books, though,' he said suspiciously.

That afternoon I had to go all over the place delivering parcels. I jumped on my bicycle and away I went. It was a job with no future – like a butcher-boy's – and sometimes humiliating. But I wish now I could go back to those gay, heedless times when I pedalled like a dare-devil through every street in the town. Sometimes I had to go to far-off,

225

Summer Storm

quiet districts where I had never been before, and could speed along over asphalt roads where cycling seemed no effort at all. Then I would dawdle back, feeling free and easy, looking at the girls and finishing a cigarette. I was paid for that.

It was nearly dark when I got back that evening. There had been a little sunshine but the muddy streets were freezing again and I could hardly feel my fingers on the handlebars. The shop was just closing as I went in. The head-clerk, looking very serious, was walking up and down by the cash-desk where Louisa seemed intent on studying her finger-nails. From the manager's office came a furious voice: 'It's as bad as stealing, you know.'

I exchanged a glance with the other two clerks, who gestured to me that someone was getting the sack. I thought they were talking about me and my legs trembled under me. Then I carried my bicycle right across the shop and down into the storeroom. The light was already out. I was standing there uncertainly on the bottom step when I heard the voice, now almost hysterical, crying: 'Get out, I tell you! And take that look off your face.'

Misogyny

The little tavern stood at a dark turn in the road, under the shadow of the mountains. The young landlord, Giusto, detested parties of trippers and would have preferred not to serve them, but this would have been unfair to his sister, who helped him run the place. Consequently his temper got worse and worse as the summer wore on.

One October evening when the place was deserted, the young fellow poured himself a glass of wine from a half-empty bottle, turned down the oil-lamp and sat with his feet on the table to glance through an old newspaper. He'd have been glad if one of his old customers had dropped in to liven things up for an hour or so.

'Mind you shut the door properly, if you're staying up,' his sister said with a sigh as she climbed listlessly up the stairs.

Giusto was left alone with his wine, staring at the paper, and thinking of his own affairs. There came a creak from behind the counter, where display-shelves with bottles of spirits stood in the shadows. Perhaps the wood was too old and rotten, or there was a rat about. No sound came from outside except a breath of night air through the half-closed window. Even the torrent that rippled noisily for most of the year was silent now. Summer was over, and all through the autumn the meadows would be filled with slow-moving mists. Indeed it was so quiet that you would

Summer Storm

have said you could hear the grass quivering or a pebble rolling down a slope. When in the end a cricket started chirping it made Giusto jump in his seat and pick up his glass.

'She's tired out, and so am I. Perhaps she's working too hard. If she married she'd have something to work for, but not even a carter will have her.'

Giusto moistened his lips again, then stopped as he heard footsteps in the courtyard and low voices. He recalled that a little while ago he had caught the sound of a car in the distance, and he raised his eyes. A human face was staring in at the window, someone said: 'Yes, yes,' hastily and the door opened.

Two young people, hand in hand, slipped inside; a thin, cautious-looking lad with broad shoulders and a dark-haired girl with big eyes, wearing a transparent mackintosh. They both halted just inside the door and stared at Giusto without speaking. The girl was carrying a suitcase and the boy, who looked at him, kept rubbing his forehead.

'Good evening,' Giusto greeted them.

The lad darted a glance at him and without coming forward asked bluntly if he could get any petrol there.

'Where's the car?' said Giusto.

The car had come to a halt on the main road. It had run out of petrol. They were in a hurry.

'I haven't any petrol,' Giusto answered placidly as he eyed the girl.

The lad turned pale and Giusto saw his eyes close for a moment. His face seemed bloodless under his bony forehead. As for the girl, she was sitting dejectedly on the suitcase, watching her companion's face as though her fate depended on him. 'Don't say anything, we'd better not say anything, Renato,' she hissed hurriedly. 'Who's to blame, anyway? Don't do anything, don't say anything. Where shall we go now, Renato?'

Misogyny

Giusto looked at the man again and saw that he had no idea what to do. He laughed and suggested they could spend the night at the inn.

'We can't do that,' the girl replied hastily. 'What about the car? We can't stay here.'

Giusto retorted crossly that they weren't the first to stay there. 'The car? We'll go and push it into the yard, I and the gentleman. Is it far away? Where d'you come from?'

They answered vaguely, Giusto persisted, and in the end they both admitted they were on their way to France. 'That's fine. In the morning we'll get the first cyclist who goes by to fetch a can from the village. Then you'll be all right. You can go where you like, but if you're going over the mountains take care you don't run dry again. You won't get any more up there.'

'Can't we go to the village ourselves, now?'

'I've already told you that's no good. The people who sell it are all fast asleep long ago.'

'Don't listen to him, Renato. Don't believe him. He's only trying to make us stay here. Let's go.'

By this time the boy had regained some self-control. He shut the door and came forward into the middle of the room. 'Tell me the real truth,' he said, 'and I'll pay double your charge for the night. Is there anywhere at all I can get petrol quickly?'

Giusto had an impulse to spit at his feet, but then realized the poor fellow was overwrought. The girl, too, huddled on the suitcase, seemed in a fever of agitation and never took her eyes from his back. He shook his head and called Tosca. Then he stood up and told them firmly: 'No petrol till tomorrow. Shall we go and get the car?'

The girl jumped up, thrust the suitcase against the wall with her foot and clutched her companion's arm, begging him not to leave her there alone. 'Here's my sister,' said

Summer Storm

Giusto. 'She's coming down now,' and he drank up the rest of his wine.

All the time they were outside, walking in the dark between fields, Giusto never opened his mouth. They found the car, switched on the headlights and slowly, laboriously, began to push it. When the other ventured to say a word or two, Giusto made no answer except to mutter that they'd both better forget the girl.

When they arrived back, panting and sweating, they found the little room empty. The girl's little motoring hat lay on the floor beside the suitcase and Giusto picked it up. He went over to the foot of the stairs and heard the two women moving about overhead. 'Here we are,' he shouted.

'They're not answering,' the boy exclaimed a moment later. Giusto reassured him and asked if they'd like to go to bed now.

'Go to sleep?'

'I suppose so,' Giusto retorted impatiently. 'Naturally, if the young lady permits.'

'Poor girl,' said the other, his fleshless face twisted in a forced smile. 'Poor little thing. No, I'm not going to bed', and he ran his hand through his hair.

Giusto stepped over to the counter, picked up a bottle, filled a couple of little glasses and invited the boy to have a drink. 'Cognac,' he said, smacking his lips. The other swallowed it in one gulp with his eyes closed, then ran up the stairs.

II

Giusto went back to his seat at the table where he had tossed the paper. For a moment there was a buzzing in

Misogyny

his ears, then all was silence except for an occasional footstep overhead. 'A dog,' he was thinking. 'That's what we want in this inn. People come and go without anybody knowing.' At that moment Tosca appeared, looking cross and preoccupied. 'She's thrown herself down on the bed,' she snapped.

'And he hasn't?'

'He's just standing there licking his hand and looking on the floor.'

'They aren't married. She isn't wearing a wedding ring. But they don't look like kids running away from home.'

'She's thirty at least. Perhaps she's his sister.'

Giusto smiled scornfully. 'They're afraid of each other. He hardly dared go upstairs. And a man doesn't drive round at night with a nervous sister and forget about petrol.'

'They haven't had any supper,' Tosca replied.

'That's what I thought. They haven't even got any rugs in the car for crossing the mountain.'

'Hush.'

The boy appeared at the top of the stairs. With that pale face of his he looked like an invalid who had just crawled out of bed.

'Anything the matter?'

He came forward uncertainly. 'The case. Where's the suitcase?'

Giusto stood up. 'Nobody's taken it,' and he went towards the door to pick it up. 'I'll do that,' the boy cried as he ran forward. 'I'll get it.'

'No you won't,' said Giusto. 'That's my job. Yours is to fill in the register. Tosca, the register.'

He walked up the stairs, but the boy came beside him and took the case from his hand. 'Listen,' he said. 'The lady isn't well. Can you give us some milk?'

Tosca carried up the milk. She was very much put out

Summer Storm

and remarked as she climbed the stairs: 'We shan't get any sleep tonight. The girl's feverish.'

'D'you think they've come here for her to have a baby?' Giusto piped up.

'Wretch!' his sister retorted. 'Go to bed! Off to bed with you.'

At this rebuff Giusto wrinkled his nose with amusement and got ready to go up. 'We'll have a baby here tomorrow,' he laughed, outside the room where the two visitors were. 'Oh, well. As long as they don't leave it here,' and he went on to his own room.

A violent shake from Tosca woke him at dead of night. She was so weary she could hardly stand. How they'd kept her at their beck and call! The woman had been delirious, thrown herself out of bed, wanted to go and get the car.

'And the baby?'

'What baby? They're scared to death, those two. They've done something. If you speak to them when they don't expect it they jump like rabbits.'

Giusto stammered something or other in the dark to reassure Tosca, and began to dress. It was cold. He wrapped his coat around him and went out on the landing, tip-toeing across to the crack of light from the other room. He heard a deep sigh and whispering voices. He shook his head and went on downstairs.

Once on the ground-floor he went across to the door and threw it open. The lamp still burned faintly but outside it was pitch dark. He could not see the sky. Chilled to the bone, he shut the door again and came over to the table to his old seat. The bottle was still there.

More than an hour went by as he dozed, woke with a start and moistened his lips now and then. That old newspaper was still before his eyes but he could not manage to read. At intervals a curl of smoke rose from the lamp.

He heard an uncertain footstep on the stairs and saw

Misogyny

a red pin-point light from a cigarette. 'Who's there?' he called.

The young man came forward, paler than ever, his eyes sunk in his head with weariness. He wanted a drink. Giusto went to fetch some cognac. 'Is the girl asleep?' he asked softly.

They sat facing one another in silence, each scrutinizing the other. The boy's two-day growth of beard made him look still more down and out. He drank at a draught, saying nothing.

'This warms the cockles of your heart,' Giusto told him. 'Takes away your palpitations. Women don't understand that.'

The other sat crouching forward and seemed to be listening. 'Doesn't anybody go past here at night?' he asked suddenly in a hoarse voice.

'Not very often,' Giusto replied. 'If they ever do it's in the summer, towards morning. Lorry drivers. Sometimes the customs officers.'

'Customs officers? Where do they go?'

'They just have a drink and then go on their rounds. But there aren't any law-breakers in these parts.'

The young man rose to his feet and began pacing up and down. Giusto followed him with his eyes.

'Is the frontier far from here?'

'Six hours by car. Anyone whose passport's in order finds it better to go by train.'

'We've got a passport,' the other broke in. 'It's just that we prefer . . .'

'To forget about petrol,' Giusto finished the sentence for him.

'You don't believe me?'

'My dear sir, it's my job to believe everybody. If an old man in a fur coat arrives in a car with a painted trollop and tells me she's his daughter, I must believe him. And if a

233

couple come with no papers and suffering from insomnia, and the fellow is so scared he'd pay me anything to get away, I don't have to punch his nose. But I can tell him, however, man to man, that getting to the frontier is nothing. It's crossing it that's the problem, especially with a woman who can't keep quiet.'

The lad halted, his hands in his pockets. He lifted his right hand to his face and gnawed at it. He said in a low voice. 'If I've given you any trouble, please excuse me. There's nothing I can say. I cannot defend myself. All I want to do is sleep.'

He dropped into a chair, utterly exhausted. 'Take it from me, you won't have any trouble. You don't know us, and we'll leave at dawn.'

Giusto looked round in annoyance. He fancied he saw eyes shining in the passage at the top of the stairs. He restrained himself. 'And all this for a woman?' he asked, his voice expressionless. 'What have you done?'

The lad raised his pale face, his pupils flickering feverishly in their sockets under his bony forehead.

'What have you done?' Giusto asked once more.

III

'Are you sure the girl's asleep?' Giusto went on. 'All that agitation, that anxiety about getting away, that fear that leaves her breathless . . . can she possibly sleep with all that on her mind?'

'No,' said the boy, 'she's not asleep. It's as if she were drugged. She's not dreaming, but she sees things. She's seeing them all the time. We've spent two nights like this.

'What does she see?'

'What we're running away from.'

Misogyny

'Prison?'

'Oh,' said the boy in a whisper, 'if I were innocent, I'd go to prison at once and stay there for years, all my life. I wouldn't mind! I'd know they were doing me an injustice. But she'd have to go there, too. She who was forced to do what she did, and in there nobody feels any pity: there's no more justice or injustice. It's remorse that prevents us from sleeping. She doesn't deserve it: she was forced. And now she must endure injustice and terror.'

From the top of the stairs came a wild uncontrollable cry: 'Renato! I'm all alone up here.'

The wretched youth started to his feet and stared wildly at Giusto. 'Was she listening to us?' he exclaimed. 'My head's splitting. I don't know what I was saying.'

'Go on up,' Giusto urged him. 'You're even more feverish than she is. But have a drink first,' and he poured him another cognac. His companion made some vague reply and rushed up the stairs.

Soon every voice was silent. Giusto felt a need to sit and think. The lamp, practically burnt out, flickered wearily among the shadows. 'And that's the man who wants to get into France,' Giusto murmured. 'How will they manage? What will they do?'

He stretched out his hand to turn up the lamp and watched it grow pale. A faint light was coming through the windows. Now he could see the chairs and the calendar on the door. The wind was whistling through the cracks. Giusto's mouth felt dry so he picked up his glass, then listlessly set it down again.

He woke to hear Tosca bustling about in her slippers. She came out of the kitchen looking grey and untidy. The lamp had gone out but it was now light enough to see. 'Did they call you in the night?' Her voice was hoarse and she sounded surprised. Giusto cleared his throat and stood up. 'I was asleep,' he said. 'It's bitterly cold.'

Summer Storm

He went to the door and threw it open. In the damp, grey light he saw the low car close by, its windows misted over. 'If they're awake they'll need something to eat,' he said. 'I'm going over to the Grange, to get them to fetch a can of petrol.'

'Who's going to pay for it?' Tosca asked sharply.

It was drizzling with rain when he got back. He found the couple sitting at table and Tosca pouring out coffee. The boy swung round in wild alarm and Giusto winked at him. Then he looked at the girl. 'There'll be some petrol soon,' he told her. 'How have you slept?'

Her drawn cheeks managed to produce a defiant smile. 'Quite well,' she replied, looking up at him.

'I heard you were feverish. Cognac's the thing for that. You should try it. Your husband does.'

Those big eyes in her little face clouded over at his words. Restlessly the boy pushed away his cup. Giusto went on: 'My sister heard you raving in the night. Be careful once you're in France. Better stuff a handkerchief in your mouth.' Tosca stood stock-still in surprise. There came a scratching at the door.

In the silence an old man entered, muffled in an army greatcoat, scraping his feet along the floor. He greeted them all in a husky voice, putting a hand to his beret and giving them a little bow. They sat watching him as if hypnotized. His face was as wrinkled as a baby's.

'It's nothing,' Giusto broke in. 'Pedrotto just wants some milk.'

The old man shook the wet from him like a dog and went to the counter. Tosca ran over and poured him a drink. 'Pedrotto.' Giusto asked casually, 'Is there still a way across the frontier?'

The old fellow spluttered over his little glass and leered round at them. 'A clever man, on foot, can always get through,' he replied cautiously in a low voice.

Misogyny

'And a woman?'

'That depends.'

Giusto bent his head down between the couple. 'D'you want him?' he asked softly. 'Don't give him more than a hundred, and then only after he's finished the job. He'll go and wait for you on the road beyond the village. But watch out! He's much craftier than you are.'

Tosca had disappeared. 'My sister will pack you a picnic basket,' Giusto went on. 'You were even forgetting that petrol. Your trip may take time. You don't want to die of hunger on the way. But think it over carefully. Once you're in his hands there can be no turning back.'

The lad's indecision showed in his eyes, but the girl looked at Giusto and said firmly: 'All right.'

The old man went out and they all stood up. 'Don't bother about showing your passport.'

'We haven't got one,' she replied.

By now dawn had broken but a thick mist was drifting in through the half-open door. While Tosca and the girl were discussing the bill, Giusto went outside with the lad, who was biting his colourless lips. 'Be on your toes at the filling station,' Giusto advised him. 'Don't act as if you're desperate.' The lad nodded obediently and paid for the petrol.

Giusto slipped stealthily upstairs, fetched a blanket from the bed and tossed it into the car. 'It's up to you to look after her. Don't let her die of cold.' Leading his companion on one side, he told him: 'All this is nothing to do with me. I don't know what you may have done. But I'm thirty, and I've always noticed that women manage to get out of trouble, leaving the man in the soup. It just can't be helped.'

The boy gave him a twisted smile. 'And how much will the blanket cost us?' he asked.

'Nothing,' Giusto retorted and they went back inside.

Summer Storm

The girl was waiting, sitting by the table. She had put on her hat ·and renewed her lipstick. Her face looked different, sharper than before and more lined. A deathly paleness made her eyes seem sunken and wisps of hair hung round her temples. Telling her companion to pay Tosca, she came to the door with the suitcase. Giusto stood aside to let her pass and then ran to open the car door for her. She jumped in.

The boy came up, and Tosca with the picnic basket. 'When you're among the snows, don't give Pedrotto anything to drink,' Giusto advised, leaning into the car. 'He's drunk enough already.'

The boy got in and switched on the engine. The car backed away, then turned into the road. 'Goodbye,' the girl cried.

'We shall always remember you,' said the boy, leaning out.

'They'd do better to forget all about us,' Giusto muttered to Tosca as she stood shivering in the fog.

Summer Storm

The sun had not yet reached the bathing-hut on the landing-stage at the foot of the hills. Great trees overshadowed it. The river gleamed an even white in the dawn, and on the far bank houses in scattered suburbs began to show lights. Over there it seemed broad daylight already. The old boat-woman, dirty and dishevelled, was going along the line of punts moored to the landing-stage, pulling them in, one by one, then bending forward with her left hand on her hip to haul in the slack ropes. Every time a boat wedged itself between two others, the bump was passed along the whole line, setting them all rocking in the current.

A hessian curtain hung across the back of the hut and from behind it came sounds of movements and voices. Somebody was undressing.

'Look at this silk blouse! Is it yours?' a harsh voice cried. 'And these silk stockings?'

The old woman looked up crossly, stopping her work. The reflection from a few pink clouds above the trees shone on the river and cast a glow over her face.

'Here's a skirt, too,' the voice went on. 'Lovely quality! And another one!'

The curtain was pulled aside and a young fellow came out, buttoning the shoulder of his swimming costume. He

Summer Storm

was short and not very muscular, but sunburnt and curly haired.

'And we meant to be first, this time! Gosh! It's cold, here,' he said, slapping his thighs, all pimply with gooseflesh, and jumping up and down. 'We talked about making it a foursome if we could get a couple of girls out of bed this early and take them boating.'

'There's a couple of girls ahead of you, all by themselves,' the old woman told him, bending to her work again. 'Alone and full of beans. Since no one was here to see them they didn't mind waking people up before it was light. They didn't even give me time to comb my hair. Women!'

'Alone!' the young fellow cried as he jumped about. 'D'you hear that, Moro? Two girls on their own ahead of us! Come on out of there!' He turned and asked the old woman: 'What are they like? What sort are they?'

'Haven't you just seen their clothes?' she answered with a grin. 'From a woman's slip to her skin is no great distance.'

'That's nothing to go by. Who are they?'

'They aren't regular customers. One is thin, her hair and skin as pale as straw. The other hadn't much to say but she's already tanned dark brown by the sun, well-built and so full of energy that she almost capsized the boat when she jumped in. Both of them were very stuck-up and stand-offish.'

'Have they been gone long?'

'An hour or so.'

'Pretty? What colour bathing costumes?'

'Ask her if they took their handbags with them, Aurelio,' the first voice called sharply from behind the curtain.

'That friend of yours sounds a bright lad,' the old woman chuckled with a wink. Raising her voice she added: 'Don't worry. They can pay for their own boat. They look as if they're worth much more than that.'

Summer Storm

'Depends who they come across,' and the second man emerged from behind the curtain, a tall, bony fellow with great sweaty feet and red hands, fastening his baggy swimsuit over shoulders as pale as the belly of a fish. He looked straight at the old woman, whose face still twinkled with mischief, and a flash of ill-temper gleamed in his eyes.

She looked him up and down stealthily and remarked: 'So we're new here, are we? Never been out in a boat all this year, by what I can see.'

Aurelio broke in: 'He looks a lot better with an oar in his hand. Then he'd beat all those family men you've tipped into the Po. Any oar! Even a bit of wood!'

'I've never seen him rowing past here though. By the look of him, I'd say the poor soul was at his last gasp after three months of sciatica. Glad to get a bit of fresh air again, eh?'

The young man screwed up his mouth and spat on the ground. Without turning round he asked his companion, out of the corner of his mouth, 'Got everything?'

Aurelio slipped behind the curtain and brought out a small case that he put into the first punt. Then he jumped aboard and stood with his legs wide apart, rocking the little boat to work it free of the others and creating tumultuous repercussions all along the line.

'It's quite ready,' the old woman cried, bringing along a paddle and a punt pole with an iron rim. 'I baled out just now, after those other two got me out of bed. All you've got to do is get in,' and with a powerful sweep of her arm she swung out the heavy pole.

'Let's hope so,' Aurelio replied.

The old woman turned with a grin to Moro, who was standing there doing nothing, and eyed him again, curiously, from head to foot. To Aurelio she said: 'Your friend still looks bleary-eyed. Watch out! If you run into a bridge there'll be damages to pay.'

Summer Storm

'You be careful nobody runs into you,' Moro retorted. He clambered awkwardly into the boat, making Aurelio nearly lose his balance. 'Hand over that paddle,' he said coldly as he turned round, 'and cast off.'

The old woman did as he told her. Aurelio looked up at the sky. By now the pink clouds had gone. Standing in the stern, Aurelio thrust the pole straight down and forced the boat out with all the power of his wrists from among the others until it swung free as the current caught it. 'Cheerio,' the old woman muttered, but neither man made any reply and she went back to the bathing-hut.

Aurelio, in his black swimsuit, kept raising and lowering the pole, probing the bottom, bending forward to exert his utmost strength against the pressure of the water. He looked steadily ahead at the smooth, shining stream, screwing up his eyes against the glare. He came out into the sunlight.

Moro was lying in the bottom of the boat, filling it completely, his hairy legs dangling over the sides. He raised his hand to shade his eyes.

'Isn't the sunshine grand, Moro?'

'It's grand to see it from here,' Moro muttered.

'It's the same everywhere,' Aurelio replied. 'But it won't be so bright for long, this morning. Look at those clouds coming up.'

'The worst of it is, when you're inside, all the sun does is heat your cell. It's not just sunshine, it's a blazing furnace.'

'Then in winter it keeps you warm.'

'In winter you freeze and you can't say a thing. But the worst thing is that in summer, when there's a sun like this, you've got to stick it out in jacket and trousers. Take your jacket off? No, sir, not on your life! Take off your jacket when they let you out in the exercise yard? You can't. Why not? You just can't.'

Summer Storm

'It's the same for soldiers, anyway.'

'No, this was worse. They shut a man up just so as to make him walk round the dustbins.'

Aurelio, bending forward to thrust in the pole, laughed down into Moro's face. Moro, raising his hand and screwing up his eyes, grinned back at him.

Covering his eyes again, Moro went on: 'Once a man's in prison it means he's a bad lot. Nobody wants no-goods like us. They tell us we must change our way of life and meantime they keep us shut up like rabbits. If we're to change our way of living they should let us get on with it, turn us loose at once. Instead, no. You've got to stay there two, three, ten years, depending on what your record says; turn yellow, green, grey – that's the only change in life you'll get. D'you know that where I was there was a man serving twenty years? He looked like my grandfather did when he was dead, yet he was only forty. Murder. All because he'd had a drop too much.'

'Still, some fools let themselves be caught when they shouldn't,' said Aurelio as he bent forward again.

Moro started up to sit facing Aurelio. 'But what if justice is worse than we are?' he exclaimed. 'Why don't they kill a man right off if they catch him at it? Or, if he's just picking pockets, give him a sound thrashing, like men? Then we'd soon see who had the best of it. It's a priests' trick to keep a man shut up for years. Don't you think so?'

'But all they gave you was a year and a half.'

'A year's nothing. It's the days that are so long.'

'You didn't used to be so dim, Moro. You haven't got the prison food out of your system, yet. It's upset your stomach and you look scared stiff.'

Moro rummaged in the attaché-case and brought out a cigarette. The pale little flame in the sunshine showed up the pale little hollows in his drawn cheeks. He tossed the match away.

Summer Storm

Aurelio said: 'What you ought to be doing is learning a bit more sense. Take care where you operate another time. Who ever heard of a stick-up in broad daylight? You're no good at that sort of job, anyway.'

'I'm all right in a boat, though,' Moro exclaimed, jumping to his feet so suddenly that Aurelio almost overbalanced. 'Give me that pole.'

Cautiously Aurelio edged over to Moro's side and passed him the pole. Then he sat down and tried to smoke. Moro, his cigarette twisted between his lips, felt for the bottom and made his first thrust, then slowly straightened up.

Bianca raised her dripping paddle and the punt glided forward under the trees into the still water. 'The sunshine's gone,' Clara grumbled.

Bianca, clenching her teeth, threw herself down on the bank and looked around. 'It's that cloud making the water seem dark,' she said. 'If the sun comes out again it will be all silvery.'

'Is it going to rain?'

'I don't think so, but even if it does, we're here to go swimming.'

'You're a real river-girl,' Clara murmured, and Bianca looked away, determined not to lose her temper at the lazy mockery in her friend's eyes.

Clara remarked: 'Why ever didn't you notice how low the swallows are flying over the Po?'

Bianca swung round to look at the river. Through the little opening where they had come in she could see the current running swiftly past in a belt of sunlight. Out in mid-stream a dredger was floating, moored to a slanting cable and rocking as the water rippled round it. It was quite deserted.

Summer Storm

'That's where we can go if it rains. I've never been on board a dredger.'

'There isn't a soul about,' Clara said. 'Once those poor sand-grubbers have gone home – and seeing they spend their life on the water they could at least wash themselves – the river is a desert. Anyone could die – or be born – here and nobody would know. It's like some bygone civilization.' She leaned over the side of the boat and added: 'Except for all those sardine tins and broken jars. They strike a different note. Actually I don't think much of your river.'

Clara's supple body in its tight-fitting yellow bathing costume threw back a pale reflection as she leaned over the greenish water. Bianca watched her almost against her will, making no reply. But then she smiled. Clara was gazing at her own face in the water and rubbing the corner of her eye with one finger. 'So any mirror's enough to put the fair lady Clara in a better humour,' Bianca mocked, conscious that her voice was shaking uncontrollably.

'Taking one mirror with another, I prefer my own. At least in that one I don't see a shoal of little fish shooting out of my mouth. and it doesn't make me look drunk. Nor does it give me a halo from a sunken bowl.'

Involuntarily, Bianca's fists clenched, but she controlled herself, stretching out her arms and relaxing her cramped fingers. At ease again, she turned her head, letting her eyes wander over the sky and the trees on the bank. Beyond their trunks stretched a pleasant beach, shining against a mass of cloud. 'I didn't promise you the River Amazon,' she said good-humouredly, 'but that's what we'll get if it rains. Why take shelter, anyway? What can be lovelier than a morning storm?'

'Listen, dear. If you want to have a swim, get on with it. It's going to pour any minute and my costume isn't meant to get wet.'

'I want to see you get in.'

Summer Storm

'Bianca! Is that why you've brought me all up here? For me to jump into that black water and get covered with filthy mud and bitten by crocodiles? Bianca! I have pretty skin and it needs looking after. It's a good thing that sun you're so fond of has been kind and respectful to a poor blonde without much on.'

'Stupid,' Bianca replied with a shrug. 'This life would do you good, make you stronger and more confident.'

'But I'm strong already. Too strong and self-reliant, really. What I need is the opposite. It's cost me one love affair, being so strong.'

Bianca bent down to undo her canvas shoes, looking sideways at Clara and listening as she went on: 'It never does to show people you're strong and self-reliant. They're only too ready to knock it out of you.'

'Why don't you give up this aimless way of life?' Bianca asked with a smile.

'It isn't as dull as some, you know.'

'I see,' Bianca murmured softly, feeling in her bag for her rubber bathing-cap.

When she stood ready she turned to Clara, who lay at full length in the bottom of the boat grinning up at her. 'So you really aren't coming?' she asked.

'You go, and come back in triumph. I'll give you a clap.'

'Won't you at least swim in here? I'll hold you up.'

'My precious, you're too silly for words. One plays that game with men, not with another girl. Off you go, and don't break your neck.'

Bianca shivered as she entered the water, and waded with uncertain steps towards the opening. Then she clenched her teeth and dived. The water was not cold. Over here in mid-stream the dredger was twinkling in the sun. She stood up again with the water up to her waist, and felt the wind cold on her shoulders.

Summer Storm

She passed the ripples swirling by the opening and saw the current running strongly ahead. The bottom was deeper now. She glanced over her shoulder at the surface of the water, the low banks, the boat, the vague blur of trees, then stretched herself in a powerful swimming stroke. Suddenly she was out into the tumbling current. She turned up-stream from the dredger, swimming straight towards the hill now veiled by the sun and clouds, and plunging her face into the dark gurgling water, catching her breath as best she could in the pauses between her arm strokes. Her progress across the current threatened to break her rhythm at any moment and she could see nothing but flashing drops of spray. Exhausted by her efforts to breathe she dropped her head for the last time and suddenly saw the water below the surface made transparent by diffused sunlight. She raised her head. The dredger was only a few yards away.

Bianca worked her way around the rocking hull, looking for somewhere to hold on. A shadow ran across the water. The last of the sunshine had gone. The chill wind blew stronger.

Bianca pulled herself up, scraping her knee on the vessel's side. The metal superstructure with its pulleys and sand-encrusted gratings took up most of the space, leaving only a narrow ledge all round. Unsteadily she made her way along it and came to a hut of rough boards tucked in among the machinery. It had an earthy floor and a pile of folded sacks in one corner. In the middle, the deck was cut away, leaving an empty space of bubbling black water – the river itself. A chain of buckets hung down into it from an opening dimly visible in the roof high above.

Bianca went outside again to watch the current rushing out from below the hull, and her eyes opened in wide amazement at the flood pouring down towards the weir, broken by stones and torn branches. She reflected that only

Summer Storm

an hour earlier they had been punting on the river, and she remembered Clara.

She ran to the side of the dredger and looked for the little break in the woods where they had landed. At first she saw nothing but the low, green bank, distant and motionless under the swaying trees. Then, behind a spit of land, she caught sight of Clara's light-coloured costume. She was standing waving the paddle, shouting shrilly and pointing at the sky.

'There's shelter here,' Bianca yelled. 'It's safe enough.'

Apparently Clara heard, for she waved her hand and disappeared behind the little promontory. The first thunder rumbled in the distance. Nervously, Bianca whipped off her rubber cap. Terrifying clouds were piling up, and a sudden bright flash of lightning darted across the sky. Bianca pressed her hands on the hull and stared down at the water swirling and foaming below her. The thunder did not come for a moment and she started shouting: 'Clara it's . . .'

There came a low roar that gradually grew louder and louder, echoing among the hills and swelling like the noise of a landslide until it crashed in the distance and died away with a dull reverberation. Bianca flushed as her fears left her. It was raining in the city, for certain. Down there in the valley the sky looked terrible.

'Clara, it's all right here. I'm coming to fetch you.' Cold wind-squalls blowing up the river whistled round the dredger, making it swing on its mooring. 'Where on earth has she got to, the silly girl!' Bianca muttered to herself, peering at the low bank and the tall trees swaying wildly against the clear streak of the horizon.

Then she saw the boat coming out of the opening with Clara in it, frenziedly straining with the paddle and raising great splashes of foam. But once out in the current she lost course, caught up in the eddies and gusts of wind.

'Careful!' Bianca yelled. 'You'll end up over the weir!'

Summer Storm

and she ran along the hull, watching the boat being swept inexorably downstream. Then Clara stood up. (The thought flashed into Bianca's mind that she looked just like a canary.) She seized the heavy, iron-rimmed pole and leaned forward to thrust it in over the stern. The punt swung further downstream. Clara was gripping the pole with all her might, holding it upright and trying to find the bottom. There was no bottom, and every time she tried to probe for it the current drove the punt hard against the pole, wrenching her wrists painfully. 'Idiot!' Bianca howled, almost beside herself. 'Go sideways! Put that pole down. Use the paddle!'

She was frantically pulling on her cap again when she heard a scream. Clara had disappeared. She had fallen into the water behind the punt. A patch of wild splashing in the wake of the boat showed where she was struggling.

Bianca dived in, at the same moment almost blinded by a lightning flash. Only in the water could she feel safe. She swam desperately, head down, seeing nothing, hearing nothing, not even the thunder clap. For the moment she was not thinking of Clara. She was straining every nerve to reach the punt and salvage the pole. Then she could save Clara.

Her arm bumped against the pole. Looking round through the spray, she could see something yellow splashing about some distance away; in the other direction, in the grip of the current, she saw the empty punt. 'Without the boat I'll never manage to pull her out' flashed through her mind, and pushing the pole ahead of her she made for the punt. She reached it and threw in the pole. Heaving herself over the side, out of the rushing water, almost tore her shoulders apart, but at last she rolled in, bruised all over and seized the paddle. When she turned round there was no longer any sign of Clara. Only then did she notice it was raining in torrents, great blasts that cut furrows in

Summer Storm

the surface of the river. Clouds of fine spray like smoke billowed everywhere and her back began to tingle, stung by the violence of the downpour.

Clara was no longer there. Bianca tossed her head to free her eyes from the matted hair that was blinding her. She had lost her cap, and had to run her fingers through her hair before she could push it away. A wild yell burst from her: 'Clara!'

All around her the water boiled, its surface unbroken. Steering the boat with the paddle and holding it steady against the current she peered into the swirling flood, trying to find the place where Clara had disappeared. Millions of tiny bubbles spread a layer of pale foam between the water and the air. Through the raindrops Bianca looked for the bank, but everything had vanished. All she could see was a vague outline. She was alone on the river.

Plying the paddle frenziedly she made some headway against the current, thankful to be still afloat, heedless of her direction. Then, through the hair still hanging over her eyes, she noticed she was level with a certain tall tree growing on the bank. Her teeth chattering with fright, she jumped to her feet in the drenching rain and put down the paddle. 'She called me a "river girl",' she murmured breathlessly and plunged in, hurting her foot badly.

Under the surface she found a great calm. The dense mass of water deadened every sound, made every effort seem remote and pointless. She strained her eyes in the darkness and groped about with her hands, but she saw nothing and felt nothing except the weight of the water. When she surfaced she was surprised by the light and the rain. She had quite forgotten them. The punt was not far away. She turned and dived again, probing about until her ears were buzzing and her arm-strokes grew weak. She surfaced again and swam to the boat, clinging to it with her whole body and tearing her costume as she clambered in.

Summer Storm

Ankle-deep in water, she picked up the paddle again and looked around her, uncertain what to do. Then her heart leapt. There in the mist was another boat with two men in it, creeping along the opposite bank and making straight for the dredger.

Bianca jumped to her feet and started shouting, waving the paddle. The warm rain splashed into her mouth. The men did not turn. 'Over here!' she yelled, loud enough to split her throat. She almost added: 'Help!', but refrained. Her bag was floating in the bottom of the punt. She pulled out a towel and waved it, still shouting.

The men were now level with the dredger and paddled round, looking up at it. As Bianca watched, one of them jumped aboard it and the other, bending forward in the rain, handed up a rope. She glanced at the foaming current as it swept past, loaded with mud, then, clenching her teeth, she turned the boat towards the dredger and paddled furiously.

Out of the rain her half-drowned head came level with the hull. 'Oh!' Aurelio was saying as he threw himself down on the sacks, 'Look at the state we're in!' Moro, standing naked at the back of the hut, wringing out his swimming trunks, did not turn.

'Here's a woman!' Aurelio exclaimed.

She clutched the rail with both hands and the little boat slid from under her feet. 'A girl's been drowned,' she cried shrilly. 'Come and help me.'

Aurelio ran forward to give her a hand. 'If you don't come aboard, you'll be drowned, too,' he cried. 'Moro, come and help!'

The girl, her hand in Aurelio's, looked back and forth from him to the river. She was steaming like a horse; her

Summer Storm

sunburnt skin looked sodden and lifeless; her arms and legs were covered with scratches.

'A friend of mine's been drowned,' she cried. 'I've got to find her. I've been calling for ages.'

'Even the fishes would drown on a day like this,' said Moro in the darkness of the hut, holding his trunks to shield his hairy stomach.

'Jump in! Jump in,' Aurelio urged again. 'You're over the worst. If it was all that time ago, she's dead by now. Where did it happen?'

'Down there,' the girl sobbed, pointing to the current and trying to release her other hand. 'Over there.'

'She went under?'

'D'you expect people to drown in the air?' Moro sneered in the background.

'Jump in,' said Aurelio. 'Too much water is bad for anyone. There's a hut here. Your boat's waterlogged already.'

Moro came forward with his costume draped around him. 'Where does she say it happened?' he asked.

'Over there. Just beyond the Sangone.' She turned her eyes in that direction and the drops fell from her matted hair like a flood of tears.

'Come on into shelter,' Aurelio persisted, pulling her by the arm. 'If that's where she went down, the current won't carry her beyond the weir. We know where to find her. Was she the same age as you?'

'Could she swim?' Moro added.

'Can you swim yourself?' the girl asked sharply.

Moro flung himself down on a seat at the edge of the hut, his trunks between his thighs. Aurelio was still bending over the side trying to pull the girl in, and Moro kicked him on the ankle. 'Don't you see?' he said out of the corner of his mouth. 'These are the girls from the landing-stage. My dear bathing beauty,' he went on, 'we can swim

Summer Storm

a lot better than people like you who come here to act the fool when other folk are working, but we swim in water, not in rain. We'll see about that later, if you like. But for the present, we'll let it rain. Leave her to get out of it by herself.'

Aurelio, uncertain what to do, relaxed his hold and went back into the hut, the water dripping from him. Slowly the boat drifted backwards. The girl stood there for a moment, raising her shoulder to rub her cheek. Then she leaned forward, picked up the paddle and brought the punt alongside the dredger again.

Without a word she pulled herself up on the hull, holding the boat's mooring chain between her teeth. Then she turned her back and crouched forward to thread the chain through a ring in the hull. As she did so, she found that her black costume was split all down the left side and torn at the hem on her thigh. Her white flesh gleamed through the holes, very different from the bronzed skin of her legs and shoulders.

Having secured the chain, she leaned forward to take her bag from the boat. Aurelio's eyes followed the play of her pale skin under her torn costume. Without looking at him, the girl staggered to her feet – she was short and dark, like him – and put down her sodden bag inside the hut. Then she sat down under the shelter, apart from the other two, her knees against her chest. She rested her elbows on them and took her cheeks in her hands, sitting very still and staring at the rain.

The whole dredger quivered and rocked as the current washed past it. Down from the opening in the roof of the hut where the pulley-chains ran came cold blasts that cut into their backs. Aurelio, crouching on his sacks, looked at Moro's long, bare spine and the girl's shoulders, shining against the background of the rain.

'Moro,' he said suddenly, breaking the silence, 'cover

Summer Storm

up your seat, or this draught'll give you a chill.'

Moro grinned across at him. 'It's not proper to put on one's trousers in the presence of a young lady.'

'D'you think you're so handsome? Young ladies don't look.'

'They're too well brought up to say anything.'

Aurelio stuffed one hand into the little case lying on the sacks. 'Want a cigarette?'

'If they're not soaked, too.'

Aurelia stood up and held out the packet to Moro, taking one out with his lips at the same time. Then he turned to the girl and offered her one. 'Let's have a smoke on it,' he said. She made no response but still sat motionless, staring at the rain.

'Thanks very much, but I don't smoke,' he prompted her as he went back to the sacks and struck a match.

'You see what women are like,' Moro told him, trying in vain to strike a match in his turn. 'The whole world at their beck and call. Acting so foolhardy and running into danger when they haven't any idea what the Po can be like. When a man reasons with them they spit at his feet and ask him if he can swim. Somebody who can really swim doesn't let anyone drown. What'll you bet, Aurelio, that the other girl couldn't swim, either?'

Irritably, Aurelio threw away his cigarette and wandered restlessly round the hut, trying out the chain that held the buckets. He thrust his hand inside his costume to rub his shivering chest and finally came to sit beside the girl at the front of the hut. Moro was watching her out of the corner of his eye. Like her, Aurelio pulled his knees against his chest and rested his cheeks on his hands. 'Pretty girls don't cry,' he told her with a wink.

She flushed, jumped to her feet and turned to go inside, but Aurelio held her by the arm and tried to pull her back. Then he let her go. 'All right, all right,' he said. 'We

Summer Storm

know each other. At least I know your friend was a blonde.'

The girl stared at him a moment with blazing eyes. 'I told you myself,' she muttered as she ran inside. Then she swung round in the gloom and asked him: 'How did you manage to find out that?'

'I'll tell you, if you tell me your name,' Aurelio smiled as he rose to his feet.

'It's Piccone,' she answered quickly. 'So what?'

Moro burst out laughing and slapped his thigh.

'Your own name,' Aurelio persisted, still smiling. 'What does your surname matter to me?'

She stood still a moment, disconcerted. Then her whole face flamed red and distorted, as if he had struck her across the mouth.

Suddenly an oath burst from Moro. He had jumped up hurriedly and his trunks had fallen overboard. Dropping to his knees he stretched his arm down but failed to reach them. Then, naked as he was, he leapt into the girl's boat with a great splash and fished them out, dripping wet. He climbed up again, still uncovered. 'Blast! They were practically dry,' he exclaimed as he threw them down in a corner and stalked into the hut.

The girl watched him come, her eyes fixed on his face. Without glancing aside, he said, from the corner of his mouth: 'Both those boats are full of water. Go and bale them out, Aurelio.' The girl backed away.

'Where have we seen the blonde, Miss Piccone?' Moro sneered, his face close to hers. 'The dead float, you fool! They can swim much better than you or me. D'you know where that blonde is now?' Moro's voice sank to a chilling whisper. The girl could see his teeth. 'She's here behind you, in this patch of water. Her eyes are open and her nails all broken. She's calling you, raising her hand. She's going to grab you!'

Summer Storm

Terrified, the girl crouched down on the sacks. Moro laughed over her shoulders. 'Silly fool,' he said, gripping her sides with his hands.

Aurelio shook him by the shoulder. 'You can't do things like that, you great lout. You're only frightening her. D'you think you're still in prison? I was the one who helped her. It's my affair.'

The girl struggled to her knees. Moro thrust her down again with his fist in her neck and his shin in the small of her back. Suddenly he turned his tense, fleshless face to Aurelio and said with a grin. 'Go and bale out those punts, I tell you. This Piccone girl has seen me; she's fallen for me; she wants me.'

'You shouldn't have got stripped. It isn't fair.'

'Sure,' Moro retorted, swaying as the girl struggled beneath him. 'I don't want any of your nonsense. Go and bale out the punts. They're sinking.'

The girl collapsed on the sacks so suddenly that Moro almost fell on top of her. Her limp body in its torn black costume lay white and slack.

'You've killed her!' Aurelio cried.

'They're like cats. They squeal if you only hold them under water.'

Out in the rain again, Aurelio stared at the current instead of seeing to the boats, watching it foaming, yellow with mud, under the water streaming from the sky. Eddies formed, swirled away and formed again round the dredger as it swung and rolled in the fierce grip of the flood, all its metal parts clanking noisily. Now and then a broken oar flashed past, glimpsed for an instant before it rolled under again. Over in the valley, everything looked vague and indistinct; the masses of trees on the deserted banks seemed in a different world. One could guess how the water must be roaring and foaming over the rapids by the weir.

Both punts were full. The one the girl had brought was

Summer Storm

half submerged. Aurelio glanced sideways at the dripping entrance to the hut, then threw himself forward and picked up a short end of wood floating in the boat. Blinded by the rain, he leaned out from the hull and made a few aimless movements with it. Then he drew back again as heavy breathing and a long, low groan reached him from the hut, and the sound of material being ripped. He looked round quickly and glimpsed in the gloom a pale, shapeless mass of struggling bodies.

He sat down again on the hull, stretching out his brown legs in the rain and staring at the punt as it rocked gently. The water inside it was clear, compared with the river, and the varnished bottom planking shone through. The iron-rimmed pole was still there. The paddle had been washed away.

He heard Moro cursing, but would not turn round. He heard sounds of a struggle and a long moan. Then, silence except for the rain.

Aurelio unbuttoned his swim-suit at the shoulder and rolled it down to his waist. He examined his chest as he breathed in and out. The cold air tasted of mud and leaves. Then he tried to purse up his lips and whistle a tune, but no sound came out.

'Aurelio! Quick!' Moro's hoarse voice broke the silence. 'Here's another one dead!'

Aurelio sprang up. Moro was sitting at the back of the hut, clutching his knees against his chest. Aurelio barely had time to glimpse the girl lying at full length before she leapt to her feet, deathly white in spite of great black bruises, her costume in tatters. She fled across the dark space, pushed Aurelio aside and fell into the water.

Aurelio had knocked his knee against the planks but he recovered his balance and turned round as a roar of laughter from Moro made his ears ring.

'She's done it on you! See! That's women for you!'

Summer Storm

The girl was already some way off, swimming spasmodically with great splashes, half out of the water. Aurelio jumped into the boat, almost capsizing it. It took him a moment or two to cast off.

'It's no good,' Moro said, coming up beside him. 'I told you to bale out. You won't do it now in the time. You've let her get away.'

Aurelio would have thrown himself into the water in his frenzy, but Moro held him back. 'She won't get far. A woman's worn out when I've finished with her. Watch!'

The girl was rolling helplessly in the current, incapable of guiding herself, and ending up in mid-stream, splashing feebly and drifting rapidly towards the weir. 'So she can't swim,' said Moro. 'Still, I gave her a good lesson.'

'She's drowning,' Aurelio cried, 'and I . . .'

'Come back in the shadow,' Moro urged, pulling him by the arm. 'Have you gone crazy? It couldn't be better. She left us of her own free will. Besides, girls like her always talk.'

Aurelio had lost sight of that black speck and stood trembling, straining his eyes.

'Now I'll have a smoke. Be glad to,' Moro said as he went back inside. When, a few minutes later, Aurelio joined him and threw himself down on the sacks, Moro went on curtly: 'Have a cigarette. Never mind. You shall do it first another time.'

The Idol

It all started again one afternoon in August. Now, whatever the sky may be, I only have to lift my head and look up between the houses to feel once more the quiet stillness of that day.

I was sitting in the little parlour that I have never seen since, where, it seems to me, only a yellowish half-light filtered through. I had come at that dead time of day to be the only one there. I still recall that when she came in I did not recognise her. All I thought was that this woman was much too thin, but I must have jumped to my feet at once, because she came across to me without the slightest hesitation and held out her hand, saying: 'How awful! It's lucky I'm dressed.' With her other hand she was buttoning her collar.

She was wearing white. A few minutes later, when she bowed her head and I felt her tears falling on my fingers, I saw where the sun had tanned the back of her neck. By contrast, her hair seemed almost blonde. I remember I managed to say: 'Let's get this straight first of all, Mina. I should be as ashamed as you of being here.'

Mina looked at me. 'It's not for shame that I'm crying,' she stammered through tense lips. 'It's just that I'm upset.'

She gave me a slow smile, but I let it die away without responding. The wrinkles at the corner of her mouth were deeper than they used to be; her old expression was now etched on her face in hard lines.

'Why d'you look at me like that?' she cried, drawing away from me. 'Trying to make me feel ashamed?'

Just then the Madame poked her head through the curtains, looked at me sharply and quickly withdrew. My eyes dropped to Mina's little slippers and the moment we were alone again I groaned, surprising myself by the sound of my own voice, 'Can this be possible, Mina? Is it possible?'

Mina gave me a quizzical look between her reddened eyelids. I looked back at her anxiously. 'Don't you fancy a sunburned girl, then?' she asked, adding as she turned away: 'I'll call another one for you.'

I clutched her shoulder. 'Let me go,' she cried shrilly, breaking away. 'Leave me alone. I'm not the sort of girl you think I am!' She rushed off through the curtains and left me standing there in the middle of the parlour.

The Madame came back and looked me up and down, severely this time. I picked up my hat and went towards the door. 'I'll come back some other time,' I murmured as I went out.

My memory of a serene deep blue sky seems to stem from that afternoon and many others that followed. When I think of it I cannot understand how the ceaseless misery that hounded me can have become linked in my mind with such lovely weather.

One Saturday, towards dusk, I was amazed to find myself strolling along those quiet streets again, well aware that my mouth was twisted in an ugly sneer. Firmly I went in and made my way to the main reception room. Mina was not there, which was almost a relief. The Madame barely glanced at me, but I was stared at by two girls sitting on the divan with their bare legs wide apart, and one of them winked at me. There were several men sitting

The Idol

round the walls, gazing absentmindedly at the empty floor. At the back of the room a fat, half-naked girl stood chatting with a sergeant.

Mina did not appear. 'She's working upstairs,' I thought, and found I was talking to myself, biting my lips at the excruciating pain round my heart. I went straight over to the Madame and asked for Mina.

'Who is Mina?'

I reminded her of that afternoon, and her hard lips smiled uncertainly.

'You mean Manuela, I expect. She isn't down yet. Adelaide, go and tell Manuela.'

One of the two girls led me upstairs, humming to herself and turning round to smile at me. Her long legs took the stairs three at a time, but she went slowly, waiting for me. Upstairs, doors slammed. She seemed an awfully nice girl. I thought about going with her.

'You men! You always want the girl who isn't about!' Adelaide said to me in the corridor. We went into a room that was dark and smelt like a bathroom. 'Put on the light, Manuela.'

I saw Mina stretched out on the bed, her arm raised to the light-switch and her hair over her eyes. She had on the dress she was wearing before, but her feet were bare. 'Wait a minute,' she said with a twisted grin, swinging up to sit on the edge of the bed. She thrust her feet into her slippers, ran across the room, looked around, then came back to the bed. 'You are naughty, Adelaide,' she said, turning her back as she swung on to it again. 'Naughty! Go away! Be off!'

When we were alone I looked at her in bewilderment. Under her outstretched legs was that horrible piece of coarse towelling. Near the bed, above her head, hung some light underwear. On the floor, a threadbare bedside mat.

'This is impossible, Mina. It's just impossible!'

Summer Storm

'I was waiting for you, Guido. I knew you'd come.'

'You stayed upstairs because you were expecting me?'

Mina shook her head, smiling at me. 'No. Actually, I'm not well. These days I'm always ill. But I knew you'd come back.'

'Mina, you must tell me everything. Why are you here? Why? I can't believe it.'

Her eyes grew hard. 'There's nothing to tell you, is there? I am here, and that's enough, I should think. What d'you want to know? I was all on my own, and I looked for a job. If you want to talk to me, leave that out of it.'

'But your father, Mina. Your father? He was always telling me I was an idle slacker. Remember?' I couldn't manage to smile. 'Does your father know? I thought you were still down there . . .'

'Papa's dead,' said Mina, and her eyes did not drop.

'Oh!' I murmured. 'But why didn't you write to me? Look me up? I thought of you so often. Felt sure you were married. Yet sometimes, in the morning – do you remember? – I wondered to myself, "Perhaps Mina's waiting for me".'

' "Mina's waiting for me! Mina's married!" ' she mocked. 'But you never managed to write to me. And now you're grumbling?' I lowered my eyes as her voice went on, more kindly now : 'Did you really think about me sometimes?'

'Oh, Mina!'

Somewhere in the corridor a little bell rang. 'Does the Madame know you're here?' she asked me abruptly as she started up.

'She called you Manuela when she spoke to me . . .'

'Guido, you can't stay here. The Madame thinks you're a client. This is her business, you know. We'll meet again tomorrow.'

'And why can't I stay? I am a client. I'll pay as if

262

The Idol

Manuela was some other girl. What does it cost for half an hour?'

Mina hid her face in the pillow. Biting my lips, I took out the fifty *lire* I had with me and I put them down on the chest-of-drawers. Mina's eyes followed me furtively, intently. Then she stretched out her arm and pressed the bell push three times . . .

'You're working? Earning a salary?' she asked.

I sat down on the bed. It was dreadfully hot and stuffy, and I should be sweating when I left, but at the time I did not notice it.

'I'm not well, you know,' Mina said. 'I get a pain in the kidneys if I sleep on my back. This isn't a really healthy life. Still, I went to the seaside this year and I'm better already. I ought always to live in the open air.'

The persian blinds were closed, making everything seem dark and mysterious. There was no sound from outside.

'What's the matter, Guido?' she asked anxiously, taking my hand. Without lifting her head from the pillow she gazed at me with those great eyes of hers. I squeezed her fingers to express the agony I was feeling.

'What do I matter to you?' she said calmly. 'Those things are far away, as far as Voghera. And you're married anyway, I expect.'

I shook my head. 'I shouldn't have come here.'

'But, poor boy,' Mina exclaimed, raising herself on her elbow, 'you were just looking for a woman.'

'I'm still looking for her,' I said.

Mina was not listening. 'What fools we were,' she went on. 'Still, I don't regret anything about that summer. What about you?'

'I regret the winter, when we left each other.'

Mina started laughing. I had forgotten that light laugh of hers.

'Oh, Mina!'

'Be good, now. I'm not well.'
'Just one kiss, Mina.'
'You'd be kissing Manuela.'
'Mina.'
'Tomorrow. We'll meet again then. Tomorrow morning. Perhaps I can come out. We shouldn't see each other here. Don't you feel it's all wrong, too?'

Now that it's all over, I'm sorry I was not tough enough, that day, to let her start her usual game. Even now I'm still wondering if that wasn't what she wanted. To hide the trembling of my lips I lit a cigarette.

'I smoke, too, you know,' Mina remarked, so we smoked together and went on talking. I turned my head and looked at her as she lay at full length behind me, watching me listlessly. Keeping my eyes averted from the corner of the washstand, all cluttered with towels and medicine bottles, I gradually fell silent. On the floor stood a big purple bottle.

'Give me that kiss, Guido,' Mina said abruptly. I twisted round, took her cheeks between my hands and with an effort kissed her. Her lips clung to mine and she murmured: 'It's still summer, Guido . . .' Then she broke away.

We both fell silent. I took her hand and squeezed it. Mina jumped from the bed. 'I'm too happy,' she exclaimed breathlessly. 'Too happy. Go away now. You might change. Yes, I'll wait for you tomorrow . . . And take the money you've left up there. You can probably do with it. I'm satisfied that I've seen you. I'm well paid today . . .' I looked at the money, reluctant to pick it up, and she went on: ' . . . Then give it to the Madame yourself. She should give you back twenty *lire*, so watch your change. But don't leave it here. That's right. Guido, good-bye.'

The next day I told her I wanted to marry her. Mina stopped dead, took a gasping breath of the fresh, quiet street air, and as the sounds from the pavement rose all

The Idol

around us she moaned, closed her eyes and murmured: 'It doesn't matter if you said it just for something to say. It doesn't matter. It's good of you.'

All that scorching Sunday afternoon I wandered round the streets, finding nowhere where I could sit and wait for the mellowing sky of evening and the return of the hour I had known the day before. Now and then I talked feverishly to myself, all alone. Towards sunset I went back to my room and threw myself down on the bed, smoking and watching the golden glow fade against the dirty windows of the house across the road.

It was dusk when I grew aware of the unusual silence and realized that for a moment I had been thinking of nothing at all. Then I felt horrified that I had asked Mina to marry me, gone out with her. Lying half-naked on the bed I let my eyes wander complacently down from my chest to my slightly sunburned legs. What was Mina's body like? I smiled cynically to think I was the only man who didn't know.

Suddenly I jumped up and dressed, my mind made up. Once again I arrived at that door, hesitant but with a forced grin, and quickly rang the bell.

This time Mina looked at me in alarm. She was standing by the door of the reception room, wearing white and chatting to the Madame. She ran over to me, shook hands and made me sit down on the sofa in the anteroom. She sat beside me, without looking at me. From the doorway the Madame gave me a faint nod.

There we sat in silence, staring down at the mosaic floor. Mina was still holding my wrist, trembling, and I was the first to look up when two young fellows went past us into the main room. 'Would you rather I went away, Mina?' I asked her quietly, finding it hard to speak.

'Why did you come?'

'I don't know.'

Summer Storm

'Aren't you satisfied with what happened this morning?'
'I want to marry you.'
Mina smiled: 'I'm not free.'
'What?'
'I've got my work.'
I twisted round to look at her and felt my face flush.
'Hush, Guido. Go away.' There was a loud conversation in the drawing-room and a woman's shrill voice. 'Go away. We'll see each other again on Tuesday morning. Madame's watching us.'
'I've got nothing to hide.'
'Guido, I implore you. Or, rather, listen,' she went on with some reluctance, 'come back when I don't see you and ask for Adelaide.'
I grinned and shrugged my shoulders. Mina gave a sigh and watched me furtively.
'Mina,' I asked without looking at her, 'have you got a disease or something?'
'Oh, no, Guido. Why don't you understand?'
A man and a young girl came down the stairs and disappeared into the corridor. The Madame looked in.
'I just don't understand,' I said. 'Forgive me, Mina.'
'We'll meet on Tuesday. Faithfully, Guido. Now go.'
We looked at each other, and I rushed outside without a backward glance.
When I had gone a hundred yards my earlier grin was back on my lips. I walked on, muttering to myself, so tensely that my cheeks soon felt numb. The freshness of the night and the Sunday evening crowd failed to distract me. Over and over again I repeated the words I should have said to Mina, feeling more and more troubled. A great bitterness filled my mouth.
Next day at dawn, on the train taking me out of town, I found a little peace. I was dozing with the movement of the train and passively enjoying the mild warmth. With

The Idol

my eyes closed I could feel, under my limp, outstretched hand, the case containing my samples. This was a good trip, as all my life had been, yet there was something new about it, a pervading, indescribable and painful sweetness. At bottom, it was just as I had always dreamed it would be. From the corner of my eye I could see the fields rushing past, wakened by the first rays of the sun. I glimpsed a moment when, with my eyes still shut, I entered a new horizon where anything, no matter how dreadful or how paltry, could happen to me.

I thought about Mina waking drowsily; thought of her body still warm from my own bed, and I could not hate her. I felt grateful to her for the sweet desire that pulsed in my blood. For certain she was alone in her room; at this hour she was alone, and I could think of her. It made me smile to think of her timid suggestion that I should try Adelaide. Who knows? Adelaide and Manuela. Perhaps they were friends.

It was Tuesday morning and we met at the station. I came back on purpose to see her, though I ought to have continued my journey by car to visit certain customers up in the hills. Mina told me she was going out too often now and this was damaging her health as well as upsetting the Madame.

'Don't you need fresh air?' I murmured.

Mina made me wait for her outside a shoe-shop and came out almost at once with a small parcel. She stood on the step between the gleaming shop windows, straight and self-possessed in her little green hat and her chestnut coat with buttons at the side, her eyes glancing round in search of me. Our elbows were close together as we crossed the street.

'Where did you get your name from?' I asked.

'Don't you like it?' she replied gaily.

'Yes, it's pretty. But where did you get it?'

Summer Storm

Mina looked up at me through her curls. 'I didn't have to look for it. It was written over the door of my room.'

We bought cigarettes that morning, then I paused in front of a stocking shop. 'If you promise me you'll wear them only on mornings like this,' I said, 'I'll buy you the nicest ones they have.'

'Come on, Guido,' she replied. 'Not here. I never buy them here.'

It was eleven o'clock and she said she must be getting back. 'Shall we sit in a café a minute, Mina?'

In the café I chose the most secluded corner and did not look up at the waiter as I gave the order.

Mina stared at me gravely, in silence, while I kept my eyes fixed on her. Then she said softly: 'You're ashamed of being out with me.'

'Mina,' I answered in surprise, 'I just want to be alone with you.'

'You don't forgive my way of life.'

'I forgive you everything that's past, Mina. Every day and every night I want to understand you. You're not the simple girl you used to be. Though I ought to grieve over so much that's happened, still, I'm not crying. I know I love you and I'm as much yours now as I was then. But marry me, Mina. Give up this life. You know you'll have to give it up some day, no matter what it costs you.'

'See? You're objecting to it. That's not forgiving.'

'D'you expect me to thank you for carrying on as you're doing now? Don't you understand what agony I endure when I'm all alone, thinking of you with all those other men?'

'But it's different with them, Guido. Quite different . . . and there aren't so many as all that.'

'I feel like murdering them!'

'Really? I know you, Guido. You'd just complain all the more if you were one of them.'

The Idol

'Mina, doesn't this life make you sick?'

'I just see that you're ashamed of me, Guido. Aren't you?'

That was the first moment when I realized I was up against immense senseless power, like a man banging his head against a brick wall. Mina sat watching me, her neck bent and her eyes bright, with tiny creases between her eyebrows. I heaved a sigh and lowered my eyes.

'See what you're thinking?' Mina went on, more tenderly. 'With you, no. But it's for your own sake. I know it would be worse, afterwards.'

'Ah,' I groaned, a fearful smile trembling on my lips. 'I'll make you work myself, if you're so keen on your job. God help me, I can go with you like all the other men, can't I?'

Mina seemed taken aback. Then in a whisper, her face close to mine, she said: 'Watch yourself, Guido. If you do this, you'll never see me again afterwards.' That was the afternoon when, after wandering aimlessly for two hours in the hot sunshine through the quiet, scorching streets, I went away from Mina's door and sought out another house I knew of, at the bottom of an alley. But though I had my fill of love, the stupid, bored complacency of the girl sent me home dissatisfied, with a strong desire to weep. Besides, it brought home to me, in every detail, what Mina's work really was. Towards evening, exhausted with agony, I found myself once more outside Mina's door. I ought to have been away on my round. I remember thinking: 'If I've come back to her tonight, it means I must love her very much.'

But I didn't dare to ring. I sat down in some pub or other, almost opposite that door. Through the railing and between several pots of plants, I could see the dimly lighted entrance hall of the house, and the closed blinds masking the various rooms. 'I'll spend my evenings here,' I said to myself, but after a quarter of an hour I was as limp as a

Summer Storm

rag. Every now and then some man or other, or a young fellow, a group of soldiers or a few riff-raff from the streets would disappear through that door, or, worse still, would hang around the doorstep, laughing and joking. One even arrived on a motor-bike, filling the night with hideous noise before he dismounted and ran up the steps, still in his leather jacket.

Then, the men who came out. Any one of them might have been with her. I saw a fat, bald man who looked furtively around before he vanished in the distance. If I hadn't run over then, I should have screamed.

This time I went to the door with no hesitation at all and rang at once. The room was crowded and full of smoke, but Mina was not there. I stood hardly breathing, staring at the door. Adelaide appeared, half-naked. She winked at me and gave me a military salute. I asked her if she wasn't afraid of catching a cold. Then I caught sight of Mina, taking something to the Madame. She was wearing a pale blue brassiere and white silk panties, showing her sunburned legs and midriff. Her face fell as she saw me standing behind Adelaide. She did not look surprised, merely resigned. Pushing Adelaide aside without a glance, she came over to me and was about to speak when a thin, fair-haired man with a high bald forehead, who until then had been standing idly by, walked across and took her by the hand. Lowering her eyes, Mina turned and followed him out, ignoring me completely. Adelaide giggled loudly and I felt I was choking.

Tears of bitter anguish filled my eyes, but could have passed for sweat. I heard Adelaide saying something or other, then several bells began ringing on Madame's desk and I went away, holding my head high but seeing nobody.

That evening, stupidly enough, I made another impossible resolve: to get drunk every night. I told myself: 'She's

The Idol

tanned on the outside, I'll get tanned on the inside.' It soon made me feel sick, but my nausea could not make me forget Mina's little pale blue brassiere. Living alone, as I did, it was hard for me to get rid of an idea, and that sardonic, blond chap with the eyebrows was grinning at me through the liquor fumes all night.

I saw Mina again on the following Sunday, during her morning walk. I had waited in the pub till she left the house, then I caught up with her in the street. She looked surprised but stopped and shook hands with me, then said, as if I was blocking the whole pavement: 'Let's walk on. I don't like standing here like this.'

She complained that I had treated her badly, played her false. She had thought a lot about me, especially in the morning when she woke up, when she was alone. Why wasn't I kind to her? I had been so nice at Voghera, when I was twenty.

I did not answer, reflecting sadly that she was a woman now. 'Played you false?' I asked abruptly. 'Who with?'

'Oh, Guido,' she replied, 'I want it, too, just as you do, but afterwards it would be worse. You'd treat me like all the other women . . .'

'There's one thing we can do, anyway. Let's get married.'

'Guido, I can't. This is my life, and I'm sure you'd come to hate me in a year or even less.'

'Mina, I love you.'

'I know' she said, taking my hand. 'I know, Guido. D'you think I don't know what you're going through? But that's exactly why I ask you to be my friend and not want anything more than that . . .' She looked up into my face. 'You'd be ashamed of me,' she whispered.

'At Voghera you said you'd marry me.'

'At Voghera you loved me, and believed me when I told you Papa would not agree.'

'And you see what came of that.'

Summer Storm

'Guido, Papa's dead, now, and the rest is my own affair.'
'You say I've been false to you. Who with?'
'Perhaps I said it because you were talking to Adelaide.'
'But she just happened to turn up. I was looking for you.'

Mina's expression clouded. 'Don't ever come to that house again,' she said. 'If you do, it's the last time you'll ever set eyes on me.'

'Mina,' I told her, steeling myself. 'I'm not going to ask anything of you, but it's obvious you feel ashamed of this sort of life, so why not give it up and let's get married? I'm the same as I always was.'

'I've got nothing to be ashamed of. I've told you that before.'

'Have you got syphilis, Mina?'

She burst out laughing. 'How could I work if I had? Oh, Guido, what a boy you are! It would be grand if we could be just good friends and forget everything else. What difference does it make to you? Just pretend I'm already married.'

We met several times after that, always in the morning. Mina would wear her green and chestnut outfit, but once she came in white, looking taller and more sophisticated in her swirling cape. To make it possible for me to spare two or three mornings a week, I began doing my travelling at night, skimping my rounds and leaving out some of my customers altogether. Some evenings as I jumped on the train by myself I longed to have Mina with me, so tall, so serene. Yet this vision could not efface my other impression of her. It was only a question of clothes. Strip her, and she would look as she always had. The very thought of how her lovely little brow wrinkled when she felt uncertain, made me tremble. Days when I knew she was going bathing were agony to me. I imagined her going there all by herself and in thought I went with her, full of tenderness; sat by her, walked beside her, whispering words

The Idol

of love; till we fell asleep side by side. Sometimes I got over the horror of those tedious afternoons by persuading myself that everything was all right; that I had found a new woman, unsullied in her humiliation. Her very firmness in resisting me seemed something to appreciate, a bitter-sweetness. It gave me a vague feeling of comfort to reflect that her inmost, secret life was lonely and proud. I felt she was my equal.

One chilly morning in September when she came to meet me, she brought a younger girl with her, a kid with too much lipstick and a hat pulled down over one eye. I think I must have looked disappointed, because they both looked at each other and started laughing. The girl's laugh was loud and deep.

'Aren't we still going to have a meal together?' I murmured to Mina as I fell into step beside her.

'Let's go,' she smiled, taking my arm. She skipped along, clinging close to me. I was surprised and delighted, because that day I had a lot of things I meant to tell her in our quiet hour over lunch. But the presence of the girl dried me up.

Mina started talking to me about my work and made me list the places I had been to in the last few days. She frowned when I explained, half-smiling, how I had cut out certain clients rather than miss her free mornings. She stopped dead on the pavement, and made a face at me. My smile faded and my eyes pleaded with her to get rid of her companion, stuck there with us.

'You'll ruin yourself by tricks like that,' Mina said dryly, 'and I don't want this to happen. I can't bear to hear of such stupid pranks. When anybody is working, they ought to work. You're on your own, with your own way to make. It means I'm ruining you, then, and we shan't see each other any more.'

Stupidly, a smile flickered over my lips again. I glanced at

Summer Storm

the profile of the other girl, who was passively staring at the ground. I did not answer Mina except by taking her arm and muttering 'Let's walk.' Mina broke away and we moved on.

After a long silence, the other girl abruptly asked her something. Adelaide had used two dozen tablets of violet scented soap in a month, and they discussed whether the Madame was justified in making so much fuss about it.

'What did she do with them?' I enquired.

'She didn't do anything with them, see?' the girl grinned, showing wrinkles at the corners of her mouth. 'That woman's just a silly fusspot.'

I looked at Mina who was staring down at the cobblestones. I compared her profile with the thin, sensual face of the other girl and noticed again its clean line and the firmness of her chin that I loved. I stroked her arm gently and squeezed it against me.

'Have you known each other long?' I asked the girl.

'Nuccia comes from Romagna,' Mina replied.

Ignoring me, Nuccia remarked to Mina, 'I've been working at Madame Martire's place in Bologna. She'd like to have you back there again.'

I shuddered. Mina looked Nuccia straight in the eyes. We quickened our steps and in silence reached the café where Nuccia had someone waiting for her.

At the little white table in our own eating-house, Mina and I looked at each other without speaking. I noticed that her hands had lost their sunburn.

'Were you very sunburned?'

'I got a lot of sunbathing. I used to take a boat, go out to sea and strip off my costume.'

'You go rowing on your own?'

'It isn't hard.'

I stared at her. Mina gave a tentative smile. 'Don't say anything, Guido. I go out to sea to have a rest.'

The Idol

'But I was thinking of coming with you.'

'That's just it. But I go there for a rest.'

Mina's plate was soon empty. As she watched me through lowered eyes, she said suddenly: 'Why do you do those things?'

'What things?'

'Why do you shirk your work? How can I trust you if that's what you do?'

'What about you? You won't marry me?'

'I've told you already, Guido.'

'No, you haven't. You just like fooling me. When are you going to Bologna?'

'I'm not going to Bologna. Perhaps I'll go to Milan.'

'How many of these houses do you go round to?'

'I've never thought of listing them.'

'Is some man keeping you? Who?'

Mina's hard look softened. 'You must have suffered a great deal, Guido, to say things like that to me. I think they hurt you, too.'

'If I'm going to be hurt, I prefer it this way. You don't want me because you've got some other man.'

'But, Guido, don't you see how I work, the sort of life I lead? If some man was keeping me . . .' she said sadly, then suddenly frowned. 'I keep myself, and you know it.'

'It's because I see the life you lead, that I want to marry you. Oh, Mina, can't you understand me, or is it that you won't? We could work together, if you like; see each other only in the evenings; if you don't want to, we won't get married, but give up this life, have pity on me, you're the only woman worth the trouble. Even in the old days, at Voghera, you wouldn't listen to me when I begged you. Tell me how I should plead with you now. This life your are leading . . .'

'I like the life I'm leading,' Mina said calmly.

My face fell. I could have hurled a stone at her. Dazedly

Summer Storm

I looked around me, struggling to control myself in my keen agony. Then a wild fury rose in my heart, and keeping my voice low I flung at her every insult I could think of.

'You see? And you wanted to marry me,' Mina remarked.

One morning she unexpectedly asked to see my room and put it tidy for me. Nervously I took her up the old, gloomy staircase and threw open the window as soon as we were inside. With fresh air and light there came a new awareness. On the floor lay my gaping suitcase near the half-open cupboard, and a pile of old catalogues from my firm. The dirty coffee cup on the side table and the untouched bed were just as I had seen but scarcely noticed as I went out a little while ago. Mina walked over to me and kissed me. Even today, when it's all over, I still tremble at the memory of the pure, firm sweetness of her hidden body. All the time, Mina gazed at me with her limpid eyes, caressing my spine. There was a fresh atmosphere about it all, such as I have never known since.

But the afternoon came and I was left alone. Mina had promised to say she was ill that day, provided that I went off to work. I nodded, and caught the train, but after one full day away I was back again at dawn. I wrote her a little note and handed it in to the foul-mouthed doorkeeper of the brothel, who opened the door in her dressing-gown and accepted it with a bad grace. Everyone in the house was still asleep, and I ran off to wait for her in our café. The streets were veiled in a slight fog. The trees in the avenues were still green, but cold.

I was already biting my nails when Mina arrived, some time later. She came in without looking at me, wearing green and chestnut. She sat down, then raised her eyes.

'Mina, you're here,' I said softly.

The Idol

'Why have you called me, Guido?'

I stammered: 'I came back to see you, and my firm's gone bankrupt. This very day,' I moaned, clenching my fist.

'Should I believe you?'

'Why should I lie to you? It's my loss.'

'How did you hear about it?'

'I looked in this morning to report and I saw the notices. I've been aware for some time they were a bit shaky, but I didn't think . . . Perhaps they may still make some sort of settlement.'

'And you? What will you do now?'

'I'll live on my savings. I've got a little. I'll look for something else. We ought to get married and look for something together.'

'Oh, poor Guido. Now you'll have to think of work.'

'Won't you help me?' I said, feeling disappointed.

'Of course I'll help you. But you shouldn't think about me any more, not in this way. Have you anything in mind?'

I watched her drinking her coffee, looked at her eyes, seeking for the Mina of yesterday. 'All the evening I dreaded that you might go down,' I told her, stroking her hand.

'I did go down, my dear . . . to supper.'

'You see, Mina, I can't get that fellow out of my mind – you remember him – the one you went off with that Tuesday evening when you were jealous of Adelaide. A languid sort of chap, wearing glasses. I was thinking, perhaps he's back again today. Who knows?'

Mina half-closed her eyes, thinking. Then she made a face. 'I remember . . . You were a bad lad that evening. Why did you come? I was very hurt about it.'

'And what about me, Mina? But hasn't that fellow been back again?'

Summer Storm

'Why him in particular?'

'Oh, Mina! With him I saw you play me false.'

'Play you false,' Mina smiled. 'Can I play any man false?'

'You can give him hell, if you want to.'

'What about yesterday, Guido? Was that hell?'

It was lovely that morning, as we sat by the window in the sunshine. Lovely, but my hands were trembling. In the end Mina noticed it and asked me: 'What's the matter with you? Why are your hands shaking?'

'They need a ring to hold them still.'

Mina laughed aloud, diverted by my little joke. 'You're a dear when you say things like that,' and she gave me a smile.

From that day on I lived like a lunatic, spreading out my journeys and trying to do a week's work in a single day, calling at offices where they rarely saw me, or shook their heads and threatened to throw me out. That month I should get barely half my usual commission. I spent long afternoons dreaming of the future, dreaming of Mina in her white dress, trying to suppress my own vivid and recent memories of her nakedness. The evening, especially, was a long drawn out agony that forced tears to my eyes, moment after moment. I could not endure it. I groaned aloud, with no one there to hear me. Sometimes I drank, but then my tears and groans broke out worse than ever. I drank till I was sick, but could not gain oblivion and at last fell into a restless doze, embracing my pillow.

My pitiless darling came back to me every now and then, treating me tenderly, obdurate only if I asked her to marry me. It made me feel so cheap that I felt reluctant to let her see the state I was in, or to ask her again. I dreaded to see the look in her eyes when I did so, or to hear her harsh reply: 'If you love me, understand me.' Sometimes the intolerable agony would wring a protest from me, where-

The Idol

upon she would smile sadly. I tried to treat it lightly but thought of killing her. I told her so, through my clenched teeth.

Since she now thought I was unemployed I waited for her every morning and went with her to do her shopping. I wouldn't have missed it for anything. Sometimes I tried to pay for something she had bought, but she would never let me. When I was alone I would walk to and fro in front of the shops where she had bought perfume or linen, trembling at the thought of her.

'Mina,' I murmured one day when we had been together, 'when I look at you or you look at me, your eyes are almost closed. Someone once said that when women do that they roll up their eyes so that only the whites can be seen. Don't you do that?'

'The things you think of!' she smiled with her cheek against mine.

'It's because I love you,' I replied softly.

'If you love me, that should be enough for you,' she said, holding me close.

As we went downstairs that day we found no need of words. It was raining and we walked arm in arm, close against the wall. I knew that any moment now I should be alone again, and shivered in anticipation.

'What's the matter, Guido?'

'Nothing. I'm quite happy.'

'Look here, Guido, do you remember what Nuccia said that day?'

'What? That you're going to Bologna?'

'No, Guido, to Milan,' she gave me a twisted smile. 'What she said first, when she was talking about Adelaide.'

I didn't remember.

'She said the Madame treated Adelaide badly. D'you remember now?'

I nodded, and she went on: 'Guido, we're all a bit like

Summer Storm

Adelaide. It comes from the life we lead. It's not too good a life, Guido.'

Staring straight in front of me but seeing nothing, I broke the silence: 'With Nuccia, Mina?'

'What does it matter who with?'

I felt a strange sense of relief and humiliation. I found it hard to breathe the damp air and stood clinging to Mina's arm without realizing it. For no reason at all, we halted at the corner.

'Now are you disgusted?' Mina asked, her wide-open eyes staring into mine.

'Oh, Mina. Anything you do is all right with me. D'you know,' I went on, letting go of her arm, 'perhaps I like it this way. I prefer it.' Mina gave me a sidelong smile and went away.

Two days later we left for Milan. I had convinced her there was nothing more I could do in Turin, and I might perhaps have found a job up there with a firm of competitors. We stayed in the hotel and Mina spent two days and nights with me. Whenever I had been in Milan before I had always been passing through, and those two days were like a dream. We walked through long, unfamiliar streets, clinging to each other, looking at the shops and going back at night with shining eyes. It filled my whole heart, that temporary room all cluttered with suitcases, but quiveringly alive with Mina's constant presence. Those were the last, serene days of October, when trees and houses were still full of mild warmth.

Then Mina went away into the brothel. I wrote to ask my employers whether they would put me in charge of this new territory. They replied that unless I resumed work in my own sector they would at once relieve me of my job as their representative. I did not even reply and started looking for new employment in the city.

November came with its rain and fog. I was living at

The Idol

the end of a courtyard in an airless room. There were no women about and I never made my bed. I never cleaned the place unless Mina was coming, but she seldom did come because she was too tired in the mornings. I spent hours at a time stretched out on the bed, listening to the rain, and later on watching the snow. I still had a thousand *lire* or so, but I missed my meals in the hope that the money might be used to marry us. I was tormented by harsh, rebellious thoughts whenever I wandered round the streets, numb with cold, envying the street-cleaners who at least had a job.

Mina stayed in a forbidding-looking villa at the end of a road that opened on a dull little park. There were carpets inside and the place was very warm, as I found one day when I escorted her to the entrance. The price was higher here, and a new rage began to burn in me. The visitors were rich men with more leisure, many of them old. She told me so herself. I'd rather have known she was in the arms of a soldier or some factory-worker. I could have gone there like any other man, but there was no question of that; some nights I wept with rage, but the memory of her hostile glance was enough to hold me back. I was alone – I told her so, once – I never found another woman; the city was so huge and strange it put me off; on some grey afternoons I was so cold I could have cried; couldn't I come and find her?

'If you had stayed in Turin . . .' she said, then added quickly. 'If you came once you'd come another time, and another, and you need all your savings.'

'If I came only for a chat, Mina?'

'No. I'll soon come to you.'

One evening as I was eating a plate of soup in a café, I heard two people, a man and a woman, talking about an agency that worked wonders. I had lost all hope of a representative's job, but it then occurred to me that I might find temporary work. We talked about it over a couple of glasses of wine. I watched their faces with infinite care. All through that period, except when I was tortured by jealousy, I felt a kind of humble tenderness when two human eyes gazed into mine. The girl was thin, with her hair hanging over her eyes and wearing a shabby mackintosh; the man, a gaunt workman, sucked gently at a cigarette. They had been out of work for months, but now he was doing a gardening job. This was the first meal they'd been able to buy. The girl said nothing but sat there nodding, devouring me with her eyes.

Next morning I rushed round to the agency, but they had nothing at the moment.

We went back to our own town at the end of March. My old landlady had kept my room for me, but I was almost ashamed to let her see my bony face. I had become the sort of man who trembles at an unexpected word.

Mina was talking of taking a holiday and playing around for a while. Her cheeks were a little sunken now; her lips were too pale and she used lipstick; the wrinkles on her forehead were deeper. She talked to me most tenderly and asked me if I still loved her.

But she went back to the house where she had been before, though I begged her not to. It was as much as her life was worth. She should go to the country for a short time, think of herself, for a change. I would stay in Turin to look for a job. All she would say was that for the first few days she would not come downstairs to work, and in fact she often came out with me for the evening, but one afternoon when I ventured to go in to look for her they told me she was working. Slowly I made my way back home.

I found casual work, where I had to wear overalls to save my ordinary clothes. I washed cars from dinner-time on, all through the night, in a garage not too far from where

The Idol

I lived. I still remember those long hours of waiting, when I sat on the bench outside, furtively smoking under the red light of the huge neon sign. Now and then some travelling salesman whom I had once known would drive in, but I avoided them all, for fear of having to talk about myself. Often enough I was quite happy, sitting there alone.

Mina would come out in the mornings, wearing a striking, flame-coloured cloak that made her stand out from the crowd, even at a distance. Her laughter-wrinkles gave her a young, gay look, like a leaf on an orange. She soon regained her bloom and developed the tantalizing habit of closing her ears to anything I said. It made her seem even more of a darling. The only indication of her inflexible determination was in the tone she unconsciously adopted when she talked about us. She was a year older than I was, and to me she seemed grown-up, superior, more mature. Compared with her, what was I but a scatter-brained boy?

We talked about that August day when I first asked her to marry me. 'I loved you for that, too,' she told me. 'The day comes when one wants a home of one's own. You gave me a feeling that I should have laughed at, once. I wish I could go back to what I was at Voghera, young and silly, but worthy of you. If only we hadn't parted then, Guido!'

'But we've found each other again, Mina. We're sure of one another. When I think of this I don't regret your past.'

'You'd regret it one day.'

'Mina, have I ever once reproached you about your past? It's the present that's killing me. Oh, Mina, now we know we could stay together. Those two days in Milan . . .'

'But you've got to work, now. You can't be thinking about women . . .'

Another time, when I was on my way back to my job and gritting my teeth to endure another night of jealousy,

Summer Storm

Mina said to me: 'You forget I've got all sorts of vices.'

'We'll take care of any vices,' I replied with a shrug, but we were both embarrassed as we exchanged a glance.

April, that year, brought none of its usual sweetness. The weather was chilly, almost cold. Rainclouds hung, every morning, above the tender green trees in the avenues. It rained often, the fresh, warm, whispering rain of spring. In my bare little room, I sometimes gazed at Mina in agony. She would give a start of surprise, compose herself and make some remark or other. Once I asked her what vices she had meant. 'Silly boy,' she cried, holding out her hand to me. 'Why must you always take me seriously?'

At last the sun broke through and a light wind freshened the streets. I thought I should soon be able to take Mina to the seaside for a rest. I had never seen the sea in springtime.

One morning I was in the pub opposite the house, not expecting to see her, just watching the sunshine slanting against the cobblestones and thinking of her asleep behind those closed blinds. All at once three figures came through the front door; a man and two women. The second woman, in blue and orange, was Mina. They passed along the pavement in front of the tubs of flowers. The other woman was Adelaide. I hardly recognized her in her little hat. The man had a jutting profile and was wearing glasses. His hat was pulled down on his forehead. He was walking arm in arm with Mina and I saw his face – the face I had hated ever since that August evening.

Next day I asked Mina about him, hardly managing to bring out the words. Mina told me it was indeed the same man. Quite casually she explained that he had come back again one evening and had taken a fancy to Adelaide. The two were now good friends. Then another girl named Mafalda, had taken him upstairs with her, leaving the other two girls alone. Adelaide had told Mina a lot of

The Idol

silly, sentimental nonsense about the poor fellow, an engineer. Mina started explaining to me how shy he was, but I harshly interrupted her: 'Did you ever go upstairs with him?' I asked in a choking voice.

Mina shrugged. 'He's a good client.' After a moment she went on: 'He wants to marry me.' She looked straight at me, then dropped her eyes. 'Now, Guido,' she murmured, her voice hard. 'Don't be a silly boy.'

I thought I had learned a bit about suffering, but that day it was like a hurricane. I knew why a man winds his cape round his throat so as not to suffocate. It's like being in a raging wind that catches your breath. Alone in my room, leaning against the wall, my every breath was a groan. I was amazed that I did not cry aloud, that I did not fall as if struck by a thunderbolt, my eyes starting from my head. I could not call out; I could not move; I just stood there choking for perhaps half an hour. Something within me was burning to ashes.

When I went out, towards evening, I was feverish and dazed. I was well aware that nothing had really changed; that the streets lay peaceful in the setting sun, people were walking up and down, night was falling and tomorrow I should see Mina as usual; I knew I was alive and unharmed, yet I looked around me frantically as if I had gone mad and the whole world had turned topsy-turvy.

Next day I asked her another silly question. 'Why did you say yes to him?'

'But I haven't said yes to him,' Mina replied.

'But you took him inside with you, which means you accept him.'

'Who knows why?' she laughed.

'Does he know you're called Mina?'

She dropped her head remorsefully. 'You see? I'm no good.'

By now my savings had dwindled and at the garage

Summer Storm

I earned barely enough to keep me. I reflected that now, even if she were willing, I couldn't have married Mina. I was seized with a blind rage against that blond lout. Either he had plenty of money or, since he went there to find her, she was keeping him herself. I said so to her once, and she answered: 'He's a decent man, just unlucky. He's a real friend to me and doesn't make scenes as you do. You're only a boy, Guido. Why don't you go back to your job?'

'But I haven't got it any more, you know that.'

'I was so proud of you, when you travelled around.'

'You mean to kill me, Mina?'

She came to see me again, one morning in May. We stayed together a long time and I watched her trembling. She clung to me like a mother, then pushed me away. 'Happy, Guido?' I told her I was, and she went on: 'You see, my dear, you should always remember me as I was that day. You've always said you forgave me. If I've made you suffer, think that I've suffered too, because of you. Perhaps more than you. Because I love you very much.'

'Mina, shan't we see each other any more?'

'Of course we'll see each other, but not here. I do you harm by coming here. You should be thinking of your work.'

'But without you, Mina...'

'With me, Guido. We'll see one another every morning...'

'And if you marry him?'

'I haven't decided yet.'

'Let me come to you, too. Then we shall fight on an equal footing.'

'But he hardly ever comes.'

There were certain empty mornings when Mina did not keep her appointment, which meant that someone had gone to find her when she was still in bed. I would sit there

The Idol

endlessly in the café, saying nothing, staring at the empty air, hardly hearing the traffic. The whim took me to affect a smile; even when I could no longer keep it up, the lines of it were fixed on my lips. I felt as if I were always drunk.

One evening I felt I could no longer breathe. All the afternoon I had wandered round, my eyes full of tears. I should have gone down to the garage, but instead I went to find Mina. I rushed up those three steps, trembled as I rang the bell and went into the room with that smile on my face. I shouted: 'Scum! The whole lot of you!'

They seemed to take it as some new form of greeting and nobody moved. The girls, Mina among them, were sitting near the door talking among themselves and they barely turned round. Instead, one of the men sitting beside them looked up sharply and stared at me. I glanced along the row of them, looking for that face. I could have murdered him.

But that face was not there. Mina followed me with her eyes, came up behind me and said softly: 'D'you want to go up with me, Guido?'

I followed her like a man in a dream. Going up the stairs I thought about the day I went up them behind Adelaide, before any of this had happened. Mina went into the same room as before. 'Manuela' was written on the door.

On the chest-of-drawers were two large suitcases, open and empty. The bed was neatly made. The room was full of a light perfume, with an underlying hint of soap and rubber. As she closed the door she asked, without turning round: 'Who were you looking for, down there?'

I replied quietly: 'I wanted to kill that fellow. You know the one. And if he does come I will kill him, even though it'll do me no good now. Oh, Mina . . .' and I fell to the floor in front of her, clasping her knees.

'You see?' she said nervously, not bending down towards

Summer Storm

me, 'You see? It's no use. Don't make me cry. You can see I'm going away.'

'You're going to Bologna?'

'No. This time it's for always. Get up. I'm going to be married.'

She said it calmly and simply, her voice quite under control, and I realized the utter futility of my position. I rose to my feet and looked around the room in complete bewilderment, gazing at the mirror, the cluttered seat, a crack in the door. 'I shall suffer later,' I told myself. 'Later, when I'm alone.'

'Do you want me?' Mina asked, bending her head to look intently at me and sliding her silk dress off her shoulders.

I'm sorry, now, that I didn't take her, tear her to pieces, destroy her. Perhaps if I had I could have got her out of my mind afterwards. Instead, the pain of that moment comes over me again even today, and I feel like a whipped dog.

Mina stood looking at me and stroking her shoulder. I stared back at her and said bluntly: 'Don't undress yourself, Mina, if you mean to get married.'

Glowing with happiness she came over to me and took my hands, holding them close to her heart. 'Forgive me, Guido. Now I know you really and truly love me.'

'I made another sacrifice for you, once.' Her eyes flashed, and I went on: 'Remember I told you my employers went bankrupt? Well, they didn't. I just wanted to be free to follow you.'

She let my hands fall. 'You did that?'

'Yes.'

'Stupid! Why don't you go back? Oh, you're such a fool! Why did you do it? Why did you want to ruin yourself? What a boy you are! Go back! Just a boy. A silly boy.'

The Idol

When I left her, those words reverberated endlessly in my brain. All night they never stopped.

The suffering that followed was beyond description. But the next morning I no longer expected Mina in the café. I no longer called at the house to see her. There was only one thing I would have liked to tell her, that left me blazing. Even now it chokes me when I think of the past. 'He got rid of your vices for you, I suppose?'

For a long time I felt shattered, as when I used to cry myself to sleep when I was a child. I thought of Mina and her husband as two grown-ups with a secret. A boy can only watch them from a distance, unaware of the joys and sorrows that make up their life. I found work in my garage for the long mornings, too, and little by little I learned to resign myself, as the summer went by. Now that I've grown old and have learned how to suffer, Mina has gone.

First Love

Before I knew Nino it never struck me that the boys I ran shouting round the streets with were ragged and filthy. Indeed, I actually envied them for going barefoot. One of them could even walk over corn-stubble without being hurt, while my pale, city-dweller's feet cringed from the very thought of treading the cobbled streets.

They taught me a lot, but nothing of it interested Nino except a few swear-words. He lived in a little villa just outside the village and had several elder sisters who scared me stiff. I would stay just beyond the low, garden wall and peep through the railings, hoping Nino would be already coming down the steps. If he kept me waiting I would give a little hiss like a snake, softly at first but getting louder, as long as the dog didn't start barking. Then Nino would come running, because he was afraid of the dog, too.

It wouldn't have done at all to suggest to Nino any idea of going barefoot or playing with the others. I never told him so, but after I had been out with him a few times I felt ashamed of those old friends. Oddly enough, from his casual remarks I gathered he knew them all, the games they played and what they talked about. Indeed, he seemed one of us, except that his shirt and shorts were even cleaner than my own. He liked to stroll along side lanes with his

First Love

hands in his pockets, peeping in at windows or between the tall grass at anyone who passed by, grinning every now and then.

We were both about thirteen or fourteen and that summer, to my surprise, I found I was beginning to dislike the urchins I used to play with; those of our own age were sloppy and stupid; any that seemed as lean and active as we were had already reached eighteen or so and didn't mix with us.

I can't clearly remember what Nino and I talked about in those early days. I know I once asked him how many sisters he had. 'None,' he replied.

'What? All those girls? Aren't they your sisters?'

'They're all like a mother to me,' he said, with his usual grimace. 'I doubt if they're really sisters, anyway.'

I told him that once I had gone hunting with a soldier on leave. I told him so many things, directly and indirectly, that one fine day Nino retorted: 'Rot!'

'What's that?' I exclaimed. 'I go hunting by myself, too. Any reason why I shouldn't?'

I took him down by the river one day. Some of the boys I played with in the mornings were fishing with creels and all soaked with water and mud. Nino stood aloof, giving me a faint smile when I called to him from the water, hoping for a glance of approval or a complimentary word. Once, when the blacksmith's son heaved out a heavy basket, creaking with the weight of fish in it, and called to him to catch hold of it, Nino moved aside and let it lie. They all yelled that he was 'dead on his feet'. I tried to make excuses for him, explaining that he was wearing a new coat, but Nino jeered back at them and shouted furiously that he had someone behind him who would soon put them in their proper place.

Nino stayed at home in the mornings, wandering round the house. The first time I went there to look for him,

Summer Storm

craning my neck up at his window, I saw a tall, handsome woman looking at me across the garden. She beckoned me to come closer, but I pretended not to notice and ran away. I was afraid Nino wouldn't speak to me any more, but it made no difference.

After that, I divided my time accordingly. Almost every morning I sneaked off to the goat pasture with the ragamuffins I had been friendly with at first. I stuffed them with exciting tales of the city – my own province – and extraordinary adventures that could happen on the trams or in lifts. Every now and then I would stop to chase a goat, peel a wand, or hunt grasshoppers. In the afternoons, instead of sheltering from the heat of the day in the hayloft or stable, as I used to do, I would go and look for Nino. I realized I was probably wasting my time and simply boring myself, yet every day I was there. When we returned from our casual stroll up the hill by the church or across the fields, I should have liked to go into the garden with him, to sit on those little chairs and risk being told off by his sisters, but the first time Nino asked me in I was too shy to accept.

After what happened at the fishing pool, I hinted that it would be best not to tell his family of our personal affairs. Nino laughed through his teeth and told me that if I was afraid the women in his home knew anything about those scruffy pals of mine, I needn't worry. His own friend was quite different.

One afternoon as we went past the open space behind the fertilizer store, I heard him laugh. Parked in the narrow street was a long, low car I had seen before. From the half-open door came the sound of many voices, suddenly dominated by a hearty laugh. Other laughs, louder still, followed the first. Nino peered forward through the stench of sulphur and manure and exclaimed: 'He's just coming out.'

First Love

Out came an old countryman who greeted us with a wink; then, flinging wide the door, he shouted: 'Toss 'em out.'

Out flew a heavy little sack that the old man caught in mid-air and put in the car. Then came another, and another.

'Give us a hand, young fellow,' said the old man, showing his gums. Nino leapt over the threshold and disappeared. I stayed by the car, trying to guess at the shadowy figures moving quickly about inside the place.

When the car was practically full and I was helping the old man readjust the bags, Nino appeared on the doorstep with a curly-haired man wearing a scarf round his neck, a red belt and Wellingtons. His sleeves were rolled up and he filled the doorway. Nino appeared at his elbow.

There was a smile in his voice as he said to Nino, and to me; 'So you've made friends, eh?' He gave me a wink and took my hand, but I broke away. He shook my forearm forcibly two or three times, then said: 'Nino, don't pick a quarrel with this one, for he's stronger than you.' Then he straightened up, looked round and said: 'Finished?'

He took out a cigarette and lit it, jumped into the car, called out 'So long' and was gone.

That evening Nino was full of excitement as he chatted to me. We went and sat on the low wall, but he couldn't stay still there. Yet his eyes hadn't the restless look they generally had and he answered my questions in a voice sparkling with gaiety.

Bruno worked as a chauffeur, but he was a real friend to Nino. He went to fetch them from the station the day they arrived, and all the way along the winding road over the hill to the villa Nino hardly bothered to answer anything his mother or sisters said, but talked to Bruno all the time, asking him about everything. Sometimes Bruno would ask him how the little heifers were getting on, meaning his

Summer Storm

sisters. (It was a saying with us: 'Silly as a heifer'.) There was only one thing that appealed to Bruno about those girls: the American cigarettes Nino brought him from them whenever he could – in their packets, of course, because the value depended on the packets.

Nino talked about all sorts of things that evening; the bathing pool at his home, that smelt even nicer than the meadows; how he wished he could get Bruno to bathe in it, too, so that he could still smell like a grown man, but clean; and especially about how he wanted to go out in the car with him, me too, touring the villages around the hills, having fun and learning to drive.

Bruno had promised to teach him, but there never seemed to be a chance. Bruno loved teasing everyone, pretending they were all stronger than he was. Then Nino gave me a pinch that almost took the skin off, and jumped clear. 'Let's see if you really are stronger,' he cried spitefully and picked up a stone.

If it had been one of those moments when we reached the gate of the villa and fell silent a moment before parting, I'd have asked Nino: 'Why do a thing like that?' But he'd never have said it, then. I couldn't understand why Nino had to spoil our friendly chat with such a spiteful remark. I couldn't go swimming in a lovely bathing pool, as he did, but I'd managed to grow stronger than he was.

'But there, he tells everyone they're stronger,' Nino went on, dropping the stone and coming over to me with a sly smile. But I couldn't trust myself to smile in return. 'So you like Bruno, eh?' he said. 'Careful. The heifers like him, too. My sisters, you know.'

'All of them?' I exclaimed.

'Yes, all of them,' Nino replied.

'But men choose just one woman,' I said.

'What a fool you are! He can't exactly marry them.'

'But you told me he talked only with you.'

First Love

'That's because they never give him an answer. They're stupid.'

I went home feeling fed up, ashamed of my father's moustaches and the dirty, wine-stained oilcloth on the table where we ate our supper. My little sister kept on whining. I had never been in a car and was thinking how nice it would be to jump in one with Nino and Bruno. But it annoyed me that his sisters could be so stupid, and Nino himself so spiteful. Luckily I'd never told him that one night I'd dreamed about them.

Next morning I didn't want to go to the pasture with the other boys, as I usually did. Instead, I felt inclined to pass the time as Nino did, enjoying a good meal, then going for a bathe or sauntering round the house and turning up at noon. But by ten o'clock I was out in the courtyard wondering what to do next. On the slopes of the valley were low apple-trees, but I already knew them by heart. I strolled past the farm entrances, each with a pile of last year's wood outside it; I met the wife of a peasant farmer, carrying a bucket. She wore a yellow kerchief over her head and her sleeves were rolled up. I understood how it was that Nino could spend the whole morning without coming out to play, just watching those sisters of his walking about in the garden. It must be fine to live with them, if even the chauffeur found them desirable. All I had to look at was my mother and the servant, who both slaved like farm labourers, and my father only came home in the evening.

The peasant farmer's wife ran to the cowshed. I heard the cow bawling loudly, as if she was in pain, and I found myself in the doorway. The woman ran over to me. 'Get out. Get out!' she cried crossly, standing behind me so that I could not see past her. 'You shouldn't be watching. Go and call Pietro. Tell him it's time. Understand?'

Pietro was digging at the bottom of a field behind the

Summer Storm

house. I came back with him. First he went into the kitchen and took a swig from a bottle, then we both ran to the shed. Again the old woman pushed me back. Pietro turned and muttered: 'Go and tell your mother we're getting a calf for her.'

I still hung around, trembling with fear at the animal groans that broke into the open air, followed by gurglings as if the creature was dying. Then came excited voices; the woman gave a sudden exclamation, followed by the splashing of water and the jingle of a chain. I thought about the shapeless mass of the cow's belly as I had seen it a day or two before.

Suddenly I thought of Nino and rushed off to find him. As I reached the villa, one of his sisters was coming out – the fair one with the dazzling white skin. I had watched her cycling past and thought how pretty she was. Now she laughed, rested her hand on my head and asked me what was the matter. I told her I was looking for Nino.

'Why?' she persisted.

'There's a new-born calf,' I stammered, red-faced. She looked at me, took her hand away and laughed aloud. 'Is it a pretty little thing?' she asked.

I didn't know what to say. She laughed again, turned away and called: 'Nino.' I heard an answering voice. She waved her hand, barely glancing at me, and went on her way, opening her parasol.

When Nino joined me – the dog was barking, rushing about and rattling his chain – I no longer wanted to take him to the cowshed. Again I felt ashamed of the filthy yard by our house. All I said was: 'Coming out?'

That morning we ended up by the river bank where the washerwomen were busy. Neither of us found anything to say. All at once I asked him: 'Ever seen a calf born? I did, this morning. It scared me.'

'Did it cry?' Nino asked.

First Love

'No, but its mother did. The cow, I mean.'

'Why didn't you call me?'

I felt annoyed, as I had done the day before. 'Silly ass!' Nino cried in a fury. 'We could have seen how babies are born. Have you ever seen how that happens?'

'Haven't you ever seen a young thing born?' I asked with an air of importance.

Nino fell silent, looking down at the ground. The washerwomen were beating sheets against the stones. One of them was a big, fat woman with bare arms. I could see her armpits, and as she laughed with one of her friends her whole body shook and quivered inside her shapeless dress.

'It's like seeing a horse pass dung,' Nino went on, his voice a little unsteady. 'Only this is bigger. Did you really see it?'

'Sure,' I replied.

'And you were born the same way,' Nino cried in a kind of rage.

'Yes, I was,' I answered calmly.

Nino gave himself a punch in the face and dropped to the ground. Standing beside him, I looked at him in some embarrassment. I crouched down to confess the truth to him, but just then he started laughing.

But his laugh sounded hollow. 'If you want to come out in the car with us,' he said, 'Tell me what it's like.'

I stared at Nino. His eyes blazing, his lips trembling with excitement. Softly he murmured: 'Have you seen your mother?'

I stared at him in amazement and said: 'You silly fool!'

'Tell me, what did you see?'

'I saw the cow.'

'You haven't seen women?'

'No,' and I looked at the ground.

Nino's voice broke out, close to my ear, 'Then you don't know what they do?'

Summer Storm

I confessed that I hadn't even seen the calf.

Nino rolled over in the grass and rose to his feet. 'I know what they do,' he said. 'Blood comes out and they've got to pull the baby away from it.'

'Blood doesn't always come.'

'Yes it does. It always comes. That's why the women cry out.'

'No,' I said. 'Listen,' and I explained that once I had seen a cow as soon as her calf was born and there was no blood. The little calf was a bit wet, that's all.

'With women there's always blood,' Nino insisted. 'You don't know anything.'

In a hoarse voice he told me how things were with women. I didn't interrupt him. I just stood staring at the grass. When he had finished I asked: 'And your sisters too?'

'Yes. It's the same with them, too.'

That afternoon Bruno came to the village unexpectedly and invited us into the car with him. He had to take a demi-john of wine to the station and there was room for us. He settled us in the back seat to hold the demi-john and off we went. All the way along the road my heart was in my mouth. As the trees and fences and passers-by flashed past us I thought I was flying. I screwed up my eyes against the sun and watched Bruno's thick neck above his red kerchief, the jerky movements of his arm resting on the wheel. I was afraid that when we stopped the demi-john would fall.

Instead, all was well and I was the one to stagger, drenched in sweat, as I set foot on the ground. Bruno, talking in a loud voice, carried the demi-john into the left-luggage office, then took us to the station tavern. Timidly I sat down in the cool shade, trying to copy Nino who looked everyone straight in the face and laughed with Bruno, throwing his head back to look up at him.

First Love

Bruno called for beer and Nino wanted an ice. We had barely moistened our lips when Nino scowled and said slyly: 'Berto, tell Bruno you've seen a baby being made.'

Bruno looked sideways at me, with one eye. He put down his glass and pursed up his lips. 'Why you . . .' I burst out wildly to Nino.

Bruno wiped away the sweat from his face and turned to Nino. 'Better tell him you're learning to act like men. You should be, at your age. For the rest, that's for women to think of.'

'There was a calf born . . .' Nino said.

'A couple of asses, you mean,' Bruno interrupted him. 'Haven't you anything else to talk about?'

He wiped his face again and looked cross. We sat silent, our eyes cast down. Nino went on eating his ice, his head bent.

'Nino, did Clara give you the cigarettes?'

Clara was the fair-haired sister. 'She's hidden them,' Nino replied.

Bruno rolled one for himself and said casually: 'Would you like to come to the Robini's tomorrow? We'll be back by midday. You can come too, Berto.'

Nino said: 'Give me a smoke.'

I watched Bruno's huge hand rolling the cigarette, not daring to ask for one myself. 'Coming tomorrow, Nino?' I said instead. Nino gave Bruno a sly look and asked softly: 'Shall we stop by the little wall?'

Bruno nodded, holding his cigarette out to him. I could not understand why Nino looked so pale. I saw his hand trembling as he lit his cigarette from Bruno's. 'Have a drink of wine,' Bruno said. 'Ice cream's for weaklings.' I knew Nino didn't like red wine, yet I watched him hold out his glass and lift it slowly to his lips. He swallowed it all.

'Fine,' Bruno exclaimed. 'While you're in town, this

Summer Storm

winter, you won't get wine like this. You'll get thin, in town. What about you, Berto? Got a girl-friend yet?'

I felt embarrassed, but managed to reply: 'There's no time for that: we're at school all the winter.'

'You have a girl in the summer, then?'

'I . . . no.'

Bruno laughed aloud. 'Bravo! You'll be seeing Nino this winter?'

'This year we shall, shan't we?' I asked Nino abruptly.

'You be careful! Nino takes fencing lessons and might run you through,' Bruno winked at me.

Nino said nothing. He drank another glass, barely listening to us. His eyes were fixed on the leather strap Bruno wore round his square wrist, and he suddenly asked what it was for.

'To bash in the face of any cheeky blighter,' Bruno explained. 'You give him a sideways blow, overhand, so as not to hurt your fingers, and it acts like a boxing glove. One night at Spigno there was a fellow who walked by the car – I was parked by the station – and he spat into it. Just spat and ran away. You must never put up with spitting, because a man who spits is afraid. I shot after him and split open his face. Like this. See how it works?'

Nino coughed over his cigarette, without taking his eyes from Bruno's fierce face. Smoking didn't worry him at all, as I knew already from the other times we had smoked together behind the church, so it must be the wine that was upsetting him. Or perhaps the argument he'd had with Bruno. Why did Bruno call his sister by her christian name?

'When your mother and sisters take that trip to Acqui they're talking about, I'll show you the market-place where I stopped a mad dog by pushing the leather in his mouth. See the marks of his teeth?'

'I'm not coming to Acqui with you,' said Nino.

First Love

Bruno started laughing: 'Berto, finish your drink. Tomorrow, then.'

We went to the Robini's, speeding all the way. Every time we rounded a curve, Bruno turned towards me and whistled through his teeth. Nino, sitting beside him, kept his chin against his chest as if someone had hit him. Two or three times his eyes wandered over the hills or up into the sky, and he gave a sudden start as though he had just woken up.

'The land is very dry, this year,' I remarked in a resigned tone of voice, as my father did.

This time Bruno did not turn towards me. Instead, he swung round into a narrow side-track between steep banks covered with flowers. For five minutes our faces were lashed by twigs. Then we came to a halt half-way up a hillside, near a little bridge whose walls overhung a rocky gorge. Bruno jumped out and said: 'You wait here. Look after the car.'

He switched off the engine and took out the key. 'Don't touch anything, and it won't move. Cheer up, Nino.' He gave us each a cigarette and lit it for us. 'If anybody comes up this way, anyone at all, sound the horn. Understand? If all goes well I'll let you drive, Nino. You, too, Berto. But keep a good look out. Anyone at all, remember.' He went up a little steep path and disappeared behind the banks.

The sun was blazing down, now. Shaded by the high banks we could watch a long stretch of the track up the hill. No one could turn into it from the main road without our seeing them. I had never been up here before, but evidently Nino had. There he sat at the wheel, never bothering to glance at the wide views spread out before our eyes, but smoking as a man does, puffing away without looking down at his cigarette.

'Will Bruno be away long?' I asked.

Nino did not answer. He jumped down and walked

Summer Storm

around the car, scrutinizing the headlamps and the dusty tyres. From the walls of the bridge he looked down at the river bed, now dry. Only when the autumn rains came would it fill again and become a raging torrent masked with foam. Now there were only knotted roots. It looked tempting to climb down by them, but for the risk of snakes. I threw away my cigarette stub, then tried to put it out by spitting at it. Nino made no move.

'Let me sit there a bit, too,' I said, turning towards him.

Nino looked at me, his eyes narrowing as they did when he felt spiteful. 'Know where he's gone?' he asked.

I shrugged my shoulders, and at that moment a dog started barking, not far away.

'See?' said Nino. 'That means he's just got to the house where the woman is. He's gone to find Martino's wife or daughter. They're expecting him. They'll tie up the dog and go to bed together.'

'But it's broad daylight!' I exclaimed.

Now Nino gave a shrug. 'They'll get on the bed as quick as they can,' he went on. 'They may be there an hour,' and he laughed, 'if nobody comes.'

'And where's Martino?'

'He's gone to the station. I heard about it yesterday.'

'And if he comes back?'

'If he comes, it's our job to sound the horn.'

I was not convinced. 'Did Bruno tell you about it?'

Nino gave me a dirty look and tossed away his cigarette end.

'I don't believe it,' I persisted. 'It would take too long. Bruno's got other things to think of. And he's got to drive the car, too.'

'What about it?'

'... He'd be too exhausted...' I faltered.

'Bruno's strong,' Nino exclaimed in a fury. 'But you'll see.'

First Love

'What?'

'You'll see.'

The narrow track still lay deserted in the hot sunshine. The very leaves before my eyes were trembling in the heat. Or perhaps it was that my heart was beating wildly. The village and my home seemed so remote from the quiet solitude around us, and from the thoughts in my mind. If only Nino didn't sound so spiteful! I thought about Clara, back in the villa and knowing nothing of what we were doing. She was a woman, too. Unsteadily I sat down on the running board of the car.

'I don't believe you,' I said abruptly. 'The Martino women attend church regularly.'

'All women go to church. They get married in church. Didn't you know? And when a couple marry it's so that they can go to bed together, isn't it?'

'I just don't believe it,' I said. 'Bruno is a good man, like us.'

'Know what I'll do to him?'

'What?'

'You'll see.'

I jumped into the car and sat beside Nino. He gave me a sly look and whistled to himself. 'At this very minute they're kissing and cuddling each other,' he said through his clenched teeth.

'Nino,' I cried. 'What'll we do if Martino comes back? He'll be sure to find him there . . .'

'He won't come back,' Nino replied. 'Is that someone coming?' He turned and surveyed the track, the main road and the whole plain. We strained our ears. There was nobody.

'Now they've stripped off their clothes,' Nino went on, and his face was pale.

'But . . .' I stammered.

'Quick, now,' Nino cried, and pressed the horn.

Summer Storm

In response came a furious barking from the dog. In the moment that followed it semed to me that the whole woodland was in an uproar. I tried to stop Nino's hand, but already the raucous blare of the horn, like the shout of a madman, was re-echoing from the hills.

When Bruno came bounding down the path, we were hiding in the long grass behind the tree-trunks, where Nino had dragged me. Bruno looked all around, especially at the track from the main road, his red belt still dangling from his hand. He strapped it around his trousers, still peering in every direction. Then, keeping his voice low, he called: 'Nino!' Nino gripped my arm.

Bruno had jumped in the car and was scrutinizing the main road far below. His lips were moving. His hair was all over the place and his face looked as if he had just held it under the pump. He got down from the car and went over to the tree, turned his back and stood with his legs wide apart. A moment later we heard him passing water. Nino stifled a giggle.

Then Bruno came over in our direction, looking up into the air and buttoning his trousers. Suddenly he leaned forward and leapt between the branches. Nino tried to flee, but he gripped him by the leg and brought him down. I had jumped to my feet and stood there watching. Without saying a word, Bruno gripped Nino's wrists in one hand and held him up like a rabbit, screeching and kicking. With the other hand he thrashed his bottom. His lips were tight together, and every blow made Nino scream. For a moment he looked at me without seeing me, and I fled down the track. The noise of a scuffle continued, then Bruno appeared, carrying Nino under his arm and throwing him into the car. To me he shouted roughly. 'Get in. We're going back.'

All the way back, Nino never said a word, held tight against Bruno's side. The wind against my face felt as

First Love

cold as if I'd had a fever. In front of the villa, Bruno stopped. He watched me get out, and for a moment I thought he was laughing. Nino raised his head, pushed my arm aside and got out unsteadily. He spat on the ground and went off through the garden, staggering as he walked.

Next day I didn't dare to call for Nino because, when I reached the gate, I saw two of his sisters – the dark ones – sitting in the garden, stretching out their legs in the sunshine. One of them was reading.

I was playing around, towards evening, when Clara rode up on her bicycle and jumped off as she came up to me. 'Where did you boys go, yesterday?' she asked me. 'What did Bruno do to Nino? Where did you go? Nino's had to stay in bed all day. What did you do to Bruno?'

'Where's Bruno?' I said.

Clara gave me a keen look and walked on towards the gate, pushing her bicycle. 'I don't know where Bruno is,' she went on. 'I don't even know him. Still, he must have done something, because Nino won't tell me about it. Did you go to the Robini's?'

'Something went wrong with the car,' I said.

'What were you doing at the Robini's?'

'Nothing. We were learning to drive.'

By now we were inside the garden, but the wicker chairs under the big umbrella were empty. The gravel scrunched under out feet. 'Did you go there to find somebody?' she asked.

'Oh, no.'

Clara said more seriously, 'Nino's in bed. Would you like to come and see him?'

'Oh, no. I'll come and call for him tomorrow. It's late, now,' I said, coming to a halt.

' How's the calf?' Clara asked with a smile.

'What calf?'

Summer Storm

'The one born the other day. Is it yours?'

I nodded in reply. Clara leaned the bicycle against the wall and went on up the steps. 'So long, for now, little calf,' she called to me as she turned away. I noticed how tall she was.

For several days after that Nino did not come out at all. I walked up and down in front of the villa, hoping to catch sight of someone or other. It was the time of year, early in August, when there's nothing much to do in the country; the apples and early plums are finished in July and the grape harvest doesn't start till September. While I was waiting for Nino to come back to me, there seemed no point in joining up with my former friends again, so I wandered aimlessly round the lanes all by myself. Still, it's a good thing to be alone sometimes when you have something on your mind, or when you've just had a glimpse of Clara through the garden railings. Still, the days seemed awfully long.

I remember there were frightful thunderstorms on some of those afternoons and the sky was cold and black, though we had no hail. They terrified my mother and the cattle in the sheds, but I rather liked them because the evenings were cool and next morning there were pools of water, with piles of leaves strewn on the ground. I thought about Clara and her sisters, wondering whether the lightning had frightened them.

At last I saw Nino again, but he hadn't much to say. Once or twice I couldn't help laughing to see how gingerly he sat down on the garden wall. He looked slyly at me, and it seemed as if we'd got back to the old days when we strolled about together with hardly a word. One day he brought along a whole packet of fine cigarettes with arabic printing on the packet. The one I had was scented and made me feel sick. One morning at the river where we swam I saw him strolling casually along with his jacket over

First Love

his shoulder. He sat on the bank and started smoking. Immediately all the other boys swarmed around him and he gave two or three of them a cigarette. He spat in the water and asked lightly: 'Have any of you seen that chauffeur lately, the one from the *Ca' Nere*?'

He discussed it with the fair-haired fellow from the Mulini, the one whose brother was a porter at the station, and decided that, if he didn't come before, Bruno would have to come through the village for the festival of the August Madonna, to load up the flour. Nino remarked calmly: 'That Martino fellow's looking for him, to skin him alive.'

The blacksmith's son remarked that his cigarette tasted of honey, yet it was strong. We four boys strolled home together. The blacksmith's boy already wore long trousers down to his bare ankles, and was always scratching his chest under his shirt. In two or three days Nino was on such good terms that they were giggling and scrapping like old friends.

Then Nino asked me one day: 'Didn't Bruno do anything to you, that time?'

'Who was it sounded the horn?' I retorted.

Nino looked sideways at me as we walked along – and his eyes were really shifty in those days. 'Berto,' he said, 'you're a fool.'

By now there were several afternoons when I did not see him at all. He went about with one of the other boys; they even went fishing, and I knew that once Nino brought along a packet of candied peaches as well as the cigarettes. On that ocasion I told him: 'Take care they don't do you an injury. They only come with you for what you bring them.' But Nino replied that he knew that, too.

On the evening of the bonfire for the Madonna, Nino kept out of sight and his sisters did not come out into the garden to watch the fires dotted all over the hills. It was

307

Summer Storm

the first time I ever spent that festival alone and uneasy. Next day a boy told me that Nino had gone with the others to make a bonfire in the Mulini's field, and when he saw a chance he had pushed the blacksmith's son right into the fire. Now that lad was out to catch Nino and threatening to slaughter him.

Next time I went by the villa, Nino sent the gardener's wife out to call me in. He begged me to go and fetch Bruno for him. The '*Ca' Nere*' was a long way off, but I went there and left word at the garage that Bruno was wanted at the villa. As I went back into the garden again, stones and lumps of earth rained against my back. The blacksmith's son and the other boys were on the watch in case Nino ever came out.

An hour or so later, Bruno arrived, very smart in his rubber Wellingtons and that hideous kerchief of his. I stopped him by the gate for a minute of two, hoping the boys would start pelting us again. Bruno believed the message was about that trip to Acqui. He gave Nino a clout, but Nino only flushed, went over close to him and asked if he'd like to make it up. Bruno seemed in no hurry to reply, and gave a casual look at the end of the garden. Then he burst out laughing and said: 'All right. What d'you want?'

That moment a clod of earth hit Nino on the back. He jumped aside, clutched at Bruno's fist and exclaimed: 'Those louts down there. Let' em have it, Bruno!' When Bruno knew who they were and why they were there, he half-turned to look at them and shouted at us: 'You kids! You're worse than women, you really are! And those fellows down there don't care, because they're all in it together.'

Just then Clara came out, spoke to Bruno and started talking about that trip to Acqui. 'Come over here if you want to see something,' Nino said to me and I went across

First Love

the garden, half-turning to look at Clara who was leaning on the gate, listening to Bruno.

The next moment a shower of stones hit Bruno in the face and Clara screamed. We ran over. Already Bruno had grabbed two of the band, one of them the blacksmith's son, and was kicking them off. I came to a halt by the gate, quivering with excitement and clenching my fists as Clara watched me. If those wretches wanted any more, I was ready. Bruno came back laughing, said good-bye to Clara and gave Nino another box on the ear. We were all a bit worked up.

We had some glorious August days after that and Nino often asked me into the garden when we came back from some excursion or other. (The dog was now tied up at the back of the villa.) Once we sat under the big sunshade and had a picnic of bread and jam. Nino, lounging in a deck chair, told me he always had jam to eat, even in town; this winter he'd take me to fencing class with him and I'd see what fun it was. Another year he'd be going to the sea in July; if I'd like to come too, we'd go in a boat together. We'd have to wear sandals, and before we went there I'd have to be able to swim.

'Aren't your sisters going to get married?' I asked him.

'One's married,' he told me, 'but she's not here. A year or so ago, Clara was going to be married, but they quarrelled.'

'And your mother?' His mother was one of the brunettes whom I had taken for one of his sisters. I couldn't believe it.

'Nothing but women in our house,' Nino said. 'At least if Clara went away . . .'

It was fine to be with Nino like this. He never said anything spiteful to me now. If we went for another run in the car with Bruno round the countryside, there was no quarrelling. Clara sent him cigarettes by us, and he stuffed them in his pocket with a laugh.

The only thing we had to worry about was the blacksmith's son. His hair was still singed and he watched us fiercely, from a distance, his mouth twisted in a snarl.

But one day he suddenly appeared at the church porch as we were passing by, and came over to us. He asked Nino for a cigarette. Nino shrugged his shoulders. Then he said: 'If you give me one, I'll tell you something that'll make you give me a whole packet.'

'Go on, give him one,' I whispered to Nino. 'Then you'll be friends again.'

But Nino hadn't any. The other laughed. 'It doesn't matter. Come round to the Orchard and I'll show you something worth seeing.'

'D'you take us for a couple of fools?' Nino answered.

The blacksmith's son put his yellow teeth close to Nino's ear and whispered breathily. Nino turned pale and jumped back; looked at me, then at him and stammered: 'Word of honour?'

'What is it?' I asked.

'Let's go,' Nino said.

The Orchard was a dairy-farm on the slope of the hill behind the villa. Between the villa and the first cleft in the rocky ground stretched a large vineyard, almost flat, shut in by a reed-bed and a patch of barren land. We reached the reeds and jumped through them, pushing our way between the rows. Silently I picked up a knotted stump in case the blacksmith's son might be leading us into an ambush.

'Seen Bruno today?' I asked suddenly, to give Nino a hint, and the other fellow, too.

Nino's lips were quivering and he made no reply. He and his companion were making their way towards the Red Shack, a deserted hut shut in by trees, at the far end

First Love

of the rows. I had played at soldiers there, a year ago.

'Quiet,' Nina murmured when we were fairly close to it. 'You stop where you are. You, Berto, keep him with you.' Then he went forward and stopped on the bare patch by the entrance. The wooden door was shut. Walking lightly, Nino went round the corner and raised himself on tiptoe by the window.

My companion gave a low laugh. 'D'you want to know what it is?' he said. 'Come and see.'

So we went forward, too, and rejoined Nino, who was supporting himself on the board that held the window-frame and staring through the filthy glass. I tried to look in, too, but saw nothing because my eyes were still dazzled by the sunshine. But something was moving inside, in the darkness.

Then I could make out a white body lying at full length and a man just breaking away from it; a man with a red kerchief. It was Bruno, and the woman was Clara. There was a kind of golden sheen over her bare body. The dusty panes masked the scene in a kind of mist.

'She's white, isn't she?' the smith's son whispered.

Nino jumped back. 'Come away,' he said softly, between his teeth. 'Come away.' I felt his nails digging into my back. The smith's son aimed a kick at him. 'If you don't come, I'll call Bruno,' Nino hissed furiously. The other tore himself away, giving Nino a dirty grin, and backed slowly away over the empty patch of ground. They stared at each other a moment, then Nino ran at him and the other fled.

I ran, too, desperately, still clutching my stump of wood. By now, Nino had caught up with him and brought him to the ground. They were rolling over and over, biting each other. I threw myself into the fight, kicking and hitting out at those patched trousers, that filthy shirt and those yellow teeth, thrashing him as if I thought Clara could see me.

Summer Storm

At last the blacksmith's son started crying and howling, and I broke away. Even Nino was exhausted. We left our enemy lying in a furrow and ran away. I think Nino had the same idea in mind as I had, because, weary and exhausted as he was, he rushed off like a horse, trying to outdistance me. Suddenly I stopped and let him go ahead. That way we avoided saying anything.

From a distance I watched him turn the corner of the villa. I stayed behind by myself, on a heap of gravel by the roadside. Only when I was nearly home did I notice that my neck was covered with blood, but to me it didn't matter; I went in through the farmyard and flung myself down on the hay. It was already dark when I struggled lazily to my feet and rubbed the dried blood from my cheeks – as if the drops had been tears – wondering whether all the sisters were like Clara.

Next day I heard that Nino had a broken arm. I didn't dare to go to the villa for fear they might have seen us. For many nights after that I stayed awake hour after hour, clutching my pillow and screwing up my eyes. One night, when there was a moon, if I hadn't been too scared I would have got up and gone to the hut to see if there were any traces. I tried to go next morning, but a man was working in the vineyard and I didn't dare go there.

Now I hardly ever went outside our own yard, for fear of having stones or lumps of earth thrown at me, but then the other boys called for me to go fishing with them – they needed my net. Since Nino had a broken arm, the smith's son didn't dare say a word. But one day, when we were talking in the hayloft with the blond fellow from Mulini's, he asked me if Nino's sister was fair, too. I felt ashamed afterwards, but on the spur of the moment I couldn't stop myself from talking. Yet my heart was in my mouth as I spoke and suddenly I felt despairing and hopeless, just as when I was a little boy sitting naked on

First Love

a chair in the kitchen, watching the water being poured into my bath. Then I stopped talking, and the blond chap fell silent, too.

At last, one morning I saw Bruno cycling by; he stopped and called to me: 'Have you quarrelled with Nino?' Now he was wearing a black neckerchief and a shirt with pockets. He told me that Nino had asked him, only yesterday, to find me and tell me to come and see him. That story he'd told about falling from a rotten tree hadn't convinced anybody. Those scratches on his face were the work of a boy. 'And if I didn't recognize your hand in it, I'd say a girl made them,' he concluded.

I stared at him incredulously. 'You go and see him,' he went on. 'No need for men to be at loggerheads. Nino wants you. He'll tell you how babies are born.'

'But have you been to see him?' I asked him with some hesitation.

'Sure. We're friends, aren't we? He's in fine form, that lad. A broken arm will set in a couple of weeks, and he wants to come out in the car with me.'

Bruno took out a cigarette, lit it, blew out a puff of smoke and straightened up his bicycle.

'What do his sisters say about it?' I asked.

'Oh, they couldn't care less, one way or the other,' Bruno replied, 'and the mother is worse than any of them. The only one who bothers about him at all is the blonde one.' He rode away down the road and I followed him with my eyes. I felt in a daze, but deep down I was happy.

Loyalty

I

When Amelio was carried home from the hospital and laid on his bed, the others put off going to see him, but Garafolo went right away. Before then he hadn't felt sure about it because, although when Amelio was taken to hospital the filth on him was more petrol than blood, word came back that his sick-bed was soaked with blood, then that he was sleeping, bandaged and encased in plaster like a bag of cement. Garafolo had seen the motor-bike and that was more than enough for him.

But when the verdict was that Amelio would never walk again, Garafolo felt he had to keep him company and give him what help he could. They'd told him at the hospital that when they put a cigarette between Amelio's lips and lit it for him he closed his eyes like a child. So Garafolo went up with his pockets full of cigarettes, but Amelio didn't seem to him at all depressed: instead, he looked him straight in the eyes as if he didn't understand. Garafolo couldn't actually remember what his face had been like before, but now there were dark cavities in the bones of his jaws and temples, showing how he had yelled and clenched his teeth.

Garafolo always found it very hard to get him to talk. One day, as they sat smoking together, Garafolo's face relaxed in a smile that ended in a wry grin.

Loyalty

'What is there to laugh at?'

'I'm laughing about Masino.'

'I don't know about him.'

'He wanted to have a go, too. His father was dismantling a machine, but Masino jumped on it just as it was and started off. The handlebars came away in his hand. Now he's got to pay for it.'

'They're an ignorant lot,' Amelio said. 'They can't even ride a push-bike, and fancy themselves as mechanics.'

It was a chilly morning, with a little light mist. The window was full of sunshine, bright but cold. Amelio lay stretched on a couch in the kitchen, his sheets trailing to the floor. The thick down covering his chest was even lighter than his fair hair. He propped himself up on his elbows and scratched at a nipple.

'It seems to me you're expecting somebody else,' Garafolo remarked, going over to open the window. 'It's fine up here. You can't even hear the street noises.' Turning round again, he saw Amelio's drawn face had dropped back on the pillow, his back still arched on his elbows. His eyes were shut and he was breathing heavily.

Before coming up, Garafolo had waited until Amelio's mother had gone past the tobacconist's shop where he lived. She went by every morning on her way to do her shopping. It didn't do to let her catch you because she never stopped gossiping, and she had such a spiteful way of talking that it was no wonder her husband hardly ever said a word. Poor fellow. His wife had been lovely as a girl. Obviously he had expended all his energy on that tough, well-set-up son of his. Now it must seem to him that he hadn't achieved much. Garafolo thought that, of the two, he was the harder hit, because, if his wife had really been as strong and beautiful as people said, having a fine stalwart son like Amelio cannot have seemed such a miracle to her as it did to her husband.

Summer Storm

The old man was a pitiful sight. A day or two ago he came into the tobacconists's to buy a cheap Tuscan cigar – he no longer came every evening as he used to do – and fumbled carefully through the box with his head bent, mumbling between his teeth through his drooping, yellow-stained moustaches as if he were paralyzed, too.

'What about Natalina?' Garafolo remarked

This time it was Amelio's turn to grin. 'It's cold,' he said.

As Garafolo turned back from the window again he saw that Amelio was laughing, his teeth gleaming as they used to do in the days when he was sunburned. 'Women are like that,' he went on. 'As long as all goes well, it's all right. But I'm not finished yet.'

'Has she come to see you?'

'She's coming this morning.'

Garafolo rose to his feet. 'So that's why you're waiting for her in bed,' he laughed.

Back in the street again, Garafolo felt happy. Actually, Amelio was better off than he was himself, he thought as he walked back along the avenue through the sunshine and the heaps of fallen leaves. This was what it meant to have a girl-friend, being with her and enjoying it.

In front of the tobacconist's he turned to look at the slim legs of a girl hurrying past, and he envied Amelio. He felt the need to talk, and the customers kept him busy as they tapped their coins on the counter and stood fingering their packets of cigarettes or their cigars. Then there was mamma, her mind on postage stamps and salt. Really, the business ran itself. Garafolo was struck with the idea that if the business were more prosperous his father could have offered Amelio a job. Amelio had to get work. Once the authorities had made up their minds to buy him a wheel chair and find him a place on ground level. But could a wheel chair move about behind a counter?

Loyalty

In came Natalina, hatless and perfumed, looking none too pleased to see Garafolo as he ran forward from the back. Natalina seldom came in – she had the little kiosk in front of the factory – but she knew Garafolo was a friend of Amelio and before the accident she had even come in with Amelio sometimes.

'It was cold this morning,' Garafolo remarked. 'Nicer to stay in bed.'

Natalina looked up at him through her hair and gave him her usual half-smile. Garafolo opened the counter and took the little bottles of perfume out of the glass showcase. As they sniffed at them, her own subtle perfume pervaded the air, warmer and more delicate. After the cologne came violet, then the 'Notturno', but Natalina was in a hurry and couldn't find anything that took her fancy.

'I'm so hungry,' she exclaimed at last, 'that I can't see straight. I'll come in another day.'

II

In the evening Garafolo still felt happy and went to the billiard saloon. Masino was there with his head bandaged up, waiting for someone to pour out his troubles to.

'How goes it?' Garafolo said.

'Not too good.'

'Get away! The motorbike had the worst of it.'

'You've got to know how to fall,' said Masino. The proprietor came up with a cup of coffee and joined in the conversation: 'What˙ you've got to know is how to stay upright.'

'If I couldn't play billiards I'd have broken my back,' Masino exclaimed, and stopped. 'Like Amelio,' he added.

All three were silent for a moment. 'Amelio's all right

Summer Storm

now,' Garafolo told them. 'He's already got his mind on the girls.'

'Is that so?' the proprietor went on. 'It doesn't give him any trouble? I'd never have believed it. Well then, he can think himself lucky.'

'What about his legs?' Masino interrupted.

'As if they were withered. The dorsal spine's affected, and the nerves are gone. That's where the controls are.'

The proprietor went on: 'Patience, patience. At least his legs are saved. The bones aren't broken. I'm really glad. He deserves a bit of luck. He needs it. It's a miracle that doesn't happen to everybody. Has he shown them to you?'

Garafolo smiled: 'Not to me.'

Garafolo was thinking that in Amelio's kitchen there must be a lingering trace of that perfume. Perhaps, who knows? when his father and mother came home, Amelio might have moved with Natalina to the big armchair in the bedroom. They behaved like a married couple and Amelio wouldn't miss a chance.

Amelio had always been the boss, with Natalina. You only had to remember how he left her outside when he came in to buy cigarettes, and when he went out she would run and take his arm. If they met anyone in the street, Amelio would stop and chat to them as if he had been on his own. One evening Masino and Garafolo had asked her to dance, and when she was half-way through a dance with Masino she had excused herself and dashed over to the door where Amelio was waiting for her. After that they were always around together and on Sundays went out on the motor-bike.

Several times Garafolo tried to get his father to take on Amelio in the shop, but his father scarcely listened to him and it was his mother who told him plainly, once for all, not to talk such nonsense. 'He couldn't even get up and down the steps.' Yet Garafolo thought something

Loyalty

could have been done if the accident had happened in his own family, or if Amelio's parents had had a tobacco shop.

But accidents never happen right. What sort of life could Amelio have, and his girl, with his wretched old mother quarrelling with everybody? Garafolo didn't go back to see Amelio next day, partly because he didn't want to get too involved, partly because he didn't know whether the old woman had gone out.

He went back one afternoon, but any trace of perfume had vanished long ago: the kitchen smelt of feet and damp. It was raining outside and the room was rather dark. They hadn't got Amelio out of bed that day, and the door was open.

Amelio had several days' growth of beard and was sitting up covered with blankets, leaning back against the cold wall. His first words were to ask for a smoke.

'When are you moving house?' (Everyone knew they wouldn't move before the spring, but it was something to say.)

Amelio lay smoking with his eyes shut. 'We had a lot of fun at the cinema last night,' Garafolo told him. 'There was a man who put his hand in the beam of the projector and made shadows on the screen. Everybody whistled and a woman screamed. Some soldiers carried her out. She looked dead and one of her stockings was torn. She had only fainted, and when she came round we saw she was hunchbacked like a witch. Imagine what people felt like, mixing with hunchbacks!'

'In the dark,' Amelio replied, 'it's all right.'

'Aren't you getting up today?' Garafolo asked.

'How can I?' Amelio said, opening his eyes. 'It needs somebody used to it, to carry me. It's always the same.'

'Where do they put you?'

'Over there in the armchair.'

Summer Storm

'And your father?'

'He manages as best he can. He's spent his last penny to get me electrical treatment, but I'm not exactly a dynamo.'

'What treatment are you having now?'

Amelio shrugged. Garafolo asked if he'd like a game of cards and took a pack from his pocket – they felt damp already. Cautiously he sat down on the sofa and dealt out a hand on the coverlet. 'There should be four of us,' he said cheerfully. Putting down the pack he added: 'How's Natalina?'

Amelio was shuffling his cards and made no reply. They began to play in silence, Amelio's bony hands and face fully concentrated on the game. Garafolo won, but with no stakes there was no taste to it. When they finished the hand no one bothered to count points. Some of the cards slithered to the floor.

Amelio's eyes shone as if he had a fever. Suddenly his lips twisted and he gave a long sigh. 'I'm sick of being shut up in here,' he moaned. To Garafolo he sounded like a child. Stooping to pick up the cards, he stammered: 'Think about building up your strength. You're half-dead. When the weather gets better we'll go out.'

'Meanwhile I'll stay in here like a plant in a cellar and I'll still have this face. I'm strong enough already. It would be better if I weren't.

'Why don't you ever open the window?' Garafolo asked.

'And if it freezes, who'll shut it?'

'There's your mother.'

'All she's afraid of is that someone will bring me a drink. She sniffs the air, and keeps the bottle under lock and key.'

'Want me to bring you some?'

Amelio shrugged his shoulders. 'I'd rather have a smoke. A smoke. Then a drink, if there is any.'

'Yes, but watch yourself,' Garafolo replied as he rose

Loyalty

to his feet. 'Any upset could be harmful.' He spoke with his eyes elsewhere.

'Are you going?' Amelio asked.

'I'll go before the old woman comes back.' He slipped three packets under the pillow.

Amelio allowed him to reach the door, then he called: 'Don't you want to see my legs?'

Garafolo turned and saw him stretched out on the bed, the sheets down by his feet and his shirt pulled up over his stomach. He had to go over. The strong, bony legs were worthy of Amelio. Only his thighs had wasted away and the bones grown twisted. Under the skin his flesh was a dirty white. Amelio slewed round and pointed to them with his hand. 'They look healthy, don't they?' he said.

III

As he walked home, Garafolo slowed to a halt on the pavement. He did not understand why Amelio had made him see his legs. As he tried to recall them he imagined instead what Natalina's body would look like, so white and firm. Thinking about them again, Amelio's legs made him aware, not so much of the paralysis as of the thick forest of hair at the top of his thighs. 'We should go naked, to get used to it,' he thought.

It was strange that a man should affect him more than women. But he calmed himself, realizing that actually he was thinking of Natalina.

Next day in the shop he looked up every time someone came in. Would she come back? A man cannot control his thoughts. But Amelio's father came in, instead, red-eyed and asking for a Tuscan. Then Garafolo remembered it was Sunday.

Summer Storm

'How's Amelio?' he asked affably.

The old man looked him up and down, blowing out his moustaches. Then he replied in a way he'd never done before. 'He should have kicked the bucket.' He paused to wipe his mouth.

Garafolo fell from the clouds, but the old man hadn't finished yet. 'He could have had a smash in the factory and claimed accident compensation, instead of flying round like a fool. Who told him to do over ninety? But when they're twenty they think they know it all . . . Never bother about a man who's over sixty . . .'

He was drunk and he wandered out. Garafolo knew his mother was standing listening at the back of the shop. She had stopped peeling potatoes for a minute and seemed satisfied, somehow. He did not dare to turn round.

He saw Natalina again because he went to her own neighbourhood to look for her. When he saw her tight skirt coming along the pavement he went forward, staring at her, caught her eye and winked. To him it was enough to have seen her again, keeping in mind the secret they shared. Natalina smiled and seemed inclined to stop.

Remembering her hanging on Amelio's arm, Garafolo was not surprised. He leaned against the wall and asked her why she hadn't come back to the tobacco shop. Natalina laughed and answered that she hadn't needed anything. Not wanting to seem like a salesman, Garafolo changed the subject and asked her how ever she managed to spend Sunday by herself. Natalina pouted like a little girl and started to walk on, saying: 'I can't trust myself with anybody: they're all cheeky to me . . .'

'Me, too?' Garafolo teased, turning his face away. Natalina smiled: 'Oh, but we know each other.'

That evening they went to the cinema, in the gallery, and Garafolo felt ashamed of having sought her out to look at her legs. Natalina had such a discreet way of

Loyalty

talking that Garafolo was astounded to remember what saucy glances she bestowed, when clinging to Amelio's arm, upon passers-by who looked at her. He didn't venture to mention it to her, but concluded it all stemmed from the accident. He thought that keeping her company in this way and taking care of her was doing Amelio a favour. Yet when he went to see him next day he didn't tell him anything about it because his mother was in the kitchen. He couldn't even give him the bottle he had in his overcoat pocket, so they smoked a cigarette together and he went away.

Natalina needed looking after. 'Bravo! Bravo!' Masino said one day when he met them walking arm in arm. Garafolo gave him a dirty look and Natalina smiled.

Garafolo quickly got used to Natalina's warm arm and the cautious words they jokingly exchanged. They talked about the old days when Natalina was all for Amelio, but they spoke as if it were something amusing and very far away. Then there had been the accident. The first time Garafolo referred to Amelio's present condition Natalina squeezed his hand, her expression changed, and she said: 'I'm thinking of him all the time. Don't let's talk about it.' Garafolo caught a flash in her glance that was by no means discreet, and he gathered that Amelio didn't count for much. Natalina clung closer to him and said: 'Let's stay together!' So they made a habit of clinging together as they walked, as long as there was nobody about.

So the days went by. There was often snow or fog, and it was nice and warm in the cinema. Garafolo found one well out of the way and Natalina liked it. She said she was sorry for the poor girl she was robbing of Garafolo's company. He laughed and told her there was nobody.

Garafolo himself had no regrets. He was pleased to be going out with a girl like Natalina, who understood everything so quickly and gave him such confidence. Natalina was bright, the fact that she was also experienced was clear from the look on her face whenever that fifth-floor flat where Amelio lived came up in conversation. Garafolo envied Amelio, and that was natural. Natalina's perfume and her gestures enflamed his blood; but still, one shouldn't run after women just because under their clothes they are naked.

'We oughtn't to see each other quite so much,' Natalina told him. 'We'd better just meet at the café. People know you're a friend of Amelio and are quick to think the worst.'

This was fair enough. They decided not to tell Amelio they were seeing one another. Being always by himself and chained to his bed, he could make something out of it.

IV

'I saw Amelio yesterday and we had a game of cards,' he told her one evening. 'I took him a drink. He's an extraordinary fellow. He never mentioned you, not even after he'd had his drink.'

'And why should he talk about me?' Natalina answered with a frown.

Garafolo didn't know what to reply.

'That's what's wrong with all you boys,' Natalina went on. 'Talk, talk, all the time. What's the point of it?'

'But . . . all I said was that Amelio didn't talk . . .'

'He'd stuffed his head down his throat, that's all. You go and do the same.'

Garafolo often wondered how things would have gone if he had been in Amelio's position and Amelio in his. Then he realized it was silly to think on those lines because in his place Amelio would have had Natalina and nothing

Loyalty

would have happened. But he at least could have gone out, since he lived on the ground floor.

Amelio couldn't go out yet. He went to see him one morning when the sun had begun to shine again. Waiting in the avenue for his mother to come down, he debated whether he would ask Amelio if Natalina had those silly fits of bad temper when she was with him, too. 'Poor chap, there's no point in bothering him,' he was saying to himself when the old woman came out, looked spitefully all around her and went off down the street.

He found Amelio in the filthy kitchen, muffled up in a cloak, busily sipping a beaker of milk. They nodded to each other. Having drunk the milk, Amelio nibbled a piece of bread soaked in a plate of cold soup. He chewed it slowly, then put the plate back on the table and sank back on the sofa.

'Anyone been to see you?'

Amelio shrugged, twisted round from the waist and stretched out a hand between the blankets. 'Give me that goose-necked bottle.' He took it in his bony fingers and slid it under the bedclothes. Garafolo went over and looked out of the shining window, turning back as Amelio lifted the covers and cautiously held the bottle out to him. 'Empty it down the washbasin,' he said. 'Who d'you expect to come and see me?' he asked when he had lit a cigarette.

'Doesn't Natalina come here to see you?'

'What are you doing to me, with Natalina?'

Garafolo raised his eyes. 'I went to the cinema with her once . . . She complains of being lonely. Who told you about it?'

Amelio laughed. 'Natalina wouldn't stay lonely long even if she was tied up. You just keep your eye on the tobacco shop.' Garafolo stood twisting his cigarette as Amelio calmly straightened the bedclothes. The washbasin in the corner gurgled as it emptied.

Summer Storm

'Listen Garafolo,' Amelio cried suddenly, 'I haven't been out of the house for three months. My father can't manage it, and my mother says it's too much trouble. It's up to you. If you don't get hold of a girl for me I'm as good as dead. Don't bring me any more drink. Use the money to hire one for me. Bring her here when there's nobody about.' He raised his voice as Garafolo gave a smile of blank amazement. '. . . And tell her I'm a cripple so that she won't make a fuss. And pick a slim one, or she'll crush me. Understand?'

A question trembled on Garafolo's lips but he didn't voice it. He fumbled his cigarette for a minute or two, then threw away the stub and said calmly: 'Any woman?'

'As long as she's not too fat, but not too skinny, either.'

'It depends on who I can find. What time?'

'This time tomorrow morning.'

'If I've found her by then. Shall I go now?'

'On your way.'

Natalina saw him by the doorway at midday and hurried away from a laughing group of her friends to run over to him. Once round the corner, Garafolo began: 'Is it true you haven't been with Amelio for three months?'

Natalina halted, clenched her fist and said quietly: 'Did you want me to go with him?'

Since it was Saturday there was no need to hurry. Strolling through the deserted back streets Natalina told him everything, without reproaching him for having talked with Amelio. 'At first I loved him very much, and you know it,' she said, looking straight in front of her. 'I told you so quite sincerely. I always went to see him at the hospital, though it was his own fault he was there. But afterwards . . .' and her mouth twisted with distaste, '. . . afterwards I just couldn't keep it up any longer. It's as if

Loyalty

his legs were of stone. Could you love a woman with legs like stone? I dream of them at night and they make me shudder.'

'Yet he's a man like everyone else,' Garafolo remarked, for something to say.

'What does that matter?' and Natalina gave him a reproachful look. 'That isn't all a girl wants, and I told him so.'

'You told him that?'

'Yes.'

They walked about till one o'clock, when Natalina smilingly lifted Garafolo's hand from around her waist. He did not detain her, thinking about the woman he had to take to Amelio. They arranged that she would call for him at the shop after supper and they parted with a kiss by a street-door bathed in sunshine.

Natalina had not told him so, but on his way home Garafolo suspected that Amelio might have treated her badly, too. Still, in the afternoon he went on that errand. He felt a sense of fastidious detachment at setting foot in that house again, now he knew that with Natalina it was only a question of time. He might even marry her. Rather breathlessly he asked for a word with the proprietress. She stood by the door of a little cubicle and listened to him without batting an eyelid. 'In the morning? At what time?' she enquired. In a side mirror, Garafolo caught a fleeting glimpse of a naked girl. 'We'd better settle terms at once,' the proprietress continued. 'It's the only way with young fellows like you. It'll be at least a hundred *lire*.'

'A hundred *lire* . . . ?'

During the afternoon Garafolo thought it over and decided he had better find a streetwalker whose price might be more within reach of Amelio's purse. There was the future to consider, too. But it was no good looking for one until after dark.

Summer Storm

Garafolo spent the evening serving at the counter, somewhat absentmindedly because he was thinking too much about Natalina's legs. If it came to the worst, a girl like that was worth the bother of marrying. If it hadn't been for that crash, Amelio would certainly have married her.

After supper they met again and went for a walk. This time Natalina no longer tried to hide, and Garafolo had to manoeuvre to get her into a dark alley.

'Silly boy,' she said. 'We've got plenty of time.' They kissed and clung together. Then they went dancing and Garafolo made sure she danced with nobody but him. Natalina looked at him as they danced, linked so closely they seemed one body.

He left her at the door. There was a moon, and as he kissed her Garafolo said in a low voice: 'I'm marrying you. Then Amelio can't say anything.'

'What d'you imagine he could say?' Natalina murmured, looking into his eyes.

Then Garafolo crossed the city as far as a central avenue where he had once been stopped by an old woman and a young man who were quarrelling. It was cold and he stood there tired to death, seeing nobody; perhaps the bright moonlight had driven them away. He turned into a side street and just past the first doorway he heard a voice inviting him. In the shadow, Garafolo stared at a pale face that seemed all eyes and mouth.

The woman listened impatiently to what he had to say, then took him by the arm. 'And don't you want me yourself?' she asked hoarsely.

Garafolo shook his head. 'You haven't any illness, I take it?'

'Just try me! Go on!'

They made an appointment for eleven in the morning. Still clinging to his arm, the woman asked for a cigarette.

Loyalty

Garafolo lit it for her and, pleased that he'd managed to avoid getting involved himself, he went on his way thinking about Natalina.

The Beggars

Even as a boy, Geri never had any sympathy for beggars who appeared on the doorstep, decently dressed – in winter wearing an overcoat – and asked in all seriousness for charity, like a man who has business to see to and makes it plain he has no time to waste. Geri had always felt an underlying antipathy towards them, as though they were of a different race, and if he hadn't been rather afraid of them he would have slammed the door in their gaunt, vaguely threatening faces, as his mother had always told him to do. Instead, he didn't instantly catch on when he answered a knock, and then realized with alarm that a beggar stood there, mumbling some demand from under his hat. With a flushed face he would stammer that there was nobody at home and would quickly shut the door, avoiding meeting those eyes. Then he would stand close behind the door as if rooted to the spot, holding his breath in the dark and staying there for several minutes, his heart beating wildly, trying to hear the breathing of the man standing outside, longing in an agony of shame and fear for the sound of his retreating footsteps. But he was glad he hadn't given the man anything, glad to have put the door between himself and that tidily-dressed adult who asked for alms as bluntly as if he had a right to expect them.

The Beggars

On one occasion, even, when Geri had run to the door to answer the bell, he found himself confronted by a woman wearing a hat and a fur round her neck, who smiled and asked if he had anything to give her. Geri ran to call his mother, who shut the door almost as soon as she reached it. For some time afterwards Geri listened to his mother talking about unheard-of impudence. After that, Geri believed that beggars who were decently dressed had wives and consequently homes, dining-rooms, working hours and days off. In short they had a job and earned wages. This made him even more bitter about them.

On the other hand, the poor he felt really sorry for, and even envied a little, were ragged street urchins, old men with the tearful look of drunkards, women carrying a baby that looked like a dirty bundle of clothes, but especially buskers who played and played on street corners, never saying a word or looking around them, the poor who never asked for anything and looked at the ground if anyone stopped by them.

One day, when he was old enough to go out by himself, Geri found an old man sitting on the bottom step of the porch by a picture he had drawn on the pavement with coloured chalks. Half hidden by the pillar, Geri studied the picture at some length and decided it was of St Joseph carrying a lily. On other days when Geri came home there would be a different picture and the old man sitting in a patch of sunshine chewing pumpkin seeds. But one day when Geri came earlier than usual the old man was kneeling by the pillar, praying fervently with bent head and his arms crossed over his breast, while passers-by stood round gossiping. Then the old man beat his breast and said a few words in a sing-song voice that made everybody laugh, but Geri did not understand what they meant. Eventually the old man picked up his chalks again and began drawing a Crucifixion. Geri never saw anyone throw him a coin.

Summer Storm

Geri was thinking about this one morning when he felt reluctant to get out of bed and through the uncurtained window the dawn was casting a dim, misty light into all the dark corners.

Suddenly he thought he heard a noise that made the door rattle, a rumble and a hoarse voice from the stairs, a thud and the sound of whispering, as if there was someone in the doorway, shuffling his feet and waiting.

Into Geri's mind flashed the memory of that timid little boy behind the front door, standing rooted to the spot with madly-beating heart and straining his ears in the darkness, as tense and stiff with terror as he was now, lying there clutching his pillow. He could see, too, that grown man muffled in a cloak, grim-eyed and haggard, standing with his fists clenched in his pockets outside the door Geri had slammed in his face. Two human beings, each hating the other whom he could not see, each listening to the other's breathing.

Geri rolled over in bed, hiding his face in the pillow and trying to catch the faintest sound from the emptiness outside. For a minute the house was quiet and still, then a distant noise from the street broke the vast silence. Gradually the warmth of his bed soothed the throbbing in his veins. The chill of the room cooled his neck and temples and he dreamed he was lying stretched out in the sunshine and the distant sounds were the noises from the swimming pool.

Years later, Geri made friends with a boy called Achille. They would stroll round the streets together for an hour or so, and when they got home each would say he had been studying at the other's house. Without Achille, the most Geri would have done was to dash into the nearest cinema, anxiously asking some soldier or other member of the audience every now and then what the time was. But Achille preferred mixing with people in the streets, pushing

The Beggars

through the crowds and turning now and then to exchange a word or two with his friend. They particularly enjoyed exploring fresh places on the spur of the moment, but Geri soon realized that Achille knew his way about, had been waiting for an opportunity and knew the places to visit.

One day he went into a café frequented by prostitutes; another time it was to hang around outside the prison, eating monkey nuts, on the offchance that some prisoner might be brought along in handcuffs; another time he would wait about outside a large tailoring shop until the seamstresses came out, in the hope of picking up something worthwhile.

So as to have his hands free, Achille would leave his books in the caretaker's office at school and pick them up in the morning. Geri admired him very much, but preferred to keep his own books with him, even though he had lost all desire to work at home in the evenings.

The best thing about these excursions was when they explored unfamiliar, out-of-the-way streets. Geri did not like crowds; all those preoccupied, anxious eyes, those trampling feet rushing hither and thither, terrified him and made him remember that he ought to be working quietly at his own little table at home and waiting for supper. But he enjoyed their walks back along the silent pavements when the cold air darkened with the dusk, the sky grew clearer and any minute the street lamps might light up one after the other.

Already Achille had tried to get Geri to go to a brothel with him, but Geri hadn't yet made up his mind. In any case, Achille had never yet been to one seriously. Still, he knew what to do, how much to pay and what to say to the doorkeeper, but once when Geri asked him about it again he muddled up the names and details so that it was obvious he was just making it up. However, Geri did not fling that accusation in his face because Achille talked so frankly and with such conviction that it was fun just to let him talk, whereas to humiliate him would have made them both unhappy.

Instead he protested: 'I'd like to know more about women, first. Let's get off with some housemaid or a seamstress, and then, when we've got more experience, we'll go there.'

He was talking just to gain time, because once, when Achille had tried to make up to a nursemaid in the park, he had only made a fool of himself. Geri had followed him a few yards behind, trembling with shame, and felt glad when the girl, a plump, dark-haired wench, had laughed in Achille's face as he spoke to her and gone away taking the baby with her. Achille followed her a short way and Geri could not see his face, but he heard his hoarse voice saying furiously:

'Let her go, you fool!'

Meanwhile spring had come again. Geri was amazed that never in his life before had he noticed how marvellous it was to be out of doors, to look around and take deep breaths of the warm air. It was not only the air and the fine weather, for even in the winter, in spite of fog or mud, he had enjoyed walking. Now, out of ill-humour, he would leave Achille on the doorstep, or they would often walk to and fro between their homes until supper time. 'It's probably because this is the first year when I've been able to go out and live as I like,' he thought to himself as he went off to school with his books under his arm. By now the cold weather had gone, the leaves were coming out and it was light until late. If only Achille wouldn't keep murmuring, whenever he passed a pretty girl: 'How I'd like to kiss you when you're naked.' Geri found it distasteful. There shouldn't be any need to say things like that to prove oneself a man ...

Evocation

I can remember the mass of poppies I could see from the window of the room. They certainly were no dream. There never are such bright colours in dreams. Besides, I have observed that one never remembers any inessential details of a dream. But those poppies covering the meadow-bank outside the window served no purpose at all: they were real. Indeed, I remember thinking: 'If this were all a dream, someone would suddenly appear in the midst of those poppies or something would happen there, because in dreams everything is significant.' Instead, when I managed to lean out of the window now and then, I realized nothing at all could happen there. Everything around, even the grass, made me feel calm and confident.

This familiar feeling comes over me whenever I am in an enclosed space and can look out at the sky, the trees and flowers, the open air. It is as if I'd doubted for a moment that these things still existed, and my glance had reassured me. There's nothing extraordinary about that, nor about the habit I adopted as a consequence, of seeking out some shut-in place so that I could enjoy that moment of liberation when I put my nose outside. Hence I am a great frequenter of cafés and taverns, and like to sit in a dark corner with my back to the window.

But it isn't a habit of mine to get drunk, still less to

Summer Storm

drop off to sleep at one of those little tables. At such times, any habit I have generally goes by the board, and sometimes I would find myself late at night wandering through some unfamiliar street in a distant suburb. Then I would go on walking, making up my mind to be still on my feet to watch the dawn break. Any pretext was enough to keep me walking, preferably in out-of-the-way places.

At certain times of day I would sit in some corner or other, sipping a drink and feeling restless. When I think back on it today, it seems strange that I remember my restlessness, really an indication that I could no longer live alone – and as a matter of fact for part of the day or night I no longer did live alone – as a craving for solitude; as if I was surfeited, almost sickened, by the only human presence I then desired. But that's how it is, they say. In short, I was in love; and I enjoyed my love whenever I could. I would leave her room at night, late in the morning or half-way through the afternoon, at the most ridiculous times, feeling sated and content. I would walk through all sorts of streets as far as my legs would carry me, thinking eagerly of our next meeting; sometimes half asleep, sometimes fresh and full of curiosity. I slept at any time of day, and every time I woke I thought it was morning. So, for me, the whole day was one long morning. Cafés and taverns were like stages in a long, never-ending journey.

That time when I noticed the poppies I was sitting at a large table below a window, leaning on my elbows. I knew there was a field outside, but I didn't bother to look at it. My eyes were still tired from the glaring sunshine I had endured; I felt exhausted and the shadows around me were filled with the buzz of mosquitoes. There was no other sound, for the room was deserted. The whole place seemed deserted, and as far as I knew I had made no move to order anything. Perhaps I was enjoying the fact that I seemed to have been forgotten, and I had no recollection of

Evocation

finding my way from the main entrance to this remote room. If, indeed, there was an entrance hall. I remember I strained my ears, hoping to catch the sound of a distant tram, and it was the absence of any such sound that suddenly made me think that I was lost, and a suspicion – my first – that, if I heard nothing, it was because there was nothing to hear, and that perhaps something had started around me that would end heaven knows how.

But it was precisely this sensation, that should have alerted me, which gave me instead a feeling of confidence, a conviction that nothing could happen to me because the man sitting at the other side of the table was a friend of mine.

This is the point. Nothing had happened since I had realized I was alone in that tavern room and had made no move to call the landlord, but had, instead, tried to fill the silence with the sound of a distant tram. And now I was calmly accepting the presence of a stranger. Yet I knew who he was, or, rather, not who he was, but something a great deal more : his feelings towards me, his usual gestures, his way of talking and of watching me. I don't think I felt any curiosity about my neighbour, because one doesn't feel curious about a man who appears with the same inevitability as one's own reflection in a mirror. This wasn't the reason for my restlessness. I accepted his company as perfectly natural; I was even glad of it. It was nothing like, for example, the uncertainty that sometimes came over me when I roused myself from a girl lying beside me and wondered for a moment what she was really like, what she meant to me. I repeat, this companion did not worry me at all : there was between us a confidence as though we shared a vast mass of memories that I couldn't fathom just then, but which were real and shared by both of us.

I said to myself : 'It's fine to be here with him. But it's better not to look into such things too closely, nor to get

Summer Storm

the idea that there's any significance in the fact that we can't hear the tram. Perhaps I can hear it without noticing it.

I should make it plain, once and for all, that ever since I was a boy, whenever I awoke from a dream, I have never been able to dismiss it and forget it, but have always gone over it again in my mind, trying to fathom its secret. It isn't easy. Still, I have clarified one thing, at least: a dream evolves, not like something really happening, but like something being told to you. For instance, you dream you are running and you lose your shoe. You think this is mere chance, but it is not. You have strange adventures and completely forget your bare foot, when suddenly you come to a table richly spread, and catch your breath, for there in the middle of it is your shoe. It has lost its laces, and you know you should on no account suck them. The operator projecting this dream – you yourself, you will say – has made you lose your shoe, kept it in reserve as a good storyteller does an intriguing detail, and served it up to you again when you have forgotten all about it.

Purely out of interest in this subject, I have for many years been so engrossed in it that now I often manage to go along with a dream and concentrate my attention on the way it works out, and by observing its minutest details try to discover what its inner meaning may be. I am still hoping – dreading – to catch that operator out in a mistake.

I admit I may have been dreaming that afternoon, but still all this needs some explanation. There was, for example, my uneasiness because I couldn't hear the trams. 'No matter why that is,' I told myself, 'it is silly to bother about it now. Much more important to observe what actually is happening. If something has really started, the first thing is to dream right through to the end. Then we'll see.'

But there was the window, and beyond it those scarlet poppies, the grass around them growing paler in the after-

Evocation

noon light. They had nothing to do with me or my mental turmoil, yet they interested me intensely because they were so brightly coloured, and so useless. To them it meant nothing at all if the trams stopped running; there they stood like shining spirits on that meadow-bank, gently nodding their heads. I remember looking quickly away because I realized at that moment they lived in a different world and I was the only one there to know it.

My neighbour sat in silence. There seemed a tacit understanding between us that we would hear nothing outside that closed room because, if we did, one of us would have to disappear. We were both well aware of it, and though my shoulders, my hands, the very expression on my face, were all sagging with drowsiness, I knew beyond question that he was, so to speak, the operator. Yet there he sat, his jacket bunched up round his waist, resting his bare elbow on the table and his jaw on his fist, absorbed in watching me.

I laughed as the thought struck me, but I could not tear my eyes away from the knuckles on his fist. They stood out in sharp relief, not only because they were so thin and strong, but because, somehow or other, they seemed connected with my present sense of confidence and my past timidity. I began to wonder why I felt like that, and I tried to surmount the barrier of those mysterious memories we had in common. I think, indeed I'm absolutely certain, that if his eyes had not looked so friendly I should have been frightened, or at least embarrassed. Any idea that the young man – suddenly I knew his name was Masino – might also feel embarrassed was utterly foreign to my nature. Never in my life, I think, has any man standing before me had any need to fear me, whatever the circumstances, though experience has taught me that people often do. However, I began to understand, or perhaps to imagine, what the basis of my confidence might be. We

Summer Storm

must have talked together a little earlier, for just as I knew his name, I knew the timbre of his voice, the way he mouthed Italian words with a slow, painful pronunciation, expressing himself like a man more used to talking in dialect, but trying to adapt himself to his questioner.

'Let's see your other hand,' I blurted out impulsively.

Masino calmly stretched out his free arm towards me, still resting his elbow and the back of his closed fist on the table. His expression did not change. He might have been suggesting a game to me, or a riddle. Quickly, eagerly, I put out my hands, took hold of his fingers and tried to force open his fist. I recall that I even half-rose from my seat. Masino, his other fist still supporting his face, did not give way. Then I pretended it was a matter of no importance and tried to look unconcerned. Masino smiled against his knuckles.

'Anything to laugh about?' I said.

Masino opened his fist. The palm was lean and dark, the fingertips roughened and hard. I scarcely looked at it, wondering what was the reason for that contest and whether I should be ashamed of it for long.

'Are you satisfied to forget all about it?' Masino asked, his voice hesitant.

'You can take it I shall go on thinking of it, and deeply,' I replied. 'Why shouldn't I think about it? Humiliations remain impressed on me more deeply than satisfactions. I'm like a boy.'

'If you listen to me, you won't think of it again,' Masino said. 'There's so little time. You should be quick and gather all the satisfaction you can, because your moment of wakefulness is over.'

I stared down at the table, muttering to myself as I often do when I'm alone. As a matter of fact, I was extraordinarily moved. I kept my eyes down, feeling empty and hopeless, so much so that tears ran down my cheeks like

Evocation

blood, and I said: 'This is my blood ebbing away. You shouldn't do things like this unless you're alone, you fool.' But I knew that the more I abased myself, the more quickly I should get over it. Choosing my moment, I said: 'That's enough. It was nothing. It doesn't matter to me.'

'Then you're convinced?' Masino asked, calm as ever.

'No,' I answered dryly. 'You don't stand on ceremony with me, nor I with you.' I spoke in fear of making things worse, but I couldn't avoid it. It was like throwing a stone into a well, hearing the reverberation and feeling the chill of the water in my very bones, but not daring to lean over the edge. Masino might even change his expression and become my enemy. Out of the tail of my eye I watched the window, half expecting that somebody would come along and fill the empty space. But I knew there was no one outside.

When I looked at Masino again, I was smiling as he had done earlier, with my hand to my mouth. 'D'you agree?' I asked. The look in Masino's eyes told me to go on talking. 'I've always been a bad lot, but more important than that, a very active boy. Some nights I didn't want to go to bed, because it seemed such a waste of time. I'd have liked to be awake all the time, out breathing the air and looking around. Looking, always looking. That would have been enough for me. It thrilled me just to go out of doors and look at the weather, the people going by; to get the smell of the street. It was fun to think it over afterwards, too. There are humiliations, too, but one must have patience.'

'To be awake in real earnest is a very different thing,' said Masino in a hard voice.

'Let me talk. It's up to me to say what I'm thinking, day and night. It will be a humiliation, the worst of all, but one must be able to tell it.'

Summer Storm

There followed a moment that, even today, I cannot connect with the rest. It seemed to me that I grinned at him and sank back exhausted into my chair, but every now and then I raised my head and threw Masino a furtive glance. He listened to me with such seriousness that for him the window might not have been there at all. But I could give it a quick look in passing, and that gave me a secret feeling of superiority. Careful to avoid being noticed, I tried to hold his eyes with mine so that he shouldn't look out. Meanwhile I thought and thought. Masino had lifted his hand from his chin and was sitting leaning forward over the table with his arms crossed.

'It's all right to talk about it,' I went on. 'I've talked about other things. If you like, I'll tell you here and now. That's all I do, day and night.'

We smiled at each other and sat there bent over the table like a couple of card players. My irritation had vanished. I felt dazed. We both wanted to talk at once.

'I tried it once,' Masino said, 'but I'm not capable. You need to know the reason for the shoe.'

'Try it again now,' I urged him.

He shrugged and made a face. 'What I know is true,' he said. 'I just can't. The silly fools might come around here and stop us talking. There are girls, too.' Masino laughed softly, nervously opening and closing his fingers on the table. 'One has to think it over and understand the why and wherefore. One can do a thing, but talking about it is something different.'

'That's true,' I said. 'No one has ever told me about what I do myself. It's not possible.'

The same idea struck us both. I read it in his eyes. He looked at me, his head bent. 'It takes two,' I said. 'Like making love.'

But even as I spoke I felt I was in a void. This was not what Masino expected from me. He was thinking of some-

Evocation

thing quite different. 'That's even better,' I cried, 'like coming into the world a second time.'

I saw Masino's face turned back to the window and again I felt the old sense of shock. 'Haven't you ever really woken up?' he asked in a low tone.

The glow of those poppies was in my eyes. I could see them vividly within myself, as if that were the only way of separating them from everything around them and hiding them from him. I almost cried out in my eagerness. My whole life was bound up with those poppies.

'What does it matter?' I said hastily. 'I'm not afraid of waking up. I'm thinking of it day and night.'

Masino replied, still turned towards the window, 'Thinking about it is no good. Waking up is worse than being afraid. From that moment there's nothing more you can do.'

'I know that,' I answered softly. By now Masino had turned away from the poppies and come back to his old place, staring at the table. My heart was heavy, for I knew now that nothing would happen; what could have happened had already come about; everything was contained in that room and that window. I heard as it were the silence throbbing in the gloom and something deep in my brain was murmuring: 'It doesn't matter . . . doesn't matter . . .'

Now I looked at Masino with pity, almost with sorrow, trying to escape his notice. Everything about him filled me with pity, and I felt that irresistible urge which pity for ourselves always induces, an instinctive desire to run away and weep, except for the dull rancour we feel against ourselves. I looked at his rough, sorrowful hands on the table.

'You don't want to know anything, Masino?' I asked him abruptly.

'No, nothing,' he replied, and his voice faded away in the distance, as if he were already outside the wall.

I don't know how long I stayed sitting there, resting my

Summer Storm

head against the wooden shutter where I had been when I first saw the poppies. I knew evening was approaching, but I was comfortable enough and did not move.

When the noise of the tram reached me, I gave myself a shake, though I was vaguely aware I had already been hearing it for some time. The dusk now filled the window, though it couldn't yet have hidden the meadow, but I didn't think of it at that moment and didn't look. Instead, at the back of the room, I saw a little door standing ajar and leading to the open air. I had no idea how long I had been there and felt apprehensive that the owners might burst in and complain that I had stayed so long without their knowledge. It was not merely apprehension, it was terror. I slipped through the little door and after crossing the meadow with a wildly beating heart, I fled around the corner of a factory building.

The Family

At one time we used to go boating as soon as summer came. We would hire a boat at the bridge, pile into it in our shorts or bathing trunks and go up-stream to the woods for the whole afternoon. In our younger days we often took a few girls with us for company, but as it turned out, we soon felt uneasy about that and one year we stopped doing it because we had come to realize that certain things shouldn't be done in the open air. Even now, when Corradino remembered those days, he felt ashamed.

By the time we were all getting on for thirty, Corradino had forgotten all about a certain experience he had had, or believed it had made no difference to him. One day he thought of going on the river again and looked over the boats from the arch of the bridge, but the idea of rowing by himself didn't appeal to him, so he got on his bicycle again and rode back home. Next day, however, he walked up to the woods through a long, dusty cart-track, then along narrow, twisting paths until he came to the bank of the Sangone, much higher up-stream than he had ever been by boat. There he discovered a clear, quiet pool ringed by thickets and reeds. He liked the place, stripped off his shorts and had a swim, then lay at full length in the sunshine, smoking and gazing at the sky above the willows. He spent an unforgettable afternoon and soon went there

Summer Storm

again, this time on his bicycle. This was last July, and he was soon going regularly. Being alone like this might have proved boring, but Corradino, who was beginning to understand himself better, took care to time his visits for the late afternoon, an hour or two before sunset. Then he knew he had to start back fairly soon.

All the same, once he reached that stretch of shingle he always did the same things: lay in the sun for a while, swam across the water, came out dripping and then got warm again by swinging from a horizontal branch of a tree, limbering up with gymnastic exercises. After that, refreshed in body and lungs, he would enjoy his usual cigarette. In the ordinary way, as we all knew, Corradino hated being alone. He lived in a furnished room, but was always in and out of our homes and dreaded nothing more than being left to spend an evening on his own. To the last minute he always hoped someone would ring or drop in to see him, but though that sort of thing can sometimes happen, even in the height of summer when the town is half empty, nobody turned up that July and Corradino was left alone. Why he didn't bring his holidays forward and join some of his friends at the seaside, he never told me. He lived and worked between boredom and expectancy, putting off any decisions from one day to the next. The only constant point in his daily round was his escape, every afternoon, to that pool among the willows. He soon got a good tan, and for him this gave a special significance to those days in the open air, just as, with certain other living creatures, their moulting period is linked with their seasonal changes.

Corradino had been a sickly child, but had cured himself by 'sweating it out' and getting brown all over in the blazing sunshine on those boating expeditions of ours. He was convinced that unless a body is well tanned before winter comes, it is in no condition to face the risk of illness. But his 'moulting period' that year, he often told me, seemed

The Family

to mean more than just hygiene; it was a retreat, a withdrawal inside himself, an active preparation for some event he felt was about to happen. He was always getting crazy ideas like that.

That year, Corradino was still telephoning a girl now and then – her name was Ernesta – and taking her to his room in the evening. She would come running – she was always available – and would leave him exhausted and out of temper. He had first met her twenty years ago; since then they had seen each other very occasionally and more recent meetings had always ended in their spending the night together. Since Corradino had started living alone he had phoned Ernesta more often. She was always willing and now had become his regular girl-friend. In the early days Corradino would take her out for walks, to a café or a theatre, but whenever he phoned her now it was understood she would come straight to his place. Ernesta, a haberdasher's daughter, would naturally have been glad to marry him. She was a simple-minded girl, incapable of running her life sensibly and finding herself a husband, as he told her she should. She preferred to depend on Corradino's recurring need of her and she would look meekly up at him with her great gentle eyes. She irritated Corradino and he was always in a bad humour the day after he had been with her.

Early in July he made up his mind to drop her. His lonely hours among the willows gave him a kind of pride, a need for creating an empty space around himself, such as he had not felt since his adolescent years. He told me : 'Instead of growing older, I'm becoming a boy again.' But now that almost everyone was away, work was so slack and the sultry weather so tedious, time hung heavily on his hands and he felt an inclination to seek that pleasure once more, unexciting though it was.

Ernesta came as usual, obviously grateful to him for

Summer Storm

remembering her. Inevitably she noticed how tanned he was getting, and Corradino gave her some evasive explanation, but when he took her out to have an ice – Ernesta adored ice cream as if she were still a child, and this annoyed Corradino, too – the conversation reverted to the subject of sunburn, and with her usual lack of tact Ernesta cried: 'Nobody ever takes me sunbathing.'

'Why don't you go by yourself?'

Ernesta smiled: 'It wouldn't be the same. I mean sunbathing in real earnest.'

Corradino looked sideways at her, doing his best to smile. 'It's not as serious as all that,' he said. 'You've amused yourself that way ever since you were a little girl.'

'I'm not a child any longer,' she snapped.

In his heart Corradino decided: 'This is the very last time.' He ruffled her hair with the tip of his finger and smiled, not looking at her. Like a dog being petted, Ernesta rubbed her cheek against his hand. Carradino said nothing else all that evening, not even while they stood waiting for a tram. Pointedly he stayed silent, and Ernesta understood. 'You're tired,' she said as they parted. 'So long,' Corradino replied, walking away.

Each day has its tomorrow, and Corradino went back to his willow trees. Lying naked in the sunshine, still in a bad mood, he smoked his usual cigarette and looked around. The same stones protruded from the muddy river bank; the same silence reigned; the same leaves hung motionless on the trees. The thought struck him that in this quiet corner nothing changed from one day to another. The same trees fringed the patch of sky; thoughts and feelings were just as changeless. Probably he had seen these same things and woven the same fancies round them in the old days when he used to row up to the woods: the water slipping by, the willow trees, a bird flying past, the steady glow of the

The Family

sun on his skin. 'What is new,' he thought, 'is that as I lie turning brown in the sun I no longer feel a need for company.'

In summer, and in the open air, ill-humour is no more than lassitude, and the bright sunshine lifts it from the mind. Corradino now had time to realize – so he told us that evening – that breaking away from Ernesta, like so many other irritating things in the past, had strengthened his old longing for solitude. It disturbed him that everything so persistently told him the same thing. As he cycled home through the empty streets at midday it struck him that the whole town was deserted.

I had several short holidays that year, but Corradino, a sedentary man, wouldn't hear of coming with me. 'You can get just as sunburned in the mountains,' I told him that evening when we talked it over, 'and if, as I believe, this craze of yours is only escapism, we'll find some distraction for you there.' But Corradino simply repeated his usual dictum about letting things take their course. He stared down at the carpet between my wife and myself with such a disconsolate air that we both smiled. The way he was frowning, his teeth and eyes white against his summer-darkened skin, told us something very different. My wife said, later, that he had something on his mind, getting married, for instance. But Corradino, who had so often talked distastefully of his contact with Ernesta, said no more about it that evening. Instead, he said something different and far more strange: that if he did decide to marry, he would do it only when he was deeply bronzed by the sun. 'Why?' my wife asked. 'Because it changes me. I feel a different man.'

'What a dandy you are!' she exclaimed.

When he left us, he hadn't yet met Cate. As usual, he didn't say a word to me about it. He talked at great length, with a curious exaltation, of the various urges that came

Summer Storm

over him; 'Crazes for tranquillity,' he called them, his longing for something to happen to change his life without robbing him of a single one of his old habits. 'What I'd really like,' he told me, 'is to become a different man without being conscious of it.'

'That's natural enough,' I answered. 'You're a man of thirty, now. The years go by for all of us.'

Corradino seemed at a loss for a reply. Then he suddenly increased the pressure and started to explain that he was not concerned to 'regularize' himself, move up the scale, gain a better position at the paper where he worked. 'You'd think of things like that if you were in love,' he explained, 'but I don't. They don't mean a thing to me. I'm more concerned with the past than the future. But I wish I were some other man.'

He couldn't seem to explain himself in more detail, not even when he was with Giusti, our friend, the only man still in Turin who could keep him company on his own level. True, Giusti was a caustic fellow, not the type best suited to act as a father confessor, but the two men understood one another and probably Corradino would have confided in him in the end if another man hadn't come up to join us. Still, in the few evenings still remaining before August, Giusti noticed that Corradino had something on his mind. It was not so much what he said as the uneasy glances he would shoot at the doorway, if they were in the café, or at the dark spaces between the trees if they were sitting in the open air.

'You don't seem to be enjoying the summer,' he remarked to him one evening. 'The heat doesn't suit everybody. If it weren't so obvious that you've got a woman in mind, I'd advise a change of air.' The other remained silent, and Giusti went on. 'I'm sure it would be helpful.'

But Corradino was ready with a reply, jokingly congratulating his friend on his powers of observation, but his

The Family

companion noticed a hint of annoyance in Corradino's casual tone.

'All right. I won't insist,' Giusti went on, noting on Corradino's lips a hint of scorn for the missed opportunity. By nature, Corradino was the sort of man who likes his friends to beg and pray him for information, as women do.

'In my opinion it's just nervousness,' Giusti said to him once when they were discussing it. 'Falling in love is fine; we all agree on that; but the man's got to be the boss. That's only right and proper! Otherwise it can't last! It isn't natural! Anything else is like giving a woman a knife by the handle.'

'It mightn't be fine at all,' Corradino countered. 'But if things go wrong, then what you say may be true enough.'

'You make me laugh,' Giusti replied. 'When a woman falls for anybody, she has already made her own calculations. It's just nervousness, I tell you.'

Corradino was silent for a moment, then he remarked that it was a question of habit. Shyness might be an advantage if the woman is offering some resistance. A timid man scores then, because nothing happens.'

'So the lady is resisting?' Giusti laughed.

'And nothing happens,' Corradino said.

'Does that state of affairs please you?'

'As a matter of fact, it does.'

During August, Giusti joined us in the mountains, leaving Corradino all alone with no company whatever, as he told us in response to our enquiry about him.

'He's mad, that fellow,' Giusti exclaimed. 'You'll see! This year he'll spend the whole summer in Turin. At least he could go to the seaside.'

Corradino had already told us he might not go to sea that year, which very much intrigued my wife, who knew a girl Corradino had met on the Riviera the year before. 'What fools you men are!' she cried. 'There's a pretty girl

Summer Storm

like Marina, so rich and distinguished, just waiting for the right man to come along, and you drop out of sight, leaving her to the mercies of anyone who understands women!'

'If there is such a man,' I retorted. At that time I didn't know about Cate; if I had anyone in mind it was Ernesta, but though she knew Corradino so well, I didn't think she was likely to disturb his dreams. 'Anyway, we'll see,' we decided. 'As long as he doesn't sacrifice his holidays. But then, it would be just like him.'

We sent him a postcard which we all signed, and then gave ourselves up to our own preoccupations, our excursions in particular. Then I had a letter from him. In it, Corradino warned me that this wasn't really a reply to our joint postcard – indeed, he begged me as his only confidant not to give him away – but our card had reminded him he had a friend, and it meant so much to him to be able to unburden himself. 'For the rest,' he went on, 'I still go up the Sangone and I'm lonely as a dog. But I was preparing myself for something – as you know – and now it has happened. I'm beginning to believe there is a Providence. People may say that if you wish for something intensely, that's enough to make it happen, but not every day is a festival. If, by staying in Turin, expecting the unexpected, I have succeeded in compelling it to manifest itself, that has created its own problem, many problems. Like stones cutting my feet as I walk or raining down upon my head. More, I cannot tell you. Now I'm incredibly confused, yet it seems to me life may be offering me a unique opportunity to become a different man – you know how. On that point my ideas are crystal clear. Until yesterday, my trouble was that I couldn't get outside myself, outside my natural sphere of limitation. If everybody knew what I know now – this morning I wept with rage – what it means to be the prisoner of one's own identity, a victim of predestination! In a child of six are already engraved all the impulses, the capabilities, the importance he will have as a man of thirty. If only people understood that, no one would dare to think of the past. Instead, they would invent a detergent to wash the memory clean. In his daily life a man thinks he is different, that he has learned from experience, feels jubilant and master of himself; but suppose some crisis arises, something that gives him a real shock, a kick in the face, and life calls on him to "get up and get on with it", then he will inevitably do what he has always done in the past, run away if he's a coward, fight it out if he has courage. That seems a silly thing to say, but it is not. The more so because it is not only a question of running away or resisting; things are more complicated than that; it's a matter of understanding, weighing one thing against another, assessing values. It's a question of taste, and as everyone knows, our tastes don't change. If a man is afraid of the dark, he's afraid of the dark.

'But now I'm on the point of being able to do things I have never done. In this, life has helped me, I don't deny. I should even be able to do something that has no real connection with anything that may happen to me; to start all over again. So you see, it was worth the trouble of staying in Turin.

'P.S. If I am so elated, don't imagine that I haven't had my black moments. I still do, but if I told you what they're like you wouldn't understand. Once again I'm convinced that it's like being at war, and it's indescribable.'

This letter seemed harmless enough to me, and naturally my wife read it too. She didn't understand a word of it, she said. Eventually, after some hesitation, I showed it to Giusti, too. He promised to say nothing about it, smiled as he read it, and remarked that Corradino had said much the same to him. 'It wouldn't surprise me if he's a father already,' he joked as he finished reading.

So I sent Corradino a telegram: 'Awaiting explanations.

Summer Storm

All the best.' I was sorry to tease him, but Giusti had so much to say that I wrote the telegram myself.

To Corradino, Cate was merely a faint memory. They had met in her student days. One of her friends used to go boating with a former colleague of Corradino, and one day they all went on a picnic together, taking a gramophone and a bottle of wine and having a thoroughly good time. Later that year, when Cate was working in an office, she and Corradino had gone on seeing each other and going boating. Then Corradino lost his temper because he wanted to have a girl-friend like anybody else. Cate satisfied him once, twice and a third time, but Corradino was the first to have had enough and he never bothered to take her out again. But a year or two later he spoke of the episode with a strange regret, calling it a silly affair, a mixture of madness and animal passion, the sort of thing that shouldn't happen, but did.

And now they had met again. Corradino maintains that everything happens because we want it to, but how he could have wanted that meeting, or let Giusti take him where he never went before, as if he had no will of his own, I simply cannot understand.

They were out for a walk and the conversation had flagged. It was then Giusti suggested joining the dancing in the Park to round off the evening.

'But aren't you tired?' Corradino answered with a grin. The idea of going dancing hadn't occurred to him for years.

'Let's make a night of it,' Giusti suggested. 'We're a good age for that, thirty.' They strolled on through the avenue in the dusk and Corradino remarked, in his usual vein, that hearing about that sort of thing was much more fun than actually doing it. He was more serious than his tone of voice implied.

The Family

'You're always the same,' Giusti replied. 'Where are you going this year? Camogli?'

They went into the Palace of Varieties, in the Park. Here there was dancing for Giusti, beer and a glance at the show for Corradino. Little tables were ranged around a large open space of asphalt and at the back by the bandstand, was a wide gilded stage whence came the noise of singing. While they were looking for seats, the ladies of the chorus screeched out their final top note and bowed to the applause. Corradino gave an embarrassed smile.

'Did you know it was as elegant as this?' Giusti enquired.

'I've never been here before.'

It was turning out a dull evening. Between one turn and the next the blood-red curtain fell and the orchestra struck up, attracting several couples on to the dance floor. Giusti soon wandered off to find a partner. Corradino called after him, betting he wouldn't find one, but he must have done so for he did not come back and soon among the dancing legs, Corradino glimpsed a pair of light trousers he thought were Giusti's. Not until after several more dances did he reappear, while Corradino gazed absentmindedly at the performers, trying to lose himself in the snatches of music and air of excitement that make up a night in the Park. At last, between the dancers, he caught sight of Giusti's eyes shining over a bare shoulder, nodding to him.

As it ended they came to the table, Giusti and the lady. Corradino rather felt he might be *de trop* and scarcely glanced at his friend's partner. Her shoulder-strap must have slipped in the heat of the dance for her dress was sliding down. Giusti made the introductions and called the waiter. The lady offered Corradino her hand, damp with perspiration, and he smiled.

'To tell the truth, I'm not dancing,' he said quickly and the girl looked at him in surprise. Giusti settled them in their chairs, the curtains swung open and a girl in Spanish

Summer Storm

costume appeared on the stage. Soon Giusti started making uncomplimentary remarks about her; his partner listened attentively, then impulsively clapped her hands like a child and exclaimed that Giusti was quite right, clasped his wrist and laughed in his face as if she were only twenty.

As they rose to have the next dance together, the girl turned to Corradino and gave him a warm smile. Left alone, he let his eyes wander round the dancing floor and at the little groups by the tables where young men were bowing to ladies who were sometimes already on their feet with arms outstretched, eager to be swept into the crowd.

Suddenly he had the impression that someone, somewhere, had been staring at him. He gazed around. There was nothing to see but a swirling crowd of heads, an old man, feminine shoulders, the flushed, laughing face of a young fellow – no one he knew. It disturbed him a little and he felt for a cigarette before settling himself back in his chair. If there really had been someone looking at him, he felt sure it was a woman. He couldn't see the other two, and thought to himself: 'That silly girl's with Giusti, anyway, so she can't be the one. It's just as well!' He imagined the unknown woman coming to his table and asking him to dance. One never knew what a woman might do! Glancing again towards the row of little tables towards the side, he noticed that the shadowy wall was really a long mirror. So that disturbing scrutiny might have come from anywhere on the dance floor. It was gone, now. Perhaps it was the music that made him think it was a woman.

He went on listening to the music, closing his eyes and trying to recapture that fleeting impression. The thudding beat of the rhythm kept pace with the throbbing in his veins. Then came scattered applause.

When the two came back, Corradino suggested a drink and started chatting gaily to the girl while Giusti watched him with amusement. She liked nothing better than a

The Family

chance to joke and toss her head. They exchanged the silliest pleasantries until the orchestra struck up again. Corradino stood up, looked at Giusti and asked the girl: 'Shall we dance?' 'Well! Well!!' Giusti exclaimed in surprise. The girl was already on her feet.

They moved into each other's arms and danced away. In the middle of the floor Corradino suggested: 'Let's go and have a drink.' They strolled over to the bar, laughing as if they were playing truant. The girl sipped a *creme de menthe*, Corradino had a liqueur. As they were standing by the bar she assured him she had not looked at him in the mirror. Corradino put his arm round her again and swung her back to the floor in time for the last few notes of the dance, holding her close to him as he performed a couple of showy steps to left and right. As the music stopped, the girl made a great fuss about recovering her breath, putting her hand on her stomach, laughing and red in the face. 'Shall we go back?' he said.

The rest of the evening he didn't touch her, just let them come and go as they chose, whispering in each other's ear. Once she made some saucy remark to him but he pretended not to understand. When at last Giusti said: 'Excuse us. We're going now,' he nodded without a word.

The curtain went up once more. After a moment's silence, out came a Japanese juggler. Corradino watched his first tricks and the swirling of his wide, flowered sleeves. Now and again came a round of applause, then that was over, too.

Corradino started walking all over the crunching gravel towards the exit. Just then the music started again, several couples began forming and blocking his way. He quickened his pace, making his way along the wall. When he reached a clump of laurel bushes forming a recess, he turned. There were those eyes again.

Corradino did not recognize her for a moment and felt

Summer Storm

embarrassed. It flashed into his mind that if Cate had only chanced to meet him by those bushes, or if she were no longer the girl she used to be, he wouldn't wait. But even before Cate could say: 'Corrado', he had already smiled at her and held out his hand. He seized hers warmly, exclaiming what a miracle it was, but only when she stepped back to draw him aside was he certain it was Cate. He recognized the gesture.

Corradino remembered that the first thing he asked her was whether she was the girl who had looked at him in the mirror, and he must have asked with peculiar insistence because, he told me, Cate gaily put him off; 'Hadn't he anything better to ask her at such a moment?' He didn't reply, because by then he had checked his memory of those eyes with the face now before him, and knew beyond question that she was the one.

She talked to him cordially in such a flexible, sonorous voice that Corradino had no time to feel ill at ease at their meeting as he would otherwise have done. A greater embarrassment overcame him at finding himself chatting on such friendly terms with a good-looking, charming woman who was almost a stranger to him.

Still holding Corradino's hand, Cate sat down on a bench by the entrance and crossed her legs in their dainty, high-heeled shoes. Her nails and lips were scarlet; she was wearing a masculine-looking jacket over a high-necked blouse, a travelling outfit, apparently. Nothing remained of the Cate he had known but her eyes and hair; he searched her face for any signs of the past years, but saw only a flush of gaiety.

I know Giusti telephoned him next morning; I know, too, that Corradino cut short his conventional excuses and told him to go to hell.

'Forgive us for leaving you on your own last night,' was

The Family

what Giusti meant to say, for he prided himself on his tact, but instead he exclaimed: 'What's got into you?'

Corradino, who was expecting a very different telephone call, said simply that he didn't yet know what he would be doing that evening. It was from then on that he became so evasive and his face took on that tense look which Giusti described to us later.

Cate was really a stranger. Even before Corradino had time to get over his first embarrassment, she suddenly stunned him by remarking with a wealth of detail that she was a variety artist now, just back from Naples. She was in Turin, resting, and had come to the show in the park because this was her world; a world of down-and-outs, perhaps, but the best one she had. Then she asked him point blank if he were 'spliced'; that was the word she used, 'spliced'. Corradino made some sort of embarrassed reply, amazed to hear her uninhibited voice saying things people seldom put into words: that she knew she was growing old and had no thought of getting married, but still she had no regrets for the past twenty years. He stared down at the toes of Cate's little shoes, listened vaguely to the orchestra playing beyond the hedge, and murmured at last: 'How you've changed!'

'What's that? A compliment?' she returned, half-smiling.

Such a response stressed how different she was – a woman, now. They were both smiling, though not at each other. Corradino was not sure whether he was laughing at himself, his own embarrassment, or her frankness. This wasn't the same Cate who once, shy and tongue-tied, walked arm in arm with him; whose little handbag concealed a worn out powder puff and a tiny, soiled handkerchief. Even her voice had changed; now she spoke by fits and starts, her candour had a forcefulness, an outspoken bluntness that smacked strongly of the stage.

'I really did think you'd be married,' she murmured.

Summer Storm

'You know I'm not the type,' he replied.

While they had been sitting there – the orchestra still playing and the chorus girls shrieking their top notes – several people had come in and out – an over-vivacious, flashily-dressed woman among them, who had called out to Cate or given her a nod. Each time she had gaily returned the greeting.

'Listen,' she said, rising to her feet. 'Let's get out of this crowd. Are you all by yourself this evening?'

So they strolled along a sidepath and Cate slipped her arm through his. From her voice it was plain this was merely a spontaneous gesture of cordiality on her part, not an assumption that she had any right to do so. A justification burned on Corradino's lips, a welcome that took no heed of the past. He wanted to hear her talk about the old days without bitterness, even amusingly, and laugh over them with him. Instead, in the dusk under the trees, where the roaring of the weir drowned the orchestra, Cate started telling him about her work, the palaces of variety, the professional jealousies. She had even been to the colonies. Tripoli was a magnificent city! 'I was a fool not to stay down there,' she said. 'More elegance than you could ever have dreamed of. People spend more there. Evenings are really festive – cafés, theatres. Here, variety business is as dull as a funeral.'

'In short, you've achieved a career,' Corradino remarked.

'I manage to keep myself,' Cate replied, squeezing his arm. 'My dear man, what a life! And you know what I've had to put up with! If it hadn't been for mummy I'd never have succeeded.' Dropping her voice, she told him her mother was dead now, her father had killed her – he treated them both so badly. When she first started singing on the stage he used to come into the theatre and shout at her to stop. He'd made her lose some good contracts.

'And can you really sing?' Corradino teased her.

The Family

Cate gave his arm a little shake. 'You're still the same as ever,' she pouted. 'Don't you believe me?'

'But how did you manage it?'

'I had lessons. I found someone to help me. He helped mummy too. Wouldn't you have helped me?'

Cate had halted, looking up at Corradino with her usual frankness. Corradino smiled.

'And what about you?' she asked as they walked on again. 'What are you doing now? Still studying?'

The night was far advanced when Corradino struck a match and looked at his watch. They decided to take a taxi. During the journey, merely to break the silence, Corradino asked if he would see her again. The request was unintentional, almost against his will, made simply to please Cate and make amends in some way for his shabby treatment of her years ago. 'Give me a ring,' he said. 'I never go to the Park, as a rule.'

It seemed to him Cate was waiting for his invitation and was pleased about it, for she squeezed his hand and whispered 'Darling' in his ear. Corradino would have kissed her impulsively but just then the taxi slowed down and Cate said : 'Here we are.'

On his way home that night, Corradino thought of Giusti's little friend and reflected that all men get the adventures they deserve. He was glad, now, that he hadn't tried to kiss Cate, not because he feared he might have been rebuffed but because everything that had happened that evening had an atmosphere of frankness and trust, all the more extraordinary in view of the past.

He smiled again next morning as he awoke. Then came Giusti's phone call – Giusti never telephoned, normally. Odd that he took it into his head to do so this particular day! There was no call from Cate, and this made Corradino so cross that he even lost all inclination to go up the Sangone. A word from Cate that morning, even only over

Summer Storm

the phone, would have meant a great deal to him. 'Why doesn't she understand that, the silly girl?' he thought. Evening came, and he missed Giusti, missed Cate, missed everybody. He could have gone to the Park and perhaps found her there, but he forced himself not to. 'No! Let her find me,' and he stuck himself in a cinema.

He saw Giusti the next day, and while they were talking about ways of starting a love affair, Corradino had an idea.

Giusti's reasoned arguments put into his head the possibility of trying to win Cate back, now she knew her way about in the world. Corradino realized that his impression of that evening was due in some degree to his own irritation, his distaste and Giusti's banter, but the same night, as he went home, he thought if Cate hadn't stopped loving him that was her own affair, and he went to bed content. Next morning the silent phone froze the smugness on his face, and the rosy dawn he had hoped for dulled to the usual torment. But Corradino did go to the Sangone and there, fresh and tanned, he gazed at the willows and regained a measure of happiness. He thought of Camogli and his own future, wondered what Marina might be doing at that moment. At this point he really smiled. He began to understand that something had happened, that his waiting had borne fruit. His meeting with Cate had brought the past to light again and justified it all. Life was full of heartwarming things; it was enough just to let them happen. He felt free indeed, free and alone – as he had always wished to be.

But Cate did not phone. Once a week Corradino did night duty, and on those occasions he would stay at work till dawn because he liked walking home in the morning through the empty streets. He wandered around while it was still cool, and one day at the entrance to a doorway he bumped into Cate.

'Hello!' they exclaimed with a laugh. In the blue, high-

The Family

necked blouse she usually wore, Cate was really a lovely woman. She carried her twenty-eight years well and seemed taller, bigger. Above all, she had a bright smile which her make-up accentuated. She was on her way to buy shoes and Corradino went with her.

She laughed with pleasure and Corradino, tired from his night's work, lacked the energy to resist and simply echoed her suggestions and counter-suggestions. They did not link arms. Their conversation was disconnected and, realizing he did not know what to say, Corradino was glad of it. Comparing Cate with Marina in his mind, he laughed. 'Whatever happens, it's plain enough we don't mix,' he was thinking. In front of the shoe-counter, Cate had a box opened, took out a shoe and stood it on her hand. 'Like it?' she asked.

As they went out, Corradino instinctively took her arm; away. Cate looked at him in some embarrassment, then they walked a few steps together, then he drew his arm enquired why he had not come back to the Park. From that moment their conversation became disjointed. Corradino looked down at his shoes and made random remarks, the gist of which was that he'd waited for her to phone, but didn't care to go·to the Park; he didn't like the sort of people there; they might find it amusing, but he had no desire to amuse himself in that way.

'But how do you spend your evenings?' Cate asked him.

'As far as yesterday evening was concerned, I worked all night,'

Cate smiled, an incredulous, spontaneous smile. 'Haven't you got a girl-friend?' she enquired.

'No,' he retorted.

Cate did not seem surprised. She went on smiling. Corradino maintains that this was the moment when he knew the die was cast. He did not speak, hesitating between self-assurance and indifference. But, he says, in that instant

Summer Storm

Cate decided the future for them both, and perhaps it was a good decision.

She herself asked him where he lived and agreed to go home with him. As they walked they started talking of their work, and Corradino boasted quite a bit about the convenience and prospects of his own job. He even went as far as remarking that in a way they were colleagues, since they both worked for the public. 'It's a good thing to support oneself,' Cate remarked.

Corradino's landlady turned a blind eye when he brought in a woman. She heard them go along the passage and contented herself with peeping from the kitchen, but on the other hand she hadn't yet made the bed from the day before. Corradino was annoyed and shut the door again, asking Cate to excuse him for a moment. He straightened out the tangle of sheets and pyjamas, smoothed the bedspread and drew the curtains over the window. Now the room took on a comfortable, rosy glow.

Corradino always remembered that tranquil light. Cate was sitting in the armchair, resting her hands on the arms and crossing her legs. 'The other day it was Ernesta sitting there,' Corradino was thinking, and now Cate was looking at him just as Ernesta did, her eyes soft, absorbed in thought. The gay words they had laughingly exchanged as they climbed the stairs seemed to be remote from this room, merely a part of the world outside like the noises in the street.

They talked about going boating and Cate smoked a cigarette. It was like any normal conversation: Corradino told her he hadn't been for a long time; Cate, exhaling smoke, listened to him seriously as though it was her duty. 'I like sun-bathing, yes,' and she fell silent.

Coming up the stairs she had said: 'I'll come and smoke a cigarette with you,' and now the cigarette was nearly finished and nothing was happening. Corradino thought resentfully of his imminent loneliness and his bitterness against Cate increased. Then he took his courage in both hands and asked her if she had ever gone boating again. He asked it through the smoke, barely looking at her.

'Would you be pleased if I had?'

'I didn't say with me,' he stammered.

Cate smiled, a smile so ambiguous that Corradino could not take his eyes away from it. 'She's coming to avenge herself,' he thought desperately. 'That's why she's here!'

'Corrado, you're still the same! Of course I've gone boating since then. And what about you? Have you thought of me even once in all these years?'

Corradino nodded without taking his eyes from her. Her smile had dawned with the greatest delicacy and was now slowly fading without any unfriendliness.

She rose to her feet and came to put down her cigarette end on the table by Corradino. He went to kiss her but she turned her face aside and gently rubbed her cheek against his. In his agitation she looked at him, a grave, solicitous look as though she were comforting a child. 'I like your room,' she said. 'Have you been here long?'

He made some reply. Cate was already by the window, pulling aside the curtain and looking out into the street. Corradino made no move: no point in running after her. She turned to him, suddenly gay. 'There's a hairdresser's just opposite your front door. Your girl-friends will be pleased.'

'I didn't want to come up,' she went on, 'but I'm curious.' Corradino had taken her hand and she let him kiss the palm – he thought her lacquered nails so odd – then she teased him. 'I'm not exactly a fine lady, you know. I was wrong to come. I must fly.'

Corradino still held her hand and couldn't joke with her nor manage to be serious. 'No, it wasn't wrong for you,' he murmured.

'I mean it was wrong for you,' Cate replied.

All he asked was if he could see her again. 'Today?' Cate thought for a minute. 'In the garden of the little square below where I live. You stopped there the other night. About four?'

Cate wouldn't go outside with him. She slipped away quickly, leaving him in the passage. Corradino waited there a little while in the gloom, until her steps had died away on the stairs, then went out furtively so that the landlady shouldn't know. He could not bear the thought of spending the rest of the morning shut up in his room.

It was ridiculous to run after her, but to the garden he went. He had to be back at work by six: everything seemed in league against him, that day. As he went he said to himself: 'I can always come away again.' He even hoped that Cate might not be there, that he would never see her again.

He remembered the garden as a few trees between blocks of flats, a fountain and a strip of open sky. He saw it from the corner, steeped in sunshine, dusty and full of shrill noises. Children were playing there; he saw women and a few nursemaids. Corradino's eyes searched the fountain. Concealed behind a tree he looked casually at the various groups. He had anticipated a private rendezvous, and the children's shrieks got on his nerves even more than usual.

Cate saw him: she was seated on a bench in the shade, helping a little boy take off his jacket. He freed himself with a final tug and ran off. Corradino came forward in a bad humour. Cate was not alone; two girls who looked like servants were sitting there too; there was even a soldier leaning against a tree, trying to get off with the girls.

Cate greeted him with a cordial 'Good afternoon.' One of the servants turned her face round to look at him. She scrutinized him thoroughly from head to foot, then smiled as Cate had done when she shook hands with him. Corra-

The Family

dino mumbled something; the servant-girl still stared; then Cate stood up, saying: 'It's a nuisance...'

She was still holding the little boy's jacket, and now she shaded her eyes to try and pick him out from among the others. Corradino was expecting Cate to move away from the bench with him and felt annoyed when she sat down again. He lost patience and said sharply: 'Cate, are you acting as nursemaid?' While they went on talking he stared at the servant girl so attentively that she pointedly turned away from him towards the soldier.

Cate said: 'I'm acting as a mother.'

'Who is that little boy?'

'My son.'

Corradino recoiled a step. He saw a flash in Cate's eyes that warned him to make no comment. The servant girl still faced the other way. When she and her friend went off at last to find their charges and the soldier had wandered away, Corradino sat down on the bench and asked Cate to explain.

'I told you he's my son. When I go on tour I leave him with my sister. She's married and lives over there on the third floor.'

'But you aren't married,' he stammered.

'So what?' Cate answered bluntly. 'Can't a woman have a baby if she's not married? It does happen, doesn't it?'

Corradino retorted that she was talking nonsense; when he asked her why she had not told him before, she answered that first she wanted to know if he disapproved.

'Well, now d'you know if I disapprove?' he asked.

'I ought to have told you this morning,' she said, fixing her eyes on him. 'I realized this morning I should have told you.'

For a moment Corradino did not know what to say. Then he returned to the attack. 'Well, now d'you know what I think?' It was like a game of hide and seek. Cate gave up,

Summer Storm

saying simply that they were friends and should try to understand each other.

Just then the boy came back, scuffing up the gravel. His name was Dino and Cate put her arms round him, straightened his hair, made him slip on his jacket again and told him to say 'Good afternoon' to Corradino.

'How old are you?' Corradino asked him.

'Six and a half,' Dino told him breathlessly in a clear voice. 'Going on for seven.'

'Who were you playing with?' Cate enquired. Dino gave her a few names, pointed out certain balconies in the blocks of flats and spoke of his class-mates.

'He goes to school, then?'

'He wants to be an engineer when he leaves school,' Cate explained, 'So he'll have to study.'

'So you want to be an engineer?' Corradino asked. The 'Yes' of the reply was lost in a spurt of gravel. Dino was off again.

'He's a real little ruffian,' Cate said.

They both stood silent a moment while Cate fumbled in her bag, not even looking at it.

'He's a marvellous kid,' Corradino remarked, watching her hands. Again he saw her red nails smoothing the child's ruffled hair, and was ashamed to remember he had meant to seduce her that morning.

'Good for you, Cate! And you live with his father? You can tell me that, anyway.'

'We brought him up ourselves, mummy and me,' Cate told him, holding herself erect again, blushing and proud. 'That's all there is to know.'

Next morning a postcard arrived from Camogli. There were several signatures on it, Marina's among them. Even her father and mother had signed it too, and Corradino looked for a long time at their names. 'So they've agreed on

The Family

something at last,' he scoffed and went out, anxiously eyeing the telephone and hoping it would not ring. That morning he wanted to be alone.

There was no time for the Sangone. He hurried off to a restaurant, but hesitated at the door and decided to go to another he seldom visited. Here at least there were no familiar faces; the waiters were obsequious and the service such that even Marina would have been satisfied. The meal cost twice as much, but his solitary way of life was generally too economical. 'I've never had a child to support,' he kept thinking all day. 'Never got involved with anyone. That's the way I'm made. I've known plenty of women and always left them in the end. If Marina were here I'd probably turn her down tomorrow, too.'

All that day he felt bad-tempered and in the evening he went out with Giusti. He did not dare suggest going to the Park and spent the whole evening listening to his friend's idle chatter. Giusti had noticed how disgruntled he looked, and was doing his best to divert him. At one point they had a difference of opinion: Corradino said that experience serves to teach us, not what we ought to do, but what we inevitably shall do. A man, no matter how bright, is like a bridge that can carry a certain weight and no more. Along comes a cart heavier than that, and the bridge collapses.

'That's good! Fine!' Giusti laughed. 'Then a man should work out what he can carry, first!'

Conversation had made Corradino more cheerful, but he did not press self-revelation to the point of asking Giusti how a man could work it out when he felt he might collapse any minute and could not even support a grasshopper. But Giusti had noticed he was brighter, now, and this was enough for him. He went on to remark: 'Talking of women – and we were talking of women, weren't we? – they manage to make the bridge take what suits them.' They both laughed, cracked a joke or two and changed the subject.

Their companionship was like that. Corradino says he often felt the need to relax with me, and was rather relieved when Giusti went away at the end of July. Then he was really on his own, and for a little while he was rather glad. That's the sort of man he was. He started bathing among the willows again.

'You see,' he said to me in his precise way, a year later, 'I was expecting something to happen that July, and when one really expects it, something does happen. But to put myself in the right state of mind I had to isolate myself. Every morning I would go up the Sangone to seek my true self in the water or in the mirror of the sun. The man who seeks, will find, they say, but what could I find, lying there naked among the willows, staring at my navel and my limbs, wondering if I were capable of producing a child of my own? I found a ridiculous, defeated creature – myself; with Cate in mind, because I thought about Cate more often than Marina, I grew to hate myself more and more; all my past rottenness came to the surface; I discovered – and this is the point – that I had always treated people, especially women, in the same way – known them, and dropped them. With no one had I made common cause; I had shirked all my responsibilities. There is no one I can truthfully call my friend, not even you.'

Corradino often returned to this question of friendship, explaining his views to me over and over, maintaining that he is not my real friend because he is jealous of my wife. From what he says, that is what annoyed him on those days when Cate did not ring him up: it meant that she had someone better, even though that someone were only a child. 'And she knew,' he added, 'that I could have come to the Park.' Another thing that upset him was the idea

The Family

that, even in the past, when he had violated and humiliated her, Cate might have absolved him with that ambiguous smile of hers. This really troubled him; the mere suspicion of it cut him to the quick.

Towards the first days of August, Corradino made up his mind to come to Camogli and applied for his holidays. Had it been possible he would have slipped off the same evening, but the office reminded him that just then almost everyone was away, and he had to wait half a week. Corradino smiled: 'Marina's unlucky, then! Too bad!'

Next day he took Cate boating. They arranged it by telephone, on the spur of the moment. The evening before he had gone to the Park where he found her wearing rather a lot of make-up and a new hat. Sometimes, on his way to meet her, he had seen, in the wings or on the stage, the typical face of a variety artist, the features haggard and over-bright, ravaged by spotlights and late hours. But Cate was much as she had always been; she had given him her hand and talked frankly to him; Corradino was quite satisfied to look at her as if he had never seen her before, trying to convince himself that this was the real Cate. At their little table they always had company – the intrusive company of some habitué of the Park determined to monopolize the conversation, or some variety artist who addressed Cate familiarly as '*tu*'. To get her to himself, Corradino asked her to dance, ('A turn with you, Corrado? Yes, I can manage that' she said), and it was while they circled the floor that he asked her to telephone him in the morning. She promised, and she did phone. Before ringing off, she herself suggested that they might go boating.

Corradino knew that her suggestion was perfectly innocent. The irritation he felt as they walked along the road sprang from a different cause. They went down to the landing stage independently, not arm in arm. Corradino slipped a hand under her elbow and with a laugh they

Summer Storm

jumped into the boat. She stumbled. Corradino caught her but almost fell himself, then they seated themselves. As all women do under such circumstances, Cate laughed and wrapped her skirt around her knees. In this gesture, and in her happy face with its lips parted to show her white teeth, Corradino captured a glimpse of those heedless by-gone days when they were children. He understood, too, Cate's whim to come boating: she wanted to rediscover and reassess her own long-distant past.

By now, Cate had regained her composure. Corradino stripped off his shirt, exposing his bare chest and displaying his sunburned skin. He started rowing and they glided along by the bank in the tender green of the Valentino.

'Why don't you bring your son to the Park?' he asked suddenly, his teeth clenched. But Cate did not catch the note of resentment in his voice and did not reply. She was looking ahead into the sunshine with her eyes half-closed, enjoying it. She had taken off her hat; her lips and bare throat did not seem quite so young, now; they betrayed the constant strain of late hours.

Corradino repeated his question, and she said that her sister was looking after Dino for the time being. He was still too young to understand that being on the variety stage was just a job like any other. Perhaps in a few years, if she could get herself organized, she could take him with her when she went on tour, but in any case he had to study, and when studying it was important to have no distractions. 'I'm always thinking of him,' she went on. 'When he's grown up I don't want him to be able to complain that I've neglected him.'

Corradino fell silent, bending forward and crossing the oars. 'But can you afford to bring him up?' he asked suddenly.

Cate answered with a smile that she had managed it so far. 'In our profession there are a good many rogues,'

The Family

she told him, 'but there are fine people, too. There is someone who helps me.'

'That fellow we saw yesterday? What is he? A musician?'

Cate went on smiling and did not reply in words, but there was something in the way she looked at him, so intently, so insistently, that made him feel uneasy.

The sun was hot and he began to sweat. He put down the oars, leaned over the side and splashed water on his shoulders with his cupped hand. Then he sluiced it over his hair. 'Don't you feel hot, too, Cate?' he asked.

She shook her head, still gazing at him with that unfathomable look in her eyes. Corradino groped for the oars again, saying to himself: 'It looks as if she's taking stock of me, thinking what I was like in those days and remembering all those silly things we used to say.' Aloud he continued: 'Wouldn't it be simpler if his father supported him?' He raised his head and added: 'I suppose you at least know who his father is?'

Cate shrugged her shoulders. She did not seem offended. Her steady glance had changed; now she looked at him almost stealthily. With the sun full on her face he could not tell if she was blushing.

'Corrado? she said softly, 'you know who his father is.'

Corradino says he let the oars go and felt his hair stand on end. Cate still looked at him, a smile of pain in her eyes. Under those eyes of hers Corradino found the strength to pull himself together, seize the oars again and draw a deep breath. 'But no!' he groaned. The faintest change in tone could have made it sound ironic, but Cate caught the note of utter amazement and her eyes suddenly narrowed.

Corradino says that in the moments that followed what he felt above all was a terrible cramp in his stomach, yet in the back of his mind was the knowledge that for days, from the time they had met, and even before, he had

Summer Storm

foreseen this agony and known that for him something irreparable was about to begin. He says that as he listened, struggling to find words, he gave a stroke of the oars now and then to keep the boat from drifting. Cate broke in on his thoughts with a forced laugh that sounded almost defensive, as if to say she had told him quite impersonally, as she might have told anybody else; or as if she were alone, chattering and joking to keep up her courage. One thing, he says, was obvious from the start: Cate was not talking to worry him or to trick him into anything. Her tone was hesitant, almost forced, as if she knew she was hurting him and wanted to make light of it, to spare him.

'I knew just after you dropped me,' she said, 'and what good would it have done to tell you then? We should both have been upset. At that time it drove me crazy, but not to such a pitch that I didn't know quite well you wanted to be rid of me.'

Corradino seized on that tone of hers because it showed him – not any way out of his problems, for he didn't dare think of the future – but a plain, simple possibility that this might not drive him mad; Cate was leaving him completely free to go on being himself. He says he raised all sorts of objections, thinking at the same time how pointless they were if this were true; but what could a man do, learning that for years he had a son whose mother he scarcely knew?

'Careful! There's a boat,' Cate warned him, and Corradino had to take the oars again and steer out of the way, but the other boat was so close it scraped along their side. The four people in it, one of them a soldier, leaned out and fended it off with their hands, laughing at Cate.

As they came into the landing-stage their bows hit the jetty with a dull crash that brought the boatwoman running up to complain, but Cate and Corradino did not stop to listen. Soon they were hurrying along the avenue, not

The Family

talking. When they slowed to a normal pace they walked arm in arm.

Plainly Cate was expecting Corradino to say something; to begin, for instance, by scolding her for having tackled such a great responsibility on her own. Instead, Corradino pointed out that the boy was six, but it was eight years since their last meeting. Cate shook her head. 'Only seven,' she said.

'You must excuse me. It's like having a mallet come down on my head.'

Cate squeezed his arm and in a calmer voice, now that they were no longer looking into each other's eyes, she began explaining it was no use being bitter; why she had told him she hardly knew herself; neither of them was to blame, unless she was for being so silly. 'All that's happened doesn't change anything, Corrado. All I want is for you to understand me,' she said.

Corradino searched anxiously for something to say that might please her. 'What? It doesn't make any difference?' he exclaimed.

'Let's go on being friends as we were before,' Cate pleaded. 'Nothing to be afraid of.'

That was when something strange happened to Corradino. Cate went on talking, though he couldn't be sure that what he remembered was what she actually said. But her words confirmed his first impression that she wanted nothing from him; she did not want help, still less to marry him. She had in fact told him her secret in confidence, an impulsive weakness, and now all she had in mind was to part with a handshake, leaving him in her debt.

As she went on talking this became even more evident. Corradino was conscious of a growing resentment, a wounded pride, as if he were the injured one. The idea that he had a son was monstrous, and to take Cate's word for it was absurd, but the realization that those three women; she,

Summer Storm

her mother and her sister, had for six years, nearly seven, treated that baby as one of their family, brought him up, looked after him, clothed him, all the time knowing the child was his, (Cate at least knew,) made his blood boil.

In his agitation, Corradino drew his arm away from Cate's and said the only kind thing that had crossed his lips that afternoon: 'Does he look like me? I do hope he does!' and he stifled a sigh, conscious of her searching eyes upon him.

'No, I don't think he does . . . Perhaps, when he's older . . .' she replied.

'So you see,' Corradino faltered, every time he talked to me about it, 'she had given him my name, but she was sure he didn't look like me. She may have been right, but is that the sort of thing to say to a man who has only that moment learned he is a father and cannot quite believe it, yet?'

Cate's strength, says Corradino was her artlessness, her utter lack of guile. She had kept nothing back, telling him everything to his face, though, true enough, she made it all sound light-hearted, to keep up her courage. She was not concerned to conceal any decision she had made or any feelings that had affected her. Or could it be that she acted like this only because she knew that with a man like Corradino it was the surest way to master him and defend herself?

'It's good of you to talk like this,' she told him in the little garden that same afternoon, 'but I couldn't ever prove to you that Corrado is your son. I was wrong to tell you about it, but one does that sort of thing on impulse or not at all.'

So Corradino, who had gone to see the boy to ask him: 'Don't you know your father?', went away with the impression that he himself had been seduced, seven years ago. As usual, Dino was playing with the others, and stayed by

The Family

Cate only long enough for her to take the picnic snacks out of her bag. Corradino had seized him by the wrists and tried to detain him, but the boy had resented the restraining arm and had broken away with the energy of a young puppy. His shrill voice as he wrenched himself free struck Corradino to the heart. He had never thought of the gulf that lies between grown-ups and young children, a perpetual distrust; or that children, all unaware of it, live in a different world. When they were alone again, Cate said that, by and large, Dino was obedient, but just now he liked to be difficult. A year or so ago he had spent an afternoon hidden under the stairs because he wouldn't talk politely to a gentleman who called.

'And he knows nothing about his father?' Corradino asked.

Cate shook her head. 'Doesn't he ask?' Corradino persisted.

'Yes, he has asked, but I've never liked to tell him his father was dead. For the moment he's quite satisfied to know his father's away.'

It was then that Corradino staked his all, and said, with frequent pauses, that Cate herself ought to understand him, ('I'm talking like a woman', he thought in dismay), let him have time to get his bearings, get to know Dino, get to know her; to convince her he loved his son, and to thank her, if he could only find the words, for all the sacrifices she must have made. And Cate, calm but determined, gave him the reply he had already told me about.

Thinking back over it all, Corradino began to feel justified. That night, (his first as a father), he wandered about alone, smoking feverishly and re-examining the whole question. It was clear that, if Cate wanted nothing from him, she was telling the truth and Dino was his son. If, on the other hand, Cate had ended by trying to trap him or get something from him – (What? Marriage? or just

Summer Storm

money?) then some doubt might remain. Facing his dilemma frankly, Corradino gave a wry grin. He no longer had the strength to laugh.

From what he remembers of that night, Corradino insists it was very different from others he had experienced in the past, when he had fled through the streets in a wild outburst of jealousy, love or enthusiasm. He says that, though he was shattered by his realization of the precarious balance in which his affairs now stood, yet underneath all the tumult he felt a calm, a certainty and a hope that would not leave him. As usual, when he spoke to me about it, he insisted that this sense of security sprang solely from what Cate had said to calm him; and, more than from her words, from her voice, so determined not to yield or let him help her. From then on, said Corradino, he understood that Cate wanted to know nothing about him. Hence the calm, the hope that sustained him.

But I know that Corradino likes to run himself down, and I tried to convince him that if, among his wild thoughts of that night, that sense of futility he had felt in other crises no longer intruded, this stemmed primarily from the fact that this time he was tackling the crisis like a man. He was now facing, not imaginary nonsense, but reality, aspects of human life, a problem of human behaviour that would snatch him out of his isolation. But Corradino shook his head and told me the truth was very different: he did not feel a scrap of love for Cate – rather he disliked her, as he did everyone else who opposed him. As for Dino, his son and a threat to him, even today he thinks of him as a stranger, though he is sure Cate told him the truth. 'I'm not made for paternal love,' he protests. 'The idea that my son might end up in other people's hands, gives me a sense of having escaped danger more than anything else; suppose, later on, he were to shame me by growing into a thief or a swindler?'

The Family

'But that's natural,' I told him. 'Fatherhood involves that, too.'

'Then explain to me,' he began, laughing, 'how it is I knew that night that within a week I should have started for Camogli, leaving Dino to Cate, and begun chasing Marina?'

'And that letter you wrote to me in the mountains?'

'That letter?' Corradino faltered. 'This had happened.' The morning after that night he had wakened with a sense of sorrow, a feeling of emptiness at his heart. Yet, as can happen, while sleeping he had reached the nadir of his grief. With the dreadful clarity some thoughts take on at dawn, he had lain in bed feeling stripped, wretched and guilty. The few women he had known began passing through his mind, creating a crescendo of remorse: Ernesta, Cate, a nameless shop-girl, faceless prostitutes and even Marina, though he had never touched her. They all said the same thing, oppressed him with the same memory, like a man in the dock facing his accusers. Powerless to defend himself in the silent dawn, Corradino saw clearly now that the recurring factor was his personality, his real self. He had treated all those women in the same way, gently; he was incapable of talking to any one of them like a man; he was too wrapped up in his self-isolation. He might at least have treated them roughly, mastered them, raped them. That morning he felt he had violated them all by letting himself be violated; first, the prostitutes, with whom he always passed for a man of good position, a gentleman of distinction; now he was thirty they took him for a student. And all of them – Ernesta, Cate, and tomorrow Marina – ended by breaking away from him, angered and disappointed by his unconquerable indolence. Now – and this shook Corradino – if he had acted like this with all of them, it meant this was his real nature and he would always act in the same way. The capacity of the bridge.

Summer Storm

That morning he went back to the Sangone to think over these things in the quiet sunshine. He stripped between the willows and then, as he smoked, looked at his body drying in the sun. Naturally his bitter humiliation on awakening had by now been dispelled by the light and his physical exercise. Now, inevitably, he thought of Cate and the boy. Looking down at his sunburned, adult body, he compared it with Dino's. That little devil's nimble legs and supple wrists were so much stronger than he would have expected, stronger, he was sure, than he could have engendered. Beyond question, the credit for making him so fine and strong must go to Cate. And then, still suspending judgement as if he were his father, he began wondering whether, in that little body, a character like his own – solitary and withdrawn – was already developing. 'It would be a real proof,' he thought, 'if, remote from me, he should grow to be like me, one day; it would mean that character is derived from birth, not from environment. It's the same with orphans.' With this thought, Corradino grew ashamed again and said to himself that at any rate he was alive and really ought to marry Cate. Just as clearly as, on waking, he had realized his own futility, he now realized he had a duty to perform. 'A duty,' he said mockingly, 'that is not unpleasant. Cate is a lovely woman and will give me other sons.'

It was in this mental state that he composed the letter he was to write to me, and especially those phrases: '. . . problems, many problems . . . raining down on my head . . . It's like being at war; it's indescribable . . . I should even be able to do something that has no real connection with anything that may happen to me . . .' And that thing, obviously, was what he did when, six days later, he got on the train for Camogli.

Such a disclosure as she had made to him in the boat

The Family

should have brought them closer together, at least for a little while, a day perhaps; they should have met again to talk it over, but they parted as usual without arranging another meeting. (Wouldn't Cate ever come up to his room again?) One thing at least was taken for granted: they could always meet in the Park, of an evening. Corradino thought this was Cate's way of bringing him into her own environment and justifying herself. One afternoon seven years ago – *which* afternoon? – he had left her on a street corner, forgetting to make another date, and they had not seen each other since.

But Corradino did go back to the little pleasure-garden, stealing the time to do so when he should have been back at the office of his paper; he peered through the trees, hiding himself behind a clump of bushes. He didn't want, or didn't dare, to let Cate catch sight of him; perhaps it was the romantic idea of concealing himself to spy on his son. His eyes followed a little boy he had seen before; along came another, then another. The third was Dino. They formed a circle, and Dino pointed a finger at each of them in turn, counting them out in some game or other. They all gave a shout and ran off, to form another group some distance away, Dino among them; they started yelling and clenching their fists. After a moment or two, Dino broke away and trotted back, head in air, to the bench where Cate was standing and calling to him. Corradino saw her take him by the arm and talk to him. 'He's a little rascal, just as I was,' he murmured, taking his eyes from the boy and leaving the garden.

That same evening he went to the Park. He fought against the impulse till the last moment – it was up to Cate to phone him – and he sat by his open window, watching the daylight turn to dusk. He says that he was thinking of Camogli and of Marina, as he usually did at that time of day.

Summer Storm

Suddenly the phone rang. Corradino went white with rage when he heard Ernesta's voice. He asked her bluntly why she had rung and she replied timidly that it was a long time since she'd heard from him; everybody seemed to be away on holiday and she was wondering if he'd gone too. She just wanted to say 'hello'.

Corradino told her in a kinder voice: 'Well, I'm still here, you see.' But Ernesta seemed to have no more to say. Corradino waited. ''Bye then,' Ernesta said softly and hung up.

Corradino took a tram and went to the Park. Cate had not arrived yet. He felt the urge to talk, walk about, do something, and he caught sight of the fellow he had seen the last time, the one who had talked to Cate about songs. Cate's eyes had been warm and friendly as she answered him. He was a good-looking man, going grey at the temples. Corradino approached him and they were chatting together when Cate appeared. 'Oh,' she cried. 'So you've made friends while waiting for me.'

An artist called Naldina was singing that evening; everyone knew her and many of them went up to greet her personally. She was blonde, a native of Florence and now rather the worse for wear; she laughed loudly all the time, gripping her public by her wildly extravagant gestures. Listening to her, Corradino wondered what Cate was like on stage. She was sitting next to him just then, her chin on her hand, listening intently to the other girl's voice. There was something so absurdly naïve about her, yet so maternal, that Corradino had to smile. 'She sings well, don't you think?' he whispered in her ear. Cate frowned for a moment, then smiled, but did not take her eyes from the stage.

Naldina, loudly applauded by their group, less warmly by people at the other tables, came over to sit with them, leaving the other couples in evening dress with whom she

The Family

had been singing. That musician friend of Cate's, with his well-trained voice and his forty-odd years, welcomed her effusively. Instantly they were all chattering away like old, intimate friends, and only then did Corradino realize from his accent that he was a native of Tuscany, too. After someone had given Naldina a light for her cigarette she looked Corradino up and down, but soon all of them, Cate included, were deep in a discussion about how audiences varied in the warmth of their reception and how different they were in Florence and Rome.

'Here you're all half-hearted, dull and hard to please,' Naldina remarked, blowing out a mouthful of smoke. Corradino had already said something complimentary, as courtesy demanded, but actually he detested her; loathed her from head to foot; hated the look of her, her voice, her profession, the way she dressed. He hated her all the more because there was something of Cate about her; they had the same habit of plain-speaking, the same self-sufficiency, the same trick of discussing mere trifles with an air of great seriousness, as all women do.

The whole group around Naldina were talking of their own affairs, using the Tuscan dialect and drawing Corradino into their discussions. He replied to their arguments as best he could, for Cate had introduced him as a journalist and he had to seem reasonably well informed. Pippo – they all called Cate's friend 'Pippo' – was full of an idea for creating a protective syndicate for members of orchestras, and from this Corradino concluded that he was definitely a musician. Even Cate looked at him now and then, listening attentively to what he said.

Pippo and Naldina stood up to dance and Naldina turned to Cate to ask with a smile : 'You don't mind, do you?' The rest all smiled or laughed outright.

Later that evening there came a moment when Corradino and Cate found themselves alone, sitting on that

Summer Storm

bench by the entrance. Cate seemed nervous, as if she was expecting someone, and lapsed into silence, barely replying to Corradino's remarks. The Park was already half-empty; Naldina and Pippo had been missing for half-an-hour. Corradino now understood the situation; he had known it ever since that last evening; there was only one thing he was not sure of, and he turned it over and over in his mind, absurd though it was.

'How long have you known this fellow Pippo?' he asked.

Cate blushed. 'Why do you ask?' she said.

'Oh, nothing,' Corradino replied. 'I can see you rely on him a great deal and I shouldn't like to think he was just a newcomer.'

Cate explained gaily that she had known him for the last two years; he was a grand companion, very keen on his work, the sort of man who could make a career for himself without running down his colleagues.

'And what is he doing in Turin?'

'You could help him,' Cate said.

'How?'

She replied that he knew nobody in Radio. 'Just a word with so and so would be quite enough,' she said warmly, but still she kept looking towards the entrance.

Corradino smiled. 'So really I ought to thank you,' he said. 'You not only give me a son, but you'd like me to help you get rid of me.'

Cate frowned. She understood, not his words, but the feeling behind them. She was puzzled for a minute but she did not blush; she was flushed already. She gave him a sidelong glance from her gentle eyes. 'Corrado,' she said, 'we're neither of us to blame,' and she clutched his wrist impulsively.

'Naturally that pianist of yours is a bachelor?' Corradino went on. Cate nodded without looking at him.

They both fell silent. Corradino, smiling to regain control

The Family

of himself, understood that Cate was already thinking of that other man, Pippo. His distress over those absurd thoughts of his was pointless, a mere waste of time. He rose to his feet, holding out his hand. 'Good night,' he said. Cate looked at him keenly and gave him her hand with some hesitation. '*Au revoir*, then,' she faltered.

For several days Corradino, when his uncertainty made him critical, satisfied himself by remembering Cate's embarrassment. Now that he felt he could consider it all from the more remote viewpoint that originated when she had smiled instead of taking offence, he felt master of the situation. 'A mere nothing,' he thought, 'is enough to take a woman by surprise when she doesn't expect it.' But was he her master? It was up to Cate to take the next move, and two long days passed without a sound from the telephone.

Corradino had made up his mind not to go back to the little pleasure garden. To regain some peace of mind he told himself that even if the boy was Pippo's son, and Cate had deceived him, she had perhaps tried to trick him into pitying her, and persuading him to regularize the situation, since he had been her lover. Yet, on the other hand, why did she wait for half a summer, make her preparations in solitude? His own need for a different sort of solitude seemed suddenly less important. Corradino could have accepted all those possibilities but could not bring himself to reject Cate herself, her firmness, her grave simplicity. Now that it had come to a question of rivalry, he needed a Cate worth the trouble of feeling jealous about. The fact that Dino might well be his son stung him like a whip lash, gave him the right to look Cate straight in the face. Even today, Corradino says: 'There are some kinds of bad luck a man might be glad to have.'

But the telephone did not ring. As he came home from the office on the third evening, thinking to himself: 'Only

Summer Storm

two more nights and I'll be starting my holidays,' Corradino found our telegram. He tells me it made him smile at first, pleased to think I had taken his letter so seriously. But then, as he read again, he began to wonder if we were pulling his leg, and wished he hadn't written that letter. He suffered keenly as he thought back over what he had written, the humiliation that had engulfed him that morning, the warm happiness he had felt all that night at the thought that he had a son, even though that son belonged to someone else. But in the end he had grown used to the idea and, as usual, done nothing about it. His real character as a man was precisely what he had known it to be when he awoke that morning. His capacity had fallen short, as it always did. There was nothing to do but weep for his own inadequacy. He told himself: 'I've got to do something about this.'

Instead, he had done nothing. He simply went to the Park and spent the evening as usual, sitting at the artists' table, listening to the songs, watching the dancing. When they happened to be left alone for a minute he asked Cate how Dino was getting on, and listened as she spoke of the care she took over him, his character and little details of his daily life. Cate was obviously happy and rather glad to be telling him such things. They had a dance together.

Then Corradino went off to the bar with Pippo, and mentioned casually that Cate had dropped a hint that he could help him in some way, but had not explained clearly what she had in mind. Would Pippo give him details of his past experience? The conversation that followed gave Corradino ample confirmation that the man had known Cate only for the past two years. Pianist though he was, he talked with a good deal of sound common-sense and seemed well aware that he was not a god. He had played in variety to earn a living, but his education was on a higher scale than that; he hinted he had studied seriously at a conservatoire,

The Family

and his colourful criticisms of the singers performing in the Park did so much to win Corradino's approval that he quite forgot to hate him. Cate came to find them.

In her presence, Corradino jokingly asked Pippo what Cate's singing was really like. Pippo, replying in the same tone, told him that the tables at the Park had heard worse and Cate, half-provocative, half-frowning, retorted that they hadn't all got as much talent as Naldina. Pippo smiled, so did Corradino, who was just on the point of enquiring 'Isn't she appearing this evening?' when Pippo added calmly: 'It's a sad thing, a girl like that.'

Obviously, he and Cate had made it up, if, indeed, they had ever quarrelled. Corradino wondered if the pianist knew about Dino and what he thought of him. During a break in the conversation he told them point blank that in a couple of days he'd be away on holiday. 'I'm off to the country.' 'What a pity!' Cate remarked, with Pippo's eyes upon her. 'But first,' Corradino added, 'I'll see about having a word with someone on the Radio.'

They chatted about being in the country and Cate said frankly she was sorry she couldn't take Dino there that year.

'You're making a mistake,' Pippo broke in. 'Only yesterday the kid told me how bored he is, and how much he wants to go to school. They're just boys ...'

Corradino felt such fierce pangs of jealousy that his eyes filled with tears. For a moment he was so dazed he did not hear what the other two were saying, nor could he remember, later. By the time he had recovered his composure they were all walking back towards their table. Then the pianist turned aside to speak to someone and Corradino took the chance to seize Cate's hand and murmur through his clenched teeth: 'I'm going the day after tomorrow and I must talk to you. Tomorrow morning I'll expect you at my place.' Cate seemed surprised and hardly looked at

387

Summer Storm

him, but she nodded her head. 'At least, phone me,' Corradino pleaded.

But Cate did not come to see him next morning, and Corradino suffered agonies of pride, jealousy, humiliation. He found some slight relief in the thought that he was being treated unfairly, and told himself over and over that he didn't deserve it. His lack of any love for Cate, his very resentment towards her, seemed to him a sacrifice he was making for the boy's sake. It was in this state of mind that he telephoned an influential man he knew in the theatrical world and recommended Pippo to him as a capable, reliable performer. He felt he was being generous.

As if to compensate him, Cate telephoned him at the office that afternoon to say she had been busy but would keep her promise to wish him good-bye. Wouldn't he come to the Park that evening?

In a gentler voice, Corradino told her he had spoken to his friend on the Radio on Pippo's behalf. Cate said nothing for a moment, and Corradino asked: 'Are you there? What's the matter?' Then Cate spoke again with sudden gaiety and thanked him warmly on Pippo's behalf.

'No,' Corradino went on, 'I shan't be coming this evening. So much to do. Besides, this is your world. I don't come into it. You come to me tonight, instead.'

'I can't, Corrado.'

'I'm alone, Cate.' He could visualize her downcast eyes, grave and regretful, and her lips, close against the mouthpiece as though to kiss it or whisper into it. At last she said: 'I'll come tomorrow, at midday.'

They met at a corner and Corradino had a sudden conviction that she would not have come up to his room. She seemed very occupied and took him with her to a shop. They gave each other only brief, fleeting glances, in spite of their cordial greeting as they met.

When he asked her again to come upstairs with him, she

The Family

shook her head. 'What are you afraid of?' he stormed. 'You're not a little girl any more.'

'If I were a little girl, I'd come,' Cate replied.

So they went and sat in a café, and still Cate found nothing to say. Corradino suddenly thought of Pippo, but he didn't venture to start a conversation. Instead he looked in the mirrors that lined the walls and saw the back of her neck, strong, supple and even more sunburned than his own. 'Whoever would imagine that we have a son, she and I?' he thought. Cate had taken off her hat and tossed back her hair. Now she was looking up at him through the chestnut curls hanging over her eyes. Did she know how attractive she looked in that pose? he wondered. She seemed younger and her breath came more quickly as she gazed at him.

'She's looking at me for the last time,' Corradino decided. 'Let's play the scene through.'

When at last Cate shook herself and smiled at him, Corradino told her: 'The more I think about you, the less I know you. You're not the same girl any more.'

They talked freely now. Cate said she was growing older. That was all the difference. Corradino did not contradict her, but simply said he was old, too. 'We might almost be celebrating our silver wedding,' Cate remarked with a smile.

They joked a little. Corradino asked her where she would be singing that winter. Cate replied that she did not know, but there was plenty of time for that, now.

'Dino will soon have a father, won't he?' Corradino asked casually, but Cate was not deceived by his careless manner. She let him go on talking while she kept looking at him, more firmly now. Then she murmured: 'He has one already.'

'He has, but he never sees him,' Corradino retorted.

Cate still sat calmly, saying no more. Then Corradino told her he wanted to marry her. He said it quite un-

389

emotionally, as if he were talking to another man about it, but once it was said he found himself deeply moved, sweating and trembling. But Cate had already given him his answer with a gesture and a slow smile. Both fell silent for a long moment. 'You see,' Cate said in her calm voice, 'you must understand that I am no longer the same; you, though, haven't changed at all. For me it was all over a long time ago, too long. You aren't sure that Dino is your son, and there's no reason why you should believe me. I was stupid to talk about it, that day.'

'And if I do believe you?' Corradino asked. She listened as if the words were written for her to see. 'If I do believe you?' he said again.

'It isn't just that,' Cate replied, turning to look straight at him. 'We live such different lives. We shouldn't even know what to talk about. You would not be happy.'

'You're the one who wouldn't be happy.'

'Corrado,' Cate said, 'Let's go home now. It's after midday.'

So they left the café and Corradino went with her as far as the entrance to the flats, caressing her elbow, moving from one side of her to the other when they crossed to a different pavement, making polite, pointless conversation. Once Cate was amused by something he said, and he noticed that actually she had a common laugh. Under the circumstances he was pleased at the outcome.

'You're not really a woman,' he told her.

'What am I?'

'Just yourself,' Corradino murmured.

When they said good-bye – and it was without ceremony, almost without embarrassment – Corradino walked across the little pleasure garden without even pausing. When he had turned the corner he lit a cigarette, trying to recall whether he had smoked in the café, but he simply could not remember.

The Name

I have forgotten who my companions were in those days; but two of them, brothers probably, lived in one of the village houses opposite our own. They ran around in their shirtsleeves, I remember, and one of them was called Pale, short for Pasquiale. That's what I called the one I played with most, though it may have been his brother's name. There were so many boys I knew in one place or another.

The one I called Pale was very tall and thin, with a face like a horse. Whenever his father gave him a thrashing he would run away from home for two or three days. When he came back his father was always looking out for him with his belt handy, ready to whip the skin off his back, so he would run away again. Then his mother would start yelling for him at the top of her voice, cursing him as she leaned out of a dirty upstairs window that overlooked the fields and the reed-beds by the river, down towards the mouth of the valley. Some mornings I was awakened by her roars of complaint from that window. Most of the old women yelled after their sons like that, but the name that deafened everyone was 'Pale!' At certain times of day it reverberated round the valley like gunshots from a hunting party. Sometimes the rest of us would start yelling his name out of bravado or as a joke. I think Pale himself shouted it for fun, now and then.

Summer Storm

Actually I'm not really sure if it was Pale who was with me, that day when we climbed the dusty hillside opposite the village. We had already explored the river bank and the clumps of reed while the sun was hot. One thing I am sure about is that my companion had protruding teeth and red hair, for he was telling me that lions living in desert lands have teeth like his and a tawny mane.

We were excited that day because we had made up our minds to go hunting snakes in real earnest. We were soaked to our waists and our necks were burnt red by the sun. Now and then a frog would shoot away from under the stones we turned over, and my ankles were all bruises. Pale was chewing grass and spitting out the green juice between his teeth. Then, in the silence of the trees and the water, there came to us in the wind, faintly but clearly, the voice of someone yelling to him to come back. I remember how I strained my ears in case someone was calling me, too.

But the shout was not repeated and soon after we left the flat river bank to climb the hillside, telling each other we would look for sloes but well aware – at least I was, and it made my heart beat quickly – that this time we meant to hunt for vipers. It was while we were climbing the path between the junipers that he started talking about lions, to keep up his courage. I had put on my shoes again, as if by that gesture to dissociate myself, like a sensible boy, from the dangers he was implying. I was whistling.

'Stop that,' he cried. 'That's no way to tempt out a viper.'

We each carried a forked stick so that we could pin a snake to the ground with it. Then it would be easier to kill. There may have been several other boys playing with us in the water, but I am certain that only the two of us climbed that path. Pale, unlike me, was walking barefoot over the stones and the thorns, heedless of danger. I was just going to speak to him about it when he suddenly

The Name

stopped by a clump of brambles and began to hiss, very very softly, leaning forward and turning his head from side to side. The brambles were growing where an old landslide had met a cleft in the rocks. I could see the sky between the stones.

Breaking the silence, I suggested: 'We'd do better if we looked for snakes by those rocks,' but my friend did not reply. He went on hissing like a little jet of water coming from a tap, but no viper came out.

All at once a sound reached us on the wind, like a howl or loud yell in the distance. Someone was shouting from the village again – the same voice as before, furious and threatening: 'Pale! Pale!'

The thought of my own family at home flashed into my mind. Pale had stopped hissing and was standing on one leg with his head poked forward. It seemed to me his lips were twisted in a fiendish grin. The silence was closing round us once more, when the same voice – it hardly sounded human, so high in the air – started shrieking again: 'Pale! Pale!'

Furiously my companion threw down his forked stick. 'Those bastards!' he cried. 'If the viper hears my name while we're hunting it, it will know who I am and come after me!'

'Let's go,' I said, my voice a mere thread of sound.

That damned old woman kept on calling him. I could see her leaning out of that window every now and then, clutching the baby she was nursing at her breast and letting out screech after screech as if she were singing. Pale held me by the wrist for a minute or two, then he said: 'Come on then! Let's run!'

We ran only as far as the level ground, pretending we weren't afraid by shouting every minute or two: 'Look! There's a viper! After it!' But our real fear – mine, at least – was something more complex, a feeling that, for

Summer Storm

all I knew, we had offended the powerful spirits of the air and the rocks.

Evening came and found us sitting on the cross timbers of the bridge. Pale kept spitting in the water, saying nothing. 'Let's go up on the balcony,' I suggested. 'It's cooler there.'

It was the time of day when all the old women in the village generally started calling their boys home, but for the moment it was wonderfully peaceful, with no sound but a cricket chirping now and then.

It was thinking: 'Nobody's called me yet,' and I asked Pale: 'Why don't you answer when they call you? You'll catch it, tonight!'

Pale shrugged his shoulders and made a face. 'Women!' he said. 'How d'you think they can understand?'

'Is it really true,' I went on, 'that if a viper knows someone's name it comes looking for him?'

Pale made no reply. Running away from home so often had taught him to be taciturn, like a man. 'But then,' I persisted, 'all the snakes on these hills must have heard your name by now.'

'And yours too,' Pale answered with a grin.

'But when anyone calls me I always answer at once.'

'That's not the point. D'you think the viper cares whether you answer like a good boy? All it wants is to kill anyone who's out hunting for it.'

But just then the yelling started again. The old woman was back at her window. I could hear cart wheels creaking and the rattle of a bucket in the well. I started strolling towards home, but Pale stayed where he was on the bridge.

Free Will

My friend Alexis says quite openly that he does not like children. Not because they are tiresome, he tells me, but because one only has to look at them to realize they live in a different world from ours. What they see and feel and hear is not the same as we do.

There are plenty of them here on the beach. We were talking, of course, about children over three, who run about and play by themselves. Some of them are delightful, especially the fair-haired ones, but one sees differences. Some just scream and shout, play some trick and run away; but now and then one will stand at the water's edge, look at the sand, try it with his bare foot or simply sit there waiting. These are the ones who interest Alexis.

The older ones, getting on for six or eight years old, make him really envious, because these are not only living a life of their own but can sum up other people, scrutinizing a man from head to foot and making up their minds about him. The little ones, if they do not like his face, just run away or start yelling; but these older ones hold their ground; they have no reason to give way; they simply look at him, or worse still, they do not deign to look at him.

'And what are you going to do now?' Alexis asked my son one day as he was hanging from one of the lower branches of an olive tree and uncertain whether to work his way

Summer Storm

back to the trunk or let himself drop to the ground below. In the end he let himself drop, but then he pretended he couldn't straighten himself and started to howl. Alexis made no move to go up to him; instead, he just looked at him, half-annoyed, half-alarmed.

'I did it on purpose,' and 'that's all right, then,' they said in turn, Alexis crossly, my son as he jumped to his feet, but it was Alexis who remained in a bad mood.

Alexis is married, but has no children. His wife tells mine that they do nothing to avoid having a child. I am convinced that if he had a son, Alexis would see the whole world through his eyes, but as things are he hasn't one and he spends his time hating the whole lot of them.

'It isn't that I wish them any harm,' he told me once. There was a group of them in front of us, chattering and playing cards on the sand. 'But just look at them! Look at what they are doing! They look like professional cardsharpers already! What frightens me about them is that they act like responsible creatures, but really they are not. See that thin boy over there? Why has he tied that handkerchief round his face to look like a moustache? It isn't just to imitate a grown man. There are other motives, deeper than they know themselves, but when they are adults they'll act accordingly.'

Actually, when we walked on the beach together, the crowd that a moment before had seemed just a noisy, happy group became a limbo of unquiet spirits, each separated from the other, big or little, in a moment of disquietude, even of agony, that did not show in their faces but remained in their memory.

We were talking of babies, and Alexis is obsessed by the idea that, subconsciously, every child is constantly testing and probing within himself the instincts, the desires, the voices he will follow when he is grown up. According to Alexis it is monstrous that during a period of mere playtime,

Free Will

of irresponsible moods and caprices, there should be forming, like a coral reef below the water-line, a whole plan of his future development. He grows quite excited when he discusses this; obviously he is talking about himself.

My son does not seem in the least concerned with listening to the voices of instinct. He is a little rascal, full of fun, but without any hidden depths. All he thinks about is having a good time and playing tricks on us when he can. Alexis says he was just the same when he was seven.

'You see,' he explains, 'it isn't that they are conscious of themselves at that age. They do not reason out what they do or try to clarify the importance of their actions. That is plain enough. It is not for nothing that children live in a different world from ours. Boys do not think, they act. That is why we call them creatures of instinct. But it is precisely this innocent choice they make within themselves that determines their future. For instance, when faced by danger or the risk of injury, one boy will run away, another will cry, another will throw himself on the ground, and another will merely whistle. They do not know it, but they will do exactly the same when they are men.'

'D'you really think so? Then what of free will?'

Alexis says he doesn't care a hoot for free will. He doesn't even like hearing it mentioned. He is prone to make these sudden, harsh outbreaks of ill-humour, but a half an hour or so later he will bring the subject up again as if to excuse himself. He has these sudden fits with his wife, too, and she always looks a little frightened. She tells my wife: 'Alexis always has to get worked up before he can make love, and then he feels ashamed...'

My wife knew her before they were married, as I had known Alexis, and had heard from her a grim story of the excesses Alexis gave way to, whenever there was a hitch in their love affair. I knew about them, too, but he hadn't precisely explained why these outbreaks served to make him

Summer Storm

feel absolved and able to re-instate himself in the good graces of the girl he was engaged to.

Alexis has clear blue eyes, and when he feels humiliated they have such a look of distraction that one cannot look at him without being deeply moved, as he well knows.

The other day I punished my son for doing something or other, I don't remember what. Alexis asked me: 'Where is he going now?'

'Hiding under the stairs, pretending he's a whipped dog,' I replied. But he, as we went out together, started telling me that when he was a child of six or seven, he did just the same. 'Sometimes I was pleased when they punished me,' he said, 'because then I would feel beyond all hope. I would stare fiercely up at the sky or shut myself up in the balcony with our cat and cry bitterly over its back. No one realized that at such moments my family, the village, the whole world existed only to torture me, and the thought pleased me so keenly that I wouldn't have changed it for any comforting kisses from anyone at all. I could feel like that then, and there was no harm in it. But what if one is still doing it at fifteen, eighteen, or twenty-five? This wallowing in self-pity like a sponge soaking up water, is it harmless, or something to be ashamed of? Nature does not contradict itself, you know.'

'Let's say that's just being sentimental.'

Alexis twisted his lips. 'Some days when I was saying "Yes, papa," I was thinking all the time how much I'd like to take off his cravat and cut his throat. Would you call that being sentimental?'

'Of course it was!' But Alexis knows I'm always joking and he did not take offence. Instead he told me that somewhere my son was savouring, at this very moment, all the sufferings he would endure in his whole future life.

We were on the beach and I tried to distract myself by looking at the bodies stretched out on the sand. There was

Free Will

a group of boys discussing some game they were playing; I recognized several of my son's friends, but him I could not see. I looked for my wife, who was lying face down on the sand sunning her shoulders. We exchanged a few words at random, but then I could contain myself no longer. I told Alexis to wait for me under the big beach umbrella and I went back to the house.

I remember I had given Guido a smart slap in public, keeping a straight face as usual on such occasions. The slap had been the culmination of a long contest of dark looks between us. Already on the previous evening there had been a stormy scene over some prank or other, and now I realized the boy might well be in the state of mind Alexis had described. I looked for him in the courtyard and all through the empty house, where the rooms all had that disordered look they get when the whole family has gone to the beach. I saw his trunks under a chair, but he himself was not to be found.

I felt annoyed, but my heart was beating faster. I was just going out again when I heard a sound from the yard, and looked up. How was it I hadn't seen him before? My son was perched on the roof of the privy, his knees drawn up to his chin, staring blankly at me and at the street as though he saw nothing. Bronzed as he was, I could not read his expression.

'What are you doing there?' I asked him.

Guido let a moment pass then he replied with a grunt.

'Why are you on the outhouse roof?'

'No reason.' He was staring fixedly at his own toes. I no longer knew what to say. Above all I did not want him to know I had come to look for him.

'Your mother's wondering where you are,' I said.

Guido smiled scornfully, a slow smile such as I had never seen on his lips before.

'Aren't you going bathing?' I asked him.

Summer Storm

'Leave me alone,' he muttered, and that smile changed into the frown I knew. It was not only scornful, but there was something cruel, something evil, in the flash I saw in his eyes. I knew well enough that if I had asked him about it he would only have lied, so I contented myself with talking kindly, telling him to come and play and helping him down.

I recall that Guido took it pleasantly enough, showing no sign of triumph at his victory. But this was exactly 'in character', judging by what Alexis had described to me.

The Leather Jacket

My father lets me spend my days hanging round the café at the boat-hire station because he thinks that way I can amuse myself and unconsciously learn a trade at the same time. A fat woman owns the place now, and she's always grousing. If I as much as touch a boat she sees me every time, even when she's down in the storeroom, and shouts at me to leave other people's property alone. Behind the café are some little tables and chairs for the customers, but this new owner doesn't employ an assistant. If I take in an order she sends her son out with the glasses. There's a part of the café I'm not allowed into any more, nor can I go upstairs to look at the water and the boats from the window of Ceresa's room. Hardly anyone comes to the place now, and my father must be crazy if he still thinks I can learn a job here.

This Madame Pina had no idea how to manage things. The customers treat her just as they do me. There's a lot more to running a business like that than just putting on a leather jacket. You've got to make people like coming. If you're the owner you must look proud of your boats and the River Po, show your customers you think it's a fine thing for them to enjoy themselves that way.

That's just the sort of man Ceresa was, always joking with everyone and more at home in the boats than his customers were. When Ceresa was here there was always something to laugh about; he would wade about in the water in his bathing trunks, baling out the boats, touching up the seams with pitch when they needed it, and in good weather he would take the trouble to put a basket of grapes on the tables under the trees.

The girls who went boating always used to stop by the shed for a laugh and a chat. One of them was always pestering Ceresa to take her up the river, but he just told her he couldn't leave the café and the landing-stage. 'You should come along one morning before the sun is up,' he teased, and one morning the silly girl actually did! 'If you get up as early as this every morning,' he told her, 'you won't have those headaches you talk about.'

Ceresa always wore the leather jacket that now the old woman throws over her shoulders when it rains. Once, I remember, when we were out in a boat and a storm blew up, he took it off and told me to wrap it round myself. Under it he was always bare to the waist, and he used to tell me that if I spent my life on the Po I'd have muscles as strong as his when I was a man. He had little moustaches and he was out in the sun so much his hair was almost white.

A year or two ago, one or two customers stopped coming, on account of Nora. To begin with she was just a waitress who took people their drinks, and she went away at night, but, before long, no matter how late I went home she was still in the café, and when I got there in the morning she was already looking out of the window. She wasn't a pretty girl – not that Ceresa ever said so, but that's what the other young fellows said, and so did the old men who came to play bowls. Nora would stand leaning against the door, cupping her elbow in one hand, wearing a red dress and staring at everybody without saying a word. Once, when I was sitting on the steps waiting for Ceresa, she said to me: 'Get along home, you fool.' But at other

The Leather Jacket

times she would laugh to see me sitting in a boat with my feet in the water, and if anyone wanted an oar or a cushion when Ceresa was not about, she would tell me to go and fetch one from the shed.

It suddenly troubled me that Nora no longer left the café. At first, when I remembered her, I would say: 'She's a pretty girl,' and think no more about it. But if she was now keeping Ceresa company, it meant there was something quite extraordinary about her, and this worried me because I didn't understand what it could be.

They took their meals together under the awning, and I would stay around for a while to help them if any boats came back, so that they did not need to get up. They would talk together, giving me a word every now and then, but most of all they would gaze into each other's eyes or wink at one another. If Nora went into the kitchen to take away a plate, Ceresa would sit in silence, watching the door. They talked to each other in a way they did not talk to me. Ceresa, who joked with everyone else, never did with her; instead he would talk softly, tapping the point of his finger on the table and looking down. Or he would play with the zip fastener of his jacket as if it were a fan, and Nora would screw up both her eyes and laugh as she watched the zipper.

It was understood that they stayed together for company, not with the intention of getting married, for Nora never wore the sort of clothes housewives wear at home. She had her red dress and an even prettier white one, and once she had washed up and swept the place she would stay by the door or come over to look at the water as girls do when they come to hire a boat. When Ceresa came looking for her he would stroll lazily along as though he had nothing to do, but actually there was plenty to do and the days were long: she served in the café, washed his shirts and still found time to smoke a cigarette.

Summer Storm

Nora was the mistress now. Ceresa told me that one day we would take a boat, he and I, and go up the Po beyond the weir, staying away until the evening. Nora never came out in a boat with us. She always said the water was too rough, and when we went off with nets and a basket to fish under the bridge she would watch us from the window and laugh. When he was going fishing, Ceresa never wore anything but his jacket and a little pair of very tight bathing trunks. We would jump in the water and fix the basket between the stones, then I would hold the boat steady while Ceresa stirred up the fish with his hands. He knew a wonderful lake up beyond the weir, where he could always fill the basket. He promised we would go up there one fine day and not come back till evening. Many mornings I arrived at the landing-stage hoping this would be the right day, but it always turned out that there was a job waiting to be done, or he had to tell Nora something, or he had to caulk a boat where a seam had opened the night before, so our outing was put off.

In the end I went up there by myself, to that lake beyond the weir. One day Ceresa had something to do in Turin so I stayed with Nora. She was washing some greens in a bucket by the shed, watching me all the time but saying nothing. I soon felt bored, so I told her I was taking a boat out and off I went. I stayed on the water till midday, thinking as I came back that I shouldn't see Ceresa that day so I might as well go home. But I was wrong. Ceresa was back already, slipping on his jacket by his bedroom window. He smiled at me and called me up. I took a step forward, but then I saw Nora blocking the door and scowling at me, so I was afraid to push past her and go upstairs. I told her: 'Ceresa called me up', but she didn't move so I went into the shed to put the oars back. Nora looked at me for some moments, then went upstairs herself.

The mornings were the best time, because then one could

The Leather Jacket

always hope something nice was going to happen, more than in the evenings. Now I was sent home in the evening, because after supper Ceresa and Nora would dress up and go off arm in arm for a walk or to a cinema in Turin. They would shut up the café even before it was really dark and leave the landing-stage deserted. At first there was usually some customer or other waiting to be served, but Ceresa would send him away. He never felt the cold and generally wore shorts, even after dark. It made me furious that Nora, who never went out in the sun and must have been as pale as the belly of a fish, should treat him as an equal, and walk arm in arm with him. I would have given a good deal to know what they talked about.

'When I get married,' Ceresa said to me one morning, 'It'll be the same as before, you'll see.' I was holding the pitch for him just then and felt like bursting into tears. I didn't cry, though, but kept my eyes on the boat, for he was smiling. I was careful not to let Nora hear me from the kitchen. 'I shouldn't get married,' I said softly, though I knew perfectly well he'd made up his mind to marry her. 'If you do, Nora won't go on wearing her red dress and you'll start quarrelling.'

'What were you talking to Zucca about yesterday while he was playing bowls?'

Ceresa always knew everything that was going on. Zucca, the one with a goitre, had remarked to another man that Nora was as obstinate as a mule and Ceresa had better not marry her. All I had done was to listen as I brought them their drinks.

'You're just a boy,' Ceresa told me. 'You shouldn't bother about what grown-ups say. But if Nora tells you anything, let me know.'

But Nora never told me anything that mattered. Often enough she drove me away. When we were working on a boat, Ceresa and I, she would watch us from the door as

Summer Storm

if she were the boss, and I never knew whether she was looking that way at me or Ceresa. By now I was only waiting for him to bring the subject up again, to tell him Nora was a bad lot.

A few days after that business about Zucca I was sitting in a boat, waiting for Ceresa to come down, but he did not come. He had slipped upstairs a couple of minutes ago to fetch something to smoke, but it was a fine evening and there might well have been a customer to detain him. I was watching his open window from the water's edge but had not seen him come down. It had been a warm afternoon and so still that I could not even hear the water lapping against the boats. Suddenly I saw Ceresa standing with his back to the window, talking to someone in the room, but he did not turn round or say anything to me.

So I sat there looking at the sun, screwing up my eyes and seeing so many red and green streaks that in the end I got tired of them. I waited I don't know how long, but at last I saw Ceresa by the shed, lighting a cigarette and calling to ask me if we were doing anything. I showed him the oar, and he made a gesture as if he didn't feel like going fishing after all, but he jumped into the boat and sat there saying nothing, just letting me take him down to the bridge. Then he dropped into the water and we started fishing. Every now and then he muttered something about the fish, still smoking and staring down into the water. I spoke of a motor-boat that went by and then asked him if it ran on petrol, but he didn't go on talking as he generally did. He just tipped the little fish into the bottom of the boat and mumbled: 'You're no good, either.'

That evening, Zucca went past in his boat and called out: 'Hello, there.' I went on pouring water over the fish and said: 'You're a sly one, all right.' Ceresa looked at him, then with a smile at me, putting his hand on my head and rubbing my hair up the wrong way.

The Leather Jacket

Yet he hadn't quarrelled with Nora, so far. Women like kicking up a fuss, or at least bursting into tears. They're different from us. But with Nora everything was quiet. I'll swear that sometimes Nora actually said to him, as she did to me: 'What a fool you are! Out of my way!' but all Ceresa did was to twist her wrist and push her away. Once, in front of two customers he asked her to sew up a cushion that had got torn in a boat. Nora took the cushion and threw it in the water. Then she shut herself away upstairs and would not open the door.

I started waiting on customers at the tables behind the café, where nobody had noticed anything. Ceresa did not speak to me at all the rest of the day. He stayed in the shed, mending a rowlock, working the forge by himself, then picking up the coals with his hands and throwing them into the Po while they were still so hot that they hissed as they struck the water.

Next day I found the door shut. I called, but no one was there, so I went away because I didn't want customers to find me there and have to tell them Ceresa had quarrelled. The landing-stage was dead for two whole days. Then one morning as I was wandering along the river bank I saw movement among the boats. Ceresa was back; Nora had come back, too, and was standing by the window, changing her blouse. Ceresa was helping a couple of girls into a boat, some of those who generally undressed in the shed, shouting a lot of stupid nonsense. Ceresa was laughing and holding the boat for them.

There was a party that night because Nora had come back. Five or six customers and other boatmen came along – Zucca, Damiano, the usual crowd – but they seemed gayer than normal and stayed there talking and laughing till midnight. They all said that Nora ought to go bathing. Tomorrow they would buy her a bathing costume and she would wear it when she waited on the ones who played bowls. Then the moon came out and the bank was as bright as noonday. Damiano brought some wine and they started playing cards. I was fit to drop with tiredness, but did not want to go away, until Nora said to me, (or I think she did), 'Aren't your family expecting you home?' so I left.

From that day on, Nora seemed nicer and happier, but she was always quick to answer Ceresa back. He just laughed and shrugged his shoulders. Sometimes I felt ashamed for him when that beast of a woman was rude to him in front of other people. She had bought a bathing costume, red like that dress of hers, and she would put it on at midday to sunbathe, walking to and fro in front of the shed. She would keep it on even later, unless Ceresa took her by the arm and glared at her. Nora's skin was as creamy butter, but she never went bathing in the Po. When Damiano came along, or Zucca's son, she would stand laughing with them and showing herself. I can't understand what people see in women. 'You will,' Ceresa told me once. 'They'll appeal even to you.' But I haven't understood it yet.

Then Ceresa quarrelled with Damiano one day when I wasn't there. I heard people talking about it in the café next day. They had come to blows and were shouting so loudly that the tram-drivers on the other side of the river could hear them. That time I had a good look at Nora's face, without her knowing, wondering if she were angry, too, but she seemed more frightened than angry. Ceresa said nothing, but came fishing with me. That day there wasn't a single fish to pay him for his trouble, and he was so furious he took the basket and smashed it against one of the piles. Then he flung himself down in the bottom of the boat and told me to take him back home.

From then on I came only reluctantly to the landing-stage, unless Ceresa told me himself there was something he wanted me to do. There were some days when I sat

The Leather Jacket

there in the shed without saying a word, and Nora was nowhere to be seen. But it was worse still when Nora bustled round the kitchen or waited on the customers, because then I was always expecting her to say something. Then one day I went to look for my own little boat, the one I had made myself on the workbench in the shed, when Ceresa let me work there. I could not find it. Ceresa was sitting on the ground leaning against a post. I asked him if he knew where my boat was, but he said he had no idea. Then I ran into the kitchen and asked Nora. I heard her say, quite calmly, that she had burned it in the fire.

Ceresa asked me one day why I was not learning a trade. 'But I want to be a boatman, like you,' I replied.

'You're mad!' he exclaimed. 'Can't you see it's a devilish job? Tell your father he should get you into a factory. Tell him that. You'd even do better as a soldier than in this damned trade.'

It upset me, not for myself, for it made no difference to me, but for his sake. It was dreadful to think he no longer enjoyed the river. I wanted to tell him he should marry Nora; then he would be the boss and things would go better, but I didn't know what his reply might be. So I put my trousers on again and went home.

Nora realized she had really annoyed me, because next day she called me into the kitchen and made me talk. She asked me if I really loved boating so much. Wasn't I afraid of drowning? I replied that I liked it because it was Ceresa's trade. Then she asked if I could manage to take her out in a boat. 'Let's ask Ceresa if he'll let us go and see the weir,' she said. 'If it's fine tomorrow, we'll go then.'

Next day she put on her bathing costume and borrowed Ceresa's jacket. We took a picnic basket and Nora sat on the cushions. Ceresa laughed as he watched us start. Once we were past the bridge I started to row with long strokes.

Summer Storm

Nora asked if we had far to go. I explained to her how to use the oar, and showed her the way. She came over close to me and we almost fell in the water. Women are all the same. She went back and sat down, then asked me if I could swim in deep water. She knew that nobody can swim below the weir, and she asked me to stop by the mouth of the Sangone where there is still water.

I tied the boat up to the bank, and she watched me as I dived in. Then I swam in the Sangone and called to her that the water was colder than in the Po. When I got back to the boat and was just going to touch it, I saw Damiano and a soldier coming to the bank. They were friends, but the soldier I had never seen before. They came up to the boat and started talking to Nora. I spoke to Damiano, but I did not trust him. I jumped into the boat myself and sat down.

Damiano made me furious, because I knew he could row better than me, and if Nora asked him to take her up to the weir I should look a fool. But Damiano and the soldier sat down on the bank and began joking. Nora joined in, and soon after she jumped on to the bank herself and said she felt like taking a walk. The soldier put his hand on the zipper of the jacket and said: 'What you really want is air.' He was a man from Naples.

I stayed alone in the boat, thinking that if Ceresa got to know about this there really would be trouble. Then I got in the water again so that if anyone were to come along they would not know it was Ceresa's boat. It was already evening when Nora came back. She told me we shouldn't tell Ceresa anything about having seen Damiano. I knew that myself, anyway.

She tried to get me to take her out again, next day, this time to the Mulini, but it wasn't my turn to come to the landing-stage. I knew that, between Ceresa's insistence and Nora looking at me as women do when they are furious, I

The Leather Jacket

couldn't say no. So I went along towards evening and found her there. She had put on her skirt, but instead of a blouse she was still wearing the leather jacket. It was plain that now she had on her bathing costume under her skirt. She gave me a dirty look, but I stayed with Ceresa.

They were lovely, those September mornings, when the Po was swathed in mist and we waited for the sun to break through at any moment. Now there was always a job to be done at the forge or with a pot of pitch, and Nora was not about so early because she went to the market. Ceresa talked less than he used to do, but I gladly stayed with him because I knew he was dazed. He let me potter about in the shed as I liked, saying something to me now and again. And so I kept him company.

At last came the grape harvest, and one afternoon we picked bunches of them from the vines that covered the café and filled the bucket. Nora was there, too, and all three of us enjoyed a picnic, laughing as we ate them. Nora said we ought to be careful in case somebody stole them at night. Then, to show us where robbers might hide them, she zipped open the jacket. I had a glimpse of something white flecked with spots, and realized that under the jacket she was naked. She had left off her costume. Hastily she closed the zipper.

While we were having our picnic, there were two soldiers drinking beer at one of the little tables, and I fancied one of them was that friend of Damiano who had joked with Nora that day on the river bank. But how can one tell? They all look alike, and Nora had not paused when she took them their beer.

But an hour later I saw the same men again, laughing and talking with Nora. Ceresa had gone into the house. I saw Nora leaning over the table, and the soldier put his hand on the zipper as he had done that day, but this time he pulled it down. Nora still stood there, bending forward

Summer Storm

and laughing. I turned only when I heard Ceresa come to the door. He called me, but said nothing more.

A moment later I was alone on the bowling green, the little tables were empty, Ceresa and Nora had gone indoors. I stood still to hear if there was any shouting, but there was no sound or movement. All I was afraid of was that a customer might come along to hire a boat or bring one back, and I should have to call Ceresa. It was quiet among the trees and evening was coming on. I was cold. Beyond the trees I could hear the birds flying low. There was not even a car on the road. Everything seemed dead.

I was seized with fear, or shame; which, I don't know. I was still thinking of Nora's white skin. It seemed to me that evening was crying aloud, or listening to me shouting. Then the window opened. Ceresa leaned out and said: 'Pino, slip along home, now.' Then shut it quickly.

Next morning I went back with my heart in my mouth. I went along the top road without going down. The landing-stage was quiet between the trees. No one was there. I had to go on an errand to Dazio, but after lunch I decided: 'Ceresa ought to know that I wasn't to blame.'

I saw a great crowd of boats going and coming in front of the landing-stage; I saw two men in city clothes standing by a car at the entrance to the path. I knew I could not go past them so I walked round the field. People were crowding in and out of the shed, but Ceresa was not there. Then I came across Zucca's son. He told me that Ceresa had throttled Nora and thrown her into the Po.

I wanted to see him to tell him about that day by the Sangone, but they made us all move back, and when he came out the only sound was the noise of the car. Then my father told me the less I said about it the better, for me and everyone else.